What Readers are Saying

I opened Virginia Hall-Apicella's new novel, Even a Sparrow, while on a cross-country trip. The annoyances of modern travel faded as I read Hall-Apicella's imaginative account of her ancestors' emigration from a small town in Germany to upstate New York in the early 19th century. Hall-Apicella's detailed descriptions brought the time period to life, and her insight into the motives and emotions of the protagonists made me care deeply about their fate. I rooted for Johann Klem, a tailor yearning for land and opportunity unavailable to him in Europe. I sympathized with Anna, his wife, comfortably enmeshed in a web of family and friends but willing to follow her husband with a mixture of anger and love. Even the minor characters come to life in Hall-Apicella's hands. Mrs. Grimsby, a hotel proprietor in New Foundland, could easily out-Havisham Dickens' famously dour character from Great Expectations. Mary, a Mi'kmaq healer, is intriguing enough to carry her own novel, as is Bernard, the Klems' brilliant son. I'd read those sequels any time!
—Geraldine Woods, author of 25 *Sentences and How They*

Got That Way (WW Norton 2020), *Basic English Grammar For Dummies, 2nd edition* (Wiley 2024), and many other books.

Even A Sparrow" immerses readers in the early 19th century, capturing the Klems' harrowing journey with vivid historical detail. Virginia Hall-Apicella masterfully portrays the trials faced by Johann and Anna as they traverse a perilous path to America. This novel is a heart-warming and riveting testament to the courage and resilience of emigrants seeking a better life.

—Cassandra King New York Times best-selling author of *Tell Me A Story: My Life With Pat Conroy.*

In *Even A Sparrow*, Virginia Hall-Apicella has created a beautiful and courageous early 19th century historical fiction based on the lives of immigrants Johann and Anna Kelm. The research is obvious from the descriptions and details of this intricately crafted story. The narrative is not romanticized nor does it hide the dark, shadowy side of the journey, yet it will capture you from the first word. Hall-Apicella reveals the way history shapes us, wounds us, and transforms us through the long line of DNA that courses through our veins. The reader will be drawn into this perilous journey—a journey based on hope that a better life awaits them and their children in Amerika. Hall-Apicella not only gives us the historical facts, but she, through Johann and Anna, tells us what it feels like to experience death, defeat, and resurrection over and over.

—Donna Keel Armer, author *Solo in Salento: A Memoir; Un'Americana in Salento; The Red Starfish;* and *Moringa~Tree of Life.*

Even a sparrow

a novel

Virginia Hall-Apicella

Susan,

Best wishes.
Happy reading!

Ginny Hall-Apicella
2024

RedPenguin BOOKS

Red Penguin Books

Bellerose Village, New York

ISBN

Print 978-1-63777-594-3 | 978-1-63777-595-0

Digital 978-1-63777-593-6

To Guy for his years of love, support, and proofreading,

Contents

New beginnings are often disguised as painful endings.

— Lao Tau

Chapter 1

The Rift

Anna

"Nein, I will not go," I shouted.

My jaw clenched as I threw the damp rag I had used to wipe table crumbs directly at Johann, my husband of eleven years. Johann ducked, and the rag sailed over his head, hit the chimney, and sputtered on the hot bricks. I had never felt so angry. My voice was too loud and too shrill. My hands shook. I bit my lip and tasted the coppery tang of blood. Yet, my face burned red with shame at what I had done. I had never thrown anything at him before in our entire marriage. We seldom even used harsh words.

"Please, *Liebchen,* listen to me, listen to reason," he urged. Johann's suggestion that I was being unreasonable increased my fury. My heart was ready to explode through my chest. I could hardly breathe, let alone calm down. I glanced at the baby's cradle to ensure my outburst had not awakened her.

Was I unreasonable? Maybe, but I did not want to hear his arguments. I did not want him to convince me that his plan to leave our home and move to far-off *Amerika,* where we knew no one was reasonable. He rubbed his hands together as if he were about to pray. If he had quoted something from the Bible, I might have thrown something else. I would not relent.

"Johann Klem, this is not the first time you talked about going to *Amerika.* Other times, you listened to *my* reasons. The decision cannot be just about what *you* want. You always tell me, 'Anna, I didn't marry you just for your pretty face.' If this is true, listen to me now."

I kept my voice low so his mother and sister-in-law on the other side of our shared wall would not hear me. Before I could speak, Johann interrupted.

"Anna, this is the best for us...and the children."

"The children?" I shot back. "The children are exactly why we cannot leave our home and travel thousands of miles to a country where no one speaks German. What do we know of *Amerika?*"

Kittersburg was home. Our town sat in the Rhine Valley, nestled between the river to our west and the Black Forest to our east. For generations, our families had lived here. I was well aware of our troubles—the overflowing river, the armies, the bad harvests—yet my mother taught me to take the bad with the good. *We belong here.* That thought hammered in my mind.

Johann began to speak, but I would not let him stop me. "How will the children see their grandmothers, their cousins? Where will they go to school?"

I looked straight into his pale blue eyes, the very eyes that had made my heart race so many years before. Sometimes, while I knit or nursed the baby at night, I would look up and find him looking at me with those beautiful eyes. Despite our years together, I would feel that wondrous pulling in my gut, the pulsing below.

Now, I had none of those sweet feelings. I couldn't stop my torrent of words. I could no longer be the accommodating woman Johann wanted me to be.

"Don't forget how dangerous that journey will be. What if the children die? What if we all die?" I demanded. The image of the two daughters we had buried seized my thoughts.

I could say no more. I sank into the oak chair Papa had made for us as a wedding present. Its carved back, adorned with a heart and two birds, was often my refuge, my place of consolation.

My tears began. Tears stop all conversation with men, even a tender man like Johann. I could not control their flood. They dripped down my cheeks and chin unabated.

Johann knelt before me. He blotted my face with a cloth he drew from his pocket—a tailor always has a fabric remnant in his pocket. His strong arms encircled me, pulling me tight to his chest. His heartbeat pounded in my ear. I felt the gentle scratch of his wool jacket on my face. Our breaths merged as we clung to each other silently. We seldom found time in our lives for our touch. I bore into his strength and warmth, savoring his smell of pipe smoke and the sun-dried shirt I had recently washed. We stayed like that for minutes until he leaned back and lifted my chin. When our eyes met, he spoke in a hushed tone. His voice was mellow as old brandy.

"The children are exactly why we must leave. What kind of life can they have here? There is no land for them." He folded his hands around mine. "After we die, our field must be divided among them. It barely feeds us. There's plenty of cheap land in *Amerika*." Here, Johann was right. I knew the small field he inherited from his father was insufficient.

"And don't forget the French. Don't forget Napoleon and his French devils."

How could I possibly forget Napoleon?

Emperor Bonaparte's army appeared in our narrow streets when Johann and I were newly married. Their horses, cannons, and soldiers dominated our lives. I remembered Napoleon's soldiers with their blue coats with red trimmed cuffs. White leather belts criss crossed their chests; one belt held a cartridge box, and the other a saber. The soldiers would curse at us if our streets were too muddy and might dirty their white breeches. Bonaparte forced Baden into an alliance. The insatiable French emperor made new rules. We had to obey him, not our former dukes and lords. Before Napoleon, General Moreau's French Revolutionary Army crossed the Rhine to occupy our village and fields. Then came the Austrian and Prussian troops. All the armies stole our food, killed the livestock, and demanded high taxes. Our village men were forced to cut down hundred-year-old oaks to build a bridge over the Rhine. They all made the same ultimatums, wanting control of the small towns whose front yard was the Rhine.

Although it lasted long, it did not last forever. Eventually, Napoleon was defeated, condemned, and isolated on a small island. A new French king, a descendant of the beheaded one, had returned. Yet, Johann repeatedly said that he did not trust the "French dogs." He thought they would return to the Duchy of Baden to sniff out a new bone.

I sighed at Johann's mention of Napoleon's dreaded army and sank deeper into my chair.

"Oh, Johann, I know. I know. I don't want that to happen again, but this is our home. It's where we belong. How can you ask me to leave my mother and my friends? How can we abandon our buried daughters, our precious girls? " I could still hear the echo of the dirt thrown on Carolina and Odelia's coffins.

"Husband, I cannot bury another child," I whispered. A lump lodged in my throat. I could not stop crying. I lifted the corner of my apron to blot the tears away.

"How can I desert them?" I asked. My heart was permanently scared at their loss.

Johann was silent. He'd been as heartbroken as I when our daughters died. Father Weber tried to convince us that the girls were with God.

"You'll have other children," he'd said.

And we did have other children. Yet, the agony of losing my girls was indelable.

As Johann held me, I closed my eyes and saw the faces of our surviving children. God had allowed us these four who were the joy and breath of our lives.

Katharina, our "Katja," was the eldest at age eleven. She was named after my mother and was as sweet and kind as Mama. My family said she was a miniature version of me with her chestnut hair and hazel-green eyes. She was my helper, my reliable daughter.

Our seven-year-old son, Bernard, resembled Johann at the same age his mother told me—bright, active, mischievous, and endlessly curious. He had his father's blue eyes and silver-blond hair. Of all the children, Bernard was the one whose lips most uttered, "Why?" Sometimes, I told him he was like a wheel on a cart, much happier moving than standing still.

Rosalia, our precious "Rosie," was still a toddler. She was fair-haired like Bernard with Johann's enthusiastic nature. She was attracted to every animal that crossed her path. She petted stray cats and clapped her hands at the sight of a sheep flock or an ambling cow. Rosie wanted to ride even the largest horse that passed under our window. Her blond curls and dimples drew attention wherever we went.

I had yet to know the personality of Odelia, our two-month-old. She was named for her sister, who had died before her birth. I could hardly say her name without feeling the stab of losing my first Odelia. My mother-in-law believed naming the baby after her sister in heaven would bring the new baby special blessings. Secretly, I thought giving her the same name might bring bad luck, yet we christened her Odelia to please Johann's mother. But we called her Delia. She was an easy baby, nursing and sleeping well. In looks, she favored Katja and me with darker hair and green-brown eyes. My constant thought was keeping her healthy.

Johann rose and pulled me up, interrupting my thoughts of our children. He wrapped his arms around me and laid his cheek on my white linen cap.

"*Schatzi,* my treasure, I am so sorry I upset you. I won't speak of *Amerika* again. I wish I could stay here with you in my arms, but I must go and meet with *Herr* Holbauer." Kissing my forehead, he released me. He walked across our creaking floor and grabbed his leather tailor's satchel hanging on a peg by the door. It held all his sewing necessities—shears, chalk, needles, pins—as essential to him as my kettle and spoons were to me.

I knew he needed to keep his appointment with Holbauer, Kittersburg's haughty mayor. Holbauer's clothing orders put bread on our table. Still, I wondered if, at this moment, Johann preferred the company of the troublesome mayor to the anger and tears of his troublesome wife.

I was still drying my face when I heard the door close and the clatter of his shoes on the wooden stairs that led from our home, over his workshop, to the village street.

For now, the disagreement was over. I knew, however, that this struggle on where to spend our lives would continue despite his words. Unlike me, Johann was a dreamer. He was always looking around the corner for a new idea, something different to try. In the past, Johann told me I clung to my roots like the turnips that resisted being yanked from the earth at harvest. I answered that his crazy idea of *Amerika* kept popping up like a pig bladder thrown into a stream.

When I knew Johann was gone, I picked up the cloth he had used to dry my tears and flung it into the fire. As I watched it hiss and burn, I resolved not to give in. I would continue to fight to stay in our home.

With Delia asleep in her cradle and Rosie visiting with Johann's mother and my sister-in-law on the other side of our shared wall, I took a moment to sit back in my chair and gaze around the room.

I knew and loved every square inch of the floor, the ceiling, the walls. On the shelf next to the fireplace was my precious copper kettle. I polished it daily to keep it shining. On the far wall was the hutch handed down from Johann's grandmother. The bottom doors were painted red and black, typical of Baden. It held the blue and white crockery where I stored my wheat and rye flours. I had bargained well with a peddler for those vessels.

In the other corner, near the steep stairs that lead to our sleeping chamber, was the heavy oak table where we shared our meals. Here, Johann sat with Katja and Bernard to help with lessons. He and his brother George made a new bench so all three could sit together. The armchair where I sat to nurse all my babies was by the four-paned window that looked out onto the street. We watched soldiers march through Kittersburg's narrow lanes from that window. The floor, which I had swept and scrubbed more times than I could ever count, slanted slightly on this side of the room. The cracks between the planks allowed crumbs to fall below into Johann's first-floor tailoring workshop.

How could I leave this room that housed everything we ever had? How could I leave the home where our children were born, where we had shared both sorrow and delight? Yet, how could I not go with Johann? He and the children were my life. I arose and paced the well-worn floor, my mind as confused as a schoolboy at his sums. I had been momentarily comforted by Johann's arms. Anger and sadness were competing bedfellows in my mind and heart.

Chapter 2

Love

Anna

I had known about Johann's dream of *Amerika* since we fell into a heady, compelling love. I had thought that when we were married and Johann was settled as a master tailor in his guild, he would forget about *Amerika*. He would realize that Kittersburg was the best place for us. I had loved listening to Johann's yearnings, but to me, they were only dreams—something you imagined while you stared at fat white clouds drifting through the sky.

In a town as small as this one, where I knew or was related to half the people, I had always known Johann. When we were young, all the village children played together, skipping stones, hitting hoops with sticks, and avoiding soldiers. By school age, when girls only played with girls and boys with boys, I took little notice of him. He was one of the boys allowed to do things forbidden to girls. After the fall harvest was tucked into barns and the fattened pigs were slaughtered, salted, or rendered into tallow, we children gathered in the one-room schoolhouse under the strict tutelage of *Herr* Remmelin.

Johann was bright, yet like the other boys, made mischief. He teased and provoked the schoolmaster, who smacked him with a pointing stick more than once. We girls laughed when we heard that the fathers paddled their sons for putting rotten fish heads in the schoolmaster's dinner pail.

I loved school. *Herr* Remmelin praised my neat letters. He commented on how well I read the Bible out loud despite my shyness. At age twelve, school ended for me and the other girls. We were sent home to learn from our mothers and help raise siblings. Washing bedding and putting up vats of sauerkraut were my new lessons. At seventeen, I was hired as a servant girl in a nearby village. It was years before I again encountered the blond-haired Johann, the tailor's son.

We were both home in Kittersburg to celebrate Easter on an early spring morning. He'd come from his journeyman year, and I from my position of tending a widower's three ill-behaved children in a town nearby. After mass, I was laughing with Magda, my best friend, when Johann, jostling with his brothers, stepped back and caught his shoe heel in the hem of my skirt. We both fell into a tangle of arms, legs, skirts, and shoes. My *fichu,* the small, triangular red-fringed shawl I wore over my shoulders, fell to the muddy ground. Johann's flat-brimmed black hat was squashed under me. When he tried to help me up, we plummeted into a jumble of limbs and clothing. A button from his sleeve twisted into my white lace cap. He stood too close as he attempted to untwist the sleeve and cap. He avoided my eyes when he handed me my cap, covered in a smear of leaves and muck. Magda picked up my shawl, which was too muddy to place over my shoulders. I stood hatless and shawl-less with my braids askew down my back. Johann mumbled an apology as I tried to brush the sludge from my skirt. Although I felt self-conscious and embarrassed, I insisted that I was fine. I heard his brothers laughing and teasing him.

"I've ruined your pretty skirt. Let me make you a new one." Johann said. His face was as flushed as mine.

When I heard his offer—something only a tailor would ever say—I stopped brushing at the dirt and looked at his face. Our eyes met and held. It was as if a stranger stood before me, not the familiar villager I had known my whole life. I could not look away. His eyes were a pale silver blue with a dark ring around the iris. They appeared as illuminated as a stained-glass window. I averted my gaze, yet my heart was pounding so hard I could feel it in my ears. I felt like an awkward colt, but a colt who could canter above the clouds. I assured him again that I was unharmed.

"The skirt will only need a good washing," I said, looking away.

We both focused on the ground as if it held the answer to our feelings. Then I turned to Magda, and he toward his brothers. Their teasing continued.

As Magda and I walked arm-in-arm away from the church, she whispered, "Well, if you have to fall all over someone, at least you found a handsome one."

On our wedding night, Johann confessed that our meeting was not an accident. He had seen me near the *Rathskeller* the previous day and planned with his brother George to casually bump into me, say, "Pardon me," and initiate a conversation. He was mortified that he had ruined my clothes and his reputation. We both laughed at the incident, grateful that it had happened.

On that evening of our muddy tumble, I only thought of him. I burned the potatoes I was frying. I dropped the beer stein I carried to Papa. I'd heard my girlfriends talk about being in love. Now I understood. I felt like I had been tipped into a vat of honey, sweet and soothing. Yet, I struggled to breathe and keep my thoughts straight. When I closed my eyes, I saw his light blue eyes looking into mine. I was jarred back to reality when my sister told me the next day that she'd heard Johann returned to his journeyman year on the road. They were guild requirements. He needed to travel and work under different masters to perfect his tailoring skills. Before he could return to Kittersburg to become a master, it was essential to finish his journeyman year. Even after such a brief encounter, I felt a stab in my heart because I did not know when I would see him again. Papa was telling me that I must marry soon, preferably to the well-established widower with the unruly children. In the next few months, Johann's face and smile were a song that did not stop playing in my head. I hid the soiled, ripped lace cap he'd touched under my pillow.

In September, months after our collision at church, I was helping prepare for the Michaelmas celebration. The impromptu tables, covered with sheets, were set up in the square in front of St. Mary Magdalena church. I set bowls of roasted harvest vegetables, bread from the new wheat, and whatever food the French had not stolen on the tables. The women stacked the twisted, salty pretzels, their arms folded as if in prayer, on a stick on the tables. Kittersburg's ramshackle band played well-known tunes. My feet began to shuffle with the music when a shadow blocked the light. I glanced up. Johann stood before me.

"*Bitte,* will you dance with me?" he asked. His uncrushed hat was in his hand, and his blue eyes glistened.

When I nodded, he took my hand. The first firm touch of his fingers on my skin rushed through me like a glowing ember. In the years since school, I had grasped many young swains' hands at festival dances, yet I had never felt like this. He not only took my hand, he intertwined his fingers in mine. Even though I hadn't drunk a single tumbler of wine, I felt warm and woozy. His eyes stayed on me as we faced corner partners in this familiar dance. We both knew the movements: right, left, backward, forward, circle your partner. When the dance finished, I was out of breath and bewitched. Johann brought me a cup of cider. As I stood shyly beside him, he cautiously touched my shoulder.

The band began another song, this time a waltz. His arm was tight around my waist as he held my right hand in the upright waltz position. We swirled and glided in time, flowing as smoothly as water over stones. When he twirled me, my skirt flew out in a perfect arc. He lowered his head, his lips close to my ear.

"You're so pretty," he whispered. I could not reply, but I briefly put my head on his chest. As we passed the older women on their wooden benches, I could see them murmuring behind their hands. I did not care.

It continued all night. The touching, the strong clasp on my waist, the brush of his hand to my cheek, the connection of our eyes as we passed, the silence at the end of the dance. We stood close together as the song ended. Some young men began a *Schuhplattler*—a dance with high knee lifts, thigh-slapping jumps, and slaps to the soles of their shoes—the single men performed it to impress the ladies. Johann called out encouragement. A crowd surrounded the dancers, everyone laughing and cheering. As if a veil had been lifted, any uneasiness between us melted. He turned and fixed me with his beguiling eyes.

"Anna, in a few days, I will return to finish the last of my journeyman year. May I see you before I leave?"

"*Ja*," I answered. I squeezed his hand. I was thrilled I would see him again and, at the same time, dismayed that he was once more bound to the road. He plucked a strand of my hair that had escaped my braid and tucked it behind my ear.

"Tomorrow." His finger touched the tip of my nose. The band had stopped playing. He smiled again before he turned to help the men dismantle the impromptu tables. I placed my hand on my nose where he had touched it. I doubted I could wait until tomorrow.

The following morning, as I was finishing my bread and cheese, Johann knocked at our door. Mama pretended it was natural for a young man to visit early when chores waited. I was glad that Papa was not home. I wiped my sweating hands on my apron before I walked outside to greet him.

"*Guten Morgen,*" we said to each other.

In the morning's bright light, I felt shy again. I scooped a cup of cool water from our well to avoid looking into his mesmerizing eyes. As I handed it to him, our hands touched. I led him to the bench in the kitchen garden where I could smell the recently cut hay and hear the call of a song thrush perched in a pine beyond the garden wall. *Do not say anything stupid*, I told myself. Magda had once advised me that men like to talk about themselves.

"Before last night, I hadn't seen you in a long time. Will you tell me about your travels?"

"Ah, Anna, I miss my family when I'm gone, but I've seen so much."

"Please tell me about it."

"Traveling is hard and wonderful at the same time. When my father would send me across the river to Strasbourg for fabric, I'd look up at the cathedral's rose window...you know how the light shines through, and it breaks into a sea of beautiful colors..."

I nodded. I could picture it.

"That made me realize that I wanted to see other wonders. *Ja*, I was quite eager to see what was beyond Kittersburg. I don't care too much about stitching a perfect buttonhole, even if it's my trade. What I like is visiting new places." He tilted his head to see my reaction. I smiled so he would continue.

"No, tailoring doesn't thrill me. Nevertheless, being a tailor's son, it's what was expected. And, it's better than being a soldier," he laughed.

I nodded again. I understood. Doing someone's bidding or fulfilling other people's expectations sounded like my life.

"Tell me what you've seen?" I prompted.

He removed his black felt hat with its flat crown and broad brim and hooked it on the trellis behind us. The sun lit his pale yellow hair. I hoped he was better at cutting fabric than he was at clipping his own hair. What had not been flattened by his hat spiked out at odd angles. I wanted to take the comb from my apron pocket and smooth it.

"I've walked through many Rhine Valley towns with huge stone castles sitting high above the river. Each town charges a toll to cross its bridge. Some of the stone bridges are from the

Romans. Can you imagine—centuries old? Do you remember *Herr* Remmelin telling us about them?"

I shook my head. It may be something you learned after you were twelve.

Johann continued, "Many towns still have walls where you can see cannonball holes from some war. Once, I walked through the ruins of a castle in Heidelberg—enormous. Built four or five hundred years ago by some prince." His hands outlined the shape of the castle in the air.

"People say lightning struck it, and the munitions turret exploded. You can still see scorch marks on some of the ramparts. There's no roof, but the walls still stand. People travel from everywhere to see it. Or they come to steal the stones to build their own houses."

"Keep going," I laughed. While he talked, I examined everything about his face—the straightness of his nose, the angle of his chin. A small, squiggly scar perched on his left cheek. I wanted to reach out and trace its pattern. His untamed hair was the same color as a butterfly that flitted by.

Johann hardly needed encouragement. The more he talked, the more I liked him. I saw far-off places through his eyes. I wished he would put his arm around my shoulder like the night before.

"I walked through amazing cathedrals with carved wooden altars gilded in gold. Their organs have more pipes than you can count. Their spires reach toward Heaven. The statues are sculpted from marble blocks or chipped away from red sandstone. It made me wonder about the people who created such beauty."

I closed my eyes, imagining what Johann described.

I never wanted to stop listening or sitting on the garden bench beside him.

"A few months ago, I saw the huge palace in Karlsruhe,

built by Baden's Grand Duke. I cannot even begin to explain how large it is. The palace and its tower are at the center of town, and all the streets radiate like spokes on a wheel." He held his arms out in a cone shape to give me a visual picture. Then he dropped his arms to his lap. He locked his eyes on mine as he clumsily took my hand.

"Anna, this is the problem. I see all these magnificent buildings which overshadow the shabby houses of the poor. I see how miserable their lives are. The dukes build their castles on the backs and taxes of unfortunate people like us."

He shook his head. "And like us in Kittersburg, the armies come and go. We suffer from wars we have nothing to do with."

Johann was not only handsome, he was caring. My heart was already in his hands.

"You know, one of the things I like best about traveling—it's certainly not sewing stitches for a master, even if he pays me—what I like is meeting new people, hearing new ideas. Once, in a tavern, I met a man, a surveyor, who'd just returned from *Amerika*. He returned to his village to collect his family and bring them to his new home. He told me about the fertile land there. 'Go to the frontier,' he said, 'the land is cheap, and every man makes his own luck. And if the streets aren't paved with gold, you can still grow plenty of golden wheat.'"

"Did he take his family back there?"

"I have no idea. We were quite drunk, and the next morning, he was gone. Still, I've met many a man my age who's bundled his fortunes on his back to cross the ocean for *Amerika*. They say there, people can become rich and happy. General Washington and Mister Jefferson wrote it down. People can be equal, unlike here, with the lords and guilds telling everyone what they can and can't do. *Liberté, Égalité, Fraternité*. That's what the French say, but the Americans try to do it."

"And is that what you want?" I asked, suddenly worried that he would leave for Washington's country.

"Yes, certainly to be happy," he said, squeezing my hand. "Being rich would not be so bad either," he added. "I think both are more possible in *Amerika* than in Baden."

He let go of my hand and picked a late squash blossom from the nearby patch. He sat quietly in thought, plucking the petals off one by one. I said nothing. He spoke again.

"I once tried to tell my father about *Amerika,* and he said..." Johann rearranged his posture to a slump, pushed out his bottom lip, and imitated his father wagging a finger and smoking his pipe.

In a growly voice, Johann repeated his father's words, "*Amerika!* Nonsense! Come home, marry a local girl, and get your papers from the guild. *Amerika!* Too far! Too new!"

I laughed at his imitation. I imagined my father would say the same thing.

We continued chatting and laughing. He mimicked the mannerisms of one of the masters he had served under. Johann was funny and handsome. Looking at his smile and full lips, I wondered if I had practiced kissing enough in Mama's small mirror.

He cleared his throat, "Anna, you should have shushed me. My mother always tells me I have more to say than the Pope on Christmas. Please...tell me about you."

I looked at my scuffed shoes. *What could I tell him? I served beer at an inn for several years and cared for other people's children. I had never been farther than fifteen miles from where I was born. I adored my mother, but I was afraid of my father. My favorite smell was the lily of the valley in spring. I would always hide when it was time to slaughter the pig in November. My best friend is Magda, and when we were ten, we'd pretend to be sick to sneak out of church on warm Sundays. Would he care about any of that?*

"There's not much to say about me," I said.

"Surely, that's not true," said this man I already loved.

He asked me gentle questions. I heard myself answering and felt relaxed. He was so easy to talk to. He did not stare at my bosom.

"Tell me," Johann said. "What's *your* dream? What do you want?" His blue eyes met mine. He moved closer. Our knees touched.

"Me?" I told myself to be brave.

"I want a house with red geraniums growing in window boxes, and I want never to pluck another chicken. I want a pretty dress like the mayor's wife wears...and a bonnet trimmed with green silk ribbons...and several children—but only if they are well behaved..." Johann chuckled. His laughter encouraged me. My cheeks burned crimson. I continued.

"And, I want a handsome husband who has dreams bigger than mine...and likes to dance."

It was Johann's turn to blush. He pressed my hand to his lips, as soft as a butterfly's landing. We sat quietly. I was glad I had shared my heart. He sighed and stood.

"I wish I could stay with you all day, Anna, but I must go and help my father cut a suit for the mayor—the same mayor whose wife wears pretty dresses. May I come back tomorrow so we can talk about your dreams again?"

I smiled and nodded. I watched as he stepped over the stone fence that surrounded our garden. His broad back disappeared down the path toward the center of town. I could barely catch my breath.

The following day, true to his word, Johann knocked on our door. When Papa answered it, I could see he was unhappy that he might lose my services for a few hours. I pushed past his scowling face and walked back into the garden. Johann sat next to me on the stone bench I now considered "ours." Johann removed a small paper packet from his breeches pocket as we sat beneath trellised pea vines whose pea pods had long since been picked and shelled. He laid the packet on my lap. I carefully unfolded the paper. Receiving gifts was rare for me—I wanted to treasure this moment. I unwrapped a length of green silk ribbon as bright and delicate as the first shoots of summer corn.

"Perhaps I can make you a bonnet and decorate it with ribbon."

What could I say to a man like that? Nothing. I leaned over and kissed his cheek.

"Anna, I did not come here only to see you. I also wanted to speak to your Papa."

My mind raced. My heart pulsed. It could only mean one thing. Nevertheless, I did not want to embarrass myself. Instead, I tried to make a joke.

"Why do you want to see my papa? Do you need your shoes resoled?" Just as the Klems were tailors, my father and his father before him were cobblers. Despite all his journeyman walking, I could see his shoes were fine.

"I did not come to ask him about shoes; I came to ask about his daughter's hand."

"Here is my hand," I said. I lifted it in the air and twisted it back and forth. "What do you want with it?" I teased. I wanted whatever would happen to be between Johann and me, not just an arrangement between men.

"I want to put a small gold ring on this finger," he said, pointing to the fourth finger of my left hand. Then he took my hand in both of his. I could feel his calluses from pushing needles and cutting fabric.

"Anna, will you honor me and be my wife?"

"Yes," I said. "Gladly." We kissed gently on the lips. It was so much better than the mirror. We walked into the house together to confront Papa and tell Mama the good news. Johann could not have come into my life a moment too soon. My father had been arguing for me to marry the fat, bald widower with the three disagreeable children I tended. I wanted the yellow-haired man with eyes like the summer sky.

In 1803, one year later, the banns were set, the financial arrangements between our two families were made, and we knelt before Father Weber under the oil paintings of Saints Mary Magdalena, Peter, and Paul in the village chapel. Two tall beeswax candles burned on either side of us. Johann wore a black wool jacket with silver buttons he had made for himself, and I wore a dark green silk skirt covered by a frilled linen apron that Magda had sewed for me. My father had made my new black shoes. My sister wove the green silk ribbons through my braids, which I wrapped around my head like a crown.

"You're beautiful," Johann whispered during mass, "and not even the mayor's wife could have such a lovely dress."

After our vows, there was a reception at my house. Neighbors and friends brought food. The table groaned with platters of grilled fish and sausage, roasted chicken, and small honey cakes. Papa made sure that there was plenty of beer and wine.

When we tried to slip into the village guesthouse to find our marriage bed, we were followed by carousing male guests banging pots and pans and singing bawdy songs. I was eager to put on the dressing gown my mother made me. The gown's white muslin was trimmed with French lace at the hem and cuffs. Magda, already married, sat with me a thousand times to tell me what to expect. With Johann as my husband, I was not afraid. I welcomed him. We yielded to each other, claiming each other's bodies—a song without a beginning or end. I could not imagine being happier. I did not need *Amerika,* only Johann, to pursue my happiness.

Within the year, Katharina was born, and Napoleon occupied Kittersburg and the towns around the Rhine.

In 1814, a decade after our marriage, the armies no longer sat on our doorstep. Emperor Bonaparte was banished to his island. The English war with the Americans in 1812 had ended. That morning, while Johann drank his coffee and dunked his bread, he had brought up going to *Amerika* again. How could I continue to ignore his vision, his dream of leaving Kittersburg? Yet what had not changed in my world was that I did not want to go. Rather than the "reasonable" wife he wanted, I raged. I had used angry words, thrown a rag, and cried. Even with his attempts to comfort me, I was distraught.

I could think of only one thing to do—talk to my mother.

Chapter 3

Mama

Anna

I needed to see Mama while Katja and Bernard were at school and Johann was measuring the mayor's expanding girth. I gathered the cups and dishes and gave them a quick rinse in the metal tub. When I heard Delia stir from her sleep, I lifted her from the cradle, untied the laces of my stays, pulled down my tunic blouse, and gave her a breast while I straightened up with my other arm. Delia liked to dawdle at feeding, but I had little time this morning. When she was finished on one side, I washed her, changed her wrappings, and swaddled her tightly. I grabbed the wooden bucket and crossed to the other side of the half-timbered house we shared with Johann's brother, Arbogast, and his family and mother. My mother-in-law sat in her usual spot by the fire with a grey cat on her lap, saying her rosary. Rosie, my tow-headed two-year-old, sat by her feet, stirring an empty pot.

"Come, Rosie, help Mama get the water," I said, wrapping a shawl around her shoulders. She was reluctant to give up her game of making stone soup.

"Come, *mein kleiner Hase*, little bunny; we're going to the well. Perhaps we'll visit *Oma* Katharina, too."

Rosie clapped her still chubby hands. She loved visiting my mother, who always had a sweet treat and a great hug for her.

"Everything all right? Your mother's well?" asked my sister-in-law.

"*Ja, ja,*" I assured her. "Just want to bring her some yarn she needs." I knew my nosey sister-in-law. Her ears always seemed attached to my wall. She probably heard Johann and me arguing.

"Thank you for watching Rosie."

"Anytime," she replied. I hurried out the door before she could ask me any more questions.

We descended the stairs past the first-floor tailor shop that Johann shared with Arbogast. Without bothering to stop to say hello to my brother-in-law, I continued as quickly as possible with a bucket in one hand, Delia swaddled in a sling over my chest, and Rosie trailing behind or wanting to be carried on my hip. We moved through the narrow streets to the other side of the village where Mama, who had borne seven children over eighteen years, lived alone after my father died. When we reached my family's old cottage, I saw Mama's bent back, pulling weeds away from the bright yellow squashes in her kitchen garden. It was the same garden where I'd sat on the bench with Johann, who had charmed me with his tales of far-off places.

"*Ach*, what is wrong? Who is hurt?" Mama exclaimed when she spied me. She wiped her dirty hands on her already-soiled apron. I had surprised her with my early morning visit.

"No one is hurt. We are all fine."

"Even the baby?" she asked as she gently pulled aside the blanket to peek at the face of her youngest granddaughter.

"Even the baby. Is it wrong to want to see my mama if it's not a Sunday or my saint's day?"

"No, no, of course not. I'm happy you've come and brought my sweet, sweet granddaughters. Come in, come in." She ushered us through the door.

Once inside, Mama removed her stained apron, rinsed her hands in a copper basin, and took Delia from my arms. She kissed the baby's tiny nose and rosebud lips. Delia opened her eyes, and she and my mother cooed at each other. Mama reluctantly handed Delia back to me and spent a few minutes playing a game with Rosie, hiding a button in one of her hands and challenging her granddaughter to find it. When Rosie discovered that throwing the button was as much fun as finding it, Mama stopped the game and looked at me.

"Anna, I have forgotten my manners. Will you have some coffee? A slice of *Kuchen?*"

I was full from breakfast but never refused a piece of Mama's honey apple cake. I unwrapped myself and gave Delia the breast I deprived her of earlier. Mama poured the coffee and cut the cake. She lifted Rosie onto a stool and gave her a mug of milk and the two ginger cookies she had taken from a small white crock below the wall clock. When Rosie was settled with her treat, Mama sat in the chair opposite me. She reached across the worn table that displayed the scars of forty years of cutting vegetables and cracking nuts. She placed her wrinkled hand on mine and gave me a slight squeeze.

"Now, tell me. Why does my capable, strong daughter with red swollen eyes decide to visit her mother on a day when 'everything is fine'?"

"*Mama,*" I began, as my tears began to flow for the second time that day. "Johann wants to go to *Amerika.*"

My mother could not control her surprise. "What? And leave his family?"

"No, no...he wants all of us to go. He'd met a fellow who lived there. He told Johann that the land was fertile and very cheap. And available. Johann wants to be a farmer full-time so he would not have to sew suits for people. You know, he thinks sewing is not a man's job. He says he would rather guide a plow than a needle. He wants lots of land, horses, cows, pigs...and whatnot..." I trailed off. My tears made my nose run. Mama pulled a towel from a hook by the wash tub and dried my face.

"Oh, Anna, I don't understand. Johann's father was a master tailor, as well as his brother."

"Johann says that he only became a tailor because his father expected it of him as the first-born son. The French were here then, and he did not want to be caught up in the fighting. And things changed for him in his *Wanderjahr*. He loved traveling. You know Johann's good nature—he loved meeting new people. He said that's when he first started to think about emigrating."

"And he never told you?"

"Yes, he did, but I thought he would change his mind once he had finished his journeyman year and we were married and had children. Now, he wants to go more than ever because the French are gone, and *Amerika's* war with the British is over. His dream is fast becoming my nightmare."

"Anna, Johann's an important man in Kittersburg, *ein Schneider und ein Burger*. Not every man can be a master tailor in the guild and be a citizen in this village. He's respected here. I'm proud to have him as a son-in-law."

"Mama, I know, I know. But Johann thinks that people here have small ideas. He says that everyone looks at every step you take and complains if you veer, even a little, off the path."

"Does he want to do something wrong?"

"No, no, of course not. He wants us to be free enough to

make our way." My tears continued to fall and stream down my face. "And the land. He talks about having more land. Here in Baden, that will never happen."

Mama took a sip of her coffee. Her cake sat untouched on the plate. She blinked away her tears as she looked at my puffy eyes. She smoothed her skirt and looked at tiny Delia and Rosie. Surprised at my crying, Rosie came and laid her head on my lap. "No tears, Mama," she said.

After I kissed her curly head, she was back on the floor, humming and stirring a pretend stew in the bucket we had brought.

Mama rose and crossed to the hearth. She stood on her toes to reach for her Bible resting on the mantle next to the prized German silver candlesticks my father had presented to her on their thirtieth anniversary. She walked back to the table and sat heavily across from me.

I pointed to the Bible on the worn table. "Are you telling me, Mama, that I must pray about this?"

Mama let out a deep sigh.

"Yes, always pray first. Oh, my darling girl, I don't want you or Johann or the children to leave me, yet there is something else we must consider."

I looked at her kind, weathered face and waited to hear what she would say. She stroked the worn leather Bible below her hand.

"Do you remember what St. Paul said?" She didn't wait for my response. Her eyes were closed as she repeated by rote, '*Wives submit to your husbands as if to the Lord because he is the head of the wife as Christ is the head of the church.*'" She opened her eyes and pointed to her forehead. "I had to tell myself that many times with your father."

I felt an immediate swelling of anger in my gut. "And didn't

St. Paul also say, '*Husbands love your wives?*'" I answered and slapped the table.

My mother ignored my fury. "Yes, he did, and we both know that Johann loves you very much, and I believe you love him as well. He's a good man. I cannot think he would do anything to hurt you or the children."

"Yes, *Mama*. Johann is a good man, but how can I leave you, my brothers and sisters, and this village? It is the only place I know."

"God will tell you how."

"I think God's ears only listen to Johann and are deaf to me," I replied.

I wanted her to defend me, to tell me that, of course, I should not go. I wanted to hear that my place was in Kittersburg with her and the rest of the family, not in a brand-new country a million miles away. For all her wisdom and kindness, my mother was a dutiful woman. She had been dutiful to my demanding father and dutiful to God. She would see no other way.

"I fear I have disappointed you."

"Mama, you never disappoint me. You were a better wife than I could ever hope to be."

"Perhaps, Anna, you should not seek advice on a journey from an old woman who has never left her home." Smiling, she picked up my hand and kissed the tip of each finger as she had done when I was a child.

There was nothing more to say.

A day's chores awaited me. I bundled the shawl back around Rosie and swaddled the baby again. I hugged Mama and kissed both of her soft, creased cheeks. Mama insisted on wrapping a clean napkin around more ginger cookies for Rosie to take to Katja and Bernard. I picked up the bucket and my daughters. We retraced our steps through the town. When we got to the church, I took a quick detour to the graveyard, where I knelt and prayed at Carolina and Odelia's stones. I promised them that I would never abandon them. We continued past the *Rathskeller* to the well. Rosie dawdled as a two-year-old does, kicking rocks and petting every dog we passed. Usually, my mind felt settled when I asked Mama for advice, but not today.

Chapter 4

Kittersburg

Johann

My feet felt heavy after I left Anna in tears at home. I knew I was to blame for her sadness. I gazed around me on the rutted, leaf-strewn lane, looking for answers where there were none. I understood Anna's feelings about our familiar home, family, and friends. Yet, to me, there were as many problems here as joys, and it wasn't only because of the bastard armies. I believed Baden was part of the old world, a world difficult to salvage.

On either side of me were the *Fachwerk* or half-timbered houses similar to the one where Anna, the children, and I lived. Built two hundred years earlier, their timber skeletons were exposed with a post-and-beam technique. Stucco was plastered in between the spaces. Walking between them, I saw that the wood on many houses had dried and split. Soon Arbogast and I would be climbing ladders to replace the wood on our own aging home. The constant need for repair was one more reason that the world Anna loved so well was crumbling and old. Anna and I lived in the same house where I was born. We shared a common wall with my brother. I toiled in the same workshop where my father and his father sewed clothing for others. It wasn't enough for me.

The lanes I passed through were so narrow that it was sometimes difficult for a horse and wagon, let alone a team of oxen with a heavy load. In my journeyman travels, I had seen similar towns with similar houses that leaned toward the crooked streets like drunken soldiers standing at half attention. They all felt too old, too the same to me. I yearned for the newness of *Amerika*. I longed for a place where everyone did not know my name or judged everything I did.

As I approached the central square, I saw the *Rathaus,* where I met with fellow villagers in the council. Nearby was the stone fountain, its cherubs' and saints' faces eroded by weather and potshots from occupying soldiers, where we often gathered to gossip and linger over buckets of dripping water. Opposite the *Rathaus* was the small medieval church where Anna and I were married. I'd hoped to hurry through the square and avoid Father Weber, the elderly priest, yet there he was, sweeping the limestone steps. He raised his reed broom like a crozier to stop me. I was in for an unwanted conversation. Sweeping was a job reserved for village women. Nevertheless, Father Weber, a fusty man with a bald head covered by a black biretta, liked to show his flock his hard work. I believed he did not want to miss any village gossip.

"Ah, Johann, please stop and visit with an old man."

"Father Weber, I always have time for you," I answered. I'd

learned years ago that the best way to deal with the sanctimonious priest was to flatter, avoid, or agree with him.

"What's this I hear about you wanting to leave us and travel to *Amerika?*"

I wondered who had told him. It was most likely Arbogast, who, despite our father's death, still harbored a brother's jealousy toward me, the firstborn.

"Father, it is just a thought, a simple idea," I said, trying to avoid his opinions.

"You know, don't you, that in *Amerika*, despite all they say about new ideals, they despise the Holy Mother Church. They call us Papists there. They say we bow to the Pope and not Jesus." With that, he lowered his head and crossed himself. I automatically did the same. "Think this through, Johann. Do you want to desert this village which has given you everything? And your mother—may the holy Blessed Virgin protect her— would grieve if you left her alone and destitute." I was growing impatient with the priest's meddling.

"My mother is very well cared for by all her sons." Arbogast had insisted that he was the best one to provide for our mother. It conveniently included moving into her house, the one on the opposite side of the dividing wall from my own.

"Father, I beg your leave. I have an appointment with *Herr* Holbauer. I will give your wise counsel great consideration." I had to stop myself from telling him not to interfere with my family. As I passed, he continued.

"Ah, yes, must not keep the mayor waiting." *For all his words for the poor, he respected the rich more,* I thought.

I bowed my head as he gave me a cursory blessing. I hurried away, glad to be away from the conversation.

The street circled behind the church to a small graveyard where our two daughters lay. Dried leaves accumulated in the corners near the crumbling rock walls. I crossed myself. It would be difficult to convince Anna to leave them.

My thoughts turned to *Herr* Holbauer. Holbauer was my best customer. But he was another example of what was wrong in Baden. Before the French army overran the town, Holbauer was a miller and not one we villagers trusted. When we brought him our wheat for grinding on his massive millstones, he skimmed off more flour than his due. We saw him tip the scale in his direction. Most of us had avoided Napoleon's officers and soldiers if we could. *Herr* Holbauer had happily dealt with the French emperor's quartermasters. While he overcharged them, he fawned and scraped to get into their good graces. Napoleon had tried to remove some of the archaic governing practices of our Rhine region and had carted off local margraves, princes, and dukes. When the Baden margrave was ousted, *Herr* Holbauer moved his family into the former lord's large gabled house. He got himself appointed the mayor of Kittersburg. The French regiments were gone, but Holbauer remained the man with the most money and power. Those of us on the council had tried to oppose him, but bribes to men who needed to feed their families often got votes to go Holbauer's way.

I wished I did not have to deal with Holbauer. The other tailors would not sew for him, so I decided I could also play the former miller's game. I never cheated him, yet it was easy to encourage him to purchase a more extensive wardrobe. Holbauer loved to show off his finery at Sunday mass. Most of the townspeople were too poor to order anything except the essential coat or wedding suit, but I could count on Holbauer to dress himself and his wife in the most elaborate clothing or the newest styles. Today, the mayor wanted a fancy outer coat.

I lifted the heavy lion's head-shaped door knocker and let it fall several times on the massive oak door. This stone manor was built at least one hundred years ago for a lord when most peasants were serfs working on the manor's land. Holbauer himself, a tall, portly man, answered my knocks. Despite the early fall weather, his ruddy face was already covered with a sweaty sheen. He wore the handsome forest green brocade vest I had sewn for him a few months before. The silver buttons strained over his ever-growing belly.

"Ah, it's you, Klem. Come in, come in. I've not much time. Must be off to Strasbourg for an important meeting." Holbauer never failed to emphasize his importance to me. He thought it kept me in my place.

"*Guten Tag, Herr* Holbauer. I need to be sure of my measurements. A great coat is long and needs to cover well. I want to be precise. I must use the best fabric and find the perfect fasteners." I did not add that every time I made him a garment, I needed to make it larger.

"*Ja, ja,* whatever you need."

"Such a fine coat will need a splendid lining, perhaps a red silk." I pantomimed him, throwing open his coat to expose a glossy, scarlet lining. His eager smile told me how pleased he would be to show it off.

"Yes, yes, the very best. Will the fabric need to be purchased in Paris?"

"*Nein,* I think I can find fine silk in Strasbourg...still, it will be dear."

"Of course, but not too much. I'm still a poor man." Holbauer tried to present himself to the townspeople as lordly and, simultaneously, a pauper like them. *Like them,* I thought, *but also one who had meat every day and never had to skip a meal so his children could eat.*

"A man in your position must look the part—only the best will do for you." I could easily humor pompous men like

Holbauer and Father Weber, but it was not what I wanted
to do.

"Now stand before the mirror and see what a handsome
sight you will present in this coat. I will look for a deep blue
worsted wool from Scotland to favor your complexion and eyes.
Imagine a stand-up collar and three short layered capes, each
lying comfortably on the other." I gestured with my hands so he
could envision the coat. "It should have silver buttons and cuffs
with more buttons." I counted out a parade of six buttons
marching up generous cuffs for him.

Herr Holbauer puffed out his chest as he looked into the
massive mirror framed by carved wooden curlicues and over-
laid with gold-leaf paint. I would make him a beautiful coat,
though I would regret every minute I hemmed that it was not
for a more worthy person.

"What a majestic vision you will present at Sunday mass.
The whole town will think only a great man could shine so
bright," I said. I was also considering all the extra fabric a coat
like this would waste: enough for a jacket for Bernard and,
perhaps, a cape for Rosie if I cut it well.

"*Auf Wiedersehen,*" I said to the overbearing mayor after I
finished my measurements. As I turned to shut the door, I
caught him still preening before the gilt-framed mirror.

Instead of heading straight home, I meandered in a circular
route around the outskirts of the town. I needed to think. How
could I convince Anna that creating fancy clothes for arrogant
men was not how I wanted to spend the rest of my life? And it
was not a life I wished for Bernard. If only she embraced my
dream. I needed to explain that we might prosper, not just get
by the way our fathers had. Could she understand that I
wanted to rise above what everyone expected? I longed for the
country across the sea where men would be paid fairly for hard

work, and a man's pockets could be filled with more than stones and crumbs or, in my case, jangling thimbles.

In the far distance, I could see the foothills of the *Schwartzwald,* the Black Forest. It loomed as both a protection and a limitation for us in Baden. The giant oaks and spruce trees paralleled our valley, covered in tidy, narrow fields of oats and hemp. The fields reached like long, thin fingers toward the village. Since the armies had come and gone, things had improved. A few good harvests that foreign troops had not stuffed down their gullets helped, but that was not enough for me.

My reverie was broken by a woman dressed entirely in black walking toward me. She tottered beneath a large bundle of hay she carried from the field to feed her cow. Some locals, especially the children, feared the crooked woman. They called her *die alte Hexa,* "the old witch," behind her back. My family knew differently.

"*Guten Tag, Frau* Metzger. How are you on this fair day?"

"Ah, Johann, you're a fine sight for an old wreck like me. My bones are old, and my feet ache, yet God wakes me every morning with his sweet breath." She dropped the heavy bundle by the side of the road. One of the many things I loved about this woman was her optimistic spirit.

"*Frau* Metzger, let me carry that hay for you."

"Johann, you're always a comfort to me. But you know that I've been carrying things for so long that my back feels lonely without a burden. I can always fend for myself."

"How is my little Bernard?" she continued, changing the subject.

"As all little boys, growing as fast as the weeds in the field and always hungry, especially for Anna's strudel," I replied.

"*Ach,* my special one."

Seven years earlier, I had met *Frau* Metzger because of our son. On the day after Bernard's birth, while Anna recuperated from hours of hard labor, I brought him to St. Mary Magdalena's church for his baptism. Arbogast and his wife, the godparents, stood beside me. Katja held onto my leg as I held my new son over the carved marble font. Father Weber poured the blessed water over my baby's brow. When he asked what name we had chosen, I answered,

"Bernard Walter."

As I said the name, I heard an exclamation from a tiny woman kneeling in the shadows of a back pew. After the anointing, as we filed from the church, the woman reached out her hand to stop me. I recognized her as the widow of *Herr* Metzger, one of the town's butchers. She leaned her face toward the blankets covering my son.

"*Bitte,* please...May I see him?" I pulled the crocheted white wrap away to reveal his fuzz of gold hair, damp from the water, and his perfect little nose. The bow of his pink lips moved as if he nursed his mother's breast in his sleep. The widow Metzger peered forward and looked at his face. She smiled an almost toothless smile and murmured a hushed blessing. Her face, creased with weather and age, shone with a mantle of kindness. Her clouded eyes found mine.

"Bernard Walter?" she repeated for confirmation.

"Yes, that's his name."

"That was my husband's name. He died ten years ago today. I came to the church to pray for his everlasting soul." She crossed herself and kissed a silver rosary. "My husband and your son have the same name. I think it is a sign, don't you?"

Before I could reply, she answered her question.

"Yes," she said, "It's a sign from God and my Bernard."

Without saying another word, she turned. I watched her black-clothed body, with its work-bent back, shuffle through the arch of St. Mary Magdalena's heavy wooden door.

When I returned home, I told Anna about my strange encounter. She shrugged her shoulders.

"A coincidence," she replied. "Mama always says, 'There are no coincidences, just God's little ways of playing a joke.'" Anna repeated. She was more interested in nuzzling and feeding her newborn son than in figuring out God's humor.

I monitored the door to greet family and friends as they arrived with good wishes and gifts of food. I had no time to ponder the strange encounter with the butcher's widow.

As I was sewing by the fading light from the window and Anna nursed Bernard the following day, we heard a loud rap at the door. Katja opened the door and stood, her mouth agape, gazing at the unexpected visitor. My daughter looked at me, uncertain if she was supposed to welcome the black-clad, stooped woman or quickly slam the door.

Frau Metzger pushed her way in.

"*Guten Tag, Fraulein,*" she said, moving Katja aside. I stood as Anna struggled to cover herself. We both attempted to welcome her, though neither knew her other than as the butcher's widow. She brushed aside greetings.

"*Guten Tag, Herr* Klem, *Frau* Klem. I have something to give to baby Bernard."

With no more introduction than that, she pulled a small, red velvet sack from her pocket. She untied the drawstrings and spilled its contents into her gnarled hand. We gazed down at a bright, gold object. It was round and wide. The domed lid had the *repousée* image of a cherub seated on a rock with a hand outstretched to a small dog. Swirls and filigree surrounded them. As we stared at the golden object in her hand, she pressed a lever on its side, and the cover sprang open, revealing an ivory-colored watch face. Its Roman numerals and silver hands pointed to the hour. I was a tailor, not a jeweler, yet I knew that this was a costly timepiece. Before we could speak, she continued as if it were the most common thing in the world to give a precious watch to almost strangers.

"This was my husband's pocket watch. He worked hard to buy it. With every slice of his meat cleaver, he thought about getting it. When the French came, he buried it in the stable. I'd laugh when the armies searched our goods while the cow stood on top of it. Of course, the army eventually took the cow but not the watch." She laughed out loud as if this was a pleasant memory. She continued as if she had not interrupted herself.

"My Bernard always wanted to pass it on to a son." She paused and wiped her eyes on her sleeve. "God did not bless us with children. Now, this watch is for your son. My Bernard Walter would want your Bernard Walter to have it."

She closed the watch cover, slipped it back into its velvet bag, and placed it in the blanket encircling our son.

"*Frau* Metzger," I protested, "We could never accept something so valuable."

"Remember, it is not for you. It's for him." She poked a crooked finger near Bernard's full pink cheek. "Just like an angel," she whispered. "The watch is for him. You'll only care for it, for him, until he is old enough."

"How can we accept it when you may need to sell it in your old..." I began, then stopped myself, realizing I might be insulting her.

"*Herr* Klem, you see, I am already old. I have a house. I have fields where I can still work. I do not need a bauble like this. Besides, why do I need a watch? When the sun rises, I wake. When the sun sets, I sleep. On Sunday, the church bells call me to mass. It was important to my Bernard but not to me. I'm a simple woman."

She finished talking. She had decided. My son, barely two days old, owned a valuable timepiece. I knew that, even if I sewed a hundred great coats for a hundred rich men like Holbauer, I could never afford such a gift for Bernard.

Anna, always better at remembering social graces, took the aged woman's knobby hand. As she looked at the woman's kind, weathered face, Anna spoke the first words since the widow had pushed her way into our home.

"We would be happy to accept this wonderful gift for our son. We will guard it with our lives until he is old enough. Now please, sit with us awhile and have coffee and *kuchen*. Everyone has brought us delicious treats to celebrate Bernard's birth. We'd be delighted if you joined us."

Frau Metzger sat and ate cake with us. We laughed as she shared stories of her early days in Kittersburg and how she and her husband had outwitted the armies.

After that day, she was generous with all our children, often pressing coins into their hands. She gave each of our children, not just Bernard, small trinkets on their saint's days and at Christmas. She became like a third *Grossmutter* to the family. The widow Metzger enriched our lives with her goodness and generosity. I always appreciated the pragmatic way she viewed the world.

Frau Metzger had been in our lives for many years, and today, I was delighted we crossed paths. Meeting her might help me forget the argument with Anna. After my encounter with Father Weber and the disagreeable Holbauer, seeing her felt like opening the window on the first spring day. Despite her crooked back and gloomy clothes, she always cheered me with her positive, simple wisdom. She said exactly what was on her mind. That day, she did not disappoint.

"Johann, what is this I hear about you leaving Kittersburg? Tell me if it's true," she challenged me.

"How fast the news travels in this town," I replied.

"I know you haven't asked my opinion, but I'll give it to you anyway—that's the privilege of the old—we can say whatever we think."

I loved her bluntness. She once told me she was too old to beat around the bush. She had no time to waste on nonsense.

"I say, you must go. I don't want to lose you and your beautiful family, but I'm not a dumb woman. I hear things. I know there is plenty of land in *Amerika*. Good opportunities. It will always be the same here—everyone meddling, telling you what you can and can't do."

I nodded my agreement. She continued as if she had been saving up her little speech all day.

"We no longer have the duke, although *Herr* Holbauer is trying to become him. He has visited me many times, wanting to buy my fields. I'll not sell my land to that fat peacock."

I chuckled at her unrestrained, accurate judgment.

She clutched at my sleeve, and I could feel the sharpness of her nails through the thickness of my wool jacket. Her clouded eyes looked directly into mine.

"Listen to me, Johann. Take your family and begin a new life far away from here. Too many wars, too many floods, too many vicious men like Holbauer. If I were a younger woman, I'd go, too."

"No one is younger in her heart than you," I said with sincerity.

"Ah, you flatter an old woman. Though ..." she grabbed my

sleeve again, "I believe you should go to *Amerika*. Have an adventure." She then turned and picked up the bundled hay she'd been carrying, "And I will help you make it come true."

Before I could ask her what she meant, she waved goodbye and trundled toward her home with her bulky load. I welcomed her opinion—today, it especially cheered me.

If only Anna felt the same. Had I been too insistent with her? Was I like other husbands bullying and insisting that, as head of the family, things must be done my way? Even if it was true, I knew my Anna. She had a will as strong as an oak. She would not bend easily.

I resolved to give it a rest. I'd try to stop persuading her that an arduous trip across a vast, dangerous ocean to a wild, undeveloped country where we knew no one and didn't speak the language was the best thing for our family.

When I returned, Anna was home. She did not turn as I entered and kept her back to me. Rosie climbed on my lap and pushed a napkin filled with crumbling cookies at me.

"Look, *Vati*, what *Oma* Katharina gave me." She opened the napkin and held out the prized confections. "Mama says we must share them with Bernard and Katja."

"Oh, you went to see your grandmother today, not to the field to help Mama dig potatoes?" I asked.

"No," she answered, "Only to see *Oma*. She gave me cookies, and Mama cried." She stuck out her bottom lip and made a sad face. She jumped from my lap and ran to hug her mother about the knees. Anna's head stayed turned away during Rosie's revelation. Despite my clumsy words of comfort earlier, Anna had not relented.

We went about our evening tasks. We didn't speak. I felt her alternating emotions. She slammed a cabinet door, then wiped tears with her shawl. As supper drew near, I watched her fry the bratwurst and slice the black bread. She attacked the bread as if it were my head on the plate. Even Katja tiptoed around her mother as she scooped sauerkraut onto our pewter dishes and poured milk into our glasses.

The children's usual chatter was hushed throughout the meal, aware of our unspoken words. After dinner, they hurried to their pallets in the loft without being asked more than once. They knew something was amiss and didn't want to be blamed for adding to it.

I felt an immense weight, a throbbing in my temples, knowing that I was the cause of the family's unease. But my mind could not ignore the thought of a different life elsewhere. It circled like a horse's continuous path around a millstone. For me, going to *Amerika* was the only way to change things for the better.

While I attempted a sketch for Holbauer's coat, Anna sat across from me silently. After nursing Delia, she placed her in the cradle and rocked her until the baby had a slow, steady breath of sleep. Picking up knitting needles and a skein of brown wool from the reed basket, Anna leaned toward the light of the fire. The woman I loved above all else now sat four feet from me and acted as if I were invisible. I could no longer stand the roar of the quiet.

"So, Anna, Rosie told me you went to see your mother today," I said in the most polite tone I could muster.

"A daughter can visit her mother whenever she wishes," Anna snapped. "I hope our daughters will come to see me when I am old and lonely."

"Certainly, Anna. Still, we've been married for eleven years. It's rare for you to visit your mother during the week."

Anna sighed and kept her gaze on her lap, where her knitting needles stopped their tapping. She remained silent.

"*Liebchen*," I said. I dropped my paper and pencil and reached my hand toward her. "Have you nothing to say?"

"Yes," she said. "I do have something to say." She looked at me for the first time since the morning argument.

"It seems your dreams are more important than mine. It seems they include more hard work thousands of miles away." Her face was red, and not just from the fire. She locked eyes with me. "Don't we have enough of that here already?"

Before I could respond, she dropped the unfinished knitting in the basket, plucked the baby from her cradle, and climbed the steep staircase to the loft following the children's path.

Chapter 5

Tumult

Anna

Sleep eluded me on this night when I had refused to go to *Amerika* with my husband. The sleeping loft was dark except for the muted glow of the candle on the corner table. I watched the candle's soft light flickering on the velvety faces of my sleeping children. Their chests rose and fell with the rhythm of their breath as they snuggled on their goose-feather pallets. Rosalia was cuddled in Katja's arms. Bernard slept on his back with his limbs splayed out as if, even in sleep, he was entitled to more space. *Why is it that men need so much room?* I wondered. *They are constantly seeking bigger margins. More bed space, grander houses, more land, larger fields, expanded boundaries; they even wanted continents.* The girls and I slept on our sides, getting more bodies into a small space. We needed only small plots of earth that could be dug and planted by hand. We would stay closer, tidier, not consuming, and not overreaching. We moved with each other, breathing in and out in a connected rhythm.

I climbed onto the far side of our cupboard bed; its roof and sides held me in its boxed-in cocoon. On our usual nights, I would sleep on the straw and feather mattress with my back to the wooden wall with the baby in the middle. When Johann clambered in, he would face me and the baby, extend his arm over Delia, and rest it on my shoulder. That night, I made it impossible. I turned my face to the cupboard's back wall; the baby curled in the crescent of my arms. I heard Johann ascend the stairs and tiptoe over the gently snoring children to blow out the candle enclosed in its glass column. The unmistakable smell of extinguished tallow scented the air. His clothes dropped to the floor. He'd missed the wall hook in the darkness. Before coming to our enclosed bed, he mumbled a low curse when his foot hit a shoe or one of the children's toys left in his path. I felt his hesitation as he assessed the new sleeping arrangement I had settled on. For the first time in our marriage, we slept back-to-back. He was as restless as I.

When I awoke to the cries of Delia searching for the breast, Johann was gone. His shoes were missing, and I could smell the coffee beans he had roasted over the fire. The smoky odor wafted up the staircase. I awakened my sleepy-headed children to hurry them into their clothes. When I descended, Johann was not there. I spied the remnants of his hasty breakfast—an empty, earthenware coffee bowl, the crumbs from his bread and butter on the table.

I could not linger on his absence because, as usual, there were children to be tended to and chores to be started.

I sent Katja to milk the cow and Bernard to collect eggs from the hens. Rosalia rocked Delia's cradle and sang her a made-up song. I reheated the coffee and buttered slices from the large rye loaf. I sprinkled sugar on each of the children's slices as a treat. They hungrily gobbled their breakfast while perched on the bench at the heavy oak table. It was the same table where I had washed and shrouded the bodies of our two dead daughters.

The children could not sustain the silence of the night before. They chattered and teased each other. Rosie pinched Bernard. He pretended that he was grievously wounded and fell to the floor moaning while his young sister laughed until milk shot from her nose. Only Katja, my most considerate daughter, noticed her father was absent.

"Where is Papa?"

"Your father has gone to buy fabric," I said, although, in truth, I did not know where he had gone. I thought that he had invented an errand to avoid his scolding wife.

"Hurry, finish your bread, and be off to school. *Geh schnell!*"

I pushed the children out the door so they would not be late. From the window, I saw Katja and Bernard racing for school before the bell was rung. Schoolmaster Remmelin was known to slap the hands of children coming late.

I busied myself for the rest of the morning: slicing and salting cabbage for sauerkraut, sitting at the loom, although today, I moved the shuttlecock as awkwardly as if I were Rosie's age. I was scrubbing the floor with sand when Johann appeared at the lunch hour. I looked at him with surprise. His hands held no fabric, nor did he carry a bucket of freshly dug potatoes. Before I could say anything, Johann began.

"I went to visit your mother today."

I put my hands on my hips and was about to sputter something, but he continued before I could.

"I wanted to apologize to her for making her daughter so unhappy. For wanting to take her firstborn and her grandchildren away from her."

"And what did my mother say?" I was suspicious and miffed that he would see *my* mother.

In a voice hardly above a whisper, he answered, "She told me that she'd quoted St. Paul to you."

"Go on," I said. I was piqued and was sure that my pursed mouth showed it.

"I told her how much I love you, and she told me you were heartbroken about leaving your home."

"Continue."

"She told me that she had no other advice, that it was up to us to weave life together as husband and wife. We are the warp and the woof and must both contribute to make a worthy cloth." He stopped talking, and I saw his eyes rotate to the loom with the shuttle lying cockeyed through the warp.

"She had nothing else to say?" I prodded.

"Only that she was old and not to stay in Kittersburg for her sake. She is ready to go to God."

Tears pooled in my eyes. With all my crying, my teardrops could have floated a thousand ships. I picked up Delia, swaddled her in my shawl, and descended the creaking stairs to the street. I looked at the dirty, narrow lane with its crooked houses.

I felt deserted by the two people who loved me the most. I had nowhere to go.

In the week that followed, my mood varied between silence and sullenness. At some moments, I was furious; at other times, I was resigned. I was too impatient with the children. Once, when Johann asked for beer, I banged his stein so hard that most of the beer splashed right onto his lap, soaking his pants and just missing Holbauer's unfinished coat.

If I was not snapping at someone, I was blubbering. I overslept or could not sleep at all. I paced the floor with Delia in my arms until she sensed my mood and wailed. Katja took her from me and lulled her back to sleep. I stayed too long at my sister's and drank too much wine at my brother's. I was not the good wife and mother Johann and the children knew—I was a woman in turmoil.

Everyone in Kittersburg seemed to have heard of the commotion at the Klems. No one hesitated to make their opinion known. I followed their words with a wintry stare.

On the ninth day after our first *Amerika* argument, I made my decision.

Johann and I sat near the hearth, trying to eke out the last light without feeding scarce sticks to the fire. The children were asleep above us when I shoved my knitting needles and yarn into the basket beside my chair.

"Johann, I have something to say." I looked directly into his silvery eyes and saw the dying fire reflected in them. My heart clenched when the memory of the Michaelmas dance flashed into my head—the night I decided that Johann was the man I wanted. Though I tried to be strong, I heard the catch in my voice.

"Johann, I agree to leave Kittersburg and everything I dearly care for and can't imagine living without...but first, you must agree to two things."

Despite my behavior, Johann had not brought up the topic of leaving since the day of his unexpected visit to my mother's. He looked at me warily. He hesitated before replying.

"Please tell me...anything..."

"First, you will agree to renew the lease for our daughters' gravesites."

In Baden, where land was precious, graves were typically rented for twenty-five years. After that, if the family did not renew, a different family could lease the graveyard plots, and new coffins could be placed on the remains of our loved ones. I shuddered at the thought. I needed to be reassured that our daughters' graves would be protected.

"Yes, of course, Anna. It's a wonderful idea. And the guild should agree. They are responsible for our burials. If we're not here, they can at least safeguard our daughters' graves."

"Yes, good," I said with impatience. I wasn't interested in guild politics or finances. I just wanted assurance that the girls' graves would be undisturbed.

"There is another condition..." This topic was more difficult for me to bring up. I took a breath before I began. My heart hammered; my voice trembled.

"Do you remember how sick I was this past year when I carried Delia and her difficult birth? How I bled?"

"Of course, I remember. She's only two months old. I was so frightened that I would lose you both. I have thanked God a thousand times that he spared you." He reached his hand toward me, though I did not clasp it.

"And do you recall how difficult my labors were with Rosie

and Bernard?" I went on, although I knew the answer. He was so worried that he bit his nails to the quick and could not sew for days. He confessed to me after Rosie's birth that he harbored a deep guilt for how I suffered giving birth to our children.

"Do you know I am afraid whenever I carry a child in my belly? I wonder if this time I will die, or the baby will die, or even both of us will die."

His eyes filled with tears, and his head dropped to his chest.

"Well..." I looked at the fire. I did not want to weaken if his rain-blue eyes looked at me. Despite our long marriage, I found it difficult to speak to Johann about certain things.

"Johann, I do not want to be big with a child and be jostled in a cart or a boat or walking down a road when I am ready to deliver. If I were to agree to go to *Amerika,* I do not want to have a child in my belly and birth it without women I know to help me."

"Anna, what are you saying?"

"I'm saying, Johann, I cannot lie with you until we are in *Amerika.* Not until we have a home and place for me and a child to lay our heads."

"Anna, children are a gift of God," Johann protested.

"Yes, and we are the ones who give him the help he needs."

A frown inched down his face. He was not happy with my proposal. In sweet times, we both looked forward to the night when we would whisper about our day. When I removed my day cap, he often unplaited my hair and took the brush from my hand to smooth the crooks and bends left from my braids. He would stroke my hair, my shoulders, my hips. We fit together like a key in a lock, a hand in a glove.

Instead of reminding me of those tender moments, he said, "Anna, as a husband, I have rights."

"And as a wife, I have rights. I do not want a child to slip from me into the sea," I exclaimed.

His lips bunched. His foot began to tap on the wood floor.

"So, tell me. When does this punishment begin?"

"Johann, you are not hearing me. This is not a punishment. If we are to travel to *Amerika*, it is the way things must be until we have a house and a cradle. A new country, a new baby."

"So until then," he said, "I must live as a monk."

"*Ja*, and I must live as a nun. When we get to *Amerika*, I will leave the convent."

"Anna, perhaps we will be the only friar and sister who have four children," he said, his voice now warmed with a smile, his usual humor returning.

"Perhaps the pope will write an encyclical about us. The nun and monk who miraculously birthed four children." My lips lifted into a grin for the first time in weeks. Despite all our toil and troubles, this felt more like our usual playful conversation.

Johann laughed out loud. My ears had been starved for that sound.

"Anna Maria Klem, you are a difficult but magnificent woman. I'm the most fortunate man in the world to be your husband," he said. "I don't like the prospect of being a deprived man, but you are the only woman I want to sleep with or without."

He arose from his chair and pulled me to my feet. He enclosed me in his arms as tenderly as a shepherd cradling a lost lamb. He gave me a deep kiss, and I kissed him back. Then I pushed him away.

"Careful," I said with a laugh. Being in his arms felt as familiar as daybreak, as special as Christmas. But I did not want his arms to wander, his hands to seek more.

"Anna, this will be torture for me."

"And for me, too," I admitted. My cheeks turned crimson even without the benefit of the fire.

"I accept your bargain," he said.

He lifted an imaginary glass as did I. We toasted to what he wanted and what I reluctantly agreed on—a strange, different life.

Chapter 6

Plans

Johann

After those two agonizing weeks, I was elated that Anna and I were finally seeing eye to eye, if not exactly, on the subject of sleeping together. Nonetheless, I was grateful to her that she was willing to let me seek my holy grail. Her agreement allowed me to plan a future. And plan I did. It was similar to what my father taught me as an apprentice. If you want to sew the button in the precise right spot, measure several times before poking the needle through the cloth. A tailor had to plan rigorously. I had to calculate twice and recalculate often. Traveling thousands of miles was much more complex than making the most intricate garment, but I was willing.

Hiding under my joy, fear peeked out. Fear that five lives depended on me. Fear that, even with the best preparation, something unexpected lurked behind a twist in the road or the next rogue wave. As a journeyman, I had put many weary miles behind me, but then I was a single man and needed only to please an exacting garment-making master and myself. My satchel and a pair of stout shoes were my only necessities. Now, in 1814, I was asking a reluctant wife and four youngsters to trek across France, a country that had only recently deposed its emperor, to cross the Atlantic, an ocean, not a river like the Rhine, in a wooden boat to reach a land that had not invited us. I felt the immensity of my burden. And I felt the excitement of going to the place I had fantasized about for years.

As soon as the news that the Klems were going to *Amerika* spread, every citizen gave us his opinion or decided he was an expert on land and sea travel. One boasted of his expertise because his fourth cousin had gotten as far as London before turning back.

Herr Remmelin, the bespectacled schoolmaster, accosted me as we left mass the following Sunday. I stepped back as he planted his gangly frame before me.

"Johann, how can you take my best student from my school? Bernard is one of the brightest students I have ever taught!" he said as a form of greeting.

I eyed the schoolmaster. I was building a high wall against interference, but I was as proud as any father to hear my son praised. I tipped my head to show Remmelin that I was listening.

"Now, you were a smart boy but so naughty. But Bernard is altogether different. I know he's only seven, yet he's so curious. He comprehends better than the older boys...I think he is destined for better things."

I couldn't help but smile at his complimentary words.

"Only last week, I told Father Weber that Bernard picks up languages so quickly. When he finishes our school, he should be sent to Stuttgart or Heidelberg to study Latin or Greek and become a real scholar."

In a small corner of my mind, I wondered if I was sacrificing my son for this journey. Without waiting for my response, he chattered on. However, as he continued, my irritation grew. How did everyone in this isolated village think they knew what was best for my family? I jangled the thimbles in my pocket. Anna always said that was a sure sign that I was annoyed or nervous. Rather than saying what I felt, I asked politely, "Don't you think there will be schools for him across the ocean?"

"I know nothing about the schools in *Amerika*. I know only that Bernard is as bright as a berry and should do more than plant potatoes."

I considered my answer before responding.

"*Herr* Remmelin, when I was young, there was only one possibility: to be a tailor like my father. It's a respectable trade, yet I want Bernard to decide for himself. If he wants to be a scholar, that's fine. Anna and I would be delighted. It will be up to him if he chooses to be a barrel maker, a glazer, or a potato planter. I understand that in *Amerika,* there is more freedom to choose. Besides, Bernard is only seven; I think there is time for him to decide."

Remmelin studied my face. Then, he put his bony hand on the lapel of my jacket. "Johann, you are right. I should not interfere with what a man wants for his family. Nevertheless, do not let that fine little mind be squandered."

He let go of my jacket, tucked his Bible under his arm, and turned to walk away. After several steps on his pipe-thin legs, he pivoted and looked back at me.

"Klem, whatever I can do to help you will be my privilege."

The next day, Holbauer's opinion came as a threat.

"Klem, you cannot leave. I forbid it!"

Holbauer had pushed his way, like an ox broken from his yoke, into the workshop I shared with Arbogast. When he collided with the low doorway, his beaver hat fell from his large head. The lintel, perfect for average-sized men like Arbogast and me, was challenging for the cranky mayor. No one bent to pick up the hat. Usually, I would appease the boisterous mayor. Not this time. I slammed my scissors on the table.

"With all due respect, I don't think that is up to you to decide."

"Of course, it is up to me whether you can leave this town," the red-faced boor insisted.

"I believe you're wrong; it's up to the *Gericht,* the town council, to decide."

"Yes, and they will do as I say."

Holbauer's bulk blocked the light from the window, and his cologne did little to mask the smell of his sweat. I turned my head while I considered my reply. He was right. I did need permission to leave from the *Gericht.* I'd need papers to present at borders to state that we were emigrating without debts and obligations.

Nonetheless, I'd grown up with most of the men on the council and knew them better than Holbauer. Most resented how the mayor had bullied and bribed his way to his position, yet men who needed to put bread on their tables could often be coaxed to vote his way. I was confident that Jacob Dertlin, the carpenter; Joseph Uber, the mason; and my good friend, Martin

Fisher, the cobbler, would not stop me with their votes. After all, we had married each other's cousins, swam naked in the stream, and gotten drunk together. I had history and friendships with these men. Not only did we serve on the *Gericht* together, but many of them considered emigrating themselves. They were happy that someone else would be the trailblazer. In this matter, they would defy Holbauer.

Holbauer continued his rant.

"And, there will be a fee to leave. Don't forget that," the mayor blustered.

Of course, I knew I had to pay a fee for the privilege of emigrating so the townspeople would not be deprived of the taxes I'd previously paid. I had included this sum in my planning.

"Who will be my tailor if you leave? I've relied only on you, and may I remind you, I've paid you handsomely."

"You have paid me exactly what the guild determined to be a fair price," I said. "*I'm* an honest man. I don't cheat," This last was a taunt to Holbauer. We all knew he'd tricked the French and, as a miller, had a heavy finger on the scale.

"There are other master tailors in the Guild, and look here." I pointed to Arbogast, who had stopped sewing to watch the drama unfold before him. His hunched shoulders displayed his discomfort. He did not like the attention on him. "My brother is a master, also taught by my father."

Arbogast nodded. He was a good tailor but less practiced than I in dealing with demanding customers like the mayor.

Holbauer looked in Arbogast's direction and harrumphed. "Well, as long as I'm not left without a tailor. You know I must dress for my position in this village." He looked Arbogast up and down from his hair to his shoes. From his scowl, I knew he wasn't sure he could trust his wardrobe with someone who might be second best.

Holbauer picked up his fallen beaver hat and brushed it off with his ham-fisted hand.

"Don't forget, Klem; this is not over yet." With that, he elbowed his way out the door.

I turned to reassure Arbogast.

"Don't worry. The mayor doesn't know a buttonhole from a hook and eye, but he orders many clothes for himself and his family. You'll make a decent income from his vanity."

On a crisp night the following week, while the younger children were asleep and Katja and Bernard sat at the table playing cards, I suggested a stroll to Anna. I handed her the heavy-knitted shawl from the hook by the door and buttoned my jacket. As I interlaced my fingers with hers, moonlight crept over the rooftops. We crunched through the dried leaves scattered on the narrow, rutted lane toward the *Platz*. I led her toward St. Mary Magdalena's church, where we walked through the small graveyard with its tombstones and markers tucked behind the church. I put my arm around her when we reached the plot where our daughters lay. We bowed our heads in silent prayer. Anna knelt and brushed the twigs and leaves from their small marker. She used her apron to wipe her cheeks and nose before we continued on the path that circled the town.

"*Liebchen*, we won't forget them. Their souls have flown to God, but their memory is sewn into our hearts."

I cleared the knot in my throat before I continued.

"Today, dear *Frau* Metzger sold a small field and gave me the proceeds for our journey. God bless her generosity. George will build us two trunks and a wagon and include a pair of oxen. I'll give him our field and our side of the house in exchange. He and Ursula will move into our house when we leave. He'll give me what he can spare for the cow and the chickens. Lorenz will buy the small field you inherited from your father. He's paying me a pittance. You know your brother, always tight-fisted."

Anna laughed. She always joked that getting milk from a bull was easier than a *pfennig* from Lorenzo.

"Arbogast will pay our emigration fee in exchange for my half of the workshop. I think he's happy that he'll be able to rent half the shop. With these arrangements, we'll be able to pay for the passage. We'll sell everything else we don't need."

Anna gasped. "We must leave behind the painted cupboard and the chair my father carved for us? The cradle, the clock?"

"*Ja*. We cannot take these things in a cart."

"Johann, exactly what may I take?"

"Whatever we can fit in the trunks. Clothing, bedding, food for the trip across France, some pots for cooking."

"My copper kettle?"

I was about to say no until I saw the anguish on her face.

"Yes, we'll take the kettle."

She squeezed my hand. As we headed home, she persisted in quizzing me on every object we owned.

I explained the rest of the plans as we sat by the hearth the following night.

"Despite *Herr* Remmelin's protest that we're stealing his best student, he's been very helpful. We've looked at maps and chosen the most direct route. First, we cross the Rhine and travel through Strasbourg..." Anna interrupted me.

"Can we stop at the *Kathedral von Notre Dame?*"

"Yes, of course, we must convince God to come with us." She loved that cathedral with its high, tarnished-copper green doors surrounding the crowned Virgin and Child statues. She loved looking at the opulently carved saints on either side of the doorway. I would not dare to pass through that city without a visit and a prayer.

"From Strasbourg, we will continue straight west to Paris..."

Anna was brought up short, "We go to Paris?"

"Yes, we may need supplies there, and I will buy fabric. I might have to work as a tailor until we plant our fields."

"Is it safe? For the children and us in that city?"

We knew of Paris as the city of a beheaded king and queen. We heard the streets ran with blood and champagne.

"Napoleon has been sent to his island. I think we'll be fine. After Paris, we continue west to Le Havre, where we will board the ship to *Neu York*. A few weeks on the ocean and then on to buy our land."

"You make it sound easy, as if we're just going for a short trek to the next village. How long will it take to get to *Amerika?*"

I wasn't sure; I did not want to alarm her. "Only a few weeks. Perhaps eight to or ten weeks at the most."

Anna let out a sigh. "Eight weeks is a long time. It's the difference between a newborn and an infant who might sleep through the night. It's the difference between planting a seed and picking the first fruit."

"Don't worry, Anna. Remmelin and I have it all figured out."

Chapter 7

Preparation

Anna

Delia's cry woke me. Before she nuzzled me to nurse, I was in the depths of a strange dream—a nightmare. I was on a raft in the middle of the Rhine, and my mother was thrashing in the water, calling my name. Every time I leaned forward to grab her, our hands missed, and the current kept pulling us farther apart. As Delia satisfied herself at my breast, I resolved to visit Mama as often as I could before we left. Besides knowing how profoundly I would miss her, I felt guilt for abandoning her. I'd hang on to the umbilical ribbon that connected us until the day the cart wheels dragged me away.

Johann and I continued our preparations through the late fall and winter. When he wasn't finishing garments for *Herr* Holbauer and the grooms who needed new waistcoats for weddings, he made boiled wool jackets for himself, Bernard, and Rosie. He fashioned long cloaks for Katja and me for the frigid days at sea. Bernard's jacket was made from scraps of navy worsted from Holbauer's greatcoat with silver buttons. Besides the long outer garments, everyone would have two sets of clothing: one to wear and one to wash. All the women on both sides of the family knit hose for us and warm shawls for the girls and me. Johann put a deep hem in Bernard's pants. Our son seemed to grow out of his clothing as soon as Johann snipped the last bit of thread. I made new linen undergarments for the children and hemmed linen for Delia's nappies. George's wife, Ursula, made a snug bonnet to cover Delia's sweet-smelling head.

I busied myself with brining sauerkraut, sealing it, and packing it in ceramic casks. After we killed the hog, we cured hams and dried sausages for the wagon ride. I threaded sliced apples on a string and hung them from the rafters to dry. Johann said we'd save money if we brought most of our food.

As the days progressed, I became sadder. Even Johann admitted that life felt strange without sowing our spring crops of wheat, cabbages, and hops. Our fields belonged to others. We would own no land. Johann sewed money into our hems and jacket linings. We did not know what would grow in *Amerika*, but I would bring some of last year's saved seed. Ursula, not I, would plant vivid pink flowers in the painted window boxes this April. The flowers always made me smile as I smelled their sweet, spicy fragrance when I opened my shutters in the morning.

We passed through all the winter holidays—Christmas Eve, the Epiphany, Katja's Saint's Day—all the occasions when the large Klem family gathered to roast nuts, eat *Sauerbraten,* and exchange homemade gifts. On those days, I thought *This is the last time I will do this with my family in Kittersburg.* I would laugh and joke, but under my smile, my heart twisted like a dog tied to a post.

To revive myself, I would pay impromptu calls to my brothers and sister; I would tarry after Sunday mass to talk with neighbors and friends, even those I had previously avoided. I needed to hang onto every precious second of my Kittersburg life.

The more dismal I felt, the more Johann blossomed. He talked about how wonderful it would be in *Amerika* with woods and streams filled with animals and fish we would be allowed to hunt. Bernard caught his father's enthusiasm for this great adventure. Rosie and the baby, of course, had no idea what this commotion was about. Only Katja seemed to shadow my feelings. I often brought her to my mother's cottage, where she would beg to stay the night with her grandmother. I always allowed it, wishing I could also spend the night. Visits to my mother were a gift I allowed myself.

Early one morning, I visited Mama's crooked house. Her kitchen garden held withered frost-damaged plants. Pointy-eared, red squirrels with bushy tails buried nuts near the old trellis. Mama had just awakened and was tying on her apron. It was too late for my mama not to have the kettle on and the bread shed of its cloth wrappings ready to be sliced.

"Ah, Anna, my precious, how good of you to visit me. Come, help me light the fire."

"It's a little late for you this morning, isn't it?"

"Every day, it is a little harder to tell my bones what to do and my knees to hold me up."

I eagerly stooped to put some kindling on the cold embers and struck the iron piece on the flint until I saw a spark. As I fanned it into a flame, I realized how difficult this would become for her. She placed a hand on my shoulder to steady herself when she leaned beside me to hang the water kettle on the iron hook.

My gentle and strong mama looked tired and weary. Enormous guilt overcame me: *how could I leave her or trust my siblings to watch over her? How could I choose between her and my husband and children? But the choice was made. There was no going back.*

I sat at her battered table, and as she settled across from me, I heard her groan in concert with the creak of her old wooden chair. My father had made this chair for her and decorated it with intricately carved knotted vines, birds, and entwined hearts on the backrest. Her knitted shawl draped across the back, its ends puddling on the floor.

She asked about the children and the plans for our journey. Then, she rose from her seat with the same difficulty she had sitting. I thought she was going for the tea tin on a shelf by the hearth. Instead, she reached up to the mantle where her prized German silver candlesticks stood like sentries on either side of the wooden clock. My father had given her these intricate candlesticks for their thirtieth anniversary.

Mama walked slowly back to the table and placed the candlesticks before me. "Anna, I want you to have these."

"*Mama,* I can't take these. *Vater* gave them to you."

"And I am giving them to you."

I looked at the precious candlesticks. They gleamed with an ornate pattern of birds and foliage encircled by serpentine scrolls and curlicues. The candlesticks had a large base; in the middle was a sphere delicately hammered to resemble a pineapple. The lip at the top where the candle was inserted was wide to catch any bees' wax drippings. Other than Mama's smile, these candlesticks were the only thing that gleamed in this simple room.

"No, *Mama*," I protested. "How can I accept these? What will Lorenz and the others say if you give them to me? They won't be happy."

"I'm an old woman with perhaps a few years left. I think I'm old enough to do as I want."

She took the towel she had thrown over her shoulder when I entered and polished the candlesticks before she continued. "Your brothers will have my field and this small house. You and I will not have each other to laugh with and scold." She lay her hand on my cheek, and I turned my face to kiss it.

"You, my first daughter, will always be in my heart."

My throat was closing. I could not get a word out beyond the large lump.

"And, sweet girl, don't be sentimental. Don't hold onto them because I gave them to you. Sell them if you need to. Do what you must to ensure you, Johann, and the *Kinder* are safe."

With these words, she plucked her shawl from the back of her chair and wrapped it around the candlesticks. She pressed them into my arms.

"Go, now, before I decide to hide you away, and don't tell Johann where you are, " Mama attempted to joke. "You don't need to see an old woman act unruly and misbehave."

"*Mama...*" It was the only word I could say as my tears flowed. I bent and kissed my mother's soft, flushed cheek.

"Go, Anna, and may God go with you," she whispered. Her hand touched my face once more. Despite her jest about hiding me, tears filled her eyes, too.

I stumbled through the low doorway to the street, where I

could smell the sizzling smoke from someone's breakfast. I walked straight home, clutching my precious gift. When I arrived at the house, I charged up the stairs, disregarding Arbogast's greeting from the workshop. I ignored Johann and the children seated at the table. I climbed to the loft and lay in my bed with the quilt over my head. I clutched my mother's gift to my breast as if it were a newborn.

Chapter 8

Feast

1815

Johann

Easter Sunday fell on March 26th that year. I had decided that we would leave the following week if the weather was fair. My family, Anna's family, and all our friends decreed that a feast was in order after the rigors and the fasting of the forty days of Lent. We would celebrate both Easter and my family's leave-taking.

Following mass, the alleluias, and the pealing of the bells, I helped the men arrange stout barrels in the central square between the church and the *Rathskeller*. We criss-crossed them with hewn planks to create make-shift tables. In their finest dresses and newly starched aprons, Katja and her friends exchanged decorated eggs. Bernard raced around with his pals, Rosie, in pursuit. Our family and neighbors brought what they

could, the food that had survived the winter or had been squir-
reled away for the Easter feast.

Every sausage, from pork to calf tongue, was displayed on
the make-do tables. Smoked hams, pork spread with spiced,
yellow mustard, roasted game birds, and a baked partridge
stuffed with dried grapes overflowed their platters. A heady,
sizzling aroma spilled onto the square as two men carried in a
pig on a long spit. The skin was crisp and brown from its long
night of roasting over an open fire. I could hardly wait to bite
into the savory flesh.

The cheesemonger's mother and the baker's wife sliced
wheels of smooth, amber *Hartekäse* and large loaves of dark rye
bread still warm from the town oven. *Frau* Metzger tottered in
with a brass cauldron of kidneys stewed with onions. Every
wife carried an earthenware crock of her favorite sauerkraut
recipe. Spoons emerged from kettles filled with crisp roasted
potatoes, buttery sautéed cabbage, and earthy baked turnips.
Ursula and her daughter brought molded cinnamon cookies,
and Anna's mama brought the molasses-infused ginger cookies
my children loved. Even *Frau* Holbauer contributed a dense
rum cake with raisins, currents, and candied orange peel.

We shared barrels of dark and light beer and casks of the
sweet, white local wine. The Romans had brought grapes to our
valley more than a thousand years before, and we Rhinelanders
were forever grateful. Pulling a bottle of *Pflaumenwasser,* a
clear brandy, from a deep jacket pocket, *Herr* Remmelin shared
it with a few select men.

After we ate more than we needed, several villagers
brought out instruments for the dancing to begin. Besides bells
and clanging pots, there was a fiddle and a guitar. My friend,
Martin Fischer, tooted along on his coiled German horn. The
young women began dancing first. I watched their braids flying
as they spun and twirled. The young men, drunk enough to

lose their shyness, joined them, an excuse to touch the *fräuleins'* hands. All the mothers and grandmothers watched so that none of the young men held a waist or a shoulder a second too long. Rosie's cheeks, as pink as her name, skipped about in imitations of the dancers. The dogs howled and got underfoot, looking for fallen tidbits. A few adult women joined the dancing, but most men watched, content to smoke pipes and continue drinking.

I bowed in front of Anna, "*Frau* Klem, will you join me in a dance?"

Anna handed Delia to Katja to hold, kissed them both, and gave me her hand.

"*Herr* Klem, I would be honored." As we swirled, I remembered our captivating first dance at Michaelmas, how her hazel eyes danced along with her feet.

When the women cleared the tables, the young men brought split logs and sticks to prepare a bonfire. Most of the older people, including Anna's mama, drifted home. The unmarried men and young women lingered, chatting and flirting. I spied Bernard, finally at a standstill, yawning and rubbing his eyes. Anna walked toward me with Rosie asleep in her arms. Katja followed with the slumbering baby.

"Johann, it's late. The children need their sleep."

I took the exhausted two-year-old from Anna and placed her curly head on my shoulder. Her arms drooped loosely around my neck. Anna fashioned a sling from her shawl and cocooned Delia inside. The older children followed us as we strolled home.

I wondered if Anna's thoughts mirrored mine. Kittersburg had given us a marvelous send-off. We would never see most of these friends again.

And it was my fault.

Chapter 9

Packing

Anna

Johann wasn't in bed when I awoke the following morning. Delia was fussy and kept me awake for part of the night. She'd both wanted and rejected the breast, and I wondered if I ate something at the celebration that was tasty for me but too spicy for my milk. Finally, she was rested and sated with a delicate dribble of milk escaping her plump lips. I lingered in the bed with her cooing and smiling. Delia looked much like Katja at the same age, with a dimple buried deep in her right cheek and long dark lashes. She would burst into a cascade of baby giggles when I planted my lips on her belly and blew a buzzy sound. She was growing too quickly—rolling from her back to her tummy and sitting if I propped her up. When she was near her brother and sisters, her eyes followed them around the room. Rosie delighted her with silly, made-up songs.

"*Meine Schatzi*, my little treasure, we must go down to the others," I told her, but the pitter-patter of rain on the steep, gabled roof made me linger to savor snuggling with my baby in my cozy bed for as long as possible. Despite Johann's eagerness to depart, I was grateful for the rain—it would delay our leave-taking another day.

When the smell of the coffee beans Johann roasted over the open fire wafted up the stairs, I knew my idleness was at an end. I struggled to find my day clothes. I was surrounded by piles to be packed or left behind. Wrapping myself with the soft shawl that Magda had knit, I descended the angled loft stairs, balancing the night jar in one arm and the baby in the other.

Johann's face beamed as he poured boiling water from the kettle over the freshly ground coffee beans. Bernard and the girls sat at the table, drinking milk and eating leftover cake from yesterday's festivities. The sturdy oak table where they ate was one more thing that would be left behind for George's family. Johann interrupted my thoughts.

"Look, Anna. George delivered them this morning," Johann pointed to two large trunks, hulking new presences under the window.

Each wooden trunk was large enough for the children to hide in. Stout leather straps with shiny buckles encircled them; a large iron latch secured the bottom and the hinged top. A fili-greed key stuck out of the lock.

"And, look at this," Johann knelt and opened one of the trunks. He lifted out a removable shelf, sectioned off to hold smaller items at the top of the trunk. Beneath that, at the bottom, he pulled out a snug-fitting board that appeared exactly like the surrounding wood.

"It's a false bottom!" he exclaimed. "We can hide our money there and, perhaps, Bernard's gold watch." He was as delighted as a little boy who had just been given a hoop and a stick.

I tried to mirror his joy but found little pleasure lurking inside. All I saw was that our entire life must be packed into two trunks.

Johann put his arm around me and handed me a steaming coffee. I attempted to smile. I would try to be happy despite all my misgivings.

"When will we leave?" I asked. I was not ready to hear his answer. I squirmed out of his arms and began to prepare a thin oat gruel for Delia. In addition to everything else happening in my life, my baby was starting to gum solid food, though she much preferred her mama's milk to anything from a bowl and spoon.

"I'm not sure," Johann answered. "The rain isn't good for the roads."

Johann walked to the window to gaze at the street. The water poured down the lane, carrying decomposing leaves and a thin mud slurry in our tiny town. As the armies traipsed through our countryside for the past ten years, some roads had been widened to accommodate their marching feet. Most highways remained miserable and deeply rutted from cannon carriages. Even the best roads washed out after heavy rains or flooding. I was silent and thanked God for his gift of rain.

Another day in my home.

Throughout the morning, I folded clothing, blankets, and eiderdown quilts and stowed them in the first trunk. Johann warned that we might sleep under the stars some nights if we could not find a guesthouse. I'd heard about the conditions in some inns and decided we would be better off sleeping on our own bedding. As I continued packing, Johann struggled into the room with a large pile of folded fabric in his arms. He added the cloth, as well as the satchel with his tailoring tools, to the trunk.

"I'll sew if we need money," he said, patting the wool and silk. "Of course, we won't, as I have planned so carefully." He descended the stairs to his workshop.

I shook my head at his certainty. I hoped his confidence could keep us safe. I tried to believe him, although the world outside our village might have other plans.

I cushioned the few household items we took with Johann's extra fabric. In the center, I gently laid my mother's candlesticks, still wrapped in her cozy shawl. My hand lingered on the shape inside their knitted envelope.

In the second trunk, I packed the bags of seed we would need in the new world—hemp, cabbage, carrots, wheat. I added the foodstuffs we had dried or salted. Johann said we would stop at markets for fresh food, though little was available so early in the spring. A crock of sauerkraut, several links of sausages and a ham, and a slab of smoked pork sheathed in waxed cloth went into the wooden chest. We'd bring a small cask of wine and one of beer, hard bread, a few pots of jam and one of honey, a sack of flour, and a sugar cone. Fabric scraps left over from Johann's workshop would protect my copper kettle. I packed two knives and a large wooden spoon. The earthenware plates would stay in Kittersburg. We would each have a tin plate, cup, knife, and spoon purchased from the peddler. Johann tried to argue against any niceties, but I insisted that the children learn to eat correctly even on the journey.

I inspected the almost-bare room. So much would be left behind. George's family would benefit from our years of thrift.

When I spied my small distaff and spindle, I tossed them in the trunk. My loom would stay.

Johann entered to pick up my fireside chair. It was going to be sold or given to a family member. I turned away. My eyes fell on the cradle that Johann and my father made for Katja's birth. A sob escaped my lips. When Johann heard my cry and followed my eyes, he knelt by me and stoked my head.

"Don't be sad. When other children come, I'll make you a cradle out of good *Amerikan* wood. Or, we will be rich enough to buy the finest one in the land." He squeezed my shoulder before he carried the carved chair down the stairs.

He's like a child, his head stuffed with dreams. I thought. *My head is stuffed with memories and grief.*

After I tucked all I could in the trunks and closed the heavy lids, I sat on the top of the blanket chest, exhausted. Still, the floors waited to be swept and scrubbed. My sister-in-law, Ursula, was a stickler for neatness. She would scrutinize every corner of her new home with critical eyes. I whisked crumbs, feathers, and mud from the children's shoes into a pile before the hearth. As I bent to sweep them into a scuttle, I stopped caring. I kicked the detritus about the room like a woman with St. Vitus dance. With a great shout, I tossed the broom out the window.

Chapter 10

The Beginning

Johann

On the following day, I awoke before the sun rose. The rain had stopped yesterday afternoon, and I didn't want to delay another day. George arrived with the newly made wagon and the team of oxen. In the previous week, he'd taught me how to yoke and control the team of oxen with a long prod stick.

Despite the early hour, we scrambled into our clothes and marched over to the home on the other side of our wall, shared by Arbogast's family and my mother, Agnes Uderi Klem. Arbogast's wife had laid a table of milk, still warm from the cow, buttered bread, and her special cherry preserves. She pressed two more loaves of her dark rye wrapped in linen cloths into Anna's arms. We gobbled down our breakfast before descending to the street. The two hefty oxen with curved horns and steaming breath were yoked to the sturdy wagon. Arbogast and I hauled the heavy trunks down the steps and hoisted them into the wagon. George had built a high bench in front for sitting and enough room in the wagon bed for the trunks and the children. There would be a cozy little nest if we needed to sleep in the wagon. A latched gate secured the back so our few precious belongings would not tumble out on an incline or over a deeply furrowed road. Hooped uprights bowed over the wagon, ready to be covered with flax canvas in rainy weather.

Rosie, our little animal lover, asked the names of the oxen.

"What would you name them?" I asked her.

"Frieda and Sophie," Rosie answered without hesitation.

"Those are girls' names," I told her gently while I lifted her to see the massive beasts closer. "These oxen are boys."

"If we put ribbons on their horns, we can pretend they're girls," she said.

"Well, I guess we can do that." I kissed her cheek before I settled her on the ground well away from the steers' cleaved hooves.

Family members had come from their homes to gather for our leave-taking. My arthritic mother, who seldom left her chair by the fire, had painstakingly descended the stairs, one by one, to stand on our narrow lane with other well-wishers. She bent, kissed her grandchildren, and pressed a sweet in each of their hands. I leaned down to hear what my mama was saying to me.

"Your father would have wanted you to stay, but you do what's best. You've always had a mind of your own. It's one of my favorite things about you, my boy. You have my blessing. I will be praying for you."

Unlike Anna, in all these months of preparation, I'd pushed aside the prospect of leaving my mother, shrugging off my feelings with the assurance that Arbogast and George would care for her. Now the thought that I might never see my *Mutter* again pierced me. My devout mother, who never missed a

Sunday mass unless she was birthing a child, had a hard life. While my father was quick with a stick, *Mama* was patient and tenderhearted. I threw my arms around her and lifted her off the ground as easily as I had lifted Rosie moments before. I wrapped my arms around my *liebe Mutter*. I could feel the knobs of her shoulders, the sharp bones of her ribs. I lay my cheek against her head. After a long hug, I placed her gently back on the ground. I blinked away unexpected tears. I bit the side of my lip so that I would not cry. Silver strands of hair escaped from mother's white cap. Everything about her appeared tiny and narrow compared to my childhood memories. When I looked into her eyes, they were the same soothing blue I'd always known. I'd inherited my eyes from her. Rosie and Bernard bore my mother's eyes as well.

"We'll all be fine, and you will be, too. *Mama*. George and Arbogast will take good care of you." I reassured her and myself as well.

"*Ja, ja,* I know," she said. She wiped her fichu across her face to collect her own tears. Waving me away, she wagged her gnarled finger as if I were still her naughty son. "Go now, and don't forget your prayers." She smiled. "God watches, you know."

Before I could sniff away more tears, she placed a hand-knotted rosary in the palm of my hand and closed my fingers around it. I embraced her fragile body once more and kissed her creased cheek. I turned quickly and busied myself, arranging everything in the wagon so I would not feel painful regret.

Anna, who was saying her goodbyes to her sisters and my mother, was the last to climb on the wheel's spokes to find her place on the high bench seat. I saw her crane her neck for a final look down the street. Katharina Ritt was not coming. Anna told me last night that she and her mother agreed it was better.

"If I see *Mama* again, I may just run off with her hiding in the Black Forest eating acorns until I know you are on a boat to *Amerika*," Anna said.

She sat upright on the bench with Delia secured on her lap. Her gaze was straight ahead. When I looked at her, she nodded her head in agreement. I tapped the muscled shoulders of the yoked Frieda and Sophie and yelled, "Come up," to get them to move forward. They began their slow tramp.

Auf Wiedersehen, Auf Wiedersehen rang out as Bernard and his sisters waved energetically to their cousins and neighbors as we headed down the street past the two- and three-story houses. The village dogs yapped as they followed the cart. I walked by the oxen's massive heads as we passed through the town's latched wooden gates and the neat, narrow fields, away from the Black Forest in the distant east, away from our old life and onto a new one.

Now the Lord said to Abram, "Go forth from your native land and from your father's house to the land where I will show you."

— Genesis 12:1

Chapter 11

The Road

Anna

Frieda and Sophie plodded slowly. I knew I could walk faster than their three-mile-per-hour lumber. The children, tired from their early rising and excited goodbyes, had become quiet and bored. Bernard had clambered down, more eager to walk by his father's side than to sit in the slow-moving cart. We were reenergized when we approached the stone bridge over the Rhine leading from Baden to the French city of Strasbourg. We could see the cathedral's spire as we waited to cross the bridge over the swirling river, high and surging from the spring rains.

Halting our little caravan in the cobbled cathedral square, Johann paid a town boy a few *pfennigs* to watch the wagon and water the oxen. As Johann had promised, we would visit the deep, cavernous *Kathedrale von Notre Dame*. Light poured through the high rose window above us. While gazing up at the high-arched ceilings and the jewel-colored, stained-glass windows with biblical scenes, I inhaled the smoky incense and the beeswax candles with their faint smell of honey. Johann stopped to speak to a cassock-robed priest. The church's spire, the good man told us, made the church the highest building in the world. He recited many facts to Johann about the pink-hued sandstone church while I guided the children to the side naves. I showed them my favorite chapels, dark and mysterious, lit only by candles near their saint's statue. I helped Katja and Bernard light votives before a statue of the Virgin Mother. We needed her assurance for a safe journey.

Johann had timed the visit just right. At half past twelve, we stood before the enormous astronomical clock. A caretaker, who was sweeping nearby, explained that the clock dated from the sixteenth century. Its various dials told the position of the sun, the moon, and zodiacal constellations, as well as the time of day. He said that the twelve mechanical figures of the apostles who circled the standing figure of Jesus at half past the hour set this clock apart. The children clapped their hands at the magical rotating figures. I smiled at their joy.

Johann signaled to me that it was time to leave. I took a deep breath as I felt the finality of each step we took farther from home. We passed through the church's arched doorways guarded by carved statues of the saints and crossed the cathedral square to *Zum Goldene Löwe*. The small tavern named for the Gold Lion on its signboard, crouched in the shadow of the imposing cathedral. As we sat at a small table by a window, an apron-clad server, her wooden shoes clattering on the worn oak floor, brought the children mugs of cider. Johann and I drank steins of excellent, dark beer.

As always, I worried about the money we were spending.

"It's important that we eat hot food when we can. We will

not find many places on the road for a wholesome meal. The food here is good, and the portions are generous," he replied.

He urged us to gobble our soup and bread. We needed to resume our trek while there was still daylight.

We left Strasbourg's main square, Johann at the shoulder of Frieda and Sophie, with me following behind him. I'd fashioned a sling from my shawl and tied Delia close to me. She pressed her sweet face on my breastbone. Her eyes fell into a pattern of slow blinks until they finally closed altogether, lulled by my footsteps into a sound sleep. Rosie and Bernard snuggled together in a nest of quilts in the wagon bed. The three youngest napped while Katja, Johann, and I trudged beside the oxen team under the afternoon sun.

We headed west, always west. Though wider than Baden's roads, the unpaved highway was sunk by years of human feet, animal hooves, and French armies. Infantrymen and artillery had rumbled over this dirt surface to reach our German principalities and to battle with the Austrians and Prussians. Napoleon had attempted to improve the roads, yet the crisscrossing of horses, oxen, boots, and cannons left the roadways rutted with collapsed shoulders. In some areas, we had the path to ourselves; sometimes, we shared the road with heavy wagons driven by hard-bitten teamsters and rickety farm carts. An occasional fancy barouche traveled in the opposite direction. The oxen pushed into their wooden yoke, making a creaking chorus to the wagon's squeaks and groans. The iron-clad wheels crunched on the gravel and dirt. The stirred-up dust created a sneezing fit with Bernard until I swaddled his nose and mouthwith my kerchief.

The landscape changed as we progressed. Although there were still a few half-timbered houses with high-pitched roofs, there were more low-slung individual stone-faced farmhouses. The newly plowed and planted fields were larger and less precise than our German ones. In the foothills of the Vosges, row after row of grape vineyards turned their leaves to face the sun. The new chartreuse shoots shouted their recent growth.

Martin Fischer, Johann's cobbler friend, had made new shoes for each of us before the trip. I chose to wear my wooden field shoes instead and save the new leather shoes for later. Despite these familiar clogs, blisters grew on my feet as we walked. Each step became more painful until I waded leaves into the shoes to cushion my toes. When the sun drifted low and gloomy clouds threatened, Johann convinced a farmer by the roadside to let us sleep in his barn. In exchange, Johann had agreed to help the farmer, Monsieur Delacroix, remove a tree that had fallen in the winter. Johann hobbled Frieda and Sophie and allowed them to graze in the farmer's meadow while I cut slabs of bread and cheese for our supper that night. With the exhilaration of the first day, we fell into an exhausted sleep in the wagon bed, comforted by the lowing of the silvery brown cow and the smell of the hay.

The following morning, after the men took care of the dead tree, the farmer's wife insisted we join them by the fire for a breakfast of coffee and rustic, crusted bread. She spread a little honey on the children's slices. She was taken with Rosie and tied red ribbons around my daughter's curls. She told Katja she was a beautiful young girl and would make some strong young man a wonderful wife. I watched my eleven-year-old pull at her braids and blush a deep crimson to the roots of her hair.

Johann told the old couple about our plans to emigrate to *Amerika*. Monsieur and Madame regaled us with stories of other travelers who had passed by on the same road. For ten years, they said, all the French armies trudged by their cottage going east, stealing this and that; now, the Swiss and the Germans trampled by in the opposite direction. Johann was eager to get us on the road, but once more, I wanted to stay. I held Madame's bread-making hand in mine and thanked her for her kindness. The generous couple blessed the baby's head, stood by their stone gate, and waved until our small caravan passed from sight.

Chapter 12

Paris

Anna

We walked for four weeks. A month of avoiding cowpats and horse dung on the road, preparing meals on makeshift fires, or eating in taverns where the food was consistently greasy and sad.

Mile after mile, from awakening sunrise to yawning sunset, we traveled. The landscape changed. The villages were more closely spaced. The villagers spoke a pronounced French dialect. Fewer and fewer people spoke or understood German. Some did not understand our French.

If I was not in the wagon, I walked with Delia in a hammocked sling lashed around my shoulders. Occasionally, I secured her on my back, where she alertly watched her brother and sisters. She continued to be an easy baby who didn't fuss at the jostle of my steps. If Johann carried her, he buttoned her up tightly in his jacket, their faces almost touching. Katja had an excellent manner with her and amused her baby sister with songs as they cuddled in a slouch of blankets in the cart's bed. Delia tasted more solid food. Little bites with her baby lips. She didn't hesitate to shower us with food spray if any nibbles displeased her. She was anxious to crawl and pull herself from place to place. I could not allow that in the squalid inns with their grimy wood-planked floors. I was relieved when we found a grassy field.

Meanwhile, my good-natured eldest daughter was becoming sullen and silent. Katja's only relief was getting to a town where she could post a letter to her grandmother or her favorite cousin. Sometimes, I heard her quiet sobs at night as she buried her head in Rosie's curls.

Bernard was filled with energy and spunk until he wasn't. When he became weepy and sad, he would snuggle close to me and let his tears flow. He had always been the center of a crowd of boisterous boys and missed their jokes and made-up games. He missed *Herr* Remmelin's lessons and even practiced writing the letters the schoolmaster taught him..

Johann tried to keep everyone's spirits up. Nevertheless, I spied a new vertical line between his brows. I heard him jangling the thimbles he carried in his pocket, a sure sign of his worry. One night, when he was going to relieve himself, he was gone longer than needed. I spied him at the edge of a wood, kneeling on the earth, praying, his head bowed and his hands clasped together. When he returned with the children settled for the night, he folded me in his arms. We silently held onto each other as if the whole earth moved on our axis; we held tight to keep each other upright.

The only ones with a steadfast, uncomplaining mood were Sophie and Frieda.

Like Johann, I was eager to arrive in Paris. One night, Johann confessed that in Paris, he would seek Klaus Fischer, the reprobate son of his friend, Martin Fischer. I remembered Klaus as a n'er-do-well who sat on a bench outside the *Rathskeller,* flirting with the young women and trying to pat the bottoms of the serving girls. The last thing I knew of Klaus was that he had been forced into Napoleon's army.

"Why do we need to see that rogue? He is the last person from Kittersburg that I would care to see again," I protested.

"I know you're not fond of him, yet I promised his father I would try. Klaus has been living in Paris since he left Napoleon's army. Martin wants me to convince him to come home."

"Johann, I'm not sure that is *our* problem."

"You're right, Anna, but we know no one else in Paris, and he may be able to help us sell Sophie and Frieda," Johann said.

I was in no hurry to renew my acquaintance with Klaus; nevertheless, I longed to arrive in Paris to stay in one place for a night and sleep in a real bed.

In late May, we spent a night at a noisy, cramped inn where plowmen played checkers in the corner, and barmaids leaned over more than needed when they served the men their ale. We shared our sleeping space with a couple from Heidelberg who snored loudly and argued when they were awake. I drew a nit comb through the children's hair when they left.

A mizzle greeted us at daybreak. Despite the rain, we

noticed the road was better, less rutted, and more elevated. The competition for space on the highway had changed. Large wagons, coaches with passengers, and carts filled with produce or grain congested the thoroughfare. A rough-sawn wooden placard nailed to a post proclaimed our nearby destination: Paris.

The parade of carriages continued—everything from a one-horse gig to a two-horse curricle haggled for space on the highway. Phaetons were followed by drays with tottering hay bales threatening to cascade onto us in a fodder fountain. A *turgotine* pulled by four unmatched geldings pulled past us while its riders poked their elbows through the coach's leather curtains. Angry teamsters shook their fists and yelled at Johann and the slow-moving oxen. We had reached the outskirts of the city famed for bejeweled kings and "enlightened" men who preferred beheadings to compromise.

I tucked the children in the wagon box and warned them not to move or lean out the cart's sloping sides. I walked anxiously behind Johann as he encouraged Sophie and Frieda over stones that were slippery and unkind to their hooves.

Before us lay the great and infamous city. We crossed an arched stone bridge over a wide, slow-moving river and suddenly were on its cobbled streets. In the past weeks, we passed many walled towns with three-story houses and imposing church steeples, but I'd never seen this forest of tiled roofs and jungle of chimneys. What had been a road widened into a boulevard. Warehouses and narrow buildings crammed together and tottered eerily close to the street. We competed for space, not only with vehicles and four-legged beasts but with a desperate stew of people. They overflowed the stalls and boardwalks. Neither Kittersburg nor Strasbourg prepared me for this patchwork of men and women. Smocked artisans merged with aproned fishwives and blue-coated Prussian soldiers. Dark-hued boys in bright livery walked behind gentlemen with tall silk hats and silver-tipped walking sticks.

"Johann, I'm afraid," I said, clutching his arm.

"Me, too," he said, pulling me closer behind him.

I only lasted a few more minutes until I joined the children in the wagon and held them close. We heard a magpie of shrieks, brays, and a cacophony of bells. People called to each other and hawked goods held above their heads: hats and brooms, woven baskets, bunches of flowers. The clattering of hooves mixed with yammering voices. Katja put her hands over the baby's ears.

Shop signs and window boxes hung at a precarious angle. A spotted dog dashed between Johann's legs and beneath the cart's wheels. The odors were overwhelming. After weeks of smelling the earth and new grass, I now smelled a blend of animal sweat and sulfur, excrement, chimney ash, hops from breweries, and the dank smell of the river. Occasionally, I caught the yeasty smell of baking bread. The sweet smell made me homesick for my mother's bread and the shiny, dark skin of her salty, twisted pretzels.

We passed through a large square, *Place du Trône-Renversé*, the Square of the Toppled Throne. Later, I learned that twelve years before, blood had sloshed on the strees from the most active guillotine in Paris. Johann drove the oxen forward with his long prod stick while the rest of us crouched down, peering out of the wagon. My eyes were alert to any object or human that might come careening towards us.

"Johann, where are we?" I leaned out of the wagon and called to him.

He glanced to the left toward a high stone pillar.

"*Avenue de Vincennes*," he answered.

"But where is that?"

"Somewhere in Paris," he shouted back to me. I was

alarmed by his tone. I knew my usually sanguine husband fretted for our safety.

"How will we ever find Klaus Fischer in all this?" I couldn't conceal the quiver in my voice.

Johann didn't respond but looked forward over the straining shoulders of the oxen. Voices erupted at our plodding ensemble, shouting words I assumed were curses.

After more jostling, we reached another large plaza with a fountain and an enormous, incongruous plaster elephant in the center. I read the letters etched onto a column: *Place de la Bastille. Herr* Remmelin had told us about this square. In 1789, a crowd of working-class folk cut the drawbridge chains and stormed the outer courtyard of a stone prison. According to Remmelin, they demanded guns and gunpowder. Instead, the commandant surrendered seven prisoners and the stronghold. The French Revolution, he'd said, had begun on that day at that place.

We continued to move with the flow of traffic. Distress was carved into the curve of Johann's neck, the arc of his shoulders. I did not ask him again where we were. I inspected the surroundings for other signs and landmarks. He commanded the oxen to "Gee" and used his goad stick to move them to the right so the more insistent drivers could pass. One man driving a coach with a footman and a family crest on a side panel leaned over and shouted.

"*Écartez-vous, paysan!*" Johann moved the wagon as far to the right as he could and glared at the man who had called him a peasant.

As we exited the square, I glimpsed a sign on a lamppost: *Rue du Faubourg Saint-Antoine.* This street was lined with workshops and small factories. Metal signs hung in front of large hinged doors depicting a shoe, a hat, and a teapot. I watched a gaggle of raggedy children push through an archway.

I guessed the building was a spinning mill from the lint cloud billowing from the windows. Johann flicked the stick on Sophie's shoulders, urging him through this commercial avenue.

The children were silent, dazed by the unending parade. Occasionally, Bernard would elbow Katja, point, and whisper something in her ear. She would nod and smile. Rosie hunched close to her brother and sucked hard on the thumb in her mouth. Oblivious to the tumult, Delia slept undisturbed in the crook of Katja's arm.

The boulevard began to narrow. When I looked, I could see the river and the twin towers of a large church. Johann directed Frieda and Sophie into a narrow lane barely wide enough for the wagon. I laid my hand on Johann's arm.

"Johann, the children are hungry."

"*Ja, ja,* we will find something to eat."

"And then, Johann, we must find Klaus Fischer." The man who had been anathema to me now seemed the only person to rescue us from the mayhem.

I recognized familiar smells floating through the door of a nearby bakery. A hard-mouthed woman wearing a filthy apron emerged with a long loaf of bread. Johann checked the francs in his pocket. He had exchanged them for German coins at our last miserable inn. He entered the shop and a few minutes later handed me a warm, paper-wrapped bundle—*brioche au fromage*—cheese buns. I placed them in the children's eager hands while Johann walked with a jug to a public fountain at the end of the lane. There, a chimney sweep, his eyes a startling green in his soot-blackened face, attempted to clean his meaty hands. His long-handled brush and a rickety ladder leaned on the fountain's top edge.

"*Pardonnez-moi Monsieur.* Sir, do you know Black Cat Street? My friend lives there," Johann said.

The man shrugged as if even a chimney sweep was superior to this foreigner with road dust and a strange accent. He looked closer to examine Johann's face. He barked at Johann in a harsh, fast French, "What are you Belgian, Austrian, Spanish?"

"No," Johann replied, "we are from Baden, *Allemagne.*"

"Aah, a German; I should have known."

"*Monsieur,* do you know the street?" Johann repeated.

"Friend, there are hundreds of streets in Paris—how should I know them all? Tell me this: is your friend rich or poor?"

"Poor, probably," answered Johann. We had never known Klaus with more than a few *pfennigs* in his pocket.

"Then he must be on the other side of the river."

"And how do I get to the other side of the river?" Johann asked.

The sweep was impatient. "You see that church with the two towers and the high spire?" Johann looked at me. I knew he wanted me to pay strict attention. Four ears are better than two, he always said. The sooty man continued.

"That is *Notre Dame.* You head towards Île de la Cité. Then take *Pont Neuf* over the Seine. You will be on the left bank, and that's probably where you will find your 'poor' friend," he proclaimed. He gestured in the general direction. Without waiting for a response or other questions, he balanced the ladder on his shoulder and carried the long-handled broom upright as he sauntered down the lane.

"*Merci beaucoup,*" Johann called to the back of the man, who didn't bother to turn around.

While we ate the delicious buns, Johann and I conferred. Although the man had spoken in a fast, clipped French, we managed to understand his route between the two of us. We headed past the vast cathedral in the direction of the bridge.

Johann "geed" and "hawed" to get Frida and Sophie to clomp over *Pont Neuf.* The long bridge sat atop sculpted arches, allowing a better view of the twin towers, the green-copper roof, and the rose window of *Cathédrale du Notre-Dame.* On any other day, I would have insisted that Johann stop to pray and compare this cathedral to the one in Strasbourg. Today was not that day. Today was the day to find that rogue Klaus Fischer and seek his help.

Chapter 13

Klaus Fischer

Johann

The *Pont Neuf* was like an eyebrow shading the Seine below. Shallow, open-air boats steered by men with long tiller poles cruised beneath. On either side of the bridge, pedestrians strolled on raised walkways past stalls selling books and candles, tin pans, and used goods.

When we reached the left or south side of the river, I saw that the chimney sweep was right. We were in a different, older part of Paris. The streets were meaner, uneven, and full of turns and corners. The light was scarce, and the buildings were menacing and gloomy, with small or boarded-up windows. The streets were barely wide enough for the wagon. The smell of urine and damp, day-old cabbage oozed from the crooked, narrow houses. Rather than the official-looking limestone, multistoried buildings we had seen on the boulevard, these structures were cramped and run-down, with hanging shutters and empty window boxes. Shabby laundry was draped from side to side overhead. With her arms wrapped around them, Anna shielded the children from the decay.

Several times, I asked passers-by if they knew *Rue du Chat Noir,* the residence of the elusive Klaus. Puzzled looks met my question. Some people merely shrugged or gestured indifferently. Maybe left, maybe right. Finally, I stopped a young man I presumed was a student judging from the heavy book he carried. He listened politely to my question.

"*Rue du Chat Noir?*" he echoed.

"*Oui,*" I answered.

"*Voilà,*" said the young man, "you have found it. This is Black Cat Street, *Monsieur.*" He pointed to a short, snaking lane to the right.

"*Merci,*" I looked around. The street was tight and dingy—I didn't think the cart could maneuver its width.

I halted Sophie and Frieda, side-stepped vegetable peelings, and a stream of liquid dribbling from a half-opened door.

"Anna, stay with the children and the cart. I will look for Klaus."

I began to knock on rough, planked doors, always asking for *Monsieur Klaus Fischer.* The doors were not answered or were abruptly slammed by men with blank looks. Shutters on second-floor windows opened as guarded eyes peered at me, an obvious stranger with an unidentifiable accent. A buxom woman with forearms the size of a blacksmith's leaned out her rotting windowsill to interrogate me.

"Who wants him? Police?" she asked in a raspy voice.

"No, no," I answered, "merely a friend from home."

The woman scoffed but pointed to a door opposite her on the ground floor.

With relief, I thumped on the door and called, *"Herr Klaus Fischer, Bitte."*

A voice called back through the closed door, *"Qui?"*

I corrected myself, *"Monsieur Klaus Fischer."*

The disembodied voice called back, "Who are you?"

"Johann Klem from Kittersburg."

The voice responded in German, "Johann Klem, the tailor?"

"Yes, that's me."

With that, I heard the screech of a sliding bolt, and the door cracked open enough to reveal a bloodshot eye appraising me. The door flew open, and a tattered Klaus Fischer flung his arms around me, almost knocking me into the mire and offal of the street. I hadn't seen Klaus in six years. Before me stood a roguishly handsome young man with uncombed curls and an unshaved jaw. His face was leaner, his eyes warier. A scar over his left brow snaked up to his hairline.

"Klem, how, why are you here? Is my father here, too?" He looked furtively down the street to see if his father had come to collect him.

"No, Klaus, it's only me, Anna, and the children." I motioned down the murky lane to the corner where my out-of-place family waited with the oxen.

"Klem, why are you here and not sitting in your workshop sewing something?"

"Because, friend, we are going to *Amerika.*"

"Amérique!" Klaus shouted. He appeared astounded by the idea.

"Yes, and we need your help. You're the only person we know in Paris. We need a place to stay and then sell the wagon and the oxen. After that, we will take a boat on the Seine to *Le Havre.*"

"But, *Freund,* I can't afford to buy a wagon, let alone a team of oxen," said Klaus, gesturing toward his shabby clothes.

"No, no, not for you. Perhaps, though, you can help us find a buyer. You were always clever with those things."

Klaus smiled at my compliment and said, still cagey as ever, "Certainly, I will help a friend of my father's, but I will need a little something for my time."

"Absolutely," I agreed. Knowing Klaus's reputation as a young man, I knew payment would be needed. If we got a good price, it would be worth it.

Once Klaus heard that money was at stake, he waved to Anna and the children and clapped my back with a strong hand, "Aah, come in, come into my humble house, and let us celebrate the Klems in Paris."

"You're kind," I said, "but we don't want to put you out in any way. We'll be grateful if you could direct us to a hotel."

I looked over Klaus's shoulder into his one-room hovel with its cold hearth and a pallet on the floor piled with a jumble of soiled linens. Anna would disapprove of the children staying in such a squalid room. She'd say she'd rather sleep in the wagon in a barn.

"*Oui, mais non?* First, let me say hello to *Frau* Klem and the *Kinder.*" With that, he ran the length of the short alley and did an elaborate bow in front of Anna.

"*Frau* Klem, you are as lovely as always. And your children are all beauties." He chucked Bernard under the chin and kissed Rosie's and Katja's cheeks.

"I'll find a place for you to lay your weary heads."

"And we will need a stable for the oxen and the wagon until we can sell them," I added.

"Just leave it to me. I know Paris like you know Kittersburg. Paris is my oyster."

For the next hour or so, Klaus led us through the warren of small streets and finally to ones that were a little brighter, less baleful. As we passed every tavern or café, barmaids, some slatternly, some just off the farm, sang out *"Bonjour"* to Klaus. It seemed that Klaus did know Paris well, or at least most of the working *mademoiselles.*

At last, we found a hotel that would take us in. We were six people with large trunks, yet we were given a small room up a steep staircase. Klaus and I hauled the trunks while Anna settled the girls.

With Bernard trailing at our heels, Klaus and I sought a livery stable to shelter Sophie, Frieda, and the cart. We found a stone carriage house, cleaner than most, where the taciturn owner, sporting a large black mustache and a battered beret, seemed to prefer the company of animals to people. Klaus negotiated a fair price to house the animals.

"Tomorrow at the market, let me talk," Klaus told me. "Your brother's made a sturdy wagon—we should get a good price. There's always someone willing to pay more for fine craftsmanship. Just let me handle it," he insisted.

"Yes, of course. I will rely on you." I had no trouble agreeing. After the long journey to Paris, I was as eager as Sophie and Frieda for someone to take the yoke from my shoulders.

As we returned to the boarding house, I told Klaus about his father, his sister, who had married, and his grandmother, who had passed the previous fall. Klaus had a thousand questions for me, yet he did not answer the one question I asked him: *Will you go back to Kittersburg as your father wishes?*

After we'd sponged off the first layer of road dirt, Klaus led us to a café, where, as usual, he knew the barmaid. She winked at him and spooned out a generous helping of *cassoulet* and gave us extra bread. We drank wine and talked about the people we knew from Kittersburg. Bernard was on the edge of his seat as Klaus regaled us with stories of his time in Spain fighting for Napoleon's army and seeing the *Mamelukes*. Other customers stopped eating as Klaus described the dark-skinned Moors who fought on horseback with the French against the Spanish Royal family. He was on his feet lunging to and fro as he pantomimed the Moors, charging the crowd with flying cutlasses.

He retook his seat, lowered his voice, and leaned across the small table for fear that former French soldiers in the café might take exception to what he was about to confess.

"There was not enough food for us soldiers, and the Spanish hated us. Since I'm not French, only a stupid German, I knew it wasn't my fight—I didn't fancy dying for Napoleon. I'd decided my soldiering days were over. By then, I could speak a little Spanish as well as French. I traveled on foot or by coach—if I could talk my way onto one. Finally, I found my way to Paris, and *voilà,* I found the place for me. I wasn't made to plow fields or fight battles, but Paris suits me."

Torn at the shoulder, his battered jacket gave truth to his adventures. The navy wool jacket, missing many buttons, was that of a French soldier. When we returned to the hotel, I convinced Klaus to leave me his tattered coat so I could mend the torn sleeve. Klaus left us with a promise to return early the following day to take me to the livestock market to sell our faithful companions who had pulled us to Paris.

That evening, as the children slept, Anna and I whispered

about our luck in finding Klaus in the chaotic city. Anna softened her attitude toward him as he found us the tidy guest-house, and we avoided Klaus's grimy room. As we talked, I replaced the buttons and holes on Klaus's former uniform. Anna gave it a good brushing. It was the least we could do for a man from Kittersburg.

The following morning, Klaus arrived early with combed hair and a clean-shaven face. He was delighted at the condition of his jacket and thanked us profusely. Klaus and I walked to the stable, which housed Frieda and Sophie. The tight-lipped owner had sloshed the beasts with water and removed the tatty red ribbons that Rosie insisted we tie on the beasts' horns earlier in our trek. Without their road dirt, they looked like the fine animals they were. We headed to the livestock market in the St. Germain quarter near the quay with the oxen yoked to pull the wagon again. This neighborhood was even dirtier than Klaus's. Yet, from this mucky livestock paddock, I could look across the Seine and see a grand, colonnaded building. Klaus told me it was called *Le Louvre*. The enormous edifice was the former home of the Bourbon kings, he said.

"Napoleon stored all the art that he had stolen in that palace," he added.

We admired the massive building until Klaus began his show. He knew how to haggle. He knew how to flatter the customers, how to push the oxen's merits, and how to walk away. A merchant who pleaded poverty and reminded me of my former nemesis, Holbauer, needed a strong team to haul lumber. He purchased my faithful friends. I stopped him long enough to teach him how to give Sophie and Frieda commands in German, the only language they knew. I was sad to see their black-and-white rumps trudge away. I was unsure how to explain their absence to my daughters, especially Rosie, who thought Sophie was her big dog.

A portly gentleman approached us to examine the wagon. Klaus demonstrated its sturdiness, the stoutness of the wheels, and the evenness of the spokes, all made by "the best cartwright in all of Baden." The gentleman bargained hard, but Klaus outlasted him. The man, whose paunch strained the buttons of a soiled, burgundy wool jacket, admitted that the workmanship was superior to those made in France. The revolution and its aftermath had stolen many craftsmen away. He was as pleased with his purchase as I was with the heavy sack of *francs* he handed to me.

I counted out the agreed-upon price in Klaus's upturned hand.

We stopped at a nearby bistro to raise a celebratory stein of beer. While Klaus flirted with a comely yet bucked-toothed serving maid, I slipped around the corner to the second-hand clothes mart. I bought Klaus a gently-used gentleman's scarlet frock coat, a pair of buff-colored breeches, and a black bicorn hat. As a tailor, I knew the value of clothing, and from watching Klaus, I also drove a bargain.

Klaus was overcome when I rejoined him at the café and presented him with the new clothes. He punched my shoulder in the casual way kinsmen often do.

"Friend, you have already paid me dearly with *francs* and a taste of home. You didn't need to buy these garments for me as well."

"Perhaps you can return to Kittersburg to see your father and show him how you have prospered in Paris."

Klaus hung his head. "All things are possible," he said, "but some things are unlikely."

We both knew that. Although this former Kittersburg man might miss his family, he was made for the city, not a tiny village. Sometimes, the prodigal son cannot return.

"Let's find Anna and tell her of our profitable morning," I said. "And the children, especially Bernard, would love to see you, too. Perhaps you can show us this city you love so well."

Chapter 14

Klaus's Paris

Anna

When the men returned to the guest house, I'd washed the dust and muck from our clothing. I'd draped damp garments over every corner and available piece of furniture in the sloped garret room. The open window was decorated with one of my petticoats. Without a place to sit but the floor, we decided that it was a good time for dinner.

Before we left, Klaus showed off the garments that Johann had bought for him. He set the bicorn hat at a jaunty angle over his dark curls and admired himself in the small looking glass above the bureau. He stood with a hand in his new red jacket as we had seen Napoleon's officers do in Kittersburg. Bernard begged to try on the hat; we laughed as it fell down his face and landed on the bridge of his nose. Our merriment continued as we walked through the streets to the café Klaus suggested. He chose a place where the food was hot, and the young servant girl knew him well. We devoured a delicious *potage* filled with ham, potatoes, and cabbage chunks. The bread was crusty; the butter sweet. The nubile server winked at Klaus over the children's heads.

After our satisfying meal, Klaus doffed his hat and bowed to me.

"*Madame,* may I escort you and your lovely family for a tour of Paris?"

He held out his arm for me to take. I love Johann beyond measure, yet I felt a tingling to the ends of my toes when I placed my hand in the crook of his elbow. We strolled down the street, and, even in my scuffed and battered shoes, I felt a bit like Marie Antoinette escorted by her Louis.

Klaus led us across the *Pont Neuf,* its old stones arching over the river. Boats sailed beneath the bridge as he pointed out the quays on the riverbank that Napoleon constructed to make it easier for the barges to load and unload.

"Napoleon was a bully—a tyrant, many say—but for Paris, he was a guardian angel," Klaus declared.

Despite deserting his army, Klaus admired the self-proclaimed emperor.

In addition to the quays, Napoleon had built sewers to help drain the sewage from the twisting lanes. *He seemed to have missed those in Klaus's part of the city,* I thought.

Continuing his tour, Klaus showed us Napoleon's straightened and enlarged streets. No longer twisted lanes, they were now the wide boulevards—the same congested roads we'd encountered when we entered Paris.

Klaus brought us to the *Rue de Rivoli,* a street the emperor created to connect the *Louvre* with the *Jardin des Tuileries.* On both sides, four-storied limestone buildings anchored the street. The ground floors boasted arcades housing fashionable shops and restaurants. The upper floors held stylish apartments with elegant chandeliers visible through the windows. They were a million miles from the dark abodes of Klaus's neighborhood and the quaint houses of our home village.

I was taken with the women I saw strolling in pairs or with their hand in the elbow of an elegant gentleman. Their graceful pastel silk or white muslin dresses had low-cut necklines and high waistlines. The skirts were long and gathered and skimmed their bodies to almost touch the ground. Peeking out under their hemlines were dainty silk or kid shoes. I glanced down with distaste at my clumsy peasant dress with its ankle-length hem and many underskirts. Even though I now wore the leather shoes Klaus's father had fashioned for me, they felt more suitable for a field. Unlike the Parisian women's delicate cadence on the cobblestones, my shoes seemed more like a horse's iron shoes. I envied these women whose white shoulders, arms, and necks were encircled in long, draping cashmere or silk shawls worn with careless abandon. Vivid-colored silk turbans or small-brimmed bonnets, decorated with trailing ribbons or flowers, perched on their heads. Those without head coverings had tucked diamond and gold pins in their looped and twisted hair. Self-consciously, I touched the close white cap covering my braided and coiled hair. I stood on my toes to whisper in Johann's ear,

"Could you make me such a dress someday?"

"Certainly," he whispered back, "but I would not let you wear it until our 'bargain' is finished."

I blushed at his tease and slapped him lightly on the arm.

Johann drew a small scrap of paper and a stub of pencil from his pocket and made quick sketches as he assessed the fashionably attired men. Their fawn-colored breeches were tight-fitting, and their frock coats had square-cut tails. They wore their cravats tied so high that their chins were partially covered. Most of the men wore black, military-style high boots and sported bicorn hats similar to the one that Johann had purchased for Klaus. I watched as Klaus adjusted his cocked hat in a shop's reflected window.

We gazed at the displays in the many arcade shops. Precious goods from Europe and China decorated the shelves. Cream and blue porcelain teacups from Meissen sat among Cloisonné vases, ivory snuff boxes, and fine china dinnerware edged with gold. Pocket watches trimmed with precious stones were artfully arranged. Bernard pointed to the watches and smiled up at his father. He knew the fine watch Frau Metzger gave him was sewn into Johann's waistcoat's inner pocket. The objects that tantalized us were ones that a family like ours, traveling from a small village to a vast, unplowed country, could not use or afford.

We left the shops and approached an enormous building.

"Here is the *Palais des Tuileries,* the palace where Napoleon lived. And these are the lovely gardens." Beyond his pointing finger lay a stunning mélange of flowers and lawns.

We explored the paths of spring magnolias, decorative stone statues, and the vibrant waving flags of daffodils, tulips, and grape hyacinths. The children were happy to chase after each other in the green space. Rosie splashed and called out to get the attention of ducks paddling in an octagonal pond.

What surprised us were the encampments of Austrian and Prussian soldiers in the vast gardens.

"You have come at an exciting time," said Klaus. "Just last

year, after being trounced in Russia, Napoleon offered to abdi-
cate in favor of his son. Nevertheless, the generals turned him
down. They shoved him off to the island of Elba. I watched him
and his 14 carriages and 400 soldiers march out of Paris. It was
a sight not to be forgotten. But, Napoleon—always clever as a
fox—escaped and returned to Paris."

We nodded. Of course, we knew of Napoleon's defeat. The
peace had emboldened Johann to propose our trek to *Amerika*.
Yet we had not heard of Napoleon's return to Paris in our
month on the road.

Klaus continued, "They say he came back here and sat
down and ate the dinner cooked for Louis XVIII. For a
hundred days, he and his supporters fought these very
soldiers," he said, gesturing at the military men in front of their
white tents. "But half of Europe was against the man; finally,
he was *kaput* in Belgium." Klaus laughed. He had enjoyed the
misadventures of the man he admired but did not want to
fight for.

"So the King is back. They say Louis is so fat they must roll
him to his throne. Only last week, he returned to this very park.
The people roared and carried on. See the people wearing
white cockades on their shoulders? A few weeks ago, these
same people wore violets to support Napoleon. These French
amuse me so. They can never make up their mind," he laughed
again.

Klaus slapped Johann on the back. "The fickleness of the
people guarantees that there's always a show to watch." Klaus
chuckled again at the changing loyalties of the Parisians.

We continued down the *Champs Élysées*. The long, broad
boulevard was lined on either side with buff-colored limestone
homes built for the nobility. Some buildings, boasting Mansard
roofs and dormers on the top level, had been confiscated during
the revolution. The street, said our tour guide Klaus, was

created by Louis XVI, but, like almost everything else in Paris in the past ten years, Napoleon had improved it.

While the stylish bourgeois walked on the sidewalks with gold-tipped canes, the ragged laborers shoveled horse manure in the street. We reached a massive memorial under construction at the end of the avenue. Klaus carried Rosie on his shoulders while he gestured toward the arch.

"You see this grand structure? Napoleon again. After winning a famous battle, he built it to honor his army and probably himself. They say it will be over 50 meters tall when it is complete. But now they are not working. I guess that fat Louis does not want to build anything to honor *Caporal La Violette*."

After we remarked on the size of the unfinished arch, we retraced our steps toward the humbler side of the Seine. I gave in when the children begged for cups of chocolate at a small shop. As they happily sipped the dark, sweet drink, my heart was filled to see them carefree and intrigued by the stories of *Onkel* Klaus.

Life in the fashionable city might not be the worst of choices. Despite my country clothes, I was charmed by the new and stylish buildings on the right bank of the river. I heard Bernard ask his father if New York would be as grand as Paris. Although he could not know, Johann assured him it would be so.

That night, while Johann and the children sat by the glowing fire in the inn's gathering room hanging on to Klaus's stories, I carried Delia up the stairs to our second-floor room. I lay her gently on the bed and began to disrobe. I removed my linen cap and the red fringed scarf that crisscrossed my bosom. I unlaced the dirndl or stays that held my breasts tightly against my ribs all day. Then, I removed my apron, embroidered skirt, and two underskirts. I stood only in my linen shift. I tugged the neck of the shift down to expose the top of my bosom, just like the Parisian women I had seen. I secured it with the laces I pulled from the dirndl's fastening holes. I swathed my head in my red scarf in a makeshift turban. I pulled a linen sheet from our trunk and attempted to drape it languidly over my shoulders and back. I stood in front of the window and examined my reflection.

I was a poor substitute for a chic Parisian woman whose only job seemed to be elegant. I stripped off my improvised outfit until I stood barefoot in my shapeless, white sheath. Crawling into the bed and under the scrubby quilt, I embraced my baby, the sleeping, silent audience to my fantasy.

That night I dreamt of wearing a pale green, high-waisted dress with a rose-colored silk shawl flowing gracefully from my shoulders. I was dancing in the arms of a man in a scarlet coat and a large black hat. When he turned to face me, he did not have Klaus's bright brown eyes but Johann's pale, blue ones.

The next day, while I sorted and folded the dry clothing, Klaus and Johann, accompanied by an excited Bernard, walked to the Seine to inquire about a boat to carry us and our baggage from Paris to *Le Havre*. We would board a vessel from that port city to cross the Atlantic.

We spent two more days in Paris. I purchased food at the outdoor market to replace the supply we had eaten on our trek through eastern France; Johann bought wool and silk and an assortment of buttons and trim. While we prepared, Klaus and one of his female friends entertained the children in the small square by our hotel. I was resolved and resigned for the next phase of our journey.

Klaus came early on the promised day with a borrowed

hand cart. As Johann pushed the cart with the trunks, we walked to the quay where our flat-bottomed barge awaited. We watched as the cargo and the other passengers boarded. The ferrymen hefted the trunks and secured them in place. Then, it was our turn to step from the solid ground via a plank to the boat. Klaus held my hand to help me aboard. I gave it an extra squeeze. I turned to thank him, and without summoning them, tears welled in my eyes.

"Thank you, Klaus, for all you have done for us." The man I had disdained before I knew him had become our rescuer. The rogue had become the hero. I owed him for opening my eyes to the ancient but ever-growing city. He leaned down and softly kissed me on the cheek.

When we were all safely on the river boat, the ferryman poled us away from the bank. Ever the charmer, Klaus swept off his black hat and bowed to the girls. They giggled and threw kisses. Bernard and Johann raised their arms in tremendous waves. Johann put his hands to both sides of his mouth and shouted.

"Don't forget your father in Baden."

"Maybe he would like to move to Paris," Klaus said.

Chapter 15

La Seine

Anna

Once I had warned the children to stay away from the sides of the barge and cautioned them against dangling their fingers in the cool water, I began to relax. The river meandered through Paris as crowded with boats as the boulevards had been with vehicles.

The landscape began to change when we passed under the newly constructed bridge at Neuilly.

I watched women rinse sheets on the bank while the men squatted and fished from the rocks. We had returned to the bucolic world of small cottages and fields with grazing animals. Black and white cows and bay horses, whose brown coats shone gold in the sun, grazed on wildflowers and meadow grass. The water's color changed from pewter to molasses, from celadon to emerald. The onshore trees threw patterns on the water. The sunlight scattered diamonds on the current as beautiful as the jeweled earrings worn by the women on the *Champs Élysées*. The cornflower-colored sky matched Bernard and Rosie's eyes. Ribbons of thready clouds streaked the heavens above. My mood mirrored the languid and unhurried flow of the river.

A man with a tobacco-stained beard and eyebrows as untamed as a bramble thicket decided to school Johann and me on the sinuous course of *La Seine*. The river, he explained, had once zigzagged until Napoleon had decided to straighten it and remove over two hundred small islands. He'd built up the embankment and dredged the shallower parts. The improved river connected Paris to *Le Havre*. According to our teacher, the river was still twisted, yet straighter than before. A network of canals tethered the numerous tributaries. *La Seine* was the Main Street to the coast, he continued. I listened and nodded, but I thought, *Napoleon, not him again. That little man decided he could improve on God's work.* I wondered if there was anything on the continent that Emperor Bonaparte had not touched.

As the barge moved slowly and smoothly in a north-westerly direction, I put Napoleon out of my mind. I watched the crew hoist a small sail. Unlike the constant jostling of life in the oxen-pulled cart, I felt myself unwind on the peaceful liquid road. I inhaled the clean air and let the sun warm me and lull me into a puddle of quiet. This was one of the first times in my marriage that I did not have a task waiting, something, or someone who needed my attention. My eyes were closed. I was drifting off until I heard a wail coming towards me.

My eyes snapped open when I saw Katja rushing toward me hand-in-hand with a sobbing Rosie.

"What's happened to Rosie?" I demanded.

"She says we have to go back to Paris."

"Whatever for?"

"Because Papa has forgotten Sophie and Frieda."

I tried not to laugh as I gathered my animal-loving now three-year-old into my arms and reassured her.

"Ah, Rosie," I said, inventing as I spoke. "While we were in Paris, Sophie and Frieda decided to swim to *Amerika* because they were hurrying to see the new country. We'll see them when we get there."

Rosie listened and blinked away her tears. I unwrapped my shawl to dry her face on a clean corner. My fabricated explanation calmed her.

"Do they swim faster than they walk?" She asked.

"I think so," I answered. "And they never get hot and sweaty when they swim. And the flies don't bother them."

"Do the fish bite them?" Rosie looked concerned.

"No, the fish only like to nibble on little fish, not big swimming oxen," I assured her.

In a few minutes, she was peaceful enough to run off to tell Bernard the news of the swimming oxen.

Katja remained and peered at me with hard eyes.

"Mama, you lied to her. That's a sin." Her tone and her plump lips accused me.

"I was trying to make her feel better. She's too young to understand." Katja was not having it.

"A lie is a lie," she insisted.

With these words, she began to sob. Her shoulders shook, and she pointed her finger at me. "You are lying just like Papa. He told us that if we left Kittersburg, we'd have a better life. Then all we do is walk. We never sleep in the same bed. And... just when we are having fun in Paris with *Onkel* Klaus, we must leave again."

"Oh, Katja, I'm sorry you're so sad," I said. I reached out my arms to her.

My Katja rarely allowed herself to be anything other than

the helpful daughter, the holder of babies, the calmer of rambunctious Rosie.

"Mama," she whimpered, "I miss *Oma* and my cousins. I miss my friends. I miss standing beside you when you knead the bread. I miss how you and I walked to the field, and you told me stories about yourself as a little girl. I miss milking the cow. And...yes...I even miss Sophie and Frieda!" Her body shook with convulsive heaves. She buried her head in my chest. As I pulled her tightly to me, I breathed in her smell of innocence and righteousness. I lay my head on hers.

"Oh, my sweet, sweet Katja, I miss them too," I said. I held her as she cried out her misery. Her heaves rocked me as she struggled to catch her breath. Her tears soaked through my bodice. She wept out weeks of loneliness. She had strangled her feelings too long in her attempt to be the good daughter who did not make trouble for her mama and papa.

In a few minutes, her sobs lessened, and her breath became regular. I stroked her back and kissed the top of her linen cap.

She lifted her head and looked at me. Her hazel eyes regarded me through pink swollen lids. "I'm sorry, Mama, for saying those things," she managed with a shaky, husky voice. She swiped at her dribbling nose and chin with her hand until I drew a handkerchief from my pocket to wipe away her tears.

"Nonsense, precious girl. You are right. Seeing all those wonderful things in Paris, I wished that Magda was beside me. I wanted to talk to her and my sisters about all the beautiful clothes the French women wore. I wanted to tell my mama how her food was more delicious than anything I ate in the nicest cafe in Paris. I wanted to tell them how much I missed laughing with them."

"And when we drank chocolate, I wished I had one of *Oma's* ginger cookies to dunk in it," Katja added with a smile.

"That would have been so delicious! You are so right, dear girl."

I kissed her cheek and continued to cradle her. I remembered when she was Delia's age. My first baby girl, my first to watch grow and crawl from my side. I hardly had time to appreciate all her little miracles when my new babies came along.

I probably embarrassed her too much. She arose from my lap, sniffed, and swabbed at any remaining tears. She shook off her cuddling to become an eleven-year-old again, a girl who thought she was as responsible as her mother in making others' lives easier or better.

"Katja, the first thing we'll do when we get to Le Havre is to write letters to all our family and friends to tell them how we miss them. And about the wonderful things we've seen."

"Yes, Mama." Katja assented. She straightened her cap and smoothed her clothing. As I watched, she turned her head to each side. *She probably wants to make sure that no one has seen her tears. She was too much like me, always having to be responsible, always waiting for that next thing to be done, the next person to protect.*

I pulled her hand to my mouth and kissed each of her fingers. Self-conscious, she began to pull away, but I did not let go of her hand.

"Katja, please come to me when you are feeling sad or I have done something to hurt you. When you love so hard, it often hurts. Some people, like you and me, look backward to the things we love. Some people, like your Papa, look forward to the things they *might* love. But still loving is always the right thing to do."

Once more, Katja nodded; her lips curved into a dimpled smile showing all her perfect little teeth. She craned her head to catch sight of Bernard and her father seated in the bow. Giving me a tiny, swift kiss, she sped away on her self-assigned duty to ensure that Rosie behaved and Bernard was not pestering anyone.

After Katja ran off, I felt immensely guilty. I had not paid her enough attention when I had been so angry with Johann all those weeks. When I was finally resigned to the inevitable trip to *Amerika*, I was caught up in our preparation. I had relied too much on my little girl's willingness to be a loyal acolyte and a considerate, cooperative child. Her still-growing shoulders had carried too much. I was a first-born daughter, so I knew well how to wear the apron of "mama's helper."

Despite that tedious month on the road, I had begun to enjoy exploring new places and seeing sights I had only dreamed of. I was understanding Johann's wanderlust. Yet, I could never forget that I was a mother first. The children God gave me and Johann must always be my first thought of the day and my last breath at night.

Chapter 16

Rouen

Johann

I sat near the barge's prow, explaining the little I knew about boats and rivers to Bernard. Rosie ran up to us, trying to tell us something about Sophie swimming to *Amerika*. I glanced back and saw Anna near the stern, embracing Katja. *All is well,* I thought. I had *francs* in my pocket and had delivered my message to Klaus. We were on the next step. I was a happy man.

The tillerman eased our way along the curving river. The tableau of people working and animals grazing on the bank was a delight. A grey-coated Percheron, its massive hindquarters hardly straining, pulled a plow, creating a furrow in a field ready for seed. I was close enough to the bank to hear the jingle of the horse's harness as the plowman turned him for the back furrow. The immense horse shook his head and snorted, his forelock bouncing, as his well-muscled shoulders pushed into the next row. I took a deep breath. Next year, I hoped, that would be me tilling the fertile soil of my new land.

The easy time on the river continued as the boat passed Conflans, Vernon, and Giverny. We passed ferrymen on barges coming toward us bound for Paris, their decks piled high with large bales of cotton and stacks of hardwood.

On the third day, the Seine bisected the lovely town of Rouen. The sun was setting in a marbled sky when the barge captain announced we would spend the night there. Some passengers were debarking, and some, like us, would continue to the ocean port of Le Havre. We stepped onto the pier as the crew readied to unload cargo. We needed a place to stay for the night.

Our bewhiskered friend, who had informed us about the bends and curves of the Seine, decided to be our guide to this wealthy, ancient city. He told us Rouen had been controlled for centuries by the dukes of Normandy.

"Here is where the English burned Joan of Arc in the main square. The tower where they kept her is right here. Be sure to take the children to see our great clock. Just follow the bells, and you'll find it," he said. He stopped long enough to light his pipe and give us a brief wave.

This city, unlike Paris, with its large, modern limestone buildings and wide streets, reminded me of Strasbourg. The tall, narrow, five-story-high half-timbered houses had probably been built three hundred years before. The streets were as abbreviated and crooked as Klaus's neighborhood, but they were well cared for here. Rainbow-colored flowers spilled from window boxes.

When we heard the thunderous clatter of church bells, we followed their call to a Gothic tower. Above an archway was an astronomical clock painted to represent the sun's golden rays on a blue sky. We continued through a curved stone arch to the town square dwarfed by a large white cathedral. Its facade with statues of saints and biblical scenes was as intricately carved as our beloved cathedral in Strasbourg. Its unmatched towers cast awkward shadows on the cobblestones below. The enormous cathedral was also named in honor of Our Lady.

This time, we had the leisure to stop for a prayer. While Anna and the children lit candles, I heard a soft banter in German. I turned to see a paunchy, pink-cheeked man with a deeply dimpled chin. He stood beside a woman I presumed to be his wife, surrounded by three blond daughters. The girls were as alike as three stairsteps. Their flaxen braids were like their mother's, while their cleft chins marked them as their father's daughters. I introduced myself to the man and asked for their destination.

"We are off to New York and then to Philadelphia, where I'll work in my brother's bakery," said the joyful-looking man. His accent marked him from Freiburg in the center of the Black Forest, not far from our home. His coat bore two embroidered lions, crossed swords, and the pretzel of the bakers' guild.

He grabbed my shoulder when I told him we were from Kittersburg. He bellowed, "Then we are almost neighbors. Delighted to meet you." He pumped my arm up and down.

"I'm Otto Hoffman, and this is my wife, Berta." He put his arm around the shoulders of the plump woman with the same pink cheeks as her husband. Otto pointed to his blond girls.

"This is Marta, Elsa, and Agnes. My lovely daughters."

I watched as Katja and Marta shyly appraised each other. They were about the same age, although Marta was taller and appeared less timid than Katja. Earlier, Anna had whispered to me of Katja's distress. I hoped a new friend would soothe her. I knew Anna was also eager to chat with another woman.

After finding a guest house with a cozy gathering room, our two families exchanged notes about our journeys. We talked about our plans over bowls of hot potato soup and steins of the delicious local cider. Otto was a chatty and easy-going sort who couldn't stop discussing the differences between French and German bread. He went on about the crusty, dense bread he baked with its distinctive crunch. *Bauernbrot, Koernerkruste, Schwarzbrot, Kaiserskemmel* he nattered on. Unlike me, Otto was not interested in being a farmer. He loved his trade and was ready to supply all of Philadelphia with good, hearty bread.

We ended the night early.

Chapter 17

Letter to Grandmother

Katja

Dear Oma,

I miss you so much. Mama said to write to tell you how much we miss you. We wish we could eat your ginger cookies. We are now in Le Havre. It's not big like Paris, and it smells like rotten fish. Papa said we must wait here for a boat to go to Amerika. There are many boats, but none is the right one to take us to New York.

I have a new friend. Her name is Marta. Like me, she is the oldest daughter, so we always help our mamas. She has no brothers to bother her, as Bernard bothers me. Her family is from Freiburg, but I don't know where that is.

Mama has a new friend, too, Marta's mutter.

She is always happy. Rosie needs lots of minding, and Delia can now sit up by herself. Mama says she looks like me when I was a baby. Papa is always worried about money.

We liked being in Paris and saw Herr Fischer's son Klaus. He was funny. Papa bought him clothes. We drank chocolate there. In Rouen, we saw where bad people burned Saint Joan. I thought it was sad. Mama made sure we said a prayer for her. They had a big church like in Strasbourg and a giant clock. I met Marta at the big church. Papa talks to everyone, so that's how we met her family. She told me that she does not want to go to Amerika either. No one listens to us.

I hope you are feeling good. I wonder if the strawberries in your garden are ready to eat. I miss you. I miss all my cousins too, even the boys.

Love from your granddaughter,
Katja

Chapter 18

Le Havre

Johann

After we arrived in Le Havre, one week turned into two while we waited for a ship to come and declare itself bound for New York. Otto and I, trailed by Bernard, walked the quay each day inspecting the schooners and brigantines. My curious son was bold enough to ask the sailors why some ships had square sails, some were gaff-rigged, and some boasted two masts and some three. Bernard proudly told us which flag came from which country. British, American, French, and, occasionally, Dutch colors flew from their towering masts. Bernard was learning not only about boats but also English words. Following my preference, Bernard declared that the *Amerikan* ships were the best. Although neither Otto nor I had ever seen an ocean-bound boat before, we discussed the merits of each one we inspected. When a ship docked, we were wary of the rough sailors and the ladies with rouged cheeks. We forbade Anna, Berta, and our daughters to walk the wharves without us. When the sailors finished unloading, they filled the quayside taverns and spilled into the streets, brawling and insulting each other in a jumble of languages. We steered clear of them.

On our second Saturday in Le Havre, our two families ambled into a dark, smoky room where we would take our evening meal. A portly man with a ruddy face and wild, stormy gray hair entered the doorway behind us. A black hat jammed on his head could hardly contain his abundant hair. He huffed and puffed his way to a table near our own. His girth collided with the table; his beefy right arm bumped into mine.

Since he couldn't be ignored, I introduced myself.

"Sir, I am Johann Klem from Baden, and these are my wife and children. This is Otto Hoffman and his family from Freiburg. We are on our way to *Amerika*," I said.

"Aah, a delight, a delight, to meet fine people from my homeland," he said with a slight bow. His voice was deep and gruff with an unmistakable northern German accent.

"I am Peter Maier from Bremen, but call me Peter. That's what the Americans do," he said. His face was red from the effort, and I assumed this was not his first beer stein for the evening.

He removed his hat, and his untamed hair jumped out like a just-released spring. He settled back in his chair. Without our asking, he began to tell us his story.

"I was a sailor myself on American ships, but that was long ago," he said.

When Peter Maier turned his chair to join our table, Berta

and Anna took the littlest girls on their laps. We crowded close together as he began his tales about the places he'd sailed: the North Sea, the Mediterranean, the Atlantic. He said Barbary pirates and the British and French navies had shot at him.

"The American ships seemed the safest, so I signed with them. Learned to speak English. Had my share of ladies," he said, winking at Otto and me. Out of the corner of my eye, I saw Anna pull our daughters closer. He continued, "Now, I'm too old to climb the ratlins, and then there's this." With that, he put his left hand on the table, which had been in his pocket for most of the meal. Katja and Marta gasped as they saw that he was missing the last three fingers of his hand.

We could not take our eyes off Mr. Maier's hand. Anna gently kneed Katja under the table, who passed the kick around to the other children to look away. Rosie looked at our new jovial friend in her usual three-year-old innocence and said, "You forgot your fingers."

"No, little miss," he replied, "...the crocodile got 'em in the West Indies."

The children shrank back, their eyes widening, then squinting at the abbreviated hand. The older girls stopped eating.

Just as he had been fascinated with Klaus, I saw that Bernard was spellbound by the seven-fingered Peter Maier.

"Did a crocodile really eat your fingers?"

"No, actually, I think it was a rhinoceros," joked the older man.

"Really?"

"Well, I might have confused it with a lion."

"*Herr* Remmelin, my teacher, said lions only live in Africa."

"Did he, though? And not in the West Indies? Well, well, what could it have been? Maybe a monkey?" teased the old sailor.

Bernard may have realized that the mischievous codger would name every animal he could conjure up, so my ever-curious son asked Mr. Maier what he truly wanted.

"Can you teach me some English words? Papa says that is what they speak in *Amerika*."

"Your father is right. But first, you must say it this way: 'America,' not *Amerika*."

Bernard practiced "America." Each of us, in turn, pronounced the word to Peter's satisfaction.

"Well, so much for getting the country's name right, but now you must have American or English-sounding names. Johann, you should be called John. Katja, you will be Katie." He continued around the table with a new name for everyone. When he saw Anna's frown, he said, "Anna will be fine."

Chapter 19

Voyage Bound

Anna

Peter Maier took Berta and me aside the morning after our first meeting.

"You'll need to bring your food for the ship when it comes. The captain will supply the fresh water, maybe some hardtack if he's generous, some porridge, but the rest you must bring."

"We've brought food from Kittersburg," I answered. "We have sausages, ham, a crock of sauerkraut, and some cheese." In truth, we had very few of those supplies because of our weeks on the road. We had only a tiny portion of what we brought from Kittersburg. I knew that Berta had even less than me.

"Well, you'll be thanking me if you listen well. This is what you'll need for the voyage."

Counting off on the fingers of his right hand only, he

enumerated, "Potatoes, eggs, cabbage, coffee, dried fruit, sugar, dried peas, and bread. Don't forget lemons for the scurvy. And a cask of wine and a water bucket."

I needed clarification. "Doesn't the ship feed us?"

"Some might, but even if they do, it's better to be safe. If they feed you a sailor's diet, you'll be lucky if it's dried bread soaked in bilge water. Better to bring your own." Peter Maier repeated without further explanation.

Berta's forehead and mouth wrinkled into a frown. She'd been listening closely to Peter's advice. "Why do we need so much?" Behind her question, I surmised that the Hoffmanns could not afford such a supply and the boat fare. I doubted the family had a *Frau* Metzger who had sold a field for them or a mother who had gifted them with silver candlesticks.

"Well, *Frau* Hoffman, you never know how long the crossing might be," Peter answered. "Could have fair winds, or you could have squalls. Can't be predicted. The sea's got a mind of her own. It's like a bobbing bottle riding the waves with some sails to help out. Never know quite where you'll wind up."

"But," I protested, "...isn't that what the captain and the sailors are supposed to do? Get us where we want to go?"

"Certainly," he said. "And nine times out of ten, the ship will behave herself. But the sea is a jealous mistress and some-times can put up a fight. I want you to be prepared. That's all."

Our faces must have mirrored our anxiety. The only thing I knew about a boat was the peaceful ride on the barge in the *Seine*.

He continued, "Trust old Peter to find you a good ship with a good captain, and you'll cross as easy as a baby finds the teat."

As we walked away from Peter, Berta grabbed my hand.

"Anna, I'm worried about the food, but I have something else to tell you."

Given the urgency in her voice, I looked at her closely.

"I'm having a baby."

I pulled her to me in a big hug.

"How wonderful! Congratulations to you and Otto." I'd had a feeling that she might have been with a child, yet it is not a question that is easily asked.

A sense of relief crossed her face.

"How far along are you?"

"A few months. I'm not quite sure. I'm feeling different than with my girls. Otto and I are sure it will be a boy. We've both longed for a son." She grinned. "I hope he'll be as smart as your little Bernard."

I embraced her again. Our conversation stopped as we reached the guest house. It was women's talk, and we would not speak of it in front of the men or the children.

While I was worried about food and Johann was concerned about finding the right ship, Bernard tagged behind Pete Maier as faithfully as a goat behind a farm girl carrying a bucket of barley. Bernard enjoyed Peter's stories of the sea, but mostly he wanted Peter to teach him English.

I watched as Bernard pointed to a ragged-eared dog that was trotting by with a stick in his mouth.

"*Hund,*" Bernard said.

"Dog," Mr. Maier corrected.

Bernard pointed to a tied-up Dutch schooner.

"*Schiff,*" Bernard said.

"Ship," said Mr. Maier.

Bernard could play this naming game for hours if the older man would allow it. I listened as their lessons went from objects to actions. Bernard would run or jump, and Peter Maier would give the English phrases for his movements. "Bernard runs, Bernard hops."

The girls paid attention but were too timid, except Rosie, to speak in front of the seven-fingered man.

Chapter 20

The Stalwart

Johann

A week after meeting Peter, a fine-looking, three-masted, gaff-rigged schooner sailed into the inner harbor and tied up at an open wharf. A red and white striped flag with fifteen white stars on a blue square billowed from the top of the main mast. I knew it was the American flag. When I saw Peter Maier march up the gangway, the French dock workers had only begun to unload enormous cotton bales. In short of an hour, he barreled back down. He shouted to Otto and me.

"I have found the ship for you. Look at her, the *Stalwart*. It's a real beauty. Straight out of New Bedford, a fine place for building boats." He patted our backs before continuing his out-of-breath narration. " Many a boat cruising the Atlantic comes from that town. She's 150 feet long with a beam of 23 feet." He recounted other facts like tonnage and draft that I did not understand. He beamed as he looked at the ship.

"And the captain is Mr. Jedidiah Henshaw, a Nantucket man. Seems like a good sort. Those Americans are fine sailors, yes, fine sailors."

"When can we leave?" I asked, trying to mask the impatience in my voice.

"Well, now, they just arrived. Got to unload, find goods to bring back, repair whatever might have come loose on the trip, and get supplies—the usual. And the sailors, they'll want a rest before venturing back. They'll be filling the taverns for a while..." He laughed loudly, his shaking belly echoing his humor.

"Yes, yes, but when can we leave for America?" I repeated.

"That all depends. I say give it a week at least."

"A week!" I yelled. "We've been waiting in Le Havre for nearly three weeks.

"Give or take," nodded Peter.

"Peter, you haven't answered the most important question. What will the captain charge us to go to America?" asked Otto.

"Reasonable. Three hundred fifty francs for adults and fewer for children. The baby will travel free."

I heard Otto groan. He hung his head and slowly wagged it from side to side. Anna told me she suspected that the Hoffmans had meager means. Unless the ship left soon, the Hoffmans might not be onboard. And Peter hadn't told us his charge for negotiating the arrangements with the estimable Captain Henshaw.

Although elated that it was finally happening, I also had to examine my funds. I had some of Baden's *gulden,* but would an American captain accept that? I had stashed the *francs* Klaus haggled for when he sold the cart and oxen. I'd felt the weight of my leather money pouch get lighter during our extended stay in Le Havre.

That night, as the children slept, I spoke quietly to Anna.

"I am afraid, Anna, that I will have to take some of the money I concealed in the false bottom of the trunk. I'd wanted it all for the land in America."

"Johann, I think the Hoffmans may not have enough money for the passage."

"Anna, what would you have me do? I must think of us and the children first."

Anna remained quiet, but I sensed that she had something more to say. Then, after a few minutes of silence, I heard her whisper while I was drifting off.

"Johann, I must tell you this. Berta is with child. She's so happy...and convinced it will be a boy after the three girls. But...I have an awful feeling about it."

I took her hand and kissed it.

"*Liebchen,* it's been so hard not to take you in my arms all these weeks when I see how brave and kind you are. But we made the right decision. I don't want anything bad to happen to us on this ship. I would be more worried if you were carrying a child."

She snuggled closer to me. I missed the times we had not permitted ourselves to hold each other.

"And one more thing, Johann," she said, her head on my shoulder.

"Tell me."

"I am afraid to be on that big sea in a small boat."

"Me too, Anna, me too."

Chapter 21

Before Boarding

Anna

The following day, Berta and I went to the open-air market and butcher shops to purchase the food Peter Maier suggested. I bought a bit extra to be safe. Berta bought just enough for the six weeks but no more.

On the way back, we encountered Peter with Bernard trailing close by.

"I may have to keep this one," the old sailor said to me, gesturing towards Bernard.

"Oh no, you won't," I laughed.

"Smart as a whip is your boy."

"Yes, he will be our translator with all the *Amerikaners.*"

"I think you are correct, my good woman," replied Peter. He then leaned over and said something in English to the seven-year-old, making him bend in a spate of giggles.

"Be at the wharf before sunrise," Peter Maier told us. "Have all your trunks and food, and have everything ready. The captain needs to leave with the right tide."

Although we struggled to wake the children and get our baggage on a handcart bound for the dock, I was glad to leave the crowded rooming house, our boisterous home for over three weeks. On the way, we passed the Our Lady's church with its twelve Corinthian columns. I longed to say a prayer and light a candle, but Johann was firm that there was no time. I later wondered if things might have been different if I'd lit the candles.

A crowd of families and single men milled around the pier where the *Stalwart* was berthed. The sailors and the stevedores, a rough-looking assortment of men in all manner of complexions and clothing, swarmed the quay. They were up and down the gangplank, rolling casks and shouldering chests. I looked over the people who I assumed were fellow passengers. Some had heavy baggage, and some held little more than a rucksack. They might be my friends and neighbors in our new country.

Peter Maier waved his hat to get our attention. As usual, he had instructions for us.

"When you board and go below, look for a berth on the port side as far aft as possible. It'll be a bit calmer there." We nodded, yet we were unsure of what he was telling us.

He continued to advise us on what to do and what not to

do. I was too nervous to take it all in. I watched as Johann pulled Peter aside to give him the agent fee.

A tall, handsome fellow with black hair tied in a queue stood at the top of the gangplank. Peter told us that he was the first mate and, after the captain, the most important man on the ship. As we climbed on board, he checked off our names. He spoke to us in English and then a schoolboy's French, telling us to go below deck and settle ourselves. The single men were to go forward, and the families aft. We must stay below and out of the sailors' way. All the sailors surrounding us were constantly moving yet kept a joking patter among themselves.

Peter had explained that the ship needed to take advantage of the falling tide and the morning's light winds. The maneuvering must be exact since many schooners and brigs were in the harbor. No clumsy passengers could stray in the way of the experienced seamen.

Before descending to the darkness below, Bernard turned and quickly waved to his portly English teacher. The old man removed his cocked hat and waved it at us. His springy gray hair was his final salute.

Greatness is not in where we stand but in what direction we are moving. We must sail sometimes with the wind and sometimes against it—but sail we must and not drift, nor lie at anchor.

— Oliver Wendell Holmes, Jr.

Chapter 22

The Crossing

Johann

From the main deck, we descended through a companionway down a steep stairway to the compartment below. This dank space would be our wooden world for the next several weeks. Despite some lanterns dangling overhead, it was very dark. The only natural light came from the overhead hatch.

On both the port and starboard sides, rough, wooden berths were stacked three rows high with barely enough room to turn over. Between the berths sat a long wooden table with benches where we would eat our meals. Our trunks would be stowed in the hold, but there was room under the bunks to hold small food chests and satchels for personal things and linens. Hooks on the timbers between the berths would hold a few garments. A small wood-fueled stove surrounded by bricks sat between the rows. I watched as Anna, Berta, and the other women jockeyed for space around the stove—they needed to establish an order, a hierarchy of who would get to cook and who would get to wait.

Anna and Berta carefully selected bunks so our families would be near. The other women staked out their territories. They shook out blankets and set about making the narrow bunks acceptable beds. Some of the single men who had boarded with us had little more than a pack on their backs and small sacks of food and had little to store. I assumed their coats would be their blankets.

We were a pastiche of nationalities and languages. Despite the summer heat, a brawny Norwegian family with two almost-grown, strapping sons, Bjorn and Birer, was dressed in heavy woolen sweaters and knitted caps. All tall, fair-haired, with weather-bronzed cheeks, they brought a barrel of pickled herring with them.

A French woman, who insisted we call her *Madame,* held a lavender-scented handkerchief to her nose. She complained about everything to her bespectacled husband and an ancient mother—a tiny bird-like woman hardly taller than Katja. The small woman was dressed entirely in black except for a small-brimmed, purple bombazine hat with jet beads on the crown. The woman with the handkerchief grumbled to anyone who would listen that they were respectable people who would not be on this ship if not for the schemes of Napoleon Bonaparte. He was to blame for their need to travel to a "savage country which probably has despicable wine."

I caught Anna rolling her eyes at the mention of Napoleon or, maybe, the prospect of traveling for weeks with *Madame.* She nudged up to me and whispered in my ear, "We're like Noah's ark on this boat; I hope the flood is less than 40 days." We did not know then that the wait would be considerably longer.

A German-speaking family from the Palatine on their way to Pennsylvania to live with a son included two marriage-aged daughters whom the sailors had ogled while they boarded. The younger daughter, with a tangle of auburn curls, had given a saucy shoulder shrug to the men. The dark-haired daughter was as silent as her sister was bold.

A tall, too-thin young man from Poland with a pallid, pock-marked face arrived with only a cask of wine. Another man, olive-skinned with a large mustache, traveled alone. He spoke in a language no one could understand. *Madame's* husband, whom she called *Professeur,* guessed he was Egyptian. The dusky man pointed to himself.

"Socrates Papadopoulos!" He proclaimed.

"Ah, he is Greek," said the professor.

His wife waved her handkerchief again and pronounced that her husband, *Professeur* Humbert Malet, was "the most brilliant man in France."

Anna turned towards me and rolled her eyes again.

As we got to know each other below deck, we heard the activity above. We were instructed, once more, to stay below deck until the ship was underway. Eventually, the first mate's deep voice called, "Prepare to weigh anchors." We heard the anchor's chain grinding and knew we were underway. The slim first mate descended the steep stairs. On closer inspection, I saw that he was barely past his twenties with a ramrod posture and a small raspberry-colored birthmark above his right eye. He nodded at the unpacking and gestured at items improperly stowed.

"I'm Officer Enoch Carothers, first mate. If you have any

problems, come to me." His manner was direct but not threatening. "It's time to meet the captain. Follow me."

He spoke first in English and then in hesitant French. We proceeded to file up the steps behind him.

When we ascended, I beheld a glorious sight. The three masts—the main mast must have been 100 feet, and the fore and mizzen masts a shade under—were covered with huge gray-white sails taut in the wind. As I looked up, I saw thousands of triangles made by the crossing of the masts, ropes, and beams converging and intersecting. I wondered how it all could be managed. A bell was attached to the main mast. I later learned it would be rung at half past the hour to advise the crew of their watches.

Behind the ship, the far-off steeples of Le Havre remained visible. The port side revealed the rugged coast of France. To the stern was a white frothy wake. It churned with fish leaping in the spumes while seabirds dove for a meal. Seagulls soared above us, gliding around the ship like rats to a piper. One landed on the prow like a feathered figurehead. I filled my lungs with fresh, salty air. The sun had risen to a luminous pink glow, and the sea was a deep, beryl green. I had once made *Herr* Holbauer a waistcoat of the same deep color.

The bell was rung to summon our attention. As we turned from the beauty overboard, we caught a gloomy sight: Captain Jedediah Henshaw. He was a short, angular man with a prominent nose and squinting eyes. His stooped shoulders made him look like he was constantly bracing himself in the prevailing wind. A tri-cornered hat sat firmly on his sparse white hair. His threadbare navy, squared-tailed jacket with tarnished brass buttons on the cuffs did not befit the ship's captain. The gold braid on the cuffs and front lapels sorely needed replacement. I didn't know much about American fashion, but I estimated he was behind it by twenty years. Even in Kittersburg, no gentleman would continue to wear such a battered coat. Nankeen britches with matching hose completed his wardrobe.

"I am Captain Jedediah Henshaw," he said in a raspy voice. " The *Stalwart* is my ship. My word is law."

I didn't think that anyone would argue with that. He continued his speech in English while the first mate tried to translate. If a passenger spoke neither French nor English, he was out of luck.

With a perfunctory gesture, Henshaw pointed to the lifeboats. Then began a recitation of on-board rules: no children on deck without a parent, everyone up at 6:00 a.m., below deck must be swept every day, lamps could be lit if the weather was suitable but must be extinguished by 10:00 every night, passengers may be allowed on deck in fair seas but must not interfere with the crew, no one was *ever* allowed to talk to the man at the helm.

The captain proceeded to point a long-nailed finger at each of his crew members. One by one, each gave his name and country. Most were Americans or British, but there was also a very young, wiry Portuguese man and Michael, a handsome Irishman with a broad smile and deep-red curls peeping from a knitted cap. An unpleasant-looking man near the captain's right elbow introduced himself as "Mr. Quimby, steward, London." He looked like he would fight any man who didn't like it. The last to introduce himself was a large, deeply muscled man who only gave his name as Sam. His dark skin emphasized his broad, large-toothed smile.

Captain Henshaw took a well-used Bible from his pocket.

"Today is the Sabbath," he said. "On every Sabbath, I will give a reading and say a few words, and you are expected to attend. This is a Christian ship. I expect Christian behavior." He read a page from James 3:4. A few passengers pulled out small Bibles and followed in their languages.

Behold the ships also: though they are great and are driven by fierce winds, they are guided by a very small rudder, wherever the inclination of the pilot directs.

The sharp-eyed captain delivered a short sermon that few, including the crew, understood. First mate Carothers did not attempt a translation. When the captain finished, he retreated to his cabin. We would see the captain infrequently except for the early mornings and Sundays. In the mornings, he carried a log book and charts. He rarely spoke to any passengers and barked orders to the crew. The disagreeable Mr. Quimby hovered near his elbow.

By then, we were well past breakfast time. The bandy-legged cook ladled out a thin, tasteless porridge. This was the only meal that the ship would supply, this gruel and the taste-less, tooth-breaking hardtack, called sea biscuit by the crew. I was glad Anna had taken Peter's advice and brought a food supply.

Following the meager breakfast, the crew hurried to their watches. Some disappeared to the forecastle—the men called it the foc'sle—to sleep. Other sailors began duties we didn't understand but would get used to. The weather was sunny with high silky clouds and steady wind. The boat was on a constant roll as it moved through the waves. I felt my stomach heave. I sprinted to the rail and lost my bland breakfast over the side.

"Johann, are you ill?" Anna asked as she held my elbow.

"I'm fine," I tried to assure her, though the queasiness in my stomach felt like I had eaten rotten fish. My skin felt clammy, and my head pounded. I was as dizzy as a drunkard after too many pints.

"I think you're seasick," said Bernard. Mr. Maier told me about it. Happens to many people," he said." Although I wished my little expert would hush at that moment, he contin-

ued. "Mr. Maier said you have to look at the horizon or something on land that doesn't move."

I tried to follow his advice, focusing on a windmill on shore.
It helped until I watched passenger after passenger, including
Berta Hoffman, follow my path to the rail to relieve themselves
of their first *Stalwart* meal. I switched my gaze to the horizon.
Its muted colors of indigo melting into pale lavender were
soothing, especially to a tailor like me who appreciated delicate
colors. Even the lovely horizon did not help as I rushed again,
fearing my innards might follow the gruel.

As the voyage continued, I was plagued by intermittent
nausea depending on the kindness or malice of the waves.

Chapter 23

Lessons

Anna

J ohann was one of many passengers to sicken. The ship's constant pitch and roll ensured that someone below deck was rushing to a slop jar or bucket. The children and I were lucky that we were spared queasy stomachs. I volunteered to empty the foul pails to have a chance to be on deck for the light and the air. I was convinced that the fresh breezes kept the heaves away.

I assigned myself the task of supervising the children when top-side. I wouldn't let them get in the crew's way or stray too close to the rails, which the crew called gunwales or gunnels. The seamen often pointed out a flying fish or a far-off ship. I was amazed at how quickly the men, some barefoot, climbed the ropes and stood on the yards adjusting the sails. We were beginning to learn the lingo: yards, ratlins, spars, sheets. I was fascinated by their hauling in or loosening the ropes—which

Bernard told me were called lines—to adjust each sail when the first mate called out his orders. I crossed myself when the spry Portuguese man, called the topman or lookout, with a dirk stuck in his waistband, would spring up the main mast to free a jammed halyard. Mr. Carothers's booming voice yelled up the instructions. When it was untangled, the wiry lad shimmied his way down and stood with a wide-legged stance on the deck, with the problem solved. I always felt relieved to see him back safely.

I was on deck with the children a few days into the voyage. The wind was constant, and the sun a brilliant, golden globe. Just like *Herr* Remmelin and Peter Maier, the sailors took a shine to my curious son. With his buttermilk hair sticking out from beneath his cap, Bernard sat close to Sam, the broad-shouldered man with a smiling, dark-skinned face. With a gentle manner, he explained to Bernard the art of tying a sailor's knot.

"Make a loop on top, then the rabbit goes out of the hole around the tree and back through the hole," Sam said. He demonstrated how the rope looped and circled the space he had formed.

Bernard repeated the phrase in German. *"Machen Sie oben eine Schlaufe, dann geht das Kaninchen aus dem Loch um den Baum herum und zurück in das Loch."*

His face scrunched with effort. Sam repeated it slowly in English and coiled the rope into the perfect knot. My little boy repeated the sailor's English words and actions until he made the knot. Sam clapped him on the back and beamed at him, a teacher pleased with an interested student.

I loved Bernard's determination. His eyes shone as

intensely as Johann's when he was intent on doing something or attempting a new skill. I thought *he is like his father with his easy way with people and endless need for something new.* With only a few cranky moments, Bernard loved our journey. I realized he would not have stayed in Kittersburg when he grew up. He would have eventually left because, like Johann, he would not have been content sitting cross-legged, squinting at threads and seams.

It wasn't just knots that Bernard wanted to learn; he was hungry for English. As he had done with Mr. Maier, he would point to an object and say the name in German. A nearby sailor would give the ship part its English name. Bernard repeated the word. Daily, his treasure chest of words increased. Neither Bernard nor I had German words for some of the ship's specific objects. Some British and American sailors had different names for the same things.

Nevertheless, Bernard persevered. Shrouds, rudder, boom, bowsprit, clew, jib, spanker, starboard, port, bilge, stanchions. When he pointed to the helm, one British seaman said, "Now, that's the *bloody* wheel."

First mate Carothers, standing nearby, reprimanded the sailor.

"We'll have none of that language on this ship. Remember, Captain Henshaw told us this is a Christian ship, and we'll behave that way, not as heathens."

Carothers reminded me of a young priest who had once visited Kittersburg. His posture was as upright as his moral code. He could be demanding of the crew but set a high standard for himself. He was polite yet aloof with the passengers. When the cabin-bound captain appeared, Carothers was respectful, though I could tell from the stern way he mashed his lips and worried his fingers behind his back that he did not always agree with the captain's commands.

From that day when Carothers scolded the cursing sailor, he took it upon himself to teach the passengers English. Bernard became his very willing assistant. Most of us wanted to know some of this strange new language except for *Madame* Malat. She thought America was only an inconvenient stopover until she could return to France, "the only civilized country," in her words.

Carothers would say to Bernard, "Where is your mouth?" Bernard pointed his finger to his mouth, ears, tongue, and so on. All the children were attentive and imitated Carothers's words. As with Peter Maier, the girls, except Rosie, were much shyer than Bernard and spoke in low, mumbled voices. Rosie danced around shouting the words like this was the best game. We adults tried but mangled the English words with our strange accents.

Those were lovely days. I did not realize how soon our luck would run out.

Chapter 24

Coffin

Johann

We sailed through the English Channel with the distant French coast on our port side. I was feeling better. With Anna's insistence, I spent more time on deck when we were allowed. Despite her early fears, I could tell that Anna was enjoying this leg of our trip. I was greatly relieved.

One Sunday after the captain's required prayer service, the wind picked up, and seemingly from nowhere, the sea got rough. The waves rose to 14 feet high, and the *Stalwart* heeled in its force. Before Carothers ordered us below, the Polish lad and Socrates lost their hats to the powerful gusts.

Below the deck, the Professor consulted one of his books. He declared that we must be in the Alderney Race, an eight-mile course between the Channel Islands and the westernmost peninsula of France.

"This is a treacherous passage," he explained, "because the wind and the current can run in opposite directions."

We heard Carothers shouting commands to "all hands."

"Lay low the main sails," he shouted.

We heard the sailors' heavy footsteps above. I almost collided with an off-watch sailor now called to duty. The sleeping sailor carried the imprint of his hammock's scaffolding on his cheeks. He scrambled up the steep steps. The crew rushed to batten or tie down anything the wind or water could carry.

Seawater began to sluice down the hatchways. The timbers screeched with the wind's battering. As the *Stalwart* was buffeted, Anna and I struggled to brace the children into the bunks with us so they would not be thrown about. Rosie and Delia set up a wail until Anna covered them with her body. While we huddled in our berths, our fellow passengers howled and prayed out loud, addressing God in several languages. No one attempted English. Below the roar of the wind, I could hear Anna leading the children in the Lord's Prayer. As the sea thrashed, water continued to dribble through the deck boards. The boat took an unexpected lurch, and we were heaved to almost a 90-degree angle. Objects we had not secured shifted to starboard. The ship righted itself, but not until we heard Madame Malat shriek.

"*Ma mère, ma mère!*" *Madame's* tiny mother, who reminded me of a baby bird, had been wrenched from her berth. Her body was tossed onto the wooden planking and crashed into the central cook stove. In a frail voice, she cried for help. Bjorn and Brier lifted her and tucked her into the bunk beside her screeching daughter. Underneath the wind's bray, the ancient woman, whom everyone called *Grand-mère*, was whimpering and moaning. *Madame* demanded that the ship stop so she could care for her mother. God didn't heed her pleas.

After an hour of plates, pans, and slop jars flung about our compartment, the sea subsided, and the ship calmed. The poor, injured woman's cries did not end.

Using a long-handled broom, I banged for the hatch to be opened. When the crew lifted it, a blessed light descended on our darkness. That's when we saw blood from a large gash on the frail woman's arm, which had saturated her clothing. *Madame's* clothes were drenched with her mother's blood as well. *Grand-mère* held her hand to her hip. She cried out when the Norwegian woman, Inger, who said she was a healer in her hometown, tried to touch her.

First-mate Carothers and Captain Henshaw descended the ladder to assess the damage. Other than the ailing, ancient French woman, we were shaken but intact. A few objects were beyond repair; the rest was salvageable. Carothers sent for the ship's carpenter to fashion a wooden cast for *Madame's* mother. Sometime later, he arrived with a contraption of wood and leather straps. This contrivance worsened the woman's pain. Anna and other women concocted tonics from the dried herbs they'd brought. Carothers brought brandy and rum. Captain Henshaw offered a dram of opium. None gave the injured woman much relief. I winced when I heard the poor woman's cries at night.

Three days later, the petite woman was dead. *Madame* could not be consoled. Her weeping forced the rest to silence. We offered the poor woman the same potions we provided her mother. She pushed them all away. Nothing her husband or any of the passengers said could calm her. We sent for the ship's carpenter again, this time to fashion a coffin. The women washed and wrapped *Grand-mère's* broken sparrow's body in linens. Anna told me the woman's wounded arm had oozed pus; she'd felt the broken hip poke through the dead woman's fragile body. I grieved, not only for *Madame* but for Anna. She had performed this chore too many times. One of the things she feared had happened—death at sea. I thanked God that it was not one of my family.

I'd watched the carpenter, who always wore a leather apron with awls and mallets peeking out of the pockets, drill holes in the coffin's side and add ballast stones to the box. After *Grand-mère's* body was nailed inside, the strong Norwegian boys carried the casket to the main deck. Captain Henshaw emerged from his cabin to read a passage from John and then a Psalm.

He caused the storm to be still.

So that the waves of the sea were hushed.

We sang a few hymns, each in our own language. The sailors lifted the casket and slid it over the stern. The greedy waves claimed their new meal; the coffin quickly slid under their white clutch. A pall descended on those on deck.

From that day on, *Madame* wore her mother's purple hat with the jet beads.

Berta Hoffman was one of the people most affected by the woman's death. Like me, she had suffered from seasickness and spent hours lying in her berth. I'd seen *Grand-mère* sit beside Berta to stroke her belly and sing her French lullabies in a soft, sweet voice. Berta would coo under the elderly woman's attention and called her "*Meine Mutter.*" The two women drew comfort from each other. With her petite comforter gone, the usually cheerful Berta grew morose. Anna urged her to come up to the open deck. Still, Berta clung to the darkness of her bunk. Even when Otto and their daughters would implore her to climb the ladder to learn Carothers's English or spot schools of fish, she would only stay for a short while and descend again to the bowels of the boat. I overheard Berta tell Anna how much she regretted leaving her home in Freiburg. She had a premonition that something ominous would happen to her hoped-for son.

The voyage continued after the terror of the storm in the Alderney Race. Day after day. Week after week. The open Atlantic was before us. The last time we saw land was on the French coast. The days passed quickly when we were allowed on deck in fair weather. We occasionally spotted a whale or a far-off ship. The children and I made a game of finding fantastical creatures and familiar objects in the layers and cushions of clouds. Yet, most days were a dull blur of sameness and monotony. A few men asked me about making jackets or waistcoats for them, but my fabric was buried in our large trunks in the hold. Sitting in my tailor's position in the shadowy passenger deck did not inspire me to ply my trade.

People who had initially enjoyed getting to know each other and learning a common language became snappish. Some young men brawled and found arguments where none had existed. Below deck, the constant creak and moan of the ship, the pitch and roll, the yaw, the reek of vomit, the odor of cooked cabbage, and the stink of the bilge water could not be avoided. Although we tried to make the best of it—the women knitting, the *Professeur* reading, the men talking about life in America—something had changed. My children and the Hoffman girls struggled on the days when they could not be above playing and dodging the spray that sprang up over the gunwales. Tempers wore thin. The crew argued among themselves. Carothers was becoming impatient even with Bernard.

Captain Henshaw was rarely seen. After his morning orders, he spent the day in his cabin. A sickly, sweet smell emanated when his door was opened. The steward, the gnarly Mr. Quimby, whose knuckles were stained with star tattoos, stood guard in front of the captain's quarters. He growled at anyone who came too close. When he walked, his knee clicked in rhythm. Most of us had no trouble keeping our distance. The sailors, especially the first mate, did not like him.

The weather, which had been mild as the voyage began, was becoming colder. The *Professeur* said we were influenced by the north-easterlies off the Scandinavian coast. I got Barnard to ask Carothers to explain where we were and how much longer we would be at sea. My son, who amazed me with his quick grasp of English, returned with the answer. We were approaching the Grand Banks, south of Greenland. Our professor scrounged through his books until he found the correct text and the right passage.

"The Grand Banks," he said, "is a relatively shallow, under-water plateau of the Atlantic where the cold Labrador Current meets the warmer waters of the Gulf Stream. It results in a gray fog, which may last all day. The area is known for abundant fishing with a profusion of cod, swordfish, and haddock."

The young Pole, who had looked ill even as he boarded with his mere wine cask, was begging for food from the rest of us. He existed on a small portion of hardtack and a bit of salt beef—the sailors' fare—reluctantly supplied by the cook. As days passed, he became worse. He was feverish and weak; he coughed continuously. The woman made him a thin soup of potatoes and carrots, but he could not swallow. He hacked up blood and phlegm. Most of us avoided him. Early one morning,

Bjorn, the Norwegian lad, found the young man's body cold and curled in a cat's curve under the steep steps to the top deck. Captain Henshaw said that the carpenter could not be spared to make a coffin for a man yet to be indentured, a man whose fare had not yet been paid. A length of sailcloth was wrapped about him, and his feet were tied together. Late that afternoon, the Norwegian boys carried him up the steep stairs. The sailors placed him on a board. After Mr. Carothers offered a quick prayer, he was slid over the stern into the sea.

The somber mood from the two deaths increased our discomfort. Otto confided to me how worried he was for Berta. As I tried to console him, Anna came to tell me that the food she had purchased in *Le Havre* was running low. The lemons and limes that Peter Maier had insisted upon had long since been sliced and sucked. She was rationing our food, yet her generosity forced her to share with others. The passengers who had initially given part of their supplies to each other were now reluctant. We all had to think of our family's needs first.

The boredom, the darkness, the hunger, and the weather were taking a toll. On top of that, I suffered guilt for putting my family through it.

Chapter 25

Storm and Death

Anna

One morning, when we awoke, the fog was gone early, and the water was alive with schools of fish. The Norwegian lads, Birer and Bjorn, and their father, who were fishermen, tossed a long line over the rail and baited it with a flying fish that had landed on the top deck. When the line went taut and heavy, they let it play out until the fish was tired. As the fish gave up its fight, they used gaffing hooks to pull up an enormous cod that flopped its heavy tail on the deck. The thought of fresh food lightened our day. We all contributed what we could, and the cook made a cauldron of fish chowder flavored with the sailors' usual salt beef. As we dined, the sun sank. The inky night sky was brilliant, with millions of stars. The *Professeur* and Mr Carothers pointed out constellations. The moon, swollen with light, reminded me of the radiant candles at Christmas Eve mass. Even Captain Henshaw emerged from his cabin looking less grim.

Michael, the Irishman with the red curls, brought out a fiddle, and big Sam, the children's favorite sailor, beat on an empty cask like a drum. The cook pulled out a penny whistle. The flirtatious girl from the Palatine swiveled her hips. She swished her skirts back and forth as close as she could get to the Irish sailor's flashing bow. Socrates did a strange solitary dance. The food and music made me remember the night I first danced with Johann at the harvest fest. On this night, we waltzed together in the middle of a continuously rolling dance floor. I was sorry for the bargain we had made.

The fair weather, with the sea as smooth as glass, lasted a few days until one morning following Captain Henshaw's Sunday service. We noticed that the olive-hued swells were higher than usual. The wind was picking up, yet the sky remained baby blue, threaded with silky clouds. I decided it was a perfect day to let laundry dry in the sunshine of the deck as the wind would encourage the clothing's quick drying.

Since Sam was off watch, he entertained the children with pony rides on his broad back. I was enjoying a glorious day until Berta approached me and grabbed my hand.

"Anna, something is wrong," she whispered to me. Her eyebrows were scrunched together, and her fingers squeezed mine too tightly.

"What do you mean?" I said, trying to release her firm grip.

Ever since the death of *Madame's* mother, Berta had not been herself. Selfishly, I did not want Berta's sadness to ruin my day.

"I am not sure, but I feel it. Something bad will happen."

Madame overheard our conversation. "You are right," she said to Berta. "My head is splitting, and whenever that happens, bad weather follows."

I began to scoff until I saw Sam stop his games with Bernard and the girls. He looked west over the bow. I followed his gaze and saw in the far distance a charcoal-colored sky. As I watched, metallic forks of lighting shredded the steely-gray cloak on the horizon.

Raised voices came from the captain's quarters. Captain Henshaw and Mr. Carothers stormed onto the deck. They stood on the quarterdeck near the wheel, pointing and gesturing, their voices raised to a resounding pitch. At the same time, we passengers and crew eavesdropped and watched from the corners of our eyes. Carothers held up a sextant in one hand and a compass in the other; Henshaw shook a roll of naval charts. Then, like the rest of us, they stood mesmerized by the darkening sky ahead.

"Captain Henshaw, sir, we may have the opportunity for the ship to sail out of this. However, if we continue directly west, we may fetch up on the shallow waters near Sable Island. We'll be pounded to pieces," Carothers said, his voice coated in urgency.

"Mr. Carothers, there is only one ship captain, and you are looking at him. My orders stand." Henshaw rejoined in an icy voice.

Carothers shoved his sextant and compass into his coat's pockets. When he turned on his heel, I could see the coming storm reflected by the set of his chin. His usual calm had disappeared, and his often friendly face was furrowed and bitter. The birthmark over his eye deepened in color. He stomped back to his quarters. Captain Henshaw, who ordinarily left the instructions for the crew to Mr. Carothers, began barking orders to the sailors. "Aloft, you go!" he screamed to the sinewy Portuguese topman, who was always the fastest sailor to climb the ratlins and shrouds. Sails were furled, lines tied off. Men moved about as Captain Henshaw and the boatswain directed the action. Then, satisfied with the preparations, the captain returned to his cabin, ignoring the few of us who huddled near the stern.

The crew mumbled among themselves. The *Professeur* took it upon himself to discover what was happening. He asked, and they explained; back and forth, it went for several minutes. They gestured and drew pictures in the air until the *Professeur* understood.

He walked back to us and took on the familiar role of a teacher to his students.

"It seems the air pressure is falling, and that's not good. It means that a storm is coming." He waved in the direction of the darkening western sky. We didn't know what air pressure was, but we surmised we were headed straight for misfortune. *Madame* elbowed me and announced triumphantly, "My head always tells me."

Her husband continued, "The Captain wants to sail straight into it because he needs to meet his schedule, and supplies are starting to run low. He thinks the ship and the men can handle it. Mr. Carothers, on the other hand, wants to sail north away from the storm into something called the Labrador Current, where the water is colder. According to the men, the colder water will slow the waves down." He paused to ensure all eyes were upon him, waiting for his discourse.

When he saw that we were listening, he continued, "The captain wants to sail straight west, but Sable Island is some-where between where we are and where we need to go. There's shallow water around the island, and the crew says that the ship will be knocked, excuse me, ladies, to shit." He wiped his nose with a silk scarf before continuing. "The crew says you should avoid land in a storm unless you can get to a safe harbor."

Most of the men nodded. This made sense to them.

"The captain thinks the *Stalwart* is sturdy enough to take on the storm and that we are headed for a cold channel between Sable Island and Nova Scotia. But the first mate says you must travel for days before getting there."

Johann said, "Please tell us what the sailors want to do."

"They want to follow Carothers out of the storm."

"And is that what will happen?" Johann asked.

"No. As you heard, the captain is the captain. We sail into the storm," *Professeur* Malat had completed his lesson.

My heart rate shot up with the rising of the waves. The sky before me had swiftly gone from cerulean to tarnished gunmetal. The winds were blowing erratically with gusts from every side. Carothers was back on the main deck instructing the crew to remove anything from the deck that might be blown or washed away. Sam and an American sailor with bulging muscles and a clenched jaw lowered the heavy scuttlebutt, the drinking water cask, from the top to a lower deck. Despite the order to go below, I was rooted to my spot, hypnotized by the crew's precarious perch on the yardarms to gather in sails. When Mr. Carothers saw me, he shouted at me to get my laundry and go. As I gathered the damp clothing and rushed to the companionway, I met Berta, trying to climb up.

"Berta, go below! A storm is coming!"

"I know, I know...but Anna, look at my skirt," She held up her skirt stained with watery blood.

I looked not understanding at first until Berta cried out, "Anna, my water has broken. The baby is coming."

I gasped in realization. The baby's birth and the storm were both arriving, as if by dead reckoning, at the same time.

I grabbed Berta's hand and pulled her down the steps with me. The other passengers were rushing about like angry ants. Carothers had demanded that all our movable belongings be tied down or stowed. Anything large enough to hurt someone would be put in the hold. Michael, the fiddle-playing Irish sailor, was already there, ensuring everything was secured. The usual darkness below deck was illuminated only by the open companionway. No lamps could be lit with the storm upon us. Pots and haversacks were jammed under the bottom bunks. After the ancient French woman had been dashed on the floor during the first storm, Johann had borrowed a hammer and nails from the ship's carpenter and banged nails into the small railings on the berths. Strips of torn and twisted clothing wound around the nails would tie us into our berths. I told Johann that he must tie in with the girls and that I would lie with Bernard and the baby. I would strap Delia to my chest, but before that happened, I had to see how Berta was progressing.

Berta was lying on her bunk, and Etta Schmidt, the mother of the bold, curly-headed girl, was stroking the swollen belly. Etta had once told us that she was the midwife in her village. She had caught so many babies, she'd bragged, that some had been named for her.

Berta was breathing heavily. Her voice betrayed her panic. "It's too early. My son should not be born until we are in America."

"Babies come when they want to," Etta replied, "...but I have seen many babies decide to come at night or when the weather changes. Now let me see how far you are."

She reached one hand under Berta's skirt while her other hand pushed on the gravid belly.

"You are not very far yet. It may be hours, or the baby may come very quickly. It's hard to tell. How are your pains?"

"So far, I can manage," Berta said until a contraction seized her.

"I will lie next to you for a while, but when the storm gets bad, I will lie next to my husband." She gently pushed Berta over and climbed onto the bunk beside her.

"Where are my girls?" Berta asked me.

"They are with their father. He'll take care of them," I answered. "Just be concerned with this one on his way. I'll be right across from you." I walked to my berth with difficulty as the waves made the deck tilt and slant. I took Delia from Katja's arms and lashed her to my chest; my eyes were on the two bodies across from me: one slender and quiet, the other writhing as much as her extended belly allowed. I climbed into the berth with Bernard and tied the strips of cloth Johann had made for us so we would not be thrown from our bunks.

The mood in our wooden room was tense. It was pitch black since the hatch had been closed and bolted. I could already hear quiet sobs. We understood that this storm would be worse than the gale off the coast of France that had broken and killed the tiny French woman. And we would be enclosed with a bellowing woman giving birth.

I began to pray but was interrupted by pounding feet and yelling from above. I could hear the first mate hollering orders to "All hands!" I imagined them swaying on the spars and cleating the sheets as I had seen in the weeks we'd been at sea. I heard a loud crash and then a horrifying scream. More feet pounded in the direction of the hard thump. I later learned that the young Portuguese sailor, a master of the crow's nest, had been catapulted from his position up high and smashed on the deck below. His leg had shattered on the landing. The sailors carried him to his hammock, yet even with the shriek of the storm, I could hear him call out in agony.

I pulled Bernard and Delia tight to me. *Jesus, Mary, and Joseph, please protect us. Please do not abandon us in our hour of need,* I prayed. When I began the Our Father out loud, some passengers joined me. Underneath their voices, I could hear Berta's laboring keens.

In the blackness, I was more aware of the uptick of the wind. Its sounds varied from a low groan to the deep resonance of a cathedral organ. Soon, it became a high screech that was no longer church-like but like a devil's howl, a shrieking madman bent on our destruction.

Worse than the howling wind were the rolling waves. I felt the *Stalwart's* bow thrust upward while it climbed the wall of the wave. It was weightless for a moment before the boat surfed down the wave at an alarming speed. When it crashed into the wave's trough, I imagined I was in a wagon falling from a cliff. I was terrified that the children would bite off their tongues, so I clamped their jaws shut with my hand. When the storm started, I heard joint prayers, but as it hurtled on, some passengers caught in this soggy hell began to cry for mercy.

After hours—I was no longer aware of the time—the others trapped with me in this watery coffin became silent.

Despite the closed hatch, an inundation of seawater had pushed through cracks, washed out calking, and leaked below.

The water sloshed over the deck board. Objects we thought safely stowed began to float. We were wet and terrified. We waited for our drowning, our sodden end.

The storm was unending, relentless, and suffocating. Somehow, Delia had fallen asleep against me. Then, almost as suddenly as it started, I heard the wind subsiding. The waves were less angry. Johann called out my name.

"Anna, are you alright? The children?"

"Yes, Johann, we are. The girls?"

"We're fine. Banged up and soaked to the skin but alive." Others murmured around us. Everyone checked on each other. We could not believe that the wind's yowl had stopped. The ship bobbed but no longer heaved to port or starboard. There was a lull. A stillness overtook the chaos. It was over. We had survived.

I could hear Johann splashing through the water on the floor and coming toward me when the hatch shot opened, and Carothers's face appeared. The light came down only in a weak funnel of gray, reaching the river of water at our feet.

"Is it over? Are we saved?" the *Professeur* called out to the first mate.

"I can't know, yet I think we're in the eye of the storm. There's no telling how long it will last. In the meantime, stay out of the crew's way. No one on deck." By now, he had descended and slogged through the sea and vomit that had accumulated on the flooring.

"You men—form a bucket line and try to get rid of this water. Only you, "he pointed to one of the brawny Norwegian boys, "on the top side."

He left as quickly as he had come.

I untied myself and the children, who whimpered and shivered. I crossed to Berta's bunk to see how she had fared. Otto leaned over his wife and called Etta to come quickly. He had placed his coat over her quivering body. He held a candle to her face. Berta's face was ashen, her lips blue. *Madame* herded Otto's girls as far as she could from their suffering mother.

"Help me, help me," Berta whispered through cracked lips. Throughout the deluge she had labored, the horror of the hurricane echoed by the pains of her body.

Etta pushed Otto to the side. "Let's see where we are now," she said. Once again, she placed one hand on Berta's round belly and one under the moist, voluminous skirt.

"This baby wants to come soon," she said. "But Berta's weak." She turned to Otto, "See if you can make her tea." Her command was impossible given the conditions, but, as Etta had told us, husbands only get in the way of birthing.

"Anna, get in the bunk behind her," she told me. "She's ready to push. I've no time to put my oils around her cervix to soften the tears. Let her lean against you. When I tell her to push, you will help with your strength." She turned around and said to the passengers who began to gather nearby, "Everyone else, stay away."

In the dull light from the opened hatch, I sat with my legs on either side of Berta, my body cushioning hers. Etta directed her when to bear down and when to relax. Berta struggled and wailed to force her baby out. I held her close against me and strained with her.

Finally, Etta spoke. "He's coming. I feel his head." Her whole body shaking and trembling, Berta let out a tremendous cry.

By now, Etta had folded back the yards of Berta's skirts. The Norwegian woman, Inger, held an oil lamp so Etta could see and feel what was delaying the infant's birth. Berta bellowed once more as she pushed. Etta cried, "He's here."

Pulling her hands from below the birthing mother's garments, Etta held up a tiny baby. The cord, his seven-month lifeline, was wrapped around his neck. His face was blue; he did not cry. Etta quickly slipped the umbilical cord from his neck, held him upside down, and slapped him on his bottom. He began to breathe in fast, shallow gasps. She wiped the blood and mucus from his body. He was so tiny that he could fit in the bowl of Etta's two open palms. His legs were scrawny and bowed. Etta immediately swaddled him in a linen cloth that Inger held out. I wondered to myself how she had found something dry.

"My son," Berta cried in a weak voice. "Let me hold my son." Etta bent down and placed the tiny bundle in her arms. While his skin had begun to pink up, he was so fragile that his blue veins could almost be seen through his skin. We all knew he was thinner and smaller than a baby should be.

"Give him the nipple right away," Etta instructed, pushing Berta's bodice away to expose her breast. Although I could see his little lips moving, he was not latching on to Berta's offered nipple.

"Your work is not over. We must get that sac the baby grew in out of you. You'll need to do more pushing," Etta said to the exhausted Berta. Berta tried to comply, grunting and pushing. Blood and fluid flowed—but not the afterbirth. As I sat behind Berta, I whispered encouragement in her ear as I felt how weak she had become. Etta called over her shoulder for more linens or blankets to stanch the gush. She sent Otto, who had returned to coo over Berta and the new baby, for beer to strengthen his wife.

Etta allowed Berta to rest for a moment, and the exhausted mother immediately dozed off, her son tucked in the crook of her arm.

Etta leaned over and whispered, "It's not good—this baby has arrived too soon. And she won't stop bleeding—the birth sac isn't out."

"How can we help?" I said quietly so as not to wake the new mother.

Etta shook her head. "Even if we weren't in this god-forsaken sea, I wouldn't know what to do. If I were back home, I would give her a tonic of nettle, artemisia, and rue. But we can't even boil water to make a strengthening tea."

As she spoke, I saw the dim light from the open hatch darkening. Carothers was once more calling out instructions to all hands in a now-hoarse voice. Heavy, rushed footfalls came from above. The second mate called down for the men to cease the bucket brigade. Once more, the hatch was closed, and we were in the darkness of our wooden tomb before we tied ourselves to our berths. The ship began to bob and yaw on the increasing waves. We had sailed through the eye—now the spinning vortex of the nightmare storm returned.

Etta yelled for Otto to get in the bunk with Berta and the infant.

"For God's sake, keep them warm," she shouted. She jammed another blanket between Berta's legs to absorb the flow and hoped the placenta would emerge. I grabbed Berta and Otto's girls. Marta tied in with me; Etta took Elsa, and Inger clutched little Agnes to her bosom before she blew out her candle. We had a woman who had not completed the birthing process and a sea that would not quit.

We'd believed the worst was over, but the storm renewed itself with unrelenting power. The vessel slammed against the eye wall with a colossal jolt. The wind screamed and threatened, then exploded on the ship.

Amid the uproar of the hurricane, we heard a tremendous

crash. The whole ship began to list to the port side. We learned later that the top part of the main mast, which was not one tree trunk but three sections stacked on each other, had cracked and slammed onto the deck. Its tremendous weight was pushing the ship askew. The vessel would be rolled on its side unless the broken mast was lifted. Capsizing was certain.

After the storm, the crew said that three brave sailors with ropes tied around their waists emerged from the fore hatch. With drawn dirks, they hacked at the heavy shrouds and rigging intended to support the topmast but instead dragged her over. If the mast could be heaved into the sea, the boat would right itself.

The sailors recounted how the men had lashed at the lines until the mast was no longer attached. Then, with a tremendous lift, they pushed the oak timber over the gunwales into the furious waves. Without the weight of the mast forcing the vessel to port, the ship self-righted. The American sailors hauled on their lifelines to regain the hatch. One sailor did not make it back. He'd gone overboard, held under the water by the shattered mast. The ocean's grasping hands claimed him.

We endured several more hours of pounding and relentless fury before the ocean lost its ire. The wind blew itself out. The waves had no more curses. God had heard our prayers and saved us. The ship, however, was not moving forward. With a broken mast and no sails to hold the wind, it bobbed like a cork on water.

Below deck, some passengers had fallen asleep from exhaustion or escape until Carothers again opened the hatch. Pale light streamed down. His appearance was interrupted by a loud wail. He backed away, leaving the open hatch but not descending the ladder. Otto was screaming.

"*Nein, Nein, sie ist tot!*" He wailed. "She is dead!"

Etta and I raced to the bunk and saw Berta's open eyes staring upward, a blanket saturated with blood lying between her legs. Her arms enfolded the swathed bundle. Only his fuzz of hair peeked out. I gently pulled the linen from the infant's face and saw the pale skin, the open mouth with the rosebud lips, and the half-open eyes. One teeny hand with perfect fingernails lay lifeless by his head. The metallic smell of blood prevailed.

"Oh, Berta, my Berta," Otto wept. With his arms encircling her, he kissed his wife's head. Her tawny braids were unpinned and spilled across her breathless chest. "My son, my son, how is my son?" Otto whispered hoarsely. I avoided his eyes as I shook my head. Otto let out another heart-wrenching howl. He sobbed without shame.

Inger and I held onto Berta and Otto's daughters to keep them away from seeing the unmoving bodies of their mother and their never-known brother.

Chapter 26

Aftermath

Johann

I climbed to the deck to inform Carothers of our situation. I was astounded by what I saw. The sky was illuminated over the stern, and the sun rose in a weak tongue of light to reveal that the uppermost part of the main mast was gone. The bulwark, where the mast had fallen, was fragmented and splintered. Without the mast and the sails, the ship reminded me of a man without his hat. The sea, the color of pickle brine, was almost as calm as before the storm. It was hard for me to believe that these easy rollers and the cloudless sky had only hours before spawned havoc. The storm sails were shredded to streaming ribbons. The once sleek schooner was like a bag of bones, a graveyard of broken planks, frayed lines, and raggedy shrouds. The Irishman and the American sailors worked the bilge pumps at a furious speed. The carpenter and the cook were hauling lumber from the hold—I assumed to repair the gunwale. The captain was nowhere in sight. However, Carothers was everywhere shouting orders. I decided it was not the time to tell him of our chaos. Instead, I retreated to our underwater world to help the others bail, sop up water, and wring out the dirty, submerged bedding.

Despite the open hatch, the area stank of blood and loosened bowels. Otto and his daughters huddled together on a berth and sobbed. Anna and Etta had laid Berta on the table we used for our meals. They washed and prepared the cold, crumpled body of their friend. I thought to myself, *the Hoffmann family, like our ship, is damaged, filled with holes*. The boat could be repaired, but I was unsure about Otto's family. Although the boat was afloat, the storm had capsized our spirits. We helped each other clean up in silence. The only sound that could be heard was the Hoffmans' continued weeping.

Our shoes squished with every step, so most of us, despite the cold water, took them off and placed them on the driest bunks. The women's hems were saturated with the rank water, so they hiked them up and tied them into their apron strings. None of them seemed to care that their petticoats and legs were showing.

Carothers abruptly descended the ladder.

"How do you fare down here?" he asked.

"Berta Hoffman delivered a baby," I said and paused. "Both mother and child are dead."

He was silent. He looked away from me as he clasped his arms awkwardly behind his back.

"I'm sorry. God can be cruel."

Before I could answer, Anna spoke up. "Sometimes it's humans, not God, who are cruel. I understand that the storm might have been avoided."

I was shocked by her frankness. Carothers said nothing.

Anna continued, "Can the carpenter make a coffin for my friend and her child?"

"No. It's not possible. The ship must be mended first. The top main needs to be replaced. I haven't enough men or timber for coffins." He shook his head and repeated, "It's not possible."

"Then what are we to do?" asked Anna. I stopped her by taking her hand and stepping closer to the first mate. I did not want Anna to argue with this man who had more to do than bury the dead.

"I'm a tailor. I'll sew a shroud for them." I said.

"Then the captain will say a few words and..." Carothers began until Anna interrupted him.

"No, we will not ask the captain to say a few words," she said. "Captain Henshaw has said enough, much of it unwise."

Anna was about to continue her rant against the captain when we heard a loud yell in a language we did not understand from the direction of the sailors' quarters.

"Is it the sailor who fell to the deck?" she asked Carothers. "How is he?"

"Suffering. He has broken his leg, and the rum riles him more."

"Poor man," Anna said. She quickly crossed herself. "We will pray for him."

Before she walked away, she turned to ask one more question.

"Mr. Carothers, where is Sam? He usually comes and checks on the children."

Carothers looked away; his eyes focused on the open hatch. Once more, he clenched his hands behind his back. It was as if only his hands revealed his true feelings. He did not look at Anna when he replied, "The sea took him last night. The mast dragged him into the water. There was no rescuing to be done."

A shadow crossed Anna's face. I knew my wife's every

mood. She carefully parsed her words, "The children will miss him." I could tell that she struggled to say no more.

"Aye, that man was soft as mush in his heart when it came to the wee ones. Some say he left little ones back on the islands. But the man never spoke to me of such." Carothers said.

Anna studied the first mate's face. "Perhaps I knew him better. He has indeed left children. Sold away from him. Perhaps Captain Henshaw can say a few words about that kind, good man, and the business that sells one's flesh and blood."

Mr. Carothers did not respond.

Later that day, I borrowed a few yards of the linen duck cloth from *Stalwart's* sailmaker that could be spared. I cut and fashioned a shroud for Berta and her infant. As I sewed, I repeated a prayer: *Thank you for not taking Anna. Thank you for saving our children. Watch over the souls of Berta, her baby, and Sam.*

I couldn't imagine Otto's grief. My prayer became a never-ending spinning wheel in my head. As hard as it has been for me not to embrace Anna and show her my love these past months, I realized that without her insistence on our bargain, I might be sewing a shroud for her, not Berta. It might have been the woman I loved since our first dance who would be buried at sea.

The women washed and prepared a body for burial for the third time on that voyage. And now, it was not for a sweet woman they hardly knew or a foolish young man who did not know how to care for himself, but for their friend, Berta, a woman with children like them. And her baby, who had not lived long enough to be named.

Anna asked Otto for a dress for Berta to be buried in. He dug through their trunk and found Berta's spruce-green Sunday dress. The cuffs had tatted lace, and the bodice was embroidered with blue and yellow flowers. Otto also discovered the baptismal gown his daughters had worn. The woman wrapped it several times around the tiny baby's body. Etta's daughter contributed blue hair ribbons that she tied around the voluminous skirt to keep it in place. The Irishman gave us several ballast stones to be placed underneath the bodies and inside the shroud so that it would sink when the cloth coffin was placed on a board and tilted into the sea. Before I stitched the ends of the sailcloth sarcophagus closed, *Madame* removed her mother's purple hat from her head and tied it over Berta's neat braids. She touched Otto's arm, "Don't worry, *ma mère* will take good care of them up there," she said and pointed heavenward.

Otto and his daughters kissed their mother's and brother's clothbound, still bodies. The Norwegian boys, Bjorn and Birer, their knit caps stuffed in their back pockets, carried the shrouded bodies to the top deck.

Otto asked me if I would read from his family's Bible. The passengers and a few sailors stood close by as I read,

But the souls of the just are in the hand of God, and no torment will touch them.

In the eyes of the foolish, they seemed to be dead, and their passing was thought an affliction, and their going forth from us utter destruction.

But they are at peace...

They shall be greatly blessed because God tried them and found them worthy of Himself.

Otto tried to say a few words but choked up, hung his head, and could not continue. I put my arm around his slumping shoulders. The Schmidt family sang a Lutheran hymn. The

Irishman appeared with his fiddle and played a melancholy tune. The cook joined in on his penny whistle. Carothers came forward with a prayer in English. Though Anna tried to soothe Berta's girls, they could not stop their sobs. Our children stood behind Anna, clutching her skirt with small hands. Little Agnes broke from Anna's arms and ran to her father, crying, "I want Mama." Most of us had tried to keep our tears in check, but we no longer could with Agnes' anguished call for her mother.

The Norwegian boys lifted and tilted the board so the sail-cloth bundle slipped over the stern into the sea below. I heard the splash but could not watch to see it sink under the consuming waves.

Captain Henshaw had not appeared on deck.

The following day was an unrelenting gray. It was difficult to distinguish the sea from the sky. They meshed together into a slate soup. If I looked aft, I could hardly make out the silhouette of the helmsman. I tasted only mist and emptiness. My guilt and sadness knew no bounds. I could not bear to think of Otto's pain. In my mood, I would not be a comfort to anyone.

When the lamp was extinguished that night, I climbed into the berth and folded my arms around Anna, who cuddled our sleeping Delia. I kissed her hair. Before I could control it, my body shook in silent sobs. She reached over to grasp my hand.

"Anna, you are so much wiser than I am. I said this would be simple: Leave Baden, a short cart ride to Paris, find a ship in Le Havre, and sail to New York—a new life for our family. You understood better than I how treacherous this trip would be. I am such a fool that I did not listen."

I stopped to wipe my tears on my sleeve. Anna said nothing, but I knew that she was listening. I choked away at the lump in my throat and continued to whisper.

"Anna, I would never forgive myself if I lost you or one of the children." Anna did not reply.

"If this has all been my folly, we can turn around when we get to New York. We can go back to Kittersburg. Just tell me, and we will do it."

Anna finally spoke, "Johann, there is no going back. Nothing remains in Kittersburg for us. We have no home, no field, no animals, no cart. We have only our family who will ache with our failure. No, Johann, we decided on a new life. We must...we will go on. If not for our sake, for people like *Grandmère* and Berta.

I took a deep breath and held her even more closely. "How was I so lucky to choose a woman who grows stronger and more beautiful daily?"

"Perhaps, husband, it was not you who chose me, but I who chose you."

"Then, indeed, I am the luckiest man in the world."

In minutes, I felt her regular breathing. Anna and the baby slept in my arms as I thanked God for them for the thousandth time that day.

Chapter 27

Mutiny

Anna

In the days following the storm and Berta's burial-at-sea, we roamed the decks like stray dogs searching for a lap for comfort. We avoided looking at each other or traded forlorn half-smiles. Three people who set out from *Le Havre* and an infant, who'd had no chance at life, were gone. *Who would be next?* I wondered.

The boat continued to bob and pitch. *Professeur* explained that with little of the sail replaced, there was less control of the boat's movement. The helmsman kept the bow pointed southwest, but the wind could not be well harnessed until the new mast was erected and a few sails hoisted.

The crew hurried about untangling or attaching new rigging. They pounded oakum into the cracks between the planks to keep her watertight; they worked longer watches than before; they hammered, greased, oiled, scrubbed, scraped,

194   Virginia Hall-Apicella

pulled, tarred, and hauled. Some set sails, while others tried to repair the main mast. Johann volunteered to help the sailmaker sew, but the sailmaker looked at Johann's hands. Although Johann had a sewer's calloused fingertips, they were not the rugged hands of an experienced ship-bound sailmaker. The sailmaker shook his head at Johann's offer.

Mr. Carothers continued to relegate us to the airless compartment below.

When allowed on deck, I noticed a change in the sailors' attitude. They were no longer joking or playfully jostling each other. No one broke into a shanty or called out a crude jest while he worked. Instead, the crewmen gathered into loose groups and looked furtively around. I sensed that they had lost a sense of camaraderie—they were now a scrum of hostile men. There was no time for *bonhomie* or enjoying the sail. If Captain Henshaw emerged from his cabin to give an order, they scattered to their posts but mumbled below their breaths. When Quimby, the steward, appeared, they brushed against him, sometimes backing him into a gunwale. A murmured insult was tossed at him. Though I seldom could understand the threat, I could understand the tone and the look. Quimby would skulk back to Captain Henshaw's cabin, muttering an oath with a vile scowl on his scarred face.

First mate Carothers seemed everywhere at once. He gave orders in his usual deep voice, scrutinizing the crew's work while looking ahead to scan the horizon. He oversaw the cook's distribution of water to us in the morning. The water, which was supposed to be fresh, was fetid after weeks in oaken casks in the hold. I ached for the rain that had gushed during the storm and was wasted in the sea. Since the hurricane, no rain had fallen. Before then, the women and I would gather each morning to receive water from the cook for each family member. It needed to last all day for cooking, drinking, and bathing. Now, it was down to a half jug. When one of the American sailors complained, I heard Carothers hush him.

"I'll get to the bottom of this," he assured the man.

Two days later, we saw that the water ration had been reduced again, as well as the portion of the thin morning gruel. I heard more complaints from the crew. Confined to the bowels of the *Stalwart,* we were a sorry lot. We were thirsty and spent from the too-long voyage.

And there was no land in sight.

Johann and I were allowed on deck for a quick stroll six days after the storm. After the reduced water ration, I pulled Johann aside so the children could not hear.

"Johann, what will happen? Our water is less every day. We have almost no food. Peter had told us to be prepared for eight weeks, but now we are at ten."

"I know Anna. But give me less. Give my portion to the children," Johann said.

I was already giving most of our share to the children. I made a thin soup with turnips and a few bacon shavings each day. The few potatoes that were left were sprouted and mealy. Cook gave us hardtack from a barrel. I needed to break it in half and knock it against the table to shake the weevils out before I gave it to the children. You could not be a finicky eater on this ship—you ate what you were given.

Bernard was thinner than he'd ever been. His ribs were visible through his shirt. Rosalia had lost her spark. She leaned listlessly against me during the day rather than displaying her usual cheerfulness. Delia continued to nurse, but my milk supply felt less and less; luckily, she needed less food than the others. I remembered giving good, hearty *Zwiebach* to my other children to chew when they were teething. Delia had only the despicable hardtack to gnaw on.. I knew it was unkind, but I regretted sharing food earlier with the young men who had come aboard ill-prepared.

Our conversation was interrupted when Carothers sprang onto the deck. His face was clouded with anger, and his usual perfect tricorn hat was at a precarious angle. He turned, surveying the sailors on deck.

"Where's Quimby?" he shouted.

One of the sailors pointed to the stern.

"Mr. Quimby, what's the meaning of this?"

The unsavory steward avoided the first mate. His cap was pulled down over his scarred face. He made for the companionway toward Captain Henshaw's cabin.

When Mr. Carothers blocked him, Quimby edged backward toward the gunwale. When there was no more room to back up, he stopped and cursed at the mate. Carothers responded with a litany of barbs and allegations. Back and forth, the accusations and insults flew. I couldn't understand the words, but I understood the language of tempers and raised fists.

Carothers lost his usual disciplined demeanor, and his fist connected with Quimby's jaw. The steward reeled back. When he regained his footing, he pulled a clasp knife from his breeches' pocket. The crew, watching and urging Carothers on, jerked their dirks from their waistbands. They stepped closer to the steward. Coming at Quimby from the side, Michael wrenched the knife from the steward's balled fist. With an arched throw, he heaved the blade over the side, and we heard it plunk in the water below. One of the Americans clapped the Irishman on the back while the others encircled the angry man. While Quimby stood alone in the middle, the crew moved closer and jeered at him.

"Got the Captain hooked on the opium pipe, you did."

Quimby stuck out his chin. "He was hooked from his days of rounding the Horn and sailing the China seas. I just found him more in Le Havre."

One by one, the sailors accused him of more crimes.

"Stole food from these fine folk."

"Gave us the worse rations, skimped on our grog, reneged on your watch..."

The taunts continued until the first mate pointed his finger into Quimby's face.

"You bloody bounder! Do you see what you've done? There should be three more casks of fresh water below," Carothers bellowed.

"You're a sniveling son of a swine, you are. If you were doin' your job as you should've, you'd have known a long time ago," Quimby shot back. He kicked hard at a scrub brush that had been discarded when the fight began. He continued.

"Back in that French port, the Cap'n, he had me take out three water casks. Instead, he tells me, 'Bring three hogsheads of that fancy wine on board. That will bring a nice price in New York, more than any rancid water,' says he."

Carothers glared at him.

"He promised me a nice profit, he did. All I had to do was help him and keep my lips sewed-up tight."

Carothers's teeth were bared. He couldn't keep his rage contained. He lashed out again.

"You were trusted to store enough water for the entire voyage." Pointing to us, he continued. "These decent people will die of thirst."

Most of our fellow passengers had climbed from below when they heard the commotion.

Quimby interrupted him.

"Hah! And that's not the 'alf of it. If they make it to shore alive, Cap'n's not headed to New York; he's headed to a southern port. Wants to sell them as redemptioners and indenture them. That'll bring a tidy bundle for the Cap'n and me."

We all heard the word and quickly translated it—from English to French to German. Soon, we were as agitated as the sailors. We all knew what "redemptioner" meant.

From the early days of the American colony, English and Irishmen who could not pay their way on a ship to the new world hired themselves as indentured servants, bargaining their service for their fare. Johann had explained it all to me. We saw the bills posted in the taverns. Redemptioner brokers advertised in our German countryside for laborers who could be quickly "redeemed" in the ports of Philadelphia and New York. Young workers from our villages were needed for the farms and factories of the growing new country. Gangs of young men, like some men aboard the *Stalwart,* signed on to have their passage paid by an American who needed their strong shoulders. Poverty forced some to commit to years of labor for passage. We'd had no doubt the brokers reaped a handsome profit from the poor man's plight.

We were not redemptionists; we had paid our fares. We buzzed with fury on hearing Quimby's announcement. The male passengers shook their fists at the churlish steward as the crew had done.

I turned toward Johann. "Am I understanding this, Johann? Did the Captain think he could sell us even though we sacrificed everything to pay for this voyage?"

"That's what I think they are saying, *Liebschen.* Please don't worry. No one is going to sell this family to the highest bidder." He took my hand.

The Irishman threw a bucket of seawater at the defiant steward.

"Ain't nothin' you can do," Quimby spat. He tried to shake off the water from his drenched clothing. "Henshaw is the cap'n, and his word goes."

"Mr. Quimby, you are dismissed," said Carothers, who had regained his usual composure. His back was straight as the mast behind him. He glared at the defiant steward and said in a fierce voice. "Please leave the deck. This matter is far from over."

Quimby turned toward the companionway, his knee clicking as he walked. Before disappearing below, he yelled to the Irishman, "You owe me for that bloody knife."

Throughout the whole confrontation, Captain Henshaw had not shown himself. The faint, sweet smell of burning opium wafted from his cabin.

The following day was Sunday, and Captain Henshaw stood by the helm, his well-thumbed Bible in hand: the crew and the rest of the passengers assembled for his required scriptural reading. Like yesterday, steward Quimby stood by himself. The captain began to read, then looked to the horizon and up at the tell-tales. He pulled his compass from the pocket of his waistcoat.

"Mr. Carothers," he called louder than usual, "what's the meaning of this? This boat should be heading in a southerly direction, and we are headed directly west!"

"Aye, Captain Henshaw. We are headed west. To Newfoundland."

"Newfoundland? This boat is commissioned to go to New York."

"Aye, sir. But that was before the food ran so low that the men had to work with only hardtack in their bellies. There's not enough water to last three days. The grog's almost gone. The salt beef's been used up."

"Nonsense. We'll be in New York harbor in several days, and these men will have plenty of food."

Carothers ignored Henshaw's reply. He continued, "...and the boat's barely seaworthy. The pumps can hardly keep up with the leaks. All the oakum in the world can't plug up these cracks. The hull's worm-eaten. If we're to hit another storm, there's not wood nor sailcloth for repairs."

Carothers's erect posture and level gaze confronted the stooped captain.

Captain Henshaw turned his back on the first mate. He pointed to the man at the helm. "Steer to the south." Then to the crew, "Prepare to come about."

We stood watching the argument, straining to understand what was happening.

The sailors walked away from the captain one by one and edged up close behind Carothers. We, passengers, followed uncertainly. Quimby was the only crew member standing behind the captain, and even he had an unsure look in his eye.

Carothers addressed the captain once more.

"Captain Henshaw, sir, it's been brought to our attention by Mr. Quimby," he spat out the steward's name. His eyes darted toward Quimby, "...he says, sir, that you intend to seek a harbor south of New York and plan to sell the labor of these people." He gestured to us all standing behind him. None of us dared to speak.

"Mr. Carothers, that is *no* concern of yours."

"Perhaps, sir. But these men and these passengers think

otherwise." With this, he pulled a piece of foolscap from his waistcoat, held it at arms-length, and read:

"We, the crew of the Stalwart schooner out of New Bedford, Massachusetts, proclaim that Captain Jedidiah Henshaw has violated his obligations under the codes of conduct and maritime law. By altering the destination, he has made the signed articles invalid. From this day, henceforth, we will heed the orders of Mr. Enoch Carothers, first mate.

He turned the paper to show Henshaw the signatures. Several were in a shaky script, but most were X's with the name written below in Carothers's neat hand.

Henshaw snatched at the paper, but the mate jerked it from his reach.

"This is mutiny! This is insufferable! Insubordination! You've all signed the articles," Captain Henshaw shouted. He glared at the crew behind the mate. He shook his gnarled finger at the seamen.

"None of you will find a place on any boat on this ocean. I'll flog you all." This time, he pointed his finger at Carothers, "...you'll be hanged!" The crew stirred themselves behind Mr. Carothers. They all knew that they had signed articles against mutiny and sedition. Death was possible.

"Captain Henshaw, you may be right," the mate answered in a polite, firm tone, "yet we do not intend to steal your ship nor sell your cargo. There'll be no bloodshed. You'll not be mistreated or held captive. But, we sail west...until we reach St. John's in Newfoundland. After repairs and resupply, the crew and passengers can decide to sail with you to New York. I doubt many will want to sail with a captain who spends most of his time under the slumber of opium, the God-forsaken poppy."

Henshaw shook his Bible. "This is an abomination, a threat to God on a Christian ship! I am Noah, and you are all only the beasts." Spittle shot from his mouth as he yelled. "It is my business what I do."

Carothers maintained his stance as if he had not heard the captain. The men mumbled behind him.

Captain Henshaw was not done with his rage.

"I'll bow down to the Pope before I let you ruffians take my ship."

Carothers once again ignored the captain's rage. In his deep voice, he continued.

"You will pay those who decide to quit you at three-quarters share. We want no profits except those we're entitled to. But we will have no more deaths of the crew or these good people under my watch."

When he finished, no one spoke. The only sounds to be heard were the constant creak of the halyards in the blocks and the incessant whir of the wind that filled the jerry-rigged sails.

Chapter 28

St. John's, Newfoundland

Johann

I might have understood Newfoundland's past better if I had been a geologist rather than a tailor. As usual, the *Professeur* tried to enlighten me. He'd consulted one of his books.

"Millions of years ago, the land was formed by continental collisions, volcanos, and an ice cap," he said. "Glaciers advanced and retreated for eons, scouring out mountains, rivers, lakes, and deep harbors."

The *Professeur* continued his narrative. He explained that native people, Vikings, Basques, Portuguese, and even pirates, had occupied this island. They'd all sought bounteous fishing, riches, and land. The English claimed that John Cabot had wandered in on the feast of St John the Baptist in 1498 and gave the port its name. Others contended that Basque fishermen named the port after a similar bay in their country. The French were the most successful as colonizers until the British fought them for it. Finally, the French surrendered in 1763 when the red-coated British outsmarted them by using signal flags from a summit called Lookout Hill. In the War of 1812, St. John's was a British anchorage.

I did not understand everything he told me. The only thing I knew from his lesson was that, according to Carothers, this was where the *Stalwart* was headed.

We sailed toward the sunset. The crew hurried to Carotherss's commands, though I sensed they were wary since the declaration of mutiny. When Captain Henshaw appeared on deck, he continued with threats and undiminished harsh words. Neither Carothers nor the crew responded. Once, Henshaw stormed from his cabin with a cat-o-nine-tails whip raised high. Standing at least seven inches taller, Carothers grabbed the whip, with its nine dangling cords attached to sharp stones, from Henshaw's hand and flung it into the waves below. Henshaw cursed at Carothers and the other sailors as he stumped toward his cabin. The odor of burning opium no longer emanated from Henshaw's cabin. No one listened when he returned to the main deck for a scriptural reading.

We began to see more birds and scraps of floating seaweed. We knew that meant land. The jury-rigged sails held the wind. Despite the ship's crippled condition, we sailed at a good clip. In the distance, rugged islands filled with vast colonies of birds the sailors called kittiwakes appeared. As we drew closer, we saw their squat gray and white bodies clinging to cliffside nests.

Their guano looked like icing dripping from a large, half-smashed cake. Their loud calls mimicked their name. Their shrieks carried over the waves to announce that *terra firma*—the *Professeur's* words—was near.

Bernard stood between my legs as I curled my arms around him to keep him warm. In minutes, the other passengers joined us on the deck. The crew wanted us below, yet they could not stop people with land-starved eyes from wanting to gaze at the horizon. One of the sailors, a former whaler, pointed out surfacing pilot whales shooting streams of mist above the water line.

"In the spring, you'd see harp seals with their pups on the ice flows as well as those humpbacks," he said.

The children shouted when fountains of water shot from the heads of the great gray beasts. Carothers took a spyglass from his pocket to let us take a closer look at the whales and the birds. Anna came beside us and nudged me with her elbow. I kissed her smiling lips. Our feet would soon be on solid ground; we would fret less when more than gunwales separated our children from disaster.

As the *Stalwart* neared Newfoundland's coast, fleets of fishing boats and other vessels headed in our direction. Their Union Jacks snapped in the off-shore gusts. Jagged reddish cliffs arched their bodies from the sea. In between the rocks were patches of verdant green lichen. Trees crowned the tops of the steep slopes.

We clapped and hurrahed as we drew closer to the harbor's craggy walls. The rocky palisades protected a slim slice of water flowing into St. John's port. The crew said the Narrows at the harbor mouth couldn't have been more than 200 feet. It was a dangerous maneuver through the protruding rocks. We held on tightly as the boat rode the current into the harbor's calm waters. When the white-knuckled helmsman steered us through, he shouted, "T'was like threading a rope through a small needle that was."

On the starboard side, one peak stood out higher than the rest. It overlooked the narrow harbor entrance. According to the crew, this was the hill the *Professor* read about where the British signaled each other in the Seven Years' War, leading to their victory over the French. The harbor's port side was greener, with more trees and less settlement.

Bernard escaped from my grasp to inch closer to the sailors and mime their lowering of the halyard. I picked up Rosalia and pressed my chin into her yellow curls. Anna held her hand over to protect Delia's fair face from the blaring sun. Katja squeezed between Anna and me, her arm around her mother's waist. Like her mother, tears flowed from her hazel eyes. Her fingers brushed them away before Bernard could notice and tease. Bernard, now close to the rail, was more interested in gazing at the buildings, boats, and steeples appearing before him. He ran toward us.

"Papa, are we here? Is this America? Is this New York? Is this where we'll live?"

"Not yet, son, but very soon," I replied. In truth, I had no idea. Back in Kittersburg, I had planned with Schoolmaster Remmelin: Strasbourg, Paris, Rouen, Le Havre, New York, up the Hudson River to western New York. We were arriving in Newfoundland. I had no idea where and how we would get to a small town on the shores of Lake Ontario that sold cheap land. I felt Anna's eyes on me. I jingled the silver thimbles in my pocket.

White gulls soared over our schooner, and a random bird landed on the mended main. The familiar roar of the sea had become a murmur of gentle waves lapping at the hull. The green-gray of the ocean had lapsed into the blue of the harbor. While the crew furled the sheets, we slipped past two and three-masted sloops and brigs. At Carothers's command, the sailors dropped anchor.

To our great relief, St. John's was a snug harbor. The Norwegian boys slapped the backs of the sailors; the Schmidt girls sang a hymn; Socrates began his solitary dance; even *Madame* fell to her knees in gladness; Anna entwined her fingers in mine.

Close to shore, small boats bobbed on their moorings. People and horse-pulled wagons went about their business on the beach. On the north side, a small fishing village with crude, wooden houses clung to a rocky bank. I imagined that if an outsized gale hit them, their planks would be launched like cannonballs in the wind. I pulled the cap from my head and wiped the sweat from my forehead. Despite the cool temperature and joy at seeing land, I was perspiring. *Is this it? Where are we? Did I force my family to leave home for this small harbor?* I asked myself.

Although grateful to be off the sea, the town disappointed me. Compared to the walled old world cities, the castles, the cathedrals, or the brand new limestone buildings of Paris, this was a make-shift place. A dirt path lay parallel to the shore, crossed over a brook, and meandered over the rocks and rills. A long wooden wharf edged the town. The houses and warehouses clustered on the waterfront were constructed of weathered wood or chinked-together stone. Chimneys sat on each side of their steep gabled roofs. I saw several burnt-out buildings huddled together at the far end of town. They looked like heaps of charcoal, with a few framing posts reaching skyward.

A handful of sheep speckled the hillsides like white spots on a green canvas. Farther inland, a whitewashed rectangular church with a truncated spire sat alone on higher ground. Behind the church, soft and hardwood trees marched up to the bluff line. Interspersed in all this green were patches of denuded, logged-out fields. *Where are the fields of wheat, the pastures with grazing cows?* I wondered.

My reverie was interrupted by Carothers, who stepped on a wooden crate in front of the main mast. As usual, his posture was erect. His uniform, despite weeks on the sea, appeared cleaned and pressed. He cleared his throat before he spoke.

"We've arrived in St. John's. We're not in America but in Newfoundland. The people here may not be fond of Americans because of the recent war, but we've no other choice. We've put in here for refitting, to make the boat seaworthy again."

Despite the offshore breeze, his tri-cornered hat remained on his head. His precise baritone carried.

"We don't know how long we'll stay, but winter is anon. Some of you may wish to leave the ship and travel to America on your own. Or you may choose to wait for repairs. That's your decision. You paid your fare, so you're due that. The owners of the *Stalwart* will be contacted about the changed plans."

While Carothers was explaining things, Captain Henshaw had climbed to the top deck. His wishbone legs and humped shoulders contrasted with Carothers' arrow-straight posture.

He shouted and pointed a knobby finger at the first mate, "Or you may linger here to watch this man be hanged."

Ignoring the jibe, Carothers continued.

"When we can tie up, we will bring your possessions ashore. From there, it will be your choice on how you will proceed."

Undeterred by the first mate's speech, Henshaw harangued Carothers and the sailors and threatened imprisonment and worse. Two burly sailors moved close and crowded him toward the rail as they had done with Quimby.

Only then did Mr. Carothers look beyond the sailors to the captain.

"We'll let the maritime court of Newfoundland determine who will be hanged and who will be found wanting in his obligations and code of conduct."

With that, Carothers turned and began to order the crew to their expected duties.

Mr. Carothers' statements left us confused. With our varying languages, we puzzled over what he said. Startled and concerned by this new proposition, we pondered our choices. *What would we do? Who was willing to wait for the ship to be repaired? Who might give Newfoundland a try? Who would find another route, another boat to New York?*

We were sure of only one thing—we had to get off this ship. We needed to pack whatever was left. What had not been destroyed by mold, salt, or the shipboard rats might be kept. Anything else would be tossed overboard. What of our previous lives could we salvage? We hurried to find and claim our few possessions.

While we packed, Bernard called down to me from the companionway.

"Papa, come look. They're taking the captain." I scrambled up the hatchway—most passengers followed—to the rail, where Bernard gazed down at the water. A longboat had been lowered from the gunwales to the water, and Captain Henshaw sat slumped, unbound, in the stern. A strapping sailor sat on one side and Carothers on the other. Bjorn and his brother, usually quiet young men, hurled insults in Norwegian at the scheming captain. The sailors were silent. I thought they might now be considering Henshaw's threats: floggings, loss of their livelihood, hanging. Being brave on the restless sea was easier than in a civilized harbor with rules and legal authorities.

Four crewmen with synchronized strokes pulled the vessel toward the pier. Quimby, whose arms were bound behind him, sat in the bow. He caught every saltwater spray that slapped at the boat. When the boat reached the wooden pier, Carothers threw a line, and a longshoreman tied her off. I squinted to watch as Carothers and the two miscreants marched along the dock toward the ramshackle town. I lost sight of them as they passed behind a building. *God will see to him. But what of us?* I hoped I would never see the greedy twosome who had changed my family's life again.

A few hours later, Otto and I stood on the deck, our belongings in order, when we spotted the longboat rowing back to the *Stalwart*. Behind it followed two more boats. Michael explained that these boats would tow the schooner to a dock to unload the cargo and the passengers. The crewmen threw lines and secured knots from the schooner to the towing boats as deftly as a weaver wielding a shuttle through the warp. The creaking and leaking *Stalwart* would be hauled to a slip at the barnacle-covered dry dock.

Carothers returned to his platform on the wooden crate.

"All off. Carry what you can. The crew will unload your trunks to the quay. Customs-men might question you and ask to see your papers. They listen better with a shilling or two put in their hand. When you're on-shore, you're on your own," he said. "You'll need to find lodging. If you've any questions, contact me at Sealy's boarding house," he indicated a clapboard-sided building tucked in between a chandlery and a two-story warehouse with a large peeling sign, Hearn & Co., All Lines of Provisions, Groceries, Feeds.

Carothers continued his parting words.

"If you are traveling back south after refitting, I need to know. No estimate of when that will be." He cleared his throat and looked away from our desperate faces.

"Best of luck to each of you. May God go with you."

We looked amongst ourselves, uncertain of our next steps. It differed from what we had planned when we paid our fares. We were abandoned in Newfoundland when we had sought the plenty of America. Carothers had saved us from Captain Henshaw's clutches, but to what end?

When the *Stalwart* was tied along the dock, the dockers began to lift and haul the cargo from the hold. The sailors appeared eager to hoist their sea chests on their shoulders and be done with the *Stalwart*. They'd be in search of a pint and a woman I knew. Michael had confessed to us men that a town filled with a willing whore and a good drink made them forget their hard work at sea. The rest of us wanted dry land, an escape from the crippled schooner, and good food.

I grabbed as much as I could with a wriggling Rosalia in my arms and walked down the creaking gangplank. When I took my first step on solid ground in more than ten weeks, my legs almost buckled beneath me. I adjusted my stance and looked back to watch Anna disembark. She clutched Delia in one arm and a satchel in the other. Bernard and Katia followed her, their few possessions in their arms. I lost sight of Otto and his girls.

We stood looking at the unpromising town. I felt like I did when we arrived in Paris—overwhelmed by the coming and going, the new smells, and the unfamiliar spaces. Unlike Paris, with its stone buildings and towering monuments, this was a tiny wooden town carved out of towering trees. Men on the dock shouted behind overloaded handcarts as women tried to sell us dried-out meat pies. Dogs scampered underfoot while horses clomped by burdened by their heavy loads. A strong odor of rotting seaweed and the fresh smell of newly sawed timber greeted us.

Drying animal pelts were tacked to a warehouse wall along the quay. Another store with peeling paint on its clapboard side proclaimed: Exporters of Dried Salt Cod, Herring, Sealskin, Whalebone and Importers of Naval Stores of All Kinds. There were signs for chandlers, sail shops, joiners, riggers, and rope works. Men sat on barrels in front of storehouses plastered with handbills.

As Carothers had said, two officious-looking gentlemen in unmatched uniforms sat at a table at the end of the quay. The first man stood, asking us to open our mouths and stick out our tongues. He gamely looked at our tongues with a magnifying glass. He thumped each of us on our backs. When Delia began to wail, he passed us on to his companion. I carefully unwrapped the papers Holbauer insisted on from their waxed canvas resting place. He took them. When he realized they were in German, he shook his head. I carefully put two French francs in his palm before he returned the documents.

"Move on," he said as he waved us ahead. "Welcome to Newfoundland. Don't stay too long."

We moved away from the table, so Socrates, who had come up behind us, tried his luck.

I turned to Anna. "This is home for the near future," I said. She gave me a brave yet uncertain smile.

"Johann, we must find a place to stay and get decent food in the children's bellies." Before our experience on the sea, Bernard and Rosie would usually run and explore a new place. Here they stayed close to us, as bewildered and unsure as Anna and I. Katja walked next to her mother, clutching her cloak tightly, her face betraying her anxiety. As happy as I was to be on shore, I wasn't certain if this sprung-up town was better than the wretched boat. We began walking up the street, and Carothers overtook us. I grabbed his arm and did not let go,

"Where are we to go? Sealy's, like you?" I said.

"No, not with a family. Water Street is only for sailors and drunkards. Go a few streets up. There should be a guest house to take you," Carothers answered.

"And remember, John. You're now in British territory. Try your English. It will go better for you."

Carothers's last piece of advice gave me more concern. I felt a churning in my empty stomach. I had no idea what to do and had to do it in my sparse English. Five people depended on my choices. I spoke German, French, and a smattering of Polish, but those tongues were insufficient. I tried to remember Carothers's shipboard lessons, yet all I recalled were nautical words—gunnel, galley, fore, and aft. These words would not help us find a place to sleep.

I touched Bernard's shoulder. "Son, can you help your father."

Anna gave me a sharp look and spoke to me in a whisper, "Johann, he is a seven-year-old boy. You might have considered this language thing when you and Remmelin planned this great adventure."

Bernard smiled up at me.

"I'll help you, Papa. I know English."

Remmelin and Peter Maier were right: Bernard was bright. He absorbed things as quickly as a mop plunged into a bucket of sudsy water. He'd listened to Carothers's lessons and spent time among the sailors when Anna allowed. By the end of the voyage, he was bantering back and forth with some crew despite Anna's worry that some words might not be appropriate for a child.

"Bernard, we need to find a place to stay and to eat, and your Mama and I need your words. Can you do it?" I asked.

"Sure, Papa. I can try. English is not so hard. When we say, '*Was ist das?*' They say, 'What is this? We say '*Wer woolen essen.*' They say, "We want to eat.'"

"Are we going to leave our fate in the hands of a little boy?" Anna asked me dubiously.

"Only when that little boy is as smart as our Bernard." I smiled at her. "And didn't Jesus say, 'and a child shall lead them?'"

We reached the street parallel to Water. These buildings seemed more permanent and stiff-upper-lip than the make-shift buildings on the quay. Two-storied brick or fieldstone houses lined this block. On a corner, a hand-painted sign identified it as Duckworth Street. Gold lettering filled the window of one of the more prominent buildings: W & G Rendell Insurance, Established in 1750. Another building identified itself by a hanging, hand-carved sign shaped like a fisherman's boot. We didn't have to wonder at the yeasty smell emitting from another: barley, hops, and good ale.

Midway down the street, we stopped to reshuffle our possessions. Anna looked at me, and I knew that she was miffed. I shrugged my shoulders; she looked away, unsatisfied. Over her shoulder, my eyes lit upon a sign: Southwick Hotel. The last was a word I knew in German, French, and now, English. I hurried to push open the heavy, wooden door.

The low-ceilinged room was dark and smelled of yesterday's food. Two soot-grimed windows on each side of the entry barely lit the room. A small fire in a grate was down to its last embers. Above the paltry fire, a massive pine mantel held several pewter tankards and a small, salt-glazed crock with feathers sticking up. A meager stock of split kindling and chopped logs was piled next to the fire, where a white-muzzled dog dozed on a ratty rug. As we entered, the dog didn't bother rising but thumped her tail on the planked wood floor.

High-backed benches, like pews, sat under the smudged windows. A steep staircase in the far corner led to a second floor. The most striking thing in the room was a massive, battered oak desk directly across from the door. A woman, undoubtedly the lady of this dubious house, glared at us from her seat behind the desk. Her gray hair was stuffed under an unfashionable bonnet, and the sharp points of her shoulders peaked through her shawl. Her lips were pinched shut on a face as wrinkled as old leather. Intense green eyes, the color of weathered copper, stared at me.

"Who might ye be, and why have ye entered my door?" she hissed. I would have turned on my heels if I felt less desperate. Bernard, my would-be translator, hid behind me.

"*Wir*...we..." I stammered. In the intimidating presence of this woman, all languages failed me. I closed my eyes and pantomimed sleep with my head tilted, and my hands placed prayer-like next to my ear.

"You want to sleep?" she said.

I nodded my head, and with my hands, I mimicked a person eating. My face flushed red to my hairline for resorting to such childlike gestures.

"And eat?" The crone said.

Bernard nudged me between my shoulders.

"*Ja*," I said.

An unexpected cackle came from the lips of the disagreeable-looking woman. Her eyes were upon Rosie, who had wriggled from my arms and was patting the aged dog by the fire.

The dog's tail smacked the ground with pleasure in universal dog language.

The old woman returned her eyes to me.

"So yer lookin' for a bed and food, are ye?"

Bernard's courage returned, and he stepped from behind me. "Yes, please, bed and food."

The woman's eyes squinted hard at the boy and then back to me.

"Not Irish, are ye?"

Irish was a word I knew from the *Stalwart*. The English sailors had teased Michael, the Irish sailor who played his fiddle with abandon and started the singing of every shanty.

"No, Irish," I replied, "*Deutsch*."

"Dutch?"

"No, *Deutsch, Allemand*."

She looked back at Bernard. She'd decided she would deal with him.

"Go two doors down," she pointed an arthritic finger at him. "Ask for Jacob Richter at the tavern," she said.

Bernard scrambled through the door and out to the street. We all followed him. Anna had to pick up Rosie, who was reluctant to leave the drowsy dog.

"She wants us to go to the *Weinstrub* and ask for a man named Jacob Richter," Bernard said.

"Let's find him."

We had no problem locating the alehouse. The noise and the prominent odors—sweet and sour, vile and enticing—drifted through the open doorway. We found ourselves in another low-ceilinged room, although a massive open-hearth fire graced this one. Large-muscled, working men hunched over a cluster of small tables. Some patrons leaned on the wide sticky bar that spanned the room's width. Most of the men held sweating mugs in their calloused hands. I approached a bald man with rolled-up sleeves and a towel flung over his shoulder, holding court behind the bar.

"Jacob Richter?" I asked.

The barkeep motioned with his chin toward a small, bald man who inclined his back on the bar as he surveyed the room. He wore a soiled fustian shirt covered by a frayed black silk weskit with a brass watch and chain dangling from a pocket. A ratty, yellow cravat covered his neck. He held a tankard in one hand and a squashed top hat in the other.

I tapped his shoulder. "*Sprechen Sie Deutsch?*" I asked.

"*Ja,*" nodded the man. "Why do you ask?" he replied in German.

I let out a grateful sigh and made a slight bow. I was so relieved to find a German-speaking man that my words came out in an avalanche. I told Jacob Richter that we'd come from Baden, crossed France, sailed on the ocean for ten weeks, endured a terrible storm, watched a mutiny, and landed in St. John's, although we were supposed to be in New York. Finally, I told him how the prickly woman at the hotel had told us to find him.

"Well, you've found me. May I buy you a drink? The beer tastes like piss, but the English can make a good whiskey," he said.

I shook my head and pointed to the rest of the family who remained by the door.

"I need to tell the old woman we need lodging and find out what we must pay."

"Well, my good man, that sounds like an easy job. Bargaining is my specialty."

Jacob Richter invited the family and me to gather around one of the irregular tables in a far corner. Laps became chairs, and a bench was dragged from one table to another. He ordered a pitcher of cider for us. Once Jacob began talking, I realized he was like my other German friend, Peter Maier, who needed a good audience and was willing to spin a tale.

"Now, Mrs. Grimsby, the old hag you met at the South-wick, is a peculiar woman. She doesn't warm up to most folks. She sits in an empty hotel half the time because she don't allow just anyone to bed down there. She's got a spinster set of mind. Years ago, they say, her heart got stuck to the coattails of an Irish sailor going to and fro from Ireland to St. John's. It seems as though he forgot to come back for her. They say it turned her from a fetching woman to bitterness in the blink of an eye. She's got no patience for the Irish. No, sir, no tolerance whatso-ever. Kind of a shame, though, because for the last thirty years, that's mainly who's coming."

I cleared my throat. We weren't Irish. As much as I liked a good story, I was anxious to secure a safe place to stay. I didn't interrupt Jacob Richter, aware that he was the kind of man who couldn't be hurried if he had a yarn to tell.

"No sir, not much sweetness in that lady. Her half-blind dog's got more feeling in the tip of her tail than Mrs. Grimsby got in her whole shriveled-up body. As far as I can tell, her only soft spot is for that dog. They say there was once a Mr. Grimsby. But the guy must have been clever enough to disappear."

Jacob Richter was finished with his tale of the infamous Mrs. Grimsby. He made a direct right turn to the story of his family.

"My family left the Palatine when I was about the age of that one." He crooked a thumb toward Bernard. "*Ja,* we fetched up in Nova Scotia and became farmers like the rest of the

Germans. It was not my kind of life, so I took a boat and have been here since. And in this tavern too often."

He might have gone on longer, but I felt Anna kick me under the table.

I interrupted, "Please help us with the old woman. The children are hungry, and we all need to sleep in a bed that doesn't move."

Jacob Richter nodded and drew a few shillings from his pocket to leave on the table. "Let's go," he said, shoving his smashed hat on his head.

We walked behind him to the Southwick.

When we followed Jacob Richter through the door, Mrs. Grimsby sat rigid and imposing. Rosie rushed over to the sleeping dog and kissed him on his muzzle. He answered with a sloppy lick to her face. Mrs. Grimsby's eyes followed the two, betraying the glimmer of a smile. Jacob removed his hat and straightened his cravat before he addressed Mrs. Grimsby.

Back and forth, the conversation went as we stood. The German gesticulated, and the woman shook or nodded her head to his queries.

Finally, Richter turned to me.

"You'll have the front room to yourself because there's so many of you, but the room's got but one bed. Breakfast is coffee and bread served no later than 8:30. Dinner's served at 4:00. It's probably some fish and cabbage. And if you don't like fish, you might stay hungry in St. John's. The privy's out back, and you'll be charged a farthing less if you empty your night jar. That one," he pointed to Rosie, who continued to pet the dog, "probably saved you a shilling or two."

When he finished, my eyes met Anna's, and I saw her relief. I held out my hand to Mrs. Grimsby, who ignored it.

"Thank you," I said in the best English I could muster. I followed it with "*Danke.*"

When the old woman turned the stained ledger toward me, I signed John Klem.

Chapter 29

Mrs. Grimsby

Anna

It was the first moment since we'd set our feet on this new land that I could let go of my caught-up breath. We had a place to stay, were off the fierce ocean, and my children would have full bellies. Yet, I felt uncomfortable with this haughty woman whom Jacob Richter said only had room in her heart for a decrepit dog.

After Johann signed his name, Mrs. Grimsby rose from her chair and bellowed, "Mary."

A short woman, smelling of smoke and onions, came through a doorway in the back of the room. She wore a colorful skirt topped by a servant's stained apron. Two long black plaits fell down her back. Her tawny cheekbones were high, and her eyes were deep brown. A wide smile lit her face. I felt immediate relief when I saw her—she was the brightest thing in this dismal dwelling. Later, I learned from Jacob that she was a member of the local Mi'kmaq. Her people had occupied this coastal environment thousands of years before the Vikings came. They hunted moose and caribou in the winter and fished by the water in the summer. For the three weeks that we resided in St. John's, I never heard Simple Mary—that was what the townspeople called her—say a word, but her face always held the radiance of daybreak.

Mrs. Grimsby led us up the narrow staircase. Mary followed with her bundles of linens and blankets. Behind her, Jacob puffed his way up, clinging to the wall for support. Mrs. Grimsby pulled open the door to a dim room with one dormer window covered in the same layer of grime and dirt as those below. In the corner, a feathered ticking covered a rope bed in need of a good turning. One wall held a battered chest of drawers. A creamware chamber pot was in a corner.

Mary placed one blanket on the bed and, pointing to the children, put two more on the floor. We looked at our grim surroundings after Mrs. Grimsby and Mary descended the stairs. I asked Johann and Jacob to go to the wharf to fetch our trunks. For better or worse, this would be our home until we could figure out our next step.

As they left, I called to Johann, "When you pass a merchant's, please bring back a large crock of vinegar and some lye. There will be some washing going on."

I was grateful that we were now in a dry space where the walls did not move and creak, with no clanking halyard or snap of sails. I knew the tasks before me: putting meat on my children's bones, washing all our clothing, and finding a church to thank God we were safe. But first, I needed to clean the grimy room.

After Johann and Jacob wrestled the trunks up the narrow staircase, we descended to the dismal main room. Mrs. Grimsby gestured for us to sit at the small table and shouted an order to Simple Mary. In a few minutes, Mary returned with steaming bowls of a pale, chunky chowder with bright carrot circles floating on top. The soup was filled with cabbage, turnips, and various fish, including the heads. On her second trip from the kitchen, Mary brought a loaf of plain, crusted bread. Beneath Mrs. Grimsby's scowl, Johann closed his eyes and asked for God's blessing on the food. As his blessing went on a bit too long, Bernard began to swing his feet, and Rosie squirmed on the wooden bench.

I hastily said, "Amen. Johann, we're hungry." After the weeks on the ship, this hot, local food tasted as satisfying as any Michaelmas or wedding feast I had ever attended.

When the meal was over, I went from the gloomy room to the kitchen dominated by a large open fireplace. The kettle of the fish soup sat on a three-legged spider warmed by the glowing embers. A bee-hive oven with a cast-iron, hinged door, bricked into the wall to the right of the fire, was the source of the hearty bread. I spied a rolled-up pallet in the corner and realized that the kitchen was Mary's bedroom. I pantomimed cheerful Mary to boil water on the large open hearth. Obligingly, she lifted a large cauldron, filled it with water from a cistern, and placed it on the trammel hook attached to a crane over the fire. I explored the kitchen until I found a wooden bucket and a bundle of rags. Once more, I signaled my intentions: scrubbing everything I saw. Simple Mary responded with a grin, showing a mouthful of tiny white teeth.

I took the flagon of vinegar Johann had bought, dumped the pungent acid into the water bucket, and carried it and the rags to the upstairs room. Mary and I set to wash the dingy window and any begrimed surface we found. We were so delighted to see the light shine through the clean panes that we descended to the entrance room and cleaned those cloudy windows. We wiped down all the furniture, and Mary swept the floor. Mrs. Grimsby, anchored to the chair behind the desk, called out to Mary.

"Don't ye be expecting more wages just because ye got a notion in yer head." Her face remained pleated with wrinkles and disdain. Her hotel was getting scrubbed without her having to part with a ha'penny. Rosie was lavishing love on her dog. Yet, Mrs. Grimsby remained sour and dismissive.

After the windows and furniture were dirt-free, we poured heated water into a giant copper tub in the back courtyard. One by one, the children would have a good sudsing.

First, shy Katja went into the tub. She held onto baby Delia, who giggled and splashed as any seven-month-old would. I wrapped them both in a large flannel when they were done. Next came Rosie. The water and suds flattened her springy blond curls. She squealed and splashed and did not want to get out. Bernard could hardly wait for his time in the tub, although he made sure that Simple Mary's head was turned when he plunged his naked body into the water.

I was so happy to see the children acting like themselves. Once the salt was washed away, their faces, sun-gilded by their weeks on the sea, glowed like summer peaches. Yet, I was alarmed at how thin they had gotten after too long on the ocean with such paltry rations. I could count their ribs and the knuckles of their spines. I vowed to sneak bread to fatten them when Mrs. Grimsby was not looking.

With the children bathed and dried, Mary heated more water and gestured for me to squeeze myself into the tub. She unbraided my hair, washed it, and rinsed it with water scented with a sweet herb I could not identify. Then she untangled my hair with a comb made from a horn. *How does this happy woman live with that sour old spinster?* I wondered. I returned her ever-present smile. Mary delighted me. I had made my first new world friend.

When the evening arrived, St. John's took on the sound of a town ready for strong spirits and conviviality. I heard the noise drifting out of every tavern and pub on the street. Music from fiddles, hornpipes, and bodhrans wafted up the street to the now clean window in the room where I stood while my children drifted off to sleep on their pallets. The fragrance of the harbor, mixed with wood smoke, filled the air. Another night, we might go and be entertained with the rest of St. John's, but I was too exhausted and knew the next day held more washing.

Without waiting for Johann to climb the stairs to our room, I snuggled onto the bed with Delia and her delicious, clean-baby smell. When he arrived minutes later, I heard him drop his clothing on the planked floor next to the bed. He placed his arm around me and our sleeping baby. His weight and warmth excited me despite our decision. On the *Stalwart*, we had each been crammed into a separate tiny berth with two children. There was no space to be close and breathe in each other at the end of the day.

"Johann..." I began.

"Remember—I am now John."

"Well then, John, you must leave my bed immediately. My husband would not look kindly on me sleeping with another man. No, Johann is very strict about that," I teased.

"Well, perhaps then I will be Johann for another night," he said, kissing that spot below my ear that made me feel that tugging below my gut. It was too soon to allow ourselves pleasure.

He whispered, "Tomorrow, Johann may have a quick funeral, and you will remarry John. The man who has adored you for so many years."

I laughed but continued as if I had not been interrupted

"So, Johann, please tell me what we will do. I cannot abide the idea of getting on that horrid ship again, even if Carothers guarantees there'll be more fresh water than flows in the Rhine. Please promise me—no more boats." I forced myself not to think of his comforting arms but to concentrate only on the next step of the trip.

"*Liebling,* I can promise nothing. Jacob and I will try to figure this out. Thank God we have found someone who can help us. He thinks we are not so far." I did not answer but thought, *Why do men believe only they get to figure things out? His planning with Remmelin and Peter Maier had not turned out too well.* In minutes, I heard Johann's soft, regular breathing.

He was asleep. Perhaps Jacob Richter would have more correct answers. I wished he was less of a jack-of-all-trades and more of a geographer.

The following morning, there was more scrubbing. All the salt-sprayed clothing and musty linens must be washed, rinsed, and sun-dried. It had been impossible to do a satisfactory job on the boat. I was happiest when I knew my children smelled soap clean. I took pride in such a simple thing.

I descended the stairs with a pile of laundry tucked in my arms. Mary knew exactly what I wanted to do. She set up the large copper tub in the courtyard and lit a fire beneath it. The two of us spent the morning boiling and stirring the linens and clothing in tubs of water and lye. The children were allowed to stay in their night clothing while their dresses and pants lay strung across bushes and shrubs, basking in the bright sun.

Later that morning, Jacob Richter arrived. He and Johann sat talking over coffee and *toutons,* the dough Mary fried and slathered in treacly, dark molasses. Not forgetting my thoughts of last night, I squeezed between the two men on a bench at the now-scrubbed table.

"Now that we've washed off the sea and filled our bellies, it is time we thanked God," I said. "Tell me, Jacob, is there a Catholic church here where we can hear mass?"

Jacob looked surreptitiously around to ensure Mrs. Grimsby was not within earshot.

"*Ja,* if you walk down Duckworth to Plymouth Road, there's a Catholic chapel on the corner. Not a ten-minute walk. You'll not miss it. Just follow the Irish. And there's a priest, Fr. Scallan, a nice fellow. As Irish as St. Patrick himself."

He looked again to confirm that Mrs. Grimsby was not eavesdropping and continued, "*Ja,* the good father's got his hands full. Most of the people who go to his church are full of sass. Those from Tipperary don't like those from Cork, and those from Wexford don't like them from Kilkenny. And they take it to the pubs and the streets sometimes."

I sighed. It seemed to me that the men of the world couldn't get along. The French and the Prussians, the Austrians and the Spanish, the captains and the crews. To me, there were more important things to consider, and the most important thing right now was getting to this place in America where Johann would find his cheap land.

Now that I knew there was a church nearby, I had my plan for Sunday. We had not been to a church since Le Havre, and I longed to dip my hand in the holy water and receive the host. I wanted to hear and repeat those Latin words. I needed to thank God that we had survived the ocean and pray for those who had not. For now, I was content with letting Johann and Jacob figure out how to get to New York.

The following week, Simple Mary and I continued cooking and cleaning. I showed Mary how to bring sand from the shore and use it to scrub the floor from years of grime and grit. Mary taught me how to cook fish. We prepared cod cheeks, cod cakes, cod chowder, cod stew, and fried cod. Once, we even made a tasty but chewy meal of seal flipper. I showed Mary how to brine cabbage for sauerkraut. It was one of the only times that the smile flew from Mary's kind face; she screwed up her nose at the smell of the sour cabbage.

Mary and I often took the children to the meadows and fields when the work was done. She pointed to the green plants we could eat and those to avoid. Mary dug the roots of one plant and laid her hand over her forehead. She picked another, crumbled the leaves in her fingers, and touched her belly. She did this to several other ferns and mosses. In this way, this native woman taught me the herbs and barks her people used to cure their ailments. I knew from my sweet mother the Baden lore on what plants helped cure or heal certain illnesses, but, of course, I knew nothing of these unfamiliar plants in this strange country until Mary's instruction. Mary searched through the damp fields for the first of the season's cloudberries, also called bake apples. After filling a bucket with the bright orange berries, we brought them to the cozy kitchen and stewed them with sugar for a delicious jam.

On other days, Mary and I walked with the children to the shore to watch the ships with lowered sails drift to anchorage. We scampered along the stony beach and scanned the sky for eagles soaring high above the waves in search of fish. We clapped with delight as we watched one dive into the sea for prey. Once, we discovered a colony of puffins with their sad-clown faces and bright orange feet among the rocks. Rosie begged to stay behind to play with Betsy some days, and I allowed it if Johann was there. If only Mrs. Grimsby skulked about, Rosie came with me.

Mary and I were two women from different backgrounds, and even with Mary's lack of speech, we were kindred spirits. I told my silent friend things that I'd only shared with Magda. Even if she did not understand, she was ready with a nod and a smile. Mary did not speak German—she spoke the language of kindness.

This was not the case with Mrs. Grimsby. The spinster took all my work around her hotel for granted. She reminded Johann daily that our bill must be paid in good British silver, not German coin. Her business improved since Mary and I cleaned the place to the standards of a Kittersburg's *Hausfrau*. A British captain and Pierre, a French fur trader, took the other second-story room at the Southwick. Johann, Jacob, and the two new occupants became fast friends over drinks at one of the many Duckworth or Water Street taverns. While Mary and I cleaned and supervised the children, the four men discussed the ideas they thought only they could solve. Unless it were time for a meal, Mrs. Grimsby would shoo the men out of the main room of her dark hotel, where she sat at her desk like the evil stepmother in one of the Grimm's tales.

Mrs. Grimsby was the same age as our old friend and third grandmother, *Frau* Metzger. However, the similarity ended there. The Kittersburg widow was compassionate and generous; Mrs. Grimsby was a harpy, a scold, a shrew. There was one exception: Mrs. Grimsby had taken a shine to our Rosie. I watched as she lurked around my little girl for too long. She invited Rosie on walks with her arthritic dog. I did not want to consent, but Rosie begged to be with the old hound. The wretched woman plied Rosie with candies and sweets while she disdained the other children. She ignored Katja or expected her to clean as hard as Mary and I did. The crone openly disliked Bernard, who had started playing with the other St. John's neighborhood boys.

"Don't ye bring any of yer Irish ragamuffins into my place," she railed at him.

I was becoming even more concerned and wary of the dour woman. I knew my children were well-behaved, yet they were children. She treated them as if they were a dreaded disease.

The sun squinted through the early morning fog when Mrs. Grimsby approached me in the kitchen one day. I was returning from the privy where I had dumped the contents of the night jar. At the same time, Jacob wandered into the room searching for his battered hat. The shrew stopped him and told him that she needed him to translate. It was not as if he had a choice in the matter—being the interpreter had become his payment for all the meals he shared with us. Without a greeting, Mrs. Grimsby stepped in front of me.

"What'll she have for the little blond one?" Mrs. Grimsby said to Jacob. I gasped in a stunned tone when he repeated that to me in German.

"What did she ask?" I said, looking bewildered at Jacob, who could hardly keep up with my quick reply.

Mrs. Grimsby turned to me and pressed a bony finger into my chest. I stepped away from her jabbing finger.

"You heard me. What'll you have for the child, the one called Rosie? I've enough to meet your price."

Jacob looked astonished as he repeated Mrs. Grimsby's question.

"Everything has its price," said Mrs. Grimsby. "And I'll meet yours."

"My child is not for sale," I screamed to Jacob as if he had been the author of those awful words. I was trembling, stunned at what I was hearing. I looked around quickly, although I knew Mary had taken all the children to the market with her.

"I've always preferred a blue-eyed child," said the crone as if she had not heard me. "You've plenty of children, and you and that husband of yours can always have another. You're young enough and appear to favor each other. You'll have others in your pack."

"Rosie and the others are *my* children. They are a gift from God." I put my face close to Mrs. Grimsby's dried-apple face. "You will not touch a hair on their heads." I was shouting at her in German, and Jacob sputtered to answer.

"Your god's not given me such a gift. If you are a true Christian woman—a Papist, I've noticed—you should share your bounty with a woman with nary a child nor a grand. I can provide for that young one better than you. She'll want for nothing. I'll teach her the King's words, not the foreign gibberish you speak."

Without waiting for my reply, Mrs. Grimsby craned her neck toward Jacob as if he was willing to barter for her. "Tell this difficult woman I'll not charge for all the room and board for the past three weeks if she leaves the blond one behind when she and her brood pack up."

My chest was heaving and my head was pounding when I

heard the last of the old hag's proposal from Jacob's lips. I dropped the slop jar and it crashed at Mrs. Grimsby's feet. I had not been this angry or frightened since Johann's demand that we go to *Amerika* all those months before. There was never a moment when I wished more that I could speak English. It would not have been pleasant if I had expressed myself in German.

I would hear no more. I pivoted, pushed Jacob aside, and rushed towards the door to find Johann. As the door slammed, Mrs. Grimsby shrieked, "I've got more than one way to get what I want."

Chapter 30

Search

Johann

I felt weary, sad, and guilty as I trudged back from walking to the dock. A ship with a New York destination had yet to arrive. Today, as on most days, I sat with Jacob, the sea captain, and Pierre, the fur trader. Some days, even Father Scallan, the Irish priest, joined us to discuss what my family must do to get out of St. John's and on our journey to New York. I showed them the much-folded, dog-eared handbill I had carried for ten years. It was my promise, my hope for a better life for my family.

Bountiful Land, Fertile Genesee River Valley, Low Prices
Holland Land Company
New York
Contact: Oliver Phelps, Canandaigua, New York

. . .

Yet, we remained here in St. John's, and my worry grew.

I was turning down Duckworth Street to return to the Southwick when I saw Anna, her white linen cap tumbling from her hair and her skirts held high in her hands, race towards me. She was shouting something I could not understand. Behind her, Jacob fought to keep up, but she continued to outdistance him. I caught her by the shoulders to stop her momentum.

"Anna, whatever is the matter?"

"It's her, the witch—she wants our Rosie!" Anna was out of breath, her chest heaving.

"Please slow down," I begged. I had no idea what she was trying to tell me in her hurried words.

By now, Jacob had caught up. He huffed, his breath erratic, his hands on his knees.

"It's true, Johann...the Grimsby woman wants to buy your little girl...says she needs Rosie more than you do," he sputtered between labored breaths.

"What?" I could not believe what they were saying.

"She says that we have too many children to care for, and she can give Rosie a better life than we can."

I shook my head, trying to understand how anyone could think we would sell one of our children.

My arms were around Anna, attempting to calm her down. She continued her struggle.

"Listen to me, Johann! We must find Rosie and the children before she does. There is no time to waste!"

"Where are they?"

"Mary took them with her to the market."

"Let's go," I said, grabbing Anna's hand. The three of us ran toward the open-air market on Water Street.

The children were not at the market square. We poked through every stall, behind every basket. We shouted their names, not caring what the St. John's residents might think. Jacob asked everyone we saw but was answered with shoulder shrugs. We searched the quays, where the children were forbidden to walk alone. We peeked into all the taverns and every mercantile. We hurried to the Irish Church, but no children or Simple Mary were found.

"Wait, I have an idea," Anna said. "The meadow where we searched for cloudberries."

Jacob and I followed behind as Anna rushed for the meadow on the far side of town. At last, we spotted them. They were laughing and chasing each other in a spirited game of tag, unaware of our drama. Mary had tied Delia in a sling on her back and played the chasing game with the others. When she reached out to tag Bernard, he darted past her. Even Katja, always so serious and responsible, ran and leaped joyfully.

And there was Rosie, her yellow curls bouncing. Safe. Unharmed. Far from Mrs. Grimsby. Mary had unknowingly brought them far from her employer's clutches. Or Simple Mary was not so simple after all. We stayed and played with Mary and the children until the children's hunger drove us back to town.

While Mary, Jacob, and the children led the way down the cobbled streets, Anna and I followed to discuss our next step quietly. As soon as we could find another place, we would leave the Southwick Hotel.

I coached Jacob on what to say to the odious woman.

As we walked through the hotel's door, she was stationed behind the bulwark of her desk. I put my coat over Rosie's yellow curls and held her tightly. Anna and the other children huddled behind me. I pushed the reluctant Jacob in front of me.

"Mr. Klem wants me to announce that he and his family will vacate your premises tomorrow. He has already paid for half his stay; tomorrow morning, he will pay you the remainder. He will not charge you for the cooking and cleaning services his wife has cheerfully rendered." Jacob stopped and took a deep breath. He might have fled from Mrs. Grimsby's stony glare if I had not stood behind him.

She said nothing. Then she rose. Despite her stooped shoulders, she was a tall woman, and at that moment, she had the presence of an enemy soldier on a spirited, well-muscled horse.

"Be gone, the lot of you," she hissed.

"Tomorrow morning," I said, drawing up my chest and looking straight into her evil eyes. I knew that much English. I turned my back to her and urged Anna and the children to walk up the staircase to our room. I closed the door, bolted it, and pushed the bureau in front. We told the children we would leave the Southwick Hotel but did not tell them why. They were relieved to hear they would be far from the woman's harsh words and looks.

Later that night, Mary snuck us food—a loaf of bread, some cheese, and a string of dried apples.

After the children were asleep, I sat beside Anna on the bed.

"Have no fear *Liebchen*. I'm going to find Fr. Scallan.

Maybe he will know where we can stay when we leave here tomorrow." Although I tried to assure her, I was sure she read the worry in my eyes.

"Johann, I'm sure the good father will help us. But then, no more secrets or conferences with only the men. You must tell me everything."

"Yes, certainly, I'll tell you the options the men have suggested. First, however, we must get away from this hotel." I kissed her. Then I knelt on the floor beside the sleeping Rosie. I carefully picked her up and placed her beside Anna and the baby on the bed. Her golden hair spilled onto the pillow.

"Don't worry, Anna. We will leave here and keep the children safe. Bar the door after I leave and open it only if you hear my voice."

I carefully avoided the third step that always creaked when stepped on.

Chapter 31

Pea Coat Man

Anna

I could not relax. I wanted to leave the hotel as soon as possible. I'd seen the vertical furrows that had developed between Johann's brows. The lines had not been there before we left Kittersburg. I wanted him to say more, confide his worries, and include me in the plans. That's how it had been before the decision to go to America.

I tucked Rosie and Delia under the blanket and opened the window's shutter to watch Johann walk down Duckworth Street toward the Irish priest's house. Across the street, in the alcove of a doorway, a man stood looking toward our dormer. I saw him more clearly when he stuck a match to light his pipe. A large scar in the shape of a crescent moon marked his face. He wore a sailor's knitted cap and a dark pea coat. When he saw me watching, he pulled his hat farther down his face and turned to stroll casually down the street. The glow from his pipe showed me his path. My mind raced with Mrs. Grimsby's last shouted threat, "I've got more than one way to get what I want!"

I paced and prayed. I could not sleep until Johann returned, and the heavy bureau was slid before the door. I could not find peace even as I watched the sleeping children in the dim light from the window. I wore a path back and forth between the youngest girls in the bed and Bernard's and Katja's pallets on the floor. At last, I heard Johann's voice and his soft knock. When he slipped inside, we barred the door and barricaded it with the bureau.

Johann whispered, "Fr. Scallan will help us. He says we can stay with Mrs. Bernadette Kavanaugh and her son until we leave. She's a laundress. And a Catholic!"

I was relieved to hear Johann's news, a safe place. I was so exhausted from worry that I fell asleep quickly. I did not have time to tell him about the scarred man in the pea coat I'd seen lurking across from the Southwick, staring up at our window.

The following day, as I sat on the edge of the bed to fasten my shoes, I watched Johann rip out the seams of a silk vest he'd sewn for himself with the remnants from a *Herr* Holbauer waistcoat. At first, he eased out the coins. Soon, he shook the vest vigorously to dislodge every last *pfennig* concealed in the lining. I knew that money had been intended for farmland. He collected the coins in a leather pouch and removed the false bottom from the trunk. He gazed at the German silver candlesticks, my mother's gift to me. Their every curve and embossed scroll reminded me of *Mutter*. When Johann realized that I was observing, he shook his head.

"Don't worry, Anna, they are safe. We have plenty of money to get us through to America."

I wondered if this could be true. We had stayed weeks longer in Le Havre than we'd anticipated. And with the damaged ship and the mutiny, we'd spent weeks in St. John's. Who knew how much longer we would need to stay? We'd paid our fare to New York and were far from her harbor. Despite his assurances, I could read every nuance, every subtle shadow on Johann's face. Johann—the dreamer, the optimist, the confident man—was as worried as any man whose daughter had been threatened with kidnapping could be. To see him so troubled gnawed at my stomach and put more racing thoughts in my mind.

One by one, the children awoke. I set each with a small task: shaking blankets, folding clothing, washing Delia, and changing her linens. I repacked our belongings in the two trunks and noticed how our possessions had dwindled in the months since we'd left Kittersburg. When I found the soft, grey shawl that Magda had knit for me, I set it aside. After I'd assured myself that I had not left out any bits or bobs, I felt better—the room was much cleaner than when we arrived. Thankfully, we would soon be out of the wretched witch's lair.

Holding the wool shawl in one arm and the baby in the other, I descended the squeaking stairs and, like Johann, omitted the third step that groaned more than the others. The children followed. We walked directly to the kitchen where Mary had prepared wheat porridge and *bannock,* the fried bread the children loved. I draped the gray shawl around Mary's shoulders and embraced her. When I let go, Mary wore her broad smile. We both had tears in our eyes.

Mary reached over to a cupboard and picked up a small seal-skin pouch decorated with the porcupine quill work of her people. Before she placed it in my hand, she reached in and took out a folded paper packet. Inside, there were dried leaves. Mary pointed to her throat. She removed another small parcel and pointed to her head. She followed this with several more wrapped packages of dried roots, berries, lichen, and fronds. Opening each packet, she indicated the body part it would cure. In her silent way, she explained to me the herbal remedies of the Mi'kmaq. Mary and I were not aligned by culture, language, or religion, yet we had learned a schoolroom of lessons from each other. Simple Mary was my first experience with kindness and generosity in the new world. I put the leather sack in my pocket and hugged Mary once more.

Johann entered the kitchen, followed by a tall, slim youth with a scramble of red hair squirting beneath an Irish fisherman's cap.

"This is Liam Kavanaugh, son of Mrs. Bernadette Kavanaugh. He'll be helping us bring the trunks to his mother's house," Johann told me and the children.

With a redhead's pale lashes and a sprinkle of freckles, the young man pulled off his cap, releasing a scramble of carroty curls. He nodded and eyed the food on the table, the hot tea and hunks of fried dough. Mary immediately placed a cup and plate in front of him. From their expressions, I knew that Bernard and Katja were immediately smitten: Bernard, because seven-year-old boys often admire the "big boys" who are willing to throw a ball or burp for fun, and Katja, our shy girl, who was becoming conscious of any handsome young man near her age. The introductions were interrupted by lumbering footsteps outside the kitchen. The furrowed face of Mrs. Grimsby, followed by her aged, white-muzzled dog, appeared in the doorway. Betsey ambled over to nose Rosie's hand until I picked up Rosie and held her close. Mrs. Grimsby did not move.

"So you're thinking of leaving without paying, are you?" she snarled.

Johann walked to the pie safe near where the wrinkled woman stood. Without saying a word, he emptied his leather, drawstring bag. He counted out precisely the amount we owed. Then he pulled an extra shilling from his pocket and pointed to Betsey.

"Get a soup bone for the dog," he said. I could feel his satisfaction in adding that.

Without touching the money, the old crone pointed a bony finger at him and Liam.

"I'll have no more balderdash or blatherskite from the likes of you. Be gone and take that Irish trash with you. I'll have no ragamuffins like him lurking around my door."

Liam, who had never met Mrs. Grimsby before, choked on his tea, astounded by the woman's harsh words. Being the subject of Mrs. Grimsby's wrath made him more of a hero in Bernard's eyes. We didn't understand the meaning of her words, but we could read the rage of her puckered red face. She hastily pocketed the coins Johann left, then eyed each one of us, including Simple Mary, with a sour scowl. When her eyes arrived on Rosie, who was cautiously peering from under my shawl, her eyes stopped. Her pursed lips began to say something but then closed. She turned and stormed away from the kitchen. Betsey followed his foul-tempered mistress, her motionless tail tucked between her legs. I relaxed my clenched jaw and breathed deeply. I urged the children to finish the last of their crumbs.

"*Schnell, schnell,* hurry, hurry," I entreated them. They rushed after Johann and Liam, who had gone upstairs to retrieve the trunks.

When we were all assembled on the street, ready to walk to Mrs. Kavanaugh's home, I looked back and glimpsed Mary exiting from the courtyard door and heading toward the meadow where sheep grazed up to the tree line. She wore no apron. The gray shawl

I'd given her was tied around her waist. The blanket she had slept on by the fire was rolled like a sausage circling her shoulders. A pair of snowshoes dangled from a small pack on her back. The strange, beaded, conical hat the Mi'kmaq women wore was on her head. I hoped she was returning to her people far from the old crone.

While we trudged up Duckworth Street and Liam and Johann alternated pushing the trunk-laden handcart, I saw the man in the pea coat lingering in a doorway. I whispered something to Johann, although I hoped his presence was only a coincidence.

We walked a mile up a gentle dirt road along the shoreline until we arrived at the cottage Liam said was his home. Beyond the small home were struggling fields and a dense thicket of trees. The view from the front of the house looked onto the beautiful harbor with its sloping cliffs. The water sparkled as the boats bobbed at their anchors. Shorebirds rode the air currents in a sky punctuated by chunky, white clouds.

Mrs. Kavanaugh stood in the doorway of the freshly white-washed home. I knew immediately that she was everything that Mrs. Grimsby was not. Her uncovered hair was a faded version of her son's orange curls, twisted into a knot at the nape of her neck. Her cheeks were as red as autumn apples, and her eyes flashed the brilliant blue of an October sky.

When Mrs. Kavanaugh saw the children, she clapped her hands.

"Holy Virgin Mother," she exclaimed, "the wee precious ones!" She bustled over and placed a wet kiss on each of their cheeks. She kissed the top of Delia's head as the baby slept in a sling across my chest.

"May the saints preserve their blessed little souls," she exclaimed and made an abbreviated sign of the cross touching her forehead, chin, and each ear.

Liam rolled his eyes and shook his head as she fussed over the children. After her extravagant welcome, Mrs. Kavanaugh gave us a tour of the small quarters we would share until we could resume our journey. Delia and I would sleep in the bed with Mrs. Kavanaugh. The girls would sleep on the rag rug by the fire. Johann, Liam, and Bernard would stay in a half-loft reached by a steep ladder leaning against the back wall. The house's rear door led to a yard where three large wash tubs rested on iron trivets. Clotheslines stretched between several trees. Long poles with Y's notched into one end kept wet clothing off the ground. Robust breezes dried an avalanche of sheets and gentlemen's breeches on the lines. On one side of the yard was a covered stone well. On the other side was a small shed with room enough for Liam's handcart and the cow that grazed in the grassy field that sloped up from the house. A small creek splashed down the hill over rocks and water-smoothed stones.

Mrs. Kavanaugh shepherded the children back into the house for buns and milk, but I caught Johann's arm before he could follow.

"Johann, this is wonderful. Mrs. Kavanaugh is like a saint after that old buzzard in town. You said she was a laundress; it's too much work for one woman. We can repay her kindness by helping her. She can take in three times the wash with Katja and me lending a hand. And we all know how to milk the cow and do other chores."

Johann smiled at me. "No one will ever say that you are not a generous woman and a hard worker. I've already told Liam I would help him pick up dirty laundry and deliver the clean back to town." He turned to reenter the tiny house, but I wasn't finished.

"Stop, Johann. Now's the time to tell me where we go next. I am not blind—I can see that St. John's is not the place to plant the acres of wheat you want to grow. Tell me what you and Jacob and the men have cooked up."

He began by apologizing to me.

"I'm sorry I did not include you, but my head spun from all I heard. I promised we wouldn't travel by boat again, but Newfoundland is an island. The only way off is by sea. I didn't want to tell you, or myself, that sailing is the only option."

He and his friends, the sea captain, Pierre, and Jacob, had discussed all the options.

"We think the best way to get to western New York is to take a boat up the St. Lawrence River and cross into New York from Montréal." I listened as he continued.

"A ship from Québec is expected soon. But no one knows when it will arrive because of the wind and the currents."

My stomach clenched at the thought of getting onto another wooden vessel. The storms had cost the lives of Berta and her newborn, the Portuguese sailor, the sweet French woman, and Sam. If I closed my eyes, I could be back on that ship again with its shrieking wind. I could feel the thunderous jolt when the schooner crashed into the trough of the waves. Even worse was having my children hungry and thirsty when I could do nothing about it. If getting on another boat was the only thing we could do, I was willing, yet I would be better prepared this time. I sighed in resignation.

"Anna, there is the other alternative of waiting for a boat traveling east back across the Atlantic to Europe. We could make our way back to Baden somehow."

On hearing this, my resignation turned to anger.

"Johann, don't you dare say that. We have talked about

this before. This was your dream—even before we married. 'Go to *Amerika*. Have a new life. Have more opportunities.' You don't get to take that back now, not after you have torn us from everything we knew. It wasn't a perfect life, but it was *our* life. We have come this far. I will not and cannot go back."

"Anna..." Johann said my name quietly.

"Johann Baptiste Klem, do *not* interrupt me. I haven't finished. It's my turn, and I have as much to say as your tavern friends."

I took a deep breath.

"Remember your tailor's advice? You always told me this: 'Anna, if you see a loose thread, never cut it. Your seam will unravel. Always pull the thread a bit and knot it off. Then weave the thread back into the fabric.' Does that sound familiar?"

Johann looked at me, his face flushed as I tossed his words at him.

"Well, husband, I have knotted off that part of my life. I am trying to weave those loose threads into making a strong fabric for us, especially the children. It will never be seamless, but I'm trying to repair the rip as much as possible. So you don't get to do it over. You already cut the thread and weakened the seam. You don't get to say, 'I was wrong. Let's go back.'" My voice rose; my arms were crossed.

"We will go to America even if it's on a *Gottverdammt* boat!"

Johann was speechless. I rarely swore, and I'd used his words in my argument.

He reached his hands toward me. I had struck a chord within him. I knew I was right. I had made my point, and he had listened. It was hard for me to stay angry with him, especially when he looked at me with those pale blue eyes that reminded me of forget-me-nots. I loved him too much to remain vexed.

I was about to walk into his arms when there was a thunderous bellow. Mrs. Kavanaugh's cow, grazing hock-deep in the meadow grass, trotted past us. We pivoted to see the source of her deep wail and saw a huge buck standing near the brook. His magnificent head was raised. His regal crown of antlers resembled a forest of bones. He was alert, his ears set wide and twitching, his nose lifted, sniffing. Then, spooked, he took off, galloping directly toward the dense pine tree line. We turned once more to see what had freighted the stag and saw—not twenty feet from us, partially hidden by one of Mrs. Kavanaugh's drying sheets—the scar-faced man. He wore the same patched-up pea coat and dark knit cap I had glimpsed the night before. I screamed when I saw him draw a knife from his waistband and raise it shoulder-high.

"The girl," he growled, "give me the girl." As I struggled to understand what he was saying, he shouted again. "Give 'er to me. I want the girl!"

Chapter 32

Harpoon

Johann

Thump! I heard something sail past my head. I immediately pulled Anna down, our faces buried deep in the prickly grass. My heart thundered as I spied the pea-coated man sprawled in the grass. Behind his head, embedded deep in a maple's bark, was a javelin-like object quivering in the dense trunk. A rope attached to the midsection of the long-shafted javelin dangled toward the ground. From our weeks in St. John's, I knew what it was—a whaler's harpoon.

The man scrambled to his knees and climbed unsteadily to his feet. He looked at the harpoon stuck only a foot above the spot where he had been standing. Without bothering to brush himself off, he took off down the dirt highway that led back to town. Liam, who had emerged from the house's back door, cursing and shouting, chased after the man. He clutched a rock in his hand. Mrs. Kavanaugh followed behind, waving a broom. I saw the glint of the abandoned knife where the scarred man had fallen. I grasped it and stuck it into the tree next to the harpoon. When I helped Anna to her feet, she was shaking and distraught.

"Johann, what just happened?" She clutched my shirt; her eyes were panicked.

"I think," I began, as I was trying to figure it out myself, "... that when that man yelled about taking Rosie, Liam heard him. Liam must have hurled that harpoon at him and scared the devil out of him. That scoundrel took off like Satan's dogs gnashed at his heels."

I hugged her close. The children burst from the cottage's back door and ran to us. Bernard held the baby while Katja clutched a sobbing Rosie close to her chest. We all stood and held onto each other in a tight embrace. I thanked God for saving our family once again.

In a few minutes, Liam and his indomitable mother returned to their small home. Mrs. Kavanaugh breathed heavily, but the lad's face held a triumphant look.

"Liam," I said, "please explain what happened."

"I was showing Bernard the harpoon—it was me Da's before he drowned—and I saw the stag out by the stream. I realized that something was spooking him, and when he bellowed, and the cow ran, we saw the cause of it all. MacDonald was standing there by the tree. He's nothing but a common cutpurse, a wretch who crawls through every crack on the pier. He'll do anyone's bidding for a price, so I knew he was up to no good. Then I heard him calling for your little girl. Me Mam told me you were staying with us because that old sourpuss wanted your girl." He stopped for a moment and nodded his head toward Rosie. "So I heaved the harpoon. Too bad I didn't get him right between his eyeballs."

While Liam spoke, Mrs. Kavanaugh repeatedly crossed herself in her abbreviated version of the forehead, chin, and ears.

"Holy Mary, Mother of God," she intoned repeatedly. She walked to Liam and threw her arms around him. Her faded curls landed on his chest as he was a good head taller.

"That harpoon couldn't save your Da, but it saved this precious little girl today. Praise be to Jesus, his angels, and saints."

We all, except Katja, who stood shyly in the corner, hugged and cheered our young hero.

Chapter 33

Michael

Johann

In the following week, we stayed close to the cottage. Anna and Katja helped Mrs. Kavanaugh with the washing as Liam, Bernard, and I walked back and forth to the town, toting soiled and clean clothing and linens. Bernard followed wherever Liam went.

One day, we ran into Michael, the Irish sailor who had led the sea shanties on the *Stalwart* and entertained us with his quick fiddle tunes. He could have been Liam's older brother with his red hair and friendly manner. The two took to speaking another language. I couldn't understand one word. My English had improved, though I wasn't near as comfortable as Bernard. I couldn't bear the thought of learning another tongue. Liam told me they were speaking Gaelic, and unless I was to immigrate to Ireland rather than America, I was safe.

Liam and Micheal got on like they had been tavern buddies

for ages, lifting pints and trading tall tales. When we parted, Liam turned to me, "A fine mate he is. And he's coming to supper tomorrow. Mam will love to make a regular Jigg's dinner and a figgy duff for that one."

The next night, Michael appeared, fiddle in hand and a brown bottle of Irish whiskey tucked under his arm. Anna and the children were thrilled to see him. We reminisced about the good nights on the boat, but no one wanted to speak of the storm or the days of hunger and thirst.

Mrs. Kavanaugh and Anna had prepared the meal. The smell of the beef boiled with carrots, cabbage, and turnips prepared in a big iron pot made me forget about the days of wormy ship biscuit dipped in a bit of watery soup. The children couldn't get enough of the figgy pudding Mrs. Kavanaugh taught Anna to make. The combination of flour, butter, sugar, molasses, ginger, cinnamon, and raisins steamed in a cloth bag was as delicious as Anna's apple strudel. After we finished our meal, Michael passed the of bottle of dark whiskey to Liam and me while Anna and Mrs. Kavanaugh drank only thimbles-full in tiny glasses. They raised their glasses to toast.

"May your big jib draw," said Michael.

Liam responded, "Fair weather to you and snow to your heels." Both men's toasts reflected their origins.

Michael removed his fiddle from its home in a canvas bag. He carefully unwrapped it from its cocoon of scarlet Indian silk and tuned it before he burst into a medley of jigs and reels. We danced as well as we could in the small confines of the single room. When Michael finished his bold, upbeat tunes, he began to play the slow, sad airs that made me think of my mother sitting by the hearth, rosary beads entwined in her hands. Delia dozed off in Mrs. Kavanaugh's arms while Rosie fell asleep on the rug before the fire. I picked her up and snuggled her on my shoulder, thanking God again that she was safe with us. As

Michael packed up his fiddle, caressing it as tenderly as I held Rosie, Bernard insisted on telling him of Liam's heroics and the evil MacDonald. Michael had heard tales of MacDonald at the pubs and agreed that the man had less merit than the barnacles on a ship's hull.

"Just need to scrape off the likes of him," Michael said.

Anna, who'd heard enough of Mrs. Grimsby and her scar-faced henchman, interrupted.

"Michael, what can you tell us of the *Stalwart* and our ship friends?"

"Well, the first thing I can report is that Cap'n Henshaw is long out of jail, and no charges are against him. I suspect he was bailed out by the ship's owners looking to make some profit on the cargo. And that slime, Quimby, left on the first ship that would take him. Back to London to crawl in the gutters, I guess. The Norwegian family, I heard, is going to stick with fishing. Last I saw them, they were headed to Nova Scotia on a fishing schooner. Your friend, who liked to talk about bread, said he paid his fare and intends to go to Philadelphia to make cakes with his brother. He and his girls are waiting for the ship to be refitted. Me? I'm going to New Orleans. I hear that they like their musicians there. I'm done with the merchant ships. No more tarring lines and climbing ratlins for me. All the grog in the world couldn't tempt me back."

"And what of Mr. Carothers?" Anna asked.

"Well, the Cap'n was right. That man could have been hanged. When he saw that these St. John's men didn't give a damn about what happened on an American merchant ship—they just finished a war with the Americans, you know—he was gone. Some said he stowed away on a ship to Liverpool. But I couldn't see the likes of him doing anything wrong. He likely found a ship headed to Boston. Some said he had a sweetheart there."

"Well, if it weren't for him, we might have all starved or had our labors sold off. If Captain Henshaw had been honest, we might be in New York today ready to buy land," I said.

Michael shrugged his shoulders.

"For me, it worked out. Landing in St. John's was the kick in the britches I needed, but it's different for you and the family. Just one more fence to climb."

"Except for us, it is one more boat to ride."

Michael stayed that night with us in the half loft. Early the following morning, Mrs. Kavanaugh cooked him an Irish breakfast. His plate overflowed with eggs, a slice of black pudding, and a generous chunk of soda bread.

"You remind me of my darlin' husband, Liam's dad, you do. Stay off the whalers and the fishing boats long enough to see your sons grow fat and sassy."

Michael hugged her as if she were his mother.

"May the Lord and the Virgin watch over you, lad. May the good Saint Patrick lead you every step of your way. And Saint Brendan, keep you safe on the sea," she said to him as he sopped up his breakfast with the last of his bread. Mrs. Kavanaugh rarely spoke a sentence without including God and one of the saints. This time she repeated prayers in both English and Gaelic. Liam shook his head again while his mother gushed over her guests.

Micheal, Liam, and I walked back down the hill to St. John's town. Michael took turns pushing the handcart with his violin nestled snuggly in the clean laundry. We parted ways at the corner of George Street and Duckworth. Michael strolled back to the "rooms" the name given to the sailors' boarding house he called home. He reminded us to visit him in New Orleans.

Liam and I finished our deliveries. When we passed the tavern I frequented with Jacob and Pierre, both gentlemen emerged and called my name.

"*Mon frère, écoute!* A ship arrived from Québec this morning on the early tide. I've spoken to the captain. Once the cargo is unloaded, they will return with new goods for a sail up the St. Lawrence back to Québec. I'll book my passage today, and I'm sure there'll be room for you and the family," Pierre said excitedly.

We'd spoken of this voyage before. He had assured me that after sailing to his home port, it was a short distance to Montréal and then a land trip down the eastern shore of the lake called Ontario. We would be at the land advertised by the Holland Company. I was as excited as he, and I felt my heart race. I would have good news to share with Anna, even if it did involve another boat.

"Please, Pierre, bring me to the captain now."

Jacob pounded me on the back with the flat of his hand.

"I'll go with you and help negotiate this. Let's not miss the opportunity. As fall grows closer, there will be fewer and fewer boats up and down the river. The ice forms early, and no one wants to be caught."

I sent Liam on his way back to his mother's, and in twenty minutes, the three of us were at the bustle and scurry of the harbor. We watched the crew of the *Earl of Wexford* and the local stevedores use ropes and pulleys to hoist the rough-cut timber from the hold of the three-masted barque. As the first mate bawled out orders, a teamster and his wagon waited to be loaded. A tall man stood nearby stroking and smoothing a tar-black beard that reached almost to his chest. He wore a faded indigo-colored frock coat and a stained white waistcoat. On the shoulders were partial epaulets, inexpertly cut off. His former naval officer's coat had been altered to fit his new command as a merchant sea captain. A bicorn hat was folded under his left armpit.

"This," said Pierre," is Captain Albion Burbank. He's the one you need to speak with."

When I was in Le Havre, my friend Peter Maier had nego-tiated our passage with the now disgraced Captain Henshaw. I had no idea what the fares would be from this remote eastern Newfoundland outpost to the inland city of Québec. Indeed, it would be different for our family of six than for a single passenger like Pierre. I had an inspiration. I would deal with him as I did the pompous Holbauer, flatter him, and barter with the help of Jacob's translation services.

"I can tell from how you manage your crew that you are a good businessman and, I am sure, a superb mariner. May I suggest that your wardrobe fit your position of honor and authority?" I said through Jacob's lips.

Captain Burbank looked at me, ignoring Jacob's translation, and listened as he stroked his fulsome beard.

"Yes, you are a man with a figure that would compliment a bespoke garment. I am a master tailor with exquisite taste. I, Sir, am the man who could tailor such a fine coat. I have recently traveled through Paris and know all the latest fashion." I was glad that I had thought to brush my jacket that morning and, thanks to Anna and Mrs. Kavanaugh, had on a sparkling white shirt.

"I can see you in a fine gray Scottish herringbone with, perhaps, a deep green lining. Both would flatter your coloring and bearing." I purchased both of those fabrics while we were in Paris.

The captain answered me in French, which was as elementary as First Mate Carothers's. "And sir, if I am to get this fashionable coat, what do you get in return?"

"Only this," I took a deep breath, "passage for my wife and I and our children to Québec—or at least the partial cost. My children take up little room and are exceptionally well-behaved. They eat very little."

"I'm not particularly fond of children, so you must do better."

"Because I know that if you wore such a coat, it would advertise my skills; I will include a handsome green brocade waistcoat." I took a deep breath. Although I had purchased beautiful fabrics in Strasbourg and Paris, my selection was limited.

Captain Burbank let out a loud laugh. "You, sir, drive a hard bargain, but you are correct. I require attire to fit my station. But those children, keep them away from me."

Chapter 34

Letter to Grandmother

Katja

Liebe Oma Katharina,

I haven't heard a word from you, but how could I, as you don't even know where we are. It is not New York but St. John's in Newfoundland. Mama says not to worry about why we are here and not in New York. Wherever we are, I will continue to write to you.

We have been in Newfoundland for ever so long. First, we stayed with a nasty old woman. Mama says not to mention anything about Rosie, so I won't, but she is fine. Now we are staying with an Irish woman and her son. His name is

Liam, and his eyes are the color of warm honey. He is strong and kind. He hardly notices me. Bernard, as usual, takes up all his time. Mama tells me not to be in a hurry. She acts like I'm a little girl, but I do everything she does.

Papa says we will soon leave and go on a trip up a river. No one wants to be on a boat again. I knew Papa planned on getting on a boat before Mama did because I listened. Papa and his friends think eleven-year-old girls are invisible, but I am not invisible. I am afraid. The farther west we go, the more certain I am that I will never see you again. Maybe you will never see any of my letters. Mama wants you to know that we are safe.

Do you think I will find someone like Papa to marry me in America? If not, I will come back and live with you, except I do not want to cross the ocean ever again.

Love,
Katja

Chapter 35

Saint Lawrence River

Anna

I was more than surprised when Johann burst through the door at Mrs. Kavanaugh's cottage, filled with news about a ship that had docked. We could board for the price of a new frock coat for the captain and a small charge for the children. Johann rifled through one of the trunks to uncover a parcel of fine woven Scottish wool he'd purchased in Paris. Almost before I could ask questions, he'd flung his leather sewing satchel over his shoulder and rushed back to find the captain.

I didn't want to step on the *Earl of Wexford* or any other ship, but I knew it was the only way. Johann was so happy and excited about the thought of moving on. I'd watched the worry pleat his face because of Rosie; I'd heard his muttered self-reproaches; I'd listened to him jangle the thimbles in his pocket.

I needed to see the light-hearted, optimistic man I'd married. I crossed my fingers and prayed that this voyage up the Saint Lawrence would take us quickly to the promised land in New York. I was so tired of the journey. The quicker we left, the sooner it would end.

We were at the harbor a week later and had readied ourselves to board the *Earl of Wexford*. I didn't regret leaving the foggy town with its constant threat to our curly-haired daughter, but I wasn't happy to leave the shelter of the Kavanaughs. No one was eager to step up the gangplank—especially the children. Tears dripped down Katja's cheeks, and Rosie made a fuss, kicking and squirming before she let Johann scoop her up. The friends we had made in the past weeks came to see us off.

Jacob Richter arrived in his usual out-of-breath run. He pulled John aside to give him final instructions. Father Scallan, who I discovered was also Newfoundland's bishop, came with letters he stuffed in John's pockets to be delivered to the Jesuits and the Ursuline sisters in Québec.

Spunky Mrs. Kavanaugh stood dockside with Liam, a wrapped loaf of her Irish soda bread cocooned in her apron. She shoved the bread into the crook of my arm and enclosed Delia and me in a robust embrace. Johann and each of the children received one of her enormous hugs before we hurried up the gangplank.

As we stood by the bulwarks peering down on her ruddy face, she pulled out a handkerchief to blot her tears and wave goodbye.

"May your troubles be less and your blessings be more.

May the day's burdens rest lightly on your shoulders," she said in her buoyant voice.

We waved back to her as she asked a litany of saints to protect us. Liam rolled his eyes.

This three-masted barque had square rigging and was far older than Captain Henshaw's American schooner. It sat high in the water. Johann pointed out the painted-on gunwales as we watched our trunks being loaded. He explained that it would look like the ship carried guns from afar. Now that the war was over, the merchant ships didn't need to carry guns or sailors to man them—they could instead take on more cargo. The owners preferred to transport hogsheads of wine and fancy French furniture. Passengers were an afterthought.

The first mate insisted we stay out of the crew's way. "Cast off the lines," he shouted.

The top gallant was raised. The ship was underway headed toward the Narrows. We glided past the little fishing huts balanced on shore. The impressive Signal Hill was on the port side, and the imposing, uncleared hills were to starboard. As usual, we were ordered to go below deck. It was the first time I saw how dark and cramped it was. It smelled of tar and mildew and the rank odor of unwashed men. There was less headroom than on the *Stalwart*.

I quickly realized that we were the only German-speaking people aboard. And the only family. Most of the passengers were men. As on the *Stalwart*, many were haunted and rough-looking. They kept to themselves and clung tightly to the few possessions they brought. We were lucky to claim a small cabin where we would share narrow berths. With the parcels we had carried on board, we struggled to find room for our family.

Two French-speaking sisters from Nova Scotia, Françoise and Clotilde, whose accents I struggled to understand, introduced themselves. They confided in me that they were searching for rich husbands and didn't want to be fishermen's wives. They said they were both well advanced in child-bearing years and needed to find husbands quickly. The older one, Françoise, had a sizable crooked nose that veered to the left; her younger sister, Clotilde, had an equally large nose that skewed to the right. Each sister had a black mole next to her distinguished nose. It was almost as if God had flipped the mold while creating them. As they chose their berths, John whispered, "They might have better luck with blind men." I elbowed him to hush; I suppressed my laugh.

Unlike the crew of the *Stalwart*, who had many nationalities, these sailors were French Canadian, while the officers were British. Jacob had given us a brief history of Canada, so we knew the country was under French control for hundreds of years until a battle in Québec. The British surprised the French army on the plains of a farmer named Abraham Martin. Finally, King George's army defeated the French, though it took them seven years. Having lived in Kittersburg when the French occupied it and then having known the British Mrs. Grimsby, I did not know where my sympathies lay. The vast land of Canada, with primarily French and native inhabitants, was in British hands. According to Jacob, even sixty years later, the French resented the English presence. It was replayed on the *Earl of Wexford*.

Through the fog, we often glimpsed the rugged granite cliffs topped by looming green balsam, as dense and thick as the coat of wintered-over sheep. Squawking gulls hovered over deep, narrow inlets interrupting the shoreline.

Pierre had taken us under his wing when we boarded. We would soon be in the Gulf of Saint Lawrence's open waters before seeing the river's mouth he explained. I had pictured a broad and winding voyage along a river like the Rhine, with castles perched atop forested hills. Instead, we were in remote waters battling strong currents. Just as on the *Stalwart,* many of the passengers became seasick. Once more, we were assaulted by the odor of vomit and urine that could not be held. And, on the *Earl of Wexford,* it was harder to escape to the open deck because of the frigid breezes and the unfriendly officers. Unlike Captain Henshaw, Captain Burbank was always present barking orders or complaining to the first mate. Johann had warned me to keep the chidren away from the captain.

After an initial bout of nausea, Johann recovered and was intent on measuring, cutting, and sewing the promised coat for Captain Burbank. Day and evening, he leaned into the glow of the hurricane lamp for his careful stitching. The rest of us gathered around him. We had become a little family with Pierre, Clotilde, and Françoise. The two French sisters enjoyed playing games with the children. I saw that if they found their wealthy husbands, they would be good mothers.

As we huddled together, Pierre regaled us with stories of Cabot, Jacques Cartier, and Champlain—his French heroes. Katja wanted to hear over and over the tale of *Les Filles du Roi* or the King's Daughters. In the late 1600s, Pierre claimed, eight hundred young French women, at the behest of King Louis XIV, arrived in New France to find husbands and help populate the vastland. Pierre claimed that his great, great, great grandmother was among them.

Pierre's tales also engaged Clotilde and Françoise until they learned he was already married to a Huron woman. Clotilde gave up on Pierre but declared that the second mate, though not wealthy, was handsome.

This voyage was darker, colder, and rainier than our trip across the endless ocean. Nevertheless, there was a captain we could trust. He needed us alive if he was to wear Johann's Paris-inspired clothes.

Chapter 36

Below Decks

Johann

Anna was right. This voyage was as challenging as our first. She did her best not to complain, but the children certainly did. They were cranky and bored. Bernard missed his English lessons, and even my gentle-tempered Katja grumbled that she was tired of carrying Delia; she hated the darkness and did not want the dried cod that was dinner. One night, she stomped around the cabin.

"I never want to smell or eat fish ever again!" she declared.

All children squabble sometimes. Since they were being forced to stay below deck, the lack of playmates made this leg of the trip even more challenging. I was too absorbed in sewing the captain's coat—Anna called it the Fare Frock—to keep them occupied. Clotilde and Françoise helped by teaching them songs and a game with a small ball and jacks, yet something more was needed.

We were almost a week into this second voyage when we heard the rain abate. The sun was playing peek-a-boo around the half-opened hatch when the first mate shouted.

"Come up. The Captain's inviting you to see a sight to behold." He slid open the hatch, and the caramel light welcomed us to a delicious day.

The timing could not have been better. I had sewn the last cuff button on the captain's square-tailed frock coat. I folded it and placed it carefully on my berth so I could join the others above.

The sun was bright butterscotch, and we needed to shade our eyes after all the darkness below. A dazzling blue sky and high, stretchy clouds dazzled us. The first mate pointed to the captain's incredible "sight."

Directly before us lay a massive rock. Percé Rock, as the captain named it, was a natural rock formation that appeared to pop up from the sea in the shallows of the Gaspé Peninsula. We were in awe of its immensity. It must have been a half-mile long and looked as high as the spire of the cathedral we loved in Strasburg. Two vast curved openings, tall enough for a ship to pass through, were scoured out of the rock. They reminded me of the arched doorways of the churches we had seen in Europe. Yet, these pillars were chiseled by God's wind and water, not man. The formation's top was flat as a table and wore a crown of green fir. Thousands of seabirds took off and descended on the cliffs. If the *Professeur* had been with us now, he would have given us information about its dimensions and the type of stone. Even the sailors who had often sailed the gulf were impressed by this enormous stone mesa emerging from the water.

Bernard forgot about using his English and shouted, "*Wunderbar, Wunderbar!*"

Clotilde and Françoise began a twirling dance with the girls.

The shipboard mood was joyful, with perfect weather and this natural wonder before us. Even the solitary male passengers seemed energized. It struck me as the ideal time to present the coat I had just completed to Captain Burbank.

I hurried below, brushed any lint or stray threads from the coat, and rushed back to the main deck.

"Captain, sir," I said slowly in French, knowing he was not facile in that language. "I have done my best to sew a coat for you, which I think will look better on you than in my humble hands."

The captain's eyes widened. He quickly cast off his frayed British Navy uniform jacket and tossed it to a nearby crewman. I stood behind him and helped him slide on the worsted wool coat. I made sure that the shoulders sat straight and tugged the cuffs so they hit the right spot on his wrist. Burbank beamed. The other passengers and crew applauded. He bowed all around. I had to admit that his tall, broad-shouldered physique showed off the coat better than the rotund body of my former client, *Herr* Holbauer. The captain sashayed up and down the deck from stern to bow as jaunty as any boulevardier on the *Champs Elysée*. He approached Clotilde and had her pirouette under his raised arm. He called for a mate to descend to his cabin and return with his looking glass. When it was in his hand, he stroked his full black beard and held the mirror in every way to capture as much of himself as possible.

"Fine job, Klem. I'm delighted. When will you get started on the waistcoat?"

"Captain, it will be done before we reach Québec. The green brocade will look wonderful with this deep gray."

"Klem, I've changed my mind. I think I deserve a gold vest. Yes, gold will set off my beard and suit these gilded buttons," he said as he pointed to the rows of buttons in the front. One hand held the mirror while he stroked and smoothed his beard with the other.

I was startled. I did have gold fabric, a shimmering, watered-silk now stowed in one of our trunks in the hold. I had bought it in Paris with the thought of making Anna the fashion-able high-waisted dress she requested after seeing the stylish *Mademoiselles* strolling near the *Tuileries*. I intended to create a lovely surprise gown for her as she had given up so much for me. Yet, I owed Burbank for our fare. I knew my Anna. She would understand.

When we were back in our tiny cabin, I explained to Anna that I needed to go to the hold below to retrieve fabric from one of the trunks. A member of the crew would accompany me. Rosie overheard me.

"Papa, I want to go with you."

"No, sweet one, you stay here with your mama and play with the baby," I said.

"I want to go; I want to go with you," she howled.

Our Rosie was different from our other children. All chil-dren her age have their own minds, but Rosie was so lively, so animated, so full of pep and vigor that it was no wonder Mrs. Grimsby wanted her in her dull, creepy life. Anna and I wanted to be firm parents, yet raising an exuberant three-year-old challenged us in these circumstances. I gave in. Anna shook her head. Gérard, the burly mate with a shaved head and a walrus-like mustache whom Clotilde fancied, would escort us down.

Gérard held the oil lamp to illuminate our descent on the

steep ladder. I held Rosie tight to my chest, and her little arms made a halo around my neck. Without the light, we would have been in total darkness. The first thing I heard was the scuttle of tiny feet. Then, the illumination caught the gleam of beady eyes. There was a frantic scrabble of rats.

"*Nom de Dieu!*" Gérard shouted. "There's more of these buggers than usual. *Merde!*" At first, I was alarmed at his curse words in front of my daughter. Rosie struggled in my arms. She wanted to get on the deck to pet them!

"Rosie, no! Those rats are dangerous. Gérard is going to take you right back to Mama," I said.

Hearing the tone of my voice, she stopped flailing. We walked to the ladder, and I transferred Rosie into Gérard's well-muscled arms. He carried her and the lamp back to the deck above. When he reached the top, he returned the light to me.

"Here you go, Klem. Watch them buggers. I think your trunks are aft on the starboard side. Be quick. The captain doesn't like passengers this far below."

"I'm only here because the captain changed his mind about the vest. Not by choice, I assure you."

When he was gone, I felt the foreboding of being alone in the dark with the sounds of the scrambling feet and the faint chirping noise of the rats. I held the lamp before me and saw a long tail disappear near a hogshead of wine. I walked warily forward. The air was dank and smelled of something that had gone bad—rancid and putrid.

At last, I spotted our trunks where Gérard had suggested, aft and starboard. I placed the lamp on one of the wooden chests. I used the key tied on a leather thong around my neck to unlock the truck that held my fabric. The silk I needed was on the bottom, wrapped in a length of muslin since I had wanted to surprise Anna with its beauty. I regretted that it was packed so low under other fabric and some household goods. Suddenly, I felt something brush against my pant leg. I cried in surprise and grabbed the lamp to see what it was. Curling around my ankle was a scrawny, marmalade-colored cat with a patchy, mangy coat. I kicked it away from me. I did not dislike cats—my mother had an agreeable, green-eyed, dove-gray cat that spent most of his life in her lap or asleep by the fire. But this cat was different. I was fearful of him as he hurried behind a large cask. I wondered how this cat could be so skinny with so many furry meals scurrying nearby. How could he spend his life in this dark, forbidding place? I knew that the ship's cats were meant to catch the ever-present rats, a constant on most vessels, but this one had hardly done his job.

The ginger cat returned as I scrounged in the trunk to find the muslin bundle. He squirmed around me and between my legs, rubbing his chin on my calf, claiming me part of his territory. I supposed he was lonely for a kind hand or a saucer of milk. At that moment, in my fear, I had neither. I booted him away once more.

At last, I found the muslin-wrapped bundle of silk and set it on the second trunk next to the lamp. While I attempted to transfer the goods back to the chest, I heard the cat again. He was perched on a nearby barrel and was growling and hissing. I lifted the lamp in the cat's direction and saw his almond-shaped, amber eyes glaring at me like the demon in a fairy tale. His ears were pinned back to his head.

"*Geh weg,* go away!" I shouted, but the cat stood his ground and swatted at me.

I placed the light down and threw the rest of the contents into the trunk as quickly as possible. The cat lunged at me before I could duck. Off-balance, I fell to the ground. I grabbed at the cat to remove him from my chest, but he dug his claws into my jacket. We were both shrieking. We wrestled on the floor for seconds, which felt like eons. As I tried to pull him away, he bit my hand. Finally, I struggled to my feet and landed a blow to his hindquarters. He let go of my hand and ran off howling. My heart raced as I stowed the silk bundle under my arm, lifted the lamp, and rushed to the ladder. When I arrived, I realized I had dropped the trunk key. My hand was on one rung of the ladder. I debated going back. I did not want to see the furious cat or the rats again. I took a deep breath. Swinging the lantern in front of me, I stamped my feet. I shouted. I heard the rats scamper in every direction. The key lay on the floor near my battle with the ginger cat. I locked the trunk, jammed the key in my pocket, and ran back to the ladder. The cat did not reappear.

When I finally ascended to the cabin deck, my heart pounding in my ears, I saw my hand was bloody from the cat's bite. I felt foolish and ashamed of my fear. I, who had easily handled two eight-hundred-pound oxen, had been terrified of a skinny cat. I went directly to the head in the bow. When the door was closed, I tried to calm myself, though the image of the cat and the rats repulsed me. I would not tell Anna of my experience because she would be even more concerned for the children. As I returned to the companionway, I spotted an abandoned bucket of salt water, washed my bloody hand, and wrapped it in a nearby rag until it stopped bleeding.

Gérard, who had just finished cleating a line, hailed me.

"Did you find what you were looking for?"

"Yes, thank you." I pointed at the bundle I had nestled back in the crook of my arm. "And thank you for taking Rosie away. I didn't realize quite how gruesome it was down there."

"I think every rat in St. John's hopped aboard for this voyage," he said. "We'll have to pick up more cats at our next port."

Chapter 37

Fever

Anna

A short while after Johann had carried Rosie off, Gérard deposited her back on my lap. We had all started noticing him after Clotilde had decided that he was handsome in a sailor-like way. I didn't see it, but I was not a woman looking for a new husband. I had listened to the flirty banter between them when we were allowed on deck. Clotilde was smitten, and Françoise, as sisters do, teased her about the sturdy sailor.

"Where is Johann?" I asked Gérard.

"He'll be back soon. No one wants to stay down there too long."

Rosie was now content; her tantrum was over. She was her usual perky self and played a clapping game with Françoise.

"Papa said I could not pet the rats," I overheard her tell Françoise.

When Johann returned, he no longer looked happy. He immediately changed his clothing. That was unusual as we had only two sets of clothes. Onboard washing and drying were unforgiving tasks with the constant rain. Later, when I began to fold the clothing he'd dropped, I saw a smear of blood on his shirt cuff. Johann was always careful with his clothes, so I knew something had happened. He merely shrugged his shoulders when I asked, and I did not pursue it. I watched as he unwrapped a muslin parcel he had brought back from the hold. It was a beautiful shimmer of silk.

"This was supposed to be a lovely dress for you," he said. "Now, it will be a waistcoat for the cocky captain. I never thought I'd find the likes of another Holbauer in my life, but there you are." He shook his head, his mouth held in a grimace. Johann had told me that feeding the vanity of pompous men was one reason he hated being a tailor—he would rather clothe the needy as Jesus wanted.

I stroked his cheek until his eyes met mine. "What need will a farmer's wife have for a fine dress? I'm proud that my husband is clever enough and skilled enough to pay our way with his craft. No dress will ever replace you and what you do for us."

We kissed while the children giggled in the background. Françoise cleared her throat to let us know she was nearby.

The next day, we reached the harbor of Gaspé. We were all eager to visit the tiny port—not more than a fishing village—yet Johann held back. He continued his somber mood since his search for the captain's gold silk.

"You go and take the children. I need to measure and cut the fabric for the waistcoat. It will be easier while the ship is at anchor. You know my motto: measure carefully and cut even more carefully. If I mess this up, I don't want the captain to abandon me at the next port for not fulfilling our bargain." Johann smiled.

So it was that the children and I, accompanied by Pierre, Françoise, and Clotilde, were rowed to the town in a boat by the burly Gérard. It was thrilling to have our feet back on solid ground. Pierre found a Mi'kmaq woman to give us tea and fried bread for a few pence. We strolled around the tiny town until it was time to return.

I found Johann back in our tiny cabin, looking glassy-eyed and worn. When I asked, he assured me he was fine.

"Don't worry, Anna. I am just concerned that I will finish this vest before arriving in Québec. I want no debt owed to Captain Burbank."

Despite his reassurance, he refused the scant dinner meal, went to his berth, and curled up in his clothing even earlier than the children that night.

In the middle of the night, despite the constant creaking of the mast and the sough of the wind, I heard a low groaning. Thinking it was one of the children, I struck a match to light my candle. Bernard was getting out of the berth he shared with his father.

"Mama, Papa has been moaning in his sleep all night."

"Bernard, go and sleep on the berth with Katja. *Schnell!* I'll see what's wrong with Papa."

Bernard stumbled over to his sister's berth, and I rushed to Johann's side. He moaned and turned toward me when I touched his shoulder.

"Johann, tell me what's wrong."

"Anna, nothing, nothing. I am fine, just a bit of a headache. Don't worry."

I put my hand on his brow and felt the heat. I had cared for enough children in my marriage and even before to know that Johann had a high fever. His forehead was perspiring and felt clammy.

"Anna, just leave your cool hand on my head," he said faintly, "it feels so good."

"Johann, you have a temperature. I will find my herbs in the morning, but I cannot now as they're buried in the satchel under the children's bunk." I moved away and found the earthen crock where we stored water for the night. I was able to pour water for him into a wooden cup. He drank as eagerly as a man in a desert. When he finished, he turned over and was soon back asleep.

I struggled to sleep as I lay back in my berth. I could not shut off my worry for Johann. Would his fever spread to the children? All the dread I had in Kittersburg came rushing back. I finally dozed off, and the next thing I knew, it was morning, and the hatch cover was being slid away. I heard footsteps around me, preparing for the start of the day. Again, Bernard was at my side.

"Mama, Papa has not awakened." He knew something was wrong. Johann was always the first to wake and take him on deck to pee over the leeward side. I pushed off my quilt and ran to Johann's berth. He was much hotter than the night before. A sheen of sweat glistened on his forehead.

"Bernard, go find Pierre, Clotilde, and Françoise, and tell them to come immediately!" He dashed off before I uttered another word.

"Katja, wake up!" I saw my sleepy-eyed oldest daughter push aside the thin, tangled blanket that covered her and Rosie.

I put Delia in her arms. "Please take your sisters away from here. And find them something to eat."

Katja hoisted the baby on her hip without questioning me and pushed Rosie through the door.

I was bathing Johann's forehead with a moistened rag—a remnant from the inner lining of Captain Burbank's frock coat —when Bernard returned, followed by Pierre, his shirt untucked.

"Pierre, please ask the captain if we can bring Johann to the sailor's sick bay," I said. "I need to keep him from the children and the others. I'll nurse him. I won't need any of the sailors' or his help. And please take Bernard up to pee. Hold onto him, or he will try to climb too high to make his pee go farther." Pierre grabbed Bernard's hand and hurried to ascend to the upper deck.

Françoise entered the small cabin. I was relieved to see her.

"Françoise, Johann is sick. He is burning up with a fever. I must find something to help him." She tied her small kerchief over her nose and mouth after she heard my words.

"I have always found that raw potato slices applied to the forehead steal some of the fire away," she answered. Although I had never heard of that solution, I was willing to try it.

"All right, let's do it," I answered. "Please ask Clotilde to help Katja mind the children for me. We must keep them away from Johann. I must nurse him."

"Anna, don't worry. I'll do all I can. In these few days we've spent together, you've felt like a sister to me. Loving and far less annoying than Clotilde." She smiled and laid a hand lightly on my shoulder. She turned and left the cabin to find her potato.

When she returned, I had dug out a leather pouch under the children's bunk with its treasure of barks and leaves. Herb use was handed down to me from my mother and her mother for illnesses, but I was low on most of the plants I had packed. I dug further into the pouch and found the packets Simple Mary had wrapped for me in the deerskin bag. I tried to picture her pointing to each piece of bark, each clump of shriveled berries or dried leaves, and remember which plant healed which part of the body. These remnants of plants from her culture were so different from those of my Rhineland home. Behind me, I heard Johann's low whimper and began to feel increasingly anxious and disturbed by his discomfort. His back was towards me, yet I knew him so well that I could read his exhaustion.

Françoise returned, her hand juicy with sliced potato. When Johann turned over, I placed slices on his forehead. He looked at me with a question. His eyes looked even bluer in his flushed face with its gleam of sweat.

"Johann, you will have to trust me. Françoise says that this will help to draw out the fever."

He was shaking when he answered.

"Promise, Anna, promise me..." His voice trailed off to a faint whisper. I did not know what he wanted me to promise him. I made my request.

"Promise me, Johann, that you will get well and take me to our new farm in America." He clumsily reached for my hand.

Pierre arrived at the cabin with Gérard in tow.

"The captain says to move him to the sick bay. But, he says he will hold Johann to the completion of the waistcoat. The captain says being sick is no excuse for not finishing it." Pierre continued, "That Burbank's a cold bastard. Excuse me for being so frank."

I nodded. I had heard the voices of demanding men before, so it did not surprise me. I did not give a tinker's curse about Burbank's vest. I only cared about getting Johann well.

Gérard, the brawnier of the two, grasped Johann under the shoulders while Pierre took his ankles. I followed behind with Johann's quilt, linen nightshirt, and my satchel of herbs.

Françoise led the way with an oil lamp. We walked past the ship's ribs to the small cabin that served as the sick bay for the crew. It was even darker and meaner than I expected. One small berth and a three-legged stool were the only accommodations. A shelf nailed to the wall held a tarnished metal basin.

The men settled Johann on the bunk and quickly left. When they had closed the door, I removed one of my cambric petticoats and folded it to make a pillow for his head. The potato slices had fallen from his forehead en route, and I felt secretly relieved. I turned to Françoise.

"Please bring me water. I will need cool water to bathe him and hot water to infuse some herbs."

"Should I bring food, too?"

"No. My mother always warned, '*Eine Erkältung füttern, ein Fieber aushungern.*' Feed a cold, starve a fever," I said.

When she'd gone, I began to remove Johann's linen shirt. That's when I saw for the first time that his chest was covered with rose-colored spots. The rash extended from his neck downwards. Johann was able to slump forward enough so I could put his head and arms through the openings of his nightshirt. He collapsed again unto the narrow bunk. I was pulling off his breeches as Françoise reentered the cabin with a crock of cool water and rags.

She gasped and pointed to a black spot surrounded by a raised red area that appeared on Johann's calf.

"*Tache noire,*" she said. "The black stain."

"What is it, Françoise? Please tell me," I said, my alarm increasing.

"I have seen it before with my nephew. He said it came from a flea bite. Said his barn cat had a bad case of the fleas."

"What happened? What did he do? Did he die?" I tried to disguise the terror in my voice.

"First, he drowned the cat," she replied. "And yes, he lived, but he was very sick."

On hearing our voices, Johann turned toward us. His eyes were closed. Through parched lips, he murmured, "The cat... the rats." He struggled to raise his head. He repeated the mantra about cats and rats several times to make us understand.

"Hush, Johann. We will take care of it. You rest." He slumped back into an uneasy sleep.

I poured some of Françoise's water into the metal basin. I showed her the bags of dried plants from Simple Mary. She shook her head at some of them, then pointed to some woody shavings. "I know that one. That's white pine bark, good to bring a fever down. And that there is broad-leaf plantain. The Mi'kmaq women used it for rashes, I think. *Oui*, they made a poultice for my nephew, if memory serves me. And those berries there," she pointed to some dried red berries in my hand, "That's teaberry. We all collected those. Some people called it wintergreen. We French call it *le petit thé de bois*, the little tea of the woods. It's good for headaches and such. I'm sure Clotilde brought some dried leaves for her monthlies."

Françoise opened the cabin door. "I'll go find her and see if she has more."

I closed my eyes and thanked God for these new friends. I would not be fighting for Johann alone. These previous strangers were willing to help. If only I could tell Simple Mary how precious her gift was to me.

I crumbled some plantain leaves into the metal basin and swished them around. I let them seep until I saw them releasing their color. When the water reached a shade of brown lighter than my mama's gingerbread, I saturated one of Françoise's rags, wrung it out, and placed it on Johann's chest under his nightshirt. I put another on his forehead. His body shivered and quieted as the moist cloths cooled the fire within.

His eyes slowly opened, and he looked at me.

"*Ja*, Anna, that feels so good." His heavy eyes drifted closed.

I was reciting a Hail Mary when a knock on the door interrupted my thoughts. Before I could say a thing, the door was pushed aside. The bulky figure of the cook—who also served as the ship's barber and surgeon—stood in the doorway. He had that wide-legged sailor's stance, always braced for the boat's bob or yaw. Despite his bald head, he had a generous, unkempt mustache. A blood-stained apron covered the lower half of his body.

"Time for a bloodlet," he said nonchalantly. He held up a three-bladed fleam with a horn handle in his right hand.

I stood quickly, almost knocking over the tottery stool I was perched on.

"*Nein!* There'll be no bloodletting here," I said too loudly in German. I repeated myself in French so he could understand my meaning.

He shrugged his shoulders. "It's how we do things on this ship," he said dismissively. "The captain won't be pleased."

"The captain is not married to this man. I am." I could feel the blood rushing to my face. I continued. "*Monsieur*, may I remind you that the captain is in charge of this boat, but I am in charge of my husband."

He shrugged his shoulders again.

"Listen," I said in a less insistent voice, "the soldiers let Jesus's blood with a sword, and He died. I will not take a chance with my husband. The women on this ship and I have other means to try."

He cocked his head at me, this time with less indifference. "The way I hear it, Jesus rose in three days, but in three days on the *Earl of Wessex,* we might be tossing your husband's body off the stern."

I strangled my response; I felt like striking him. I knew he might be correct, but I could not allow myself to think that. If Johann died, what would the children and I do? We would not have the money, patience, or bravery to return to Baden. And how could a widowed woman and four children go alone to New York? How could I go on without my Johann? I said nothing to the cook until I took a deep breath to control my anger and the helpless, scared feeling throbbing in my head.

"I'm guessing you won't want any of my leeches, either," he said. He held up a small, cylindrical, pewter box. There were small holes on the top.

"No, *Monsieur*, I will not try them," I said as I clenched my fists.

"Have it your way, but you better hope the man up there," he pointed his finger upward, "and I don't mean Captain Burbank is listening."

Yes. I needed God and all the saints to help me save Johann.

The cook turned to go and almost collided with Françoise. She gingerly carried my copper tea kettle in her right hand while her left hand held a ceramic cup.

"*Bonjour,*" he said to her brusquely and stomped toward the galley. His original indifference had turned into surliness.

"What did he want?" she asked, frowning.

"To let Johann's blood or to leech him."

"Let's try the teaberry tea first," she said pragmatically. "I have brought the leaves, and you have the berries."

We put the dried plant material in her cup and poured it into the hot water. We sat and whispered while the leaves and berries softened in the cup, releasing the medicine I hoped would cure Johann.

"François, please join me in prayer," I urged. She nodded and began to mumble the *Notre Père* in French. I started the same prayer in German because that's the language in which God heard me best. I hoped He was listening well. We stayed that way as the tea steeped and listened to Johann's labored breathing.

Later, when Johann awoke, I supported him as well as I could, my arms wrapped around his hunched shoulders. I held the cup for him to drink. Much of the precious tea dribbled down his chin. He was so thirsty that he tried again. This time, he consumed most of the liquid and fell back again on the makeshift pillow. I kept my vigil with Johann for hours, often changing the cooling rags and brewing more tea. Once, I put most of Mary's herbs into his teacup. I did not recall her instructions but was willing to give anything a chance until Johann's fever broke.

As I watched Johann, Françoise came in and out with cool or hot water as needed. She reminded me she was praying and tucked her rosary in my apron pocket. Once, Clotilde stopped by to assure me that the children were fine. She had, she told me, run a nit comb through their hair to ensure me that no lice eggs crept about. She and Katja had also aired out all the linens in our cabin and sprinkled them with vinegar.

"Clotilde," I said to her with great sincerity, "I hope you find your husband because you will make a wonderful mother."

She grinned at my statement. Then she whispered, "Gérard is helping with the children. He told me..." A deep flush rose in her cheeks.

I patted her hand. I wanted the best for her, and if this tall, thickset sailor was the one, I was happy for her.

I kept my vigil at Johann's side. Often, I drifted off, my

head falling on the bunk beside him. I could not keep track of time. His fever fell and rose again. I alternately piled blankets on or removed them from his body. I gave him as much tea as possible, sometimes mixing it with honey or maple syrup.

One night, Katja came to bring me Delia for bedtime nursing. Delia was almost weaned, yet we were both comforted by this nightly ritual. After I returned the sleeping baby to Katja, I removed my second petticoat and gave it to her.

"Katja, after you bring Delia back to Clotilde, take the petticoat on the deck and ask Gérard to dunk it in the cold river. Wring out as much water as possible. I'll try wrapping Papa in the cold petticoat to keep his fever down." She ran to do what I had asked.

I don't know if being enveloped in the cool fabric or if the tortuous fever was running its course, but Johann seemed to improve.

Captain Burbank filled the doorway on the third or fourth day —I could not keep track of time. He held a handkerchief in front of his nose.

"How's the tailor?" he barked. His eyes traveled to the collapsed form of Johann on the narrow berth.

"Improving," I said. The rash was fading; the *tache noiré* had formed a scab. He was weak and sleeping most of the time. He no longer called out my name or murmured about cats and rats.

"Well, let him know that I want that waistcoat. That was the agreement—your passage for the frock coat and waistcoat. If it's not done, you'll pay your fare. No sluggards on my boat." He stroked his full black beard. He was not wearing the beautiful coat Johann had fashioned. I assumed he was saving it for the gentry of Québec.

"Tomorrow, we'll anchor briefly at Tadoussac, and then it's onto Québec. Given the wind and current, we'll be there in a few days."

"My husband's a man of his word. The waistcoat will be finished," I said.

With another stroke of his beard and a sniff, he was out the door.

Johann had slept through the conversation; the damp cloth had fallen from his head. Though I knew he was getting better —the flexuous fever was subsiding—it would be days before he could sit upright in his tailor's crossed-legged position, his head bent over his flying needle.

Later, Katja came to bring me food and some broth for her father.

"Katja, please bring me Papa's sewing satchel."

She looked at me quizzically.

"Say nothing to anyone, sweet girl, but bring it here."

In a few minutes, she returned with his sewing case. Once I had my hands on it, I shooed her off to be with her sisters and Clotilde. I carefully pulled out the pieces. The face of the waistcoat was the gold silk he had purchased in Paris, the lining was a rust taffeta, and the interlining was linen. They were pinned to the paper pattern he had cut. I was no tailor, but like every girl growing up in a village in those days, I knew how to sew. After living with Johann for so long in his workshop below our home, I watched him construct his beautiful pieces.

With a shaking hand, I threaded the first needle. I basted the interlining to the gold silk from the center outward to minimize any bunching of the fabric. I knew from Johann's work that the interlining would help the waistcoat maintain its shape. Johann would never take shortcuts with any garment he made. I overlocked the silk and the lining's pieces at their edges. I pinned the right sides of the silk and the taffeta together. I measured and chalked off where the shoulder seams and buttons would go. He, of course, would have sought out the captain to check the fit, but I could not take that chance. The captain was expecting a waistcoat from a guild master, not a woman. My shoulders ached as I curled toward the lamp's small cone of illumination. My eyes blurred from my squinting. I had no idea how long I worked. I was rubbing my neck when I heard him stirring.

"Anna," he said in his weak voice, "what are you doing?"

"Johann, tell me first, how are you feeling?" I laid the half-finished waistcoat aside and slid the stool close to his berth.

"I feel so much better, thanks to you. My head continues to pound but is no longer on fire."

I placed my hand on his forehead. The fever was gone. I peeked under his shirt and saw that the pink, angry rash was now faint.

"Thank God," I said. I squeezed Françoise's rosary that lay in my apron pocket.

"But, Anna, what *are* you doing?" he repeated.

"Captain Burbank came by. He said we'd soon be in Québec and needed to pay the fare if he did not have his waist-coat. I didn't know what to do, so I began to sew it myself."

"Let me see."

I handed the incomplete waistcoat to him. I knew my stitches were not as precise and exacting as his. I hung my head.

He looked at the vest from all sides and held it under the tunnel of lamplight.

"Fine work," he pronounced. "I don't think you are ready to be a guild master, but you are ready for your journeyman's year," he teased me. His returning humor told me that he would recover.

"Help me up," he said. After I guided him to a seated position, he took the garment on his lap and asked me to thread a needle. He worked on the vest for an hour before falling back into a deep sleep.

I listened to his regular breathing. For the first time in the days since Gaspée, I felt relief. Johann would be all right, the waistcoat would be sewn, and we could continue our journey. I would have my Johann back. My anchor, my rock.

Chapter 38

Québec

Johann

I don't remember ever being as exhausted as those days after my illness. Pierre, Clotilde, and Françoise told me that Anna had never left my side. Pierre described her as being the indestructible force that made me survive.

"You had no choice," he said. "Anna willed you to live." He laughed, "...And she poured tea down your throat, massaged your hands and feet, and ensured the rest of us were on call if you so much as turned over in your sleep."

I never felt closer to my Anna. At night, when I went on the deck to relieve myself, I looked at the blanket of stars above me and thanked God for my life and Anna. My work was not done, and I could not tarry. I needed to complete the waistcoat Anna had valiantly begun to sew. Even when I felt no energy, I sat and sewed. If allowed, I did my work on the deck of *The Earl* where the light was better and the air fresher. I stitched the right sides together, clipped the corners, and bound the edges before reversing the fabrics. I cut and bound seven buttonholes and fastened seven shiny brass buttons. I added a watch pocket and gold-braid trim. It turned out as well as hoped, given my weariness and the river roll. I appreciated my apprentice's early work.

Before encountering the frantic sprawl of rats, the flea-mad cat, and my illness, we'd been in the immense Gulf of St Lawrence. We were now in a broad river valley, and I was astounded by its bosky beauty. On each side of the river were rugged high banks and uplands covered by leafless hardwoods and conifers with a harlequin coat of green. In some areas, sandbanks with small beaches and wild grasses provided a small margin between the river and a small inhabited area.

To everyone's delight, Pierre pointed out an occasional moose or deer wading in one of the streams that emptied into the *San Laurent*. The air smelled different. Gérard explained that the river was fresher and less salty, flowing east from Lake Ontario to its mouth at the sea.

We continued the zigzag course of a sailing ship. Anna and I noticed how different the St. Lawrence was from the Rhine River Valley. On the Rhine, small castles and churches over-looked its flow, and row upon row of staked grape vines climbed its sloping hillsides. From Kittersburg, I was within walking distance of many small towns. An ancient bridge crossed the Rhine to the grand city of Strasbourg. No bridges crossed the wide St Lawrence. I saw only isolated settlements with rough-hewn houses and small boats pulled to the shoreline. More lumber was being harvested than bushels of wheat. Occasion-ally, we spotted a paddled birch bark canoe and the encamp-ments of native peoples. Gérard explained that both sides of the river were still Canada, but the south bank would be America as we progressed. As I gazed at the vast uninhabited forests, this scantily populated vastness, I was sure there would be enough land for a poor tailor and his family.

When I presented Burbank with his finished waistcoat, he was as pleased as he had been with the frock coat. As before, he sauntered back and forth in his new finery. He was right. The yellow silk vest with brass buttons looked beautiful against the deep charcoal of the outer coat. He was an impressive sight: tall and broad, with his bespoke clothing and luxurious beard.

We Klems, on the other hand, looked a sorry lot. We were all too thin, and the clothes we had worn since Kittersburg were now raggedy, patched, and faded. Anna had sacrificed her two petticoats for me. I could see her hip bones through the folds of her skirt. I was embarrassed that I had allowed my family to become so bedraggled. It reminded me of an expression my father would quote, "A blacksmith's home has only wooden spoons." I wanted more than wooden spoons for my family. Yet, here we were, looking like the village beggars.

Unlike Burbank, my beard was anything but luxurious. It was scrubby and sparse, and gray hairs presented themselves for the first time. I prayed that our fortunes would soon change.

The day after Captain Burbank paraded in his new waistcoat, he called all the passengers to the main deck.

"If all goes as planned, we will reach Québec tomorrow. As we prepare to drop anchor, you will all stay out of the crew's path. A *bateau* will transport you to the town. If you have any trunks or other merchandise on board, you will find them on the wharf." He said a few other things I could not understand.

All I cared about then was getting my family well-fed and into better clothing. We had things to pack up. Anna would insist on tidying up our space. I was still determining what we would do when we reached the city.

I approached Pierre as he confirmed that the goods he had traded for his fur pelts in St. John's were in order. He was in a jubilant mood. He would see his wife and young son for the first time in months. Pierre' had told us that his wife was of the Wyandot nation or, as the French called them, Huron. They had a young son together. When I met Pierre in the tavern in St. John's, he walked the muddy streets in high leather boots, but on *The Earl of Wessex,* he wore heavily beaded moccasins that his wife had made for him. He often wore a soft deerskin tunic with fringe and beads under his waistcoat.

"Pierre, where can I find a place for my family to stay once we have reached the shore?"

"*Mon ami,* you are welcome to stay with us. I'll show you my beloved town, but first, I need to hold my wife in my arms," he winked and made a kissing noise. "I need to get reacquainted with my son. I need to make sure my trade goods are intact. Then, *mon ami*, I am at your disposal."

The following morning was cool. Cloudy skies appeared in the west. As the crew set anchor, a wind raised the choppy water into white-capped troughs. Through a lifting fog, we saw the city of Québec.

The town consisted of two parts: the lower section close to the river looked like a hub of activity. It was the commercial center, I surmised. Stone and wood-constructed houses were visible, similar to our half-timbered home in Kittersburg, with exposed wooden frames filled in with mortar or crude cement. All the buildings had steep wooden roofs "for snow melt," Pierre told us. Several more excellent houses farther from the river were two-storied with several chimneys. A steep road climbed the distance between the lower and upper towns. Midway up the road in a clearing off to the side was the palisaded profile of a native village.

"That's where my wife's people live," Pierre pointed out, " I want you to come to meet her and Jacques Little Turtle, my son," he said

Pierre lent me his spyglass, and I could see that the higher town had large stone buildings. He pointed out the Jesuit seminary, a hospital, and the Ursuline Convent, where Bishop Scallan had entrusted me to deliver a letter. That was the second thing on my agenda after I found a place for our family to stay in this city.

We were all on the deck, ready to be assisted down the rope ladder to the waiting boat, when Gérard said he had an announcement. He cleared his throat.

"This will be my last voyage. This beautiful lady here," he pointed to a blushing Clotilde, "has consented to be my wife."

We all clapped, patted him on the back, and kissed Clotilde on both cheeks. With her beaming face, she looked beautiful, and her smile straightened the curve of her right-leaning nose.

We gathered around the happy couple while Gérard told us he would gladly leave the sailing business to run a hostelry with his brother. Clotilde would run the kitchen.

"She makes the best *tourtière,* she tells me." Clotilde nodded and told us of all the savory ingredients in her meat pie. Their happiness reminded me of the day I proposed to Anna in her parents' garden. How could we ever have foreseen that twelve years later, we would be disembarking from a ship into a rough little city in Canada at the beginning of winter?

I saw Anna take Françoise aside.

"What will you do?" Anna asked Clotilde's elder sister.

Françoise replied, "I'll help them, of course, but after I saw how you cared so desperately for Johann, I knew I couldn't do it. I couldn't give that much. I'm content. I don't need to let my heart be torn apart. I'm happy for Clotilde and Gérard. But for me, children and doing a man's bidding are more than I want. I'll be happy to be the wise aunt."

"You will be the best aunt," Anna laughed. "You'll probably also be the family healer."

When it was our turn to disembark, the river was rough, and getting from *The Earl of Wessex* to the boat below was difficult. By the time we were ashore, it was afternoon, and we were drenched. We were assured that our two trunks would safely wait for us the next day.

We began our trudge to find a place to stay. The first inn we approached was filled with tippling sailors and coarse-looking lost souls. Anna shook her head. She wouldn't have the repeat of the pea-coated man, she said.

The second public house, a short distance away, had no more rooms to let.

"If it were one of you, I could make do," the keeper told us, "but not with the whole tribe of young ones."

We walked through the doorway of a better establishment in the lower city. It turned out that it was the pub owned by Gérard's brother.

"Sorry," he said. "My soon-to-be-wedded brother and the two women just filled my last room."

I felt anxious and cranky. Once more, I failed to provide for my family as a man should. It was with guilt and self-reproach that I told Anna that we must walk the muddy road to the upper town. Not only did we need a place to stay, but I needed to return Fr. Scallan's kindness and deliver a letter.

We shivered with cold when I let the knocker fall on the solid door of the Ursuline Convent. The heavy brass knocker was shaped like a *fleur-de-lis*.

A small peep door opened. I heard a voice, but I could not see a face. I explained that I had a letter for the Mother Superior from the bishop of Newfoundland. There was a hesitation until the disembodied voice responded, "You may put it in the turn." She indicated the small door where items could be placed in a revolving turnstile so bundles or mail could be taken to the inside the convent without opening the massive door.

"Father Scallen asked that I deliver it to the hands of the Mother Superior," I replied.

"*Oui,*" the voice replied.

I heard the sound of a bolt being slid across the door.

Look at the birds of the air, they do not sow, nor reap or gather into barns, and yet your heavenly Father feeds them.

— Matthew 6:26

Chapter 39

The Convent

Anna

The old nun who opened the door was dressed in a familiar sister's attire. Her black serge tunic was belted. A rosary dangled down from the cincture. Tiny strands of gray hair escaped from her white wimple. Her kind face regarded us from the tops of our heads to our muddy, drenched shoes. Her sharp eyes missed nothing. I wished I had a rag to clean up our mess in the dark, vaulted corridor. She held a veined, knobby hand toward Johann, who withdrew the letter from his pocket. He laid it on her open palm.

He introduced us and waited for her to respond.

"I am Mother Joséphine," she responded. There was an edge of authority in her voice.

Breaking the seal, she quickly read. The gray eyes were on us again. I saw how embarrassed Johann looked. He must have realized that the bishop had written about us.

"Come," she said in refined French. It was very different from the country dialect of the Acadian sisters and crew we had sailed with for the past two weeks.

"Let us warm you and find your nourishment."

We followed her past two tall doors, one ajar. A high-ceilinged chapel with several candles on a gilded altar was visible. She led us down the flagstone hallway to an open door. Light and savory odors flooded out. A plump sister stood by an arched fireplace, stirring a large kettle with a wooden paddle. The blackened pot hung from a hook over bright coals. She looked at us suspiciously. We were, indeed, pathetic looking. Johann always wanted us to appear neatly attired, but today, we were muddy and shabby.

Johann, usually so pleasant and proud, was silent. The two Ursulines conferred, their veiled heads almost touching. The plump one glared at us over the shoulder of the older sister. Finally, the disagreeable-looking cook nodded, and the old sister gestured us to a table in the corner.

The stout sister, introduced as Sister Céleste, plunked steaming bowls of a thick ochre-colored soup before us. Nothing had ever tasted so good.

Mother Joséphine sat with us and began to play with the children. I could see that she was affectionate and open-hearted beyond her calling to God. She was especially drawn to Delia. She held out her arms, and I placed my baby on her lap. The nun's face wrinkled with a generous smile. She sang a little French song to Delia and bounced her on her knee. The baby rewarded the old nun with her dimpled smile.

Handing the baby back to me, she turned to Johann.

"*Monsieur*, you may stay here this evening, but please remember that this is a convent. You and your son will not be permitted beyond these doors." She pointed outside the open doorway of the kitchen to a pair of double doors in the corridor.

"You will stay in the room provided to Paul, our caretaker. Your wife and daughters may stay in the cell of one of our sisters who has recently passed on to our heavenly Father. You will dine only in this kitchen as the sisters and students eat in the refectory. This can only be temporary as we have students to teach and other ministries to perform. In exchange, *Monsieur* Klem, I hope you will enlighten and, perhaps, entertain us with the details of your journey."

Johann and I bowed our heads to her. God had once more looked out for us and brought us to this kind woman. Because of her generosity, our family was fed and safe.

In the following days, I tried to be of service to these holy women. I offered to help cook, yet unlike Simple Mary, Sister Céleste was not looking for anyone else's recipes or skills in dicing carrots. One of the novices helped prepare the meal, and other postulants performed scullery duties. I volunteered my assistance in embroidering or laundering the chaplain's vestments. Mother Joséphine looked at me with a smile.

"Dear Anna. We are a convent and school. While I am sure you do lovely work, we have taught these tasks for hundreds of years. You take care of your children. The rest is well under control."

And indeed, it was. The ringing of a bell controlled all the activities of the sisters and the students. I watched as the black-habited nuns and their proteges moved silently from music class to the refectory to chapel prayers, all at the clang of the hand-held bell.

I observed the nuns instruct the young girls in reading, drawing, writing, needlework, and lace-making. I was entranced by a young sister who, surrounded by her students, sat with a small pillow before her and skillfully manipulated the pins and 22 bobbins of thread to make a dainty lace ribbon. Katja looked at the students with envy. I was sure that if her life had been different, she would have chosen to learn these gentler crafts in this protected environment rather than what lay before her—the back-breaking life of a farm.

For three nights, after our last meal and before completing the evening prayers, we sat in the warmth of the convent kitchen. Mother Superior perched close by the small table where we enjoyed Sr. Céleste's delicious stews. A few other sisters sat behind a screen so they wouldn't be seen by Johann or Bernard. Johann, an accomplished storyteller, embellished certain parts of our journey and chose not to describe our difficulties. Mother Joséphine would sit and hold sleeping Delia in her arms and listen intently. Her body often shook with amusement as he imitated some of the people we met. Even Sister Céleste, scandalized that the mother superior had allowed a man to penetrate this far into the convent, listened, and paid attention. He began with the charitable widow, Frau Metzger, who'd sold a field to enable us to start our journey.

Rosie interrupted, "Papa, talk about Sophie and Frieda!"

So, her father included a description of the two oxen who wore ribbons on their horns. Johann described Paris and all its new construction and how Klaus Fischer, a German who had deserted the French army, was our guide to the treasures of the City of Lights. He did not include Klaus's lusty behavior to avoid offending the nuns. He praised the loveliness of our trip down the Seine and the soaring cathedrals in towns such as

Rouen. He described the hustle and bustle of Le Havre and the vastness of the misbehaving ocean. He recounted how we encountered schools of fish and spouting whales. He did not mention the coffins we had lowered overboard or a negligent captain who spent his days smoking opium.

He began to speak of the storm until Katja asked him not to. I could see that even bringing it up brought fear to her eyes. She nervously looked at her booted feet and tugged at her ear lobe.

Johann painted a picture of the engaging sailors, such as Michael, who played the fiddle for us under the stars. When he told of Mr. Carothers, the straight-laced first mate who tried to teach us English, Sister smiled at Bernard. He always attempted to speak to her in English, Sister's third language after French and Abenaki. Bernard's face blushed with recognition of her attention. Johann chronicled life in St. John's and our friendship with Simple Mary. He spoke of our stay with the welcoming Kavanaughs and how Katja and I helped Bernadette with tub after tub of laundry. He did not mention the horrible Mrs. Grimsby or the pea-coated MacDonald. Johann did not play false notes. Instead, he composed a beautiful melody from the better parts of our journey. Through all his worry and concern, he tried to perform the most harmonic music.

Johann recounted the beauty of the Saint Lawrence and how the immense Percé Rock jutted up from the gulf. Rosie, who had difficulty understanding all her father's words in French, asked him to tell them about Mrs. Grimsby's old dog and all the birds that followed our ship. Smiling, he told of the colonies of puffins we had spotted and the gannets who perched on the yardarms of the boat looking for a free meal.

Mother Joséphine remarked that we had seen more of her country than she. She had barely gone beyond the walls of

Québec City and had never dreamed of crossing the ocean to France, the home of her ancestors and her branch of the Ursulines.

Johann praised every person who assisted us.

"Indeed, God is good. He provided you with many guardian angels," the good abbess said. She suggested we all say a decade of the rosary for them.

It was a wonderful time for us.

We knew we had to leave the convent. While Johann and Bernard were out trying to find a new place to stay, I entered the chapel and sat by myself to pray. I looked at the gilded altar and the light streaming through the rose window. Over the doors was a large painting of Jesus blessing a native woman with Mary Magdalene at his feet. I breathed in the faint odor of incense and the familiar smell of the burning beeswax candles when Mother Joséphine entered and sat beside me in the pew. Her eyelids closed for a few minutes, and her lips moved in silent prayer. I was about to leave as quietly as possible when her eyes opened, and she looked at me. She laid her soft hand on mine.

"Anna, you needn't be so hard on yourself. God is on your shoulder, watching and protecting you. He will give you strength."

I said nothing, though tears stung my eyes.

With effort, Mother Joséphine rose and climbed the curving steps to the pulpit. The ambo was capped by a small roof with an angel blowing a trumpet. When she reached the spot where the priest would stand to preach, she bent and picked up a book. I saw she held a Bible in her hand. I was transported to my mother's kitchen on the day I pounced on her to save me from Johann's plan for *Amerika*. The two older women, the embodiment of kindness and wisdom, relied on God's word. When Mother Joséphine rejoined me in the pew, her fingers carefully turned the thin pages until she found what she was searching for. She read out loud.

"Psalms 84." I caught her last words, "Even the sparrow finds a home, and the swallow her nest."

I tasted the saltiness of my tears as I understood her words. She withdrew a handkerchief from under her starched, white guimpe and brushed my cheek.

"Anna, do not worry. You will get there. Your children will be safe. You will find your new home just as the sparrow has."

I could not answer as I was overwhelmed by her kindness.

Mother Joséphine patted my hand. "Matthew tells us that not a sparrow falls to the ground without our Father's knowledge. You, dear Anna, are worth more than many sparrows."

She reached into her pocket again and withdrew a silver cross on a black cord. She laid it on my lap.

"This belonged to Geneviève, one of our postulants who, a few weeks ago, decided that convent life was not for her. When she did not answer her call, Sister Céleste found her folded habit and this crucifix on the cot in her cell."

Mother Joséphine's eyes rose to the large crucifix over the altar before they returned to me.

"In most cases, I would save it for the next novice, but I think it's in better hands with you." Smiling, she lifted the chain over my head until the cross dangled over my bodice.

I embraced her. My linen cap brushed against her wimple.

I vowed never to remove the cross—her token of a mother's love. I had two mothers who gave me gifts of silver and more love than I ever deserved.

Chapter 40

Huron Life

Johann

While Anna and the girls enjoyed the solitude of the convent, Bernard and I walked the Québec streets to discover how to manage the overland trip to Montréal. We passed the sturdy houses of the well-to-do with their red wooden shutters and third-story dormers. We stopped in the main square to watch the masons rebuild the Cathedral damaged in the war with the British. Although it was tiny compared to our beloved cathedral in Strasbourg, this cathedral also had a single-spired steeple. In front of the church's doors, a market with several stalls and vendors was in progress. I'd decided to search for second-hand clothing to alter for my family when I heard a familiar voice.

"*Mon ami,* I have been looking for you."

When I turned, I saw Pierre striding toward me. Like St.

Christopher carrying the Christ Child, he held the legs of a young boy perched on his shoulders. The boy's large dark eyes peeked around two feathers connected by a beaded band framing chubby cheeks. The boy lay his head on his father's fur trader's cap. Next to them stood a lissome woman whose long black braids, tied off with deer hide stripes, cascaded down her back. Small ornaments had been woven into the thick plaits. Her earrings were made from shells; her eyes were large and dark like her son's. She and Pierre wore clothing that was a combination of European style and native dress. Red fabric bands surrounded the hem of her cloth skirt.

I could understand why Pierre had been so eager to get home to her. High coppery cheekbones set off her beautiful face. She looked at me timidly as Pierre introduced her. He first pronounced her Huron name, which I could not attempt to repeat. He then gave her French name, Marie Yvette, a name as lovely as she. Their son was Jacques Little Turtle.

"Johann, no one knew where you had gone. Where have you been hiding?"

"At the convent of the Ursuline sisters," I said.

"*Quoi?* Not thinking of taking the veil, are you?"

Pierre laughed at his joke. I explained to him how the good sisters had rescued us and taken us in.

"Now that we've found you, you must be our guests. We have a small house in *La Basse Ville,* the lower town, where Yvette and I will be happy to have you. It will be crowded, but we're all used to that from the *Earl of Wessex, n'est-ce pas?*"

Jacques squirmed from his seat on his father's shoulders to the ground to gaze at Bernard, who leaned to shake the little boy's hand. With his arms free, Pierre clasped my shoulder and pulled me towards him. There was nothing I could say to argue with my congenial Canadian friend. On that crisp sunny day with the smell of the river wafting up towards us, I was rescued once more by the willingness of a stranger to befriend me. Throughout this difficult journey, we had been assisted over and over by people who reached out to us to become companions and helpmates.

On the following day, we moved into Pierre's small home. Anna had reluctantly left the Ursuline abbey's peaceful atmosphere and the mother superior's solace. We could no longer impose on the patient nuns. The children were happy to have a new playmate. Jacques taught them a game using half-scorched peach stones tossed into an earthen bowl. As Pierre and I smoked our pipes by the fire that evening—and there was always a well-stoked fire, as Canada did not lack wood—he recounted how he'd met Marie Yvette. When he went to a Huron compound to buy pelts, Pierre saw Yvette sitting quietly in the longhouse weaving a basket from black ash strips and marsh grasses. She looked at him shyly, and he knew he had found the woman he desired. Her smile confirmed it.

"It took quite a while to convince the older women of her clan that I was worthy. They're the ones who have a say with the Huron," Pierre said. "They eventually agreed; they knew my father had been a fair trader with them. In the end, I became partners with her brothers and her kinsmen. They catch the game, cure the hides, and I trade it for them. Knives, scissors, blankets, kettles, what have you."

Pierre took another puff from his pipe.

"I provide them with the guns and traps. It's become a risky business. It is hard to be a single trader when large companies want all the trade. The Europeans are so hungry for the furs that newcomers hunt out of season and kill pregnant does.

There is no respect for the animal. That is not the Huron way. There are fewer and fewer animals to feed the people. Americans like John Astor get fat on the money from the pelts, and my wife's people have less and less."

Pierre looked into the fire and was silent for a while. I said nothing. Knocking out the ashes from his clay pipe on the side of the hearth, he interrupted his reverie.

"But let us not be dour tonight. Let us celebrate our families being together."

He arose and filled his glass and mine with a French brandy he'd brought from St. John's. Yvette filled gourd bowls with the richly flavored Indian pudding she'd made with the corn she had grown and pounded. She'd laced it with sweet maple syrup.

Early the following day, Pierre insisted on giving us a tour of his beloved city. I couldn't help but think that Pierre was the married version of Klaus Fischer: ebullient, buoyant, high-spirited, and proud of the city surrounding him.

"This was an entirely French city founded by Samuel Champlain himself in the early 1600s," he said.

While Pierre narrated the history of his Québec, I thought that our little village of Kittersburg had houses older than this city. Compared to Europe's worn-out fields and minds, Canada was brand new, like a toddler taking its first steps.

Pierre bounded around the city, showing us the high walls and the ramparts built for the city's defense. A huge black cannon sat pointed toward the river. The big guns had been unable to stave off the British. Still, they had worked well in 1775 when the American Continental Army failed in its attempt to invade Canada and rally the French Canadians to support the Patriot movement.

A Latin hymn floated through the windows as we walked past the Jesuit seminary. Pierre explained that the British expelled the Jesuits and only recently allowed them back into Canada. Strolling by the *Hôtel-Dieu,* Pierre described how the Augustinian nuns had arrived early to tend to the needs of sick colonists and natives alike.

"If Anna had not been able to mend you, we could have given the good sisters a try at it," he joked.

From the high bluffs, he pointed to the locale where the British had scaled the cliffs in the infamous battle on the fields of a farmer named Abraham. Here, General Wolfe had defeated *Général* Montcalm's French forces. Both generals were wounded and died. Pierre remarked that Montcalm was buried in a shell hole under the Ursuline choir, the same convent where we had enjoyed our meals. Mother Joséphine had never mentioned that the French general's bones rotted beneath our feet. The battle was fought in 1759, well before Pierre was born—nevertheless, it was clear that he resented the British who controlled his city.

As much as I wanted to see all that Québec held, I was not fully recuperated from my illness. It was hard to compete with Pierre's energy and enthusiasm. The children were restless with Pierre's history lessons.

"Pierre, you would have been a boon companion to a *Professeur* we knew. But, friend, we can no longer tarry. We need to get to Montréal before winter," I said. I had discussed buying another wagon and oxen to drive overland, but Pierre convinced me that the trip would be faster and easier by coach.

"We'll go to the coach depot *tout de suite,*" he said, leading us back to the lower city.

While Anna and the children returned to Pierre's small

home, Pierre led me to a merchant building where the stage-coach left daily for Montréal.

Royal Mail Line, William Weller, Proprietor, was painted over the doorway. I could hear the whiny of horses and the pungent smell of their manure from a stable in the courtyard. Pierre asked the agent about the schedule and fares. I was glad that I had negotiated with Captain Burbank for the voyage on the *Earl of Wessex,* but I did not want to cut and sew another frock coat to exchange for our coach fares.

On the day we were set to leave, Pierre went to his house's loft and returned with a brown, wooly bundle in his arms. He tossed it on the floor before the hearth. It was about four feet wide with plush, cinnamon-brown fur. I could see where an animal's legs and tail had been. A large grin spread across his face.

"*Mon ami,* this bear skin is for you and your family."

He must have read my quizzical expression.

"It will keep you warm on the ride to *Montréal.* Do you think they will have a nice fire like mine in that coach to keep you cozy? *Non, mon ami.*"

"Pierre, I cannot possibly pay you for this," I said. I knew this was a sought-after pelt I could not afford. A flush rose to my cheeks. He had already been more than generous with me.

"Johann, I give this to you because I have been delighted to know all six of you. And you have been more than accepting of me and my family. Someday, perhaps, I will visit you on your vast land in *Amérique,* and you will give me exclusive rights to hunt your animals." He exploded into a great laugh.

We embraced. We were two friends, both husbands and fathers. We both knew the challenges the world presented to keep our families warm and protected.

Chapter 41

The King's Highway

Anna

When Johann told me we would leave Québec, I felt a tug in my heart. I loved the French feel of the city high on the bluffs. Though much smaller, it reminded me of Paris without the commotion and the crowds of people sporting cockades on their hats. The air was fresh. The view of the St. Lawrence, polka-dotted with white sails from the schooners and barques, was lovely and peaceful. In this city, fresh, warm food had filled my children's bellies and added pink to Johann's pale cheeks.

The worst part of leaving was knowing I would never see Mother Joséphine again. It felt like being torn one more time from the arms of Mama. Both women were as holy and kind as the Virgin Mother herself. I would also miss the jaunty Pierre and his quiet, lovely wife. They welcomed us as if we were born in their longhouse, raised as part of the turtle clan. The children were also unhappy to leave. Rosie pestered us to bring little Jacques with us. Katja became sullen and wrote a very long letter to her grandmother. Only Bernard was as eager as his father to continue the trek.

Johann discovered that there was room for only one of our trunks on top of the stagecoach we would ride to Montréal. One would be left behind. It was an easy choice. One chest, so finely crafted by Johann's brother, had been cracked in the great storm on the *Stalwart*. Rats had gnawed on its corners on the *Earl of Wessex*. We shuffled through its contents. I held on to my copper kettle, spoons, a crock to hold my flour, and Mama's silver candlesticks. The mildewed bedding and a brass pot had to go. Pierre thought he could repair the chest, and Yvette was glad to receive an extra cooking pan. I watched as Johann dug into his breeches' pocket and presented Yvette with one of the silver thimbles he often unconsciously jingled. This long trip gave us new friends and separated us further from our former life.

We arrived at William Weller's depot the following Monday to board the Montréal bound stage. Pierre, Yvette, and Jacques were there. We were also surprised when Clotilde, Françoise, and Gérard appeared. Gérard's brother's tavern was nearby, and Pierre had told them that the long-traveling Klem family was on the road again. It was a joyous reunion and farewell.

With a smile that showed her teeth and crinkled her eyes, Clotilde told us that the banns were published. Gérard's arm was around her shoulders as she said she and her former sailor would wed the following month. I held her hand and told her I was sorry we could not help celebrate or bring a tasty dish for the wedding festivities.

"Your good thoughts are all I need," she assured me.

Françoise, always ready with her wit, leaned forward and whispered in my ear. "I'm getting bored with all this happiness. I should travel with you for a bit more mishap and adventure."

"You, friend, are always welcome wherever we land. And don't forget your herbs. You never know when one of us will take sick again," I answered.

The passengers included the six of us and two gentlemen, well-off, judging from their beaver hats and well-shined high boots. When we were assembled, a surly-looking man wearing a low-crowned hat and a great coat spattered by roadway mire called from the driver's box.

"Ladies and gentlemen, welcome to the Royal Mail Line. I'm your driver. Silas Hingham, by name. This coach leaves in five minutes. If you're not in it, you're left behind. Trip will take four to six days depending on...well, depending on me, the horses, the weather, and anything else that gets thrown at us. I'm not inclined for it to be any longer. God willing, it'll be shorter, but we got one hundred and seventy-nine miles to cover. The ladies ride in the rear seats, facing forward to prevent road sickness. The young ones ride on the laps. We stop to change horses every twenty miles or so. We stop at villages to deliver the mail. No one gets in or out of the coach without my say-so."

He stopped to take a breath before continuing his singsong speech. I imagined he had recited this a thousand times.

"When we stay at a depot inn for the night, be ready to leave at first light. As I said, and I won't repeat it, if you're not there, you're left behind. It's all about the mail getting there on time. As far as I see it, you passengers make it harder. When we halt for a fresh team, do your necessaries; if not, you hold it to the next station. If you got any other problem, bang on the roof, but I can't promise I'll stop."

He paused and looked down at us. "Any questions?"

It was clear from his quick descent from the driver's box that Silas Hingham wasn't willing to answer any.

The coach itself was well used. It had once been bright, but now the blue and green paint was chipped or stained by weather and age. *Royal Mail Line* was barely discernible on the coach's door. The spoked wheels on the back axle—at least four feet high, by my guess—were larger than those in the front. Lanterns hugged each side of the box where Silas Hingham would drive. I saw a whip sticking up from the small compartment near his seat.

We watched Silas Hingham heave a few more leather satchels into the rear boot storage. He secured the buckles while a young boy, not much older than Bernard, applied grease to the front and back axles. Four bay horses, one with four white stockings, had been hitched and pawed the ground. Rosie, of course, wanted to pet each one. I distracted her as I didn't think the crusty coachman would allow it.

After hugging our friends, we climbed the high step to the coach's inner compartment. Given Mr. Hingham's instructions, Johann, Katja, and I sat in the forward-facing seats with Delia on my lap and Rosie on Johann's. Katja rode between us. Bernard squeezed between the gentlemen with the shiny leather boots. Johann snuggled the bear skin rug over our laps.

"Good idea, that," said the portlier of the two gentlemen. He had introduced himself as Mr. Cooper and his companion as Mr. Wycliff. Mr. Cooper pointed to Pierre's bear skin gift. "It'll get colder as we travel west."

Pierre had explained that the highway we would travel was called *Chemin du Roy* or the King's Highway. A road was needed from Québec to Montréal to connect all the settlements along the river. I presumed that the king who ordered the road was one of the French kings named Louie. He'd given vast properties to his noblemen, called *seigneuries*. They, in turn, granted chunks of land to families to clear trees, break sod, and farm. Each family was required to give a certain amount of grain, fish, wood, and labor as rent to the *seigneur* or lord. According to Pierre, the plan aimed to settle New France, although it sounded suspiciously like the old way of life we had come from. Johann told me that the Revolution and the beheadings in France were all about getting out from under the feet of the nobility. This part of Canada had not gotten that news. Johann assured me that it was different in America. There were no lords and peons. I hoped he was right. We had put thousands of miles between ourselves and Europe, and I did not want to be beholden to a nobleman or a pretender like *Herr* Holbauer.

As the coach followed the course of the St. Lawrence, we gazed through the small windows and watched the river's course narrow. Soon, we needed to draw the grimy curtains to save ourselves from the dust that spiraled in. Pierre and Mr. Hingham had prepared us for the stops and tollgates, yet nothing prepared us for the thrusts and thwacks of the road. As we sat in the coach, we felt every thump and bang. The impact elevated us from the hard seat beneath us, slamming us down again. The memory of the storm on the *Stalwart* returned. Mr. Cooper's head hit the roof with one wallop, smashing his tall black hat. He attempted to punch it back into shape while his companion, Mr.Wycliff, cradled his Wellington hat on his lap. The hat's curled brim and flared crown would not suffer a *chapeau* disaster like Mr. Cooper's. The two gentlemen may have been accustomed to this buffeting as they kept a steady conversation about something I could not decipher. When I later asked Bernard about their conversation, he said he did not understand much, but it was always about money.

"Money this and money that."

Meanwhile, Delia and Rosie were less tolerant of the jarring ride; they began to fuss and cry. Johann and I did our best to smooth them. They would quiet until the next thump and then whimper again.

Clunk, crack, clank, clomp. I longed for our slow trip to Paris with Frieda and Sophie's unrushed and steady gait. This road was wider and newer than those in France but still rutted, and the sturdy horses were at least twice as fast. If a vehicle approached us from the opposite direction, slowing down was not in Silas Hingham's vocabulary. He plunged on through.

Despite being in the forward-facing seat, which, according to Mr. Hingham, would preserve a woman's delicate constitution and prevent road sickness, Johann was as nauseous as he had been on the ocean. I could see the sweat on his brow, and regardless of the dust, he stuck his head around the sooty curtain for air. When we halted at the first turnstile, Johann lost the delicious breakfast Yvette had prepared out the window.

Finally, we stopped for a change of horses and a quick visit to the privy. We welcomed the fresh breeze, although, as Mr. Cooper had warned us, it was beginning to feel cooler as the road wandered inland from the river. Fresh horses were harnessed, and we soon returned to the stuffy stagecoach.

We stopped at toll gates and various towns where a depot attendant flung open the boot to retrieve his mail satchel. We learned to brace ourselves against the doors when we heard the crack of Silas Hingham's whip as it signaled that the four horses, nostrils steaming, would jolt ahead.

Onward, we drove. The first overnight stop was in Trois-

Rivières, a city larger than the towns we had passed early in the day. Like Québec, it sat high on a bluff over the St. Lawrence. There was no time for a tour of this city. We were exhausted, though we had done little that day except to fight off the bumps and keep the children pacified. The guest house was surprisingly clean, and the dinner was hot and savory. We climbed into our beds as soon as possible, fearing being left behind if we dallied the following day. No one wanted to be on the wrong side of the choleric Mr. Hingham.

The next few days were a blur of towns and rivers. Many were named for the saints and martyrs. *Saint-Barthélemy, Saint Cuthbert, Sainte Geneviève-de-Berthier, Saint-Sulpice, Sainte-Anne.* It was like a litany sung by the priest at Easter vigil.

We crossed several rivers, most without incident. One particular river was at least a half-mile wide, and Mr. Hingham demanded we step out of the coach. He and the ferrymen skillfully maneuvered the coach and the horses from a flat rock outcropping onto a large, broad scow. Mr. Hingham tied rags around the horses' eyes so they would not spook. The children and I huddled in the prow. I clutched them close as the gunwales on this vessel were lower than the two boats we had sailed before. None of us—except Johann, barely—could swim. Despite the cool late autumn weather, the ferrymen sweated through their shirts, exposing massive shoulders and muscles. A man on each side, with another at the stern, steered the ferry to the opposite bank with long poles called sweeps. Hand over hand, they pushed and lifted the poles, holding the boat steady against the wind and current. I was relieved when the boat drifted onto the western bank.

A constant rain bloated a stream on the fourth day, and we were asked once more to descend from the carriage. Silas Hingham required all the gentlemen to push the coach from behind when a back wheel stuck. Mr. Cooper's poor smashed hat landed in a puddle of sludge and muck. He was forced to his knees in an attempt to retrieve it. His hands and his mole-skin breeches were covered with the ooze. When we returned to the coach's compartment, neither man's fine leather knee-high boots had kept their gleaming high polish. I gave Mr. Cooper my scarf to help him remove at least the first coating of the slick mud, but he shook it off.

"My dear lady, I appreciate your kind offer. Yet, the mud gives me a fine excuse to visit the haberdasher in Montréal. My wife is not the only one to spend my money."

The two gentlemen laughed as if this were a great joke. In my world, the need for a new hat would have meant one less acre of land for Johann's farm.

Chapter 42

Montréal

Johann

At the end of the fourth day of the stagecoach journey, we crossed one more racing river to the island that housed the city of Montréal. Although we were within the time window that Silas Hingham had proposed, he was as cantankerous as usual. He wanted to break a record without breaking his horses. I was relieved that the bone-shattering trip was over. We had all survived without concussions or bitten-off tongues. We rejoiced that there would not be a fifth day on the road.

I was pleased with my first sighting of Montréal. Spires and steeples, tin roofs, and turrets caught my eye. The air was crisp and colder than Québec, and I could spy ice forming where three rivers joined. While the upper part of Québec sat high on a bluff, Montréal, long and narrow, was built on a low hillock parallel to the river. A low mountain interrupted the view north of the city. Mr. Cooper said that hill was the city's name-sake. *Mont Réal* or Mount Royal. Beyond the remains of a forti-fying wall lay orchards and fields. When Silas Hingham finally pulled the horses to a halt, we were in front of the LeBlanc Hotel near the *Place de la Douane.* Dusk had crept in, and we had no choice but to stay the night at the hotel. Whenever we stayed at a hotel, I worried about the contents of my pocketbook.

Mr. Wycliff, who now deemed it safe to place his hand-some hat back on his head, asked if he could assist. His French was better than his companion's, and on the last two days of the travail on the *Chemin du Roy,* we'd all attempted conversation. As in other cities and places we had landed before, I knew I would need any offered help. A sense of shame seized me. I must rely on others; I could not make this journey alone.

We walked into LeBlanc Hotel together, where Wycliff borrowed paper and a quill from a mustachioed clerk who sat imperiously behind a mahogany writing table. Our stage companion wrote a quick note on the paper and fanned it in the air to dry the ink. It read: Mr. Barnwell T. Wycliff, Purveyor of Fine Goods, 12 Rue Saint-Paul. After he handed the paper to me, he doffed his fine hat to Anna and Katja and left.

The night at the warm hotel made us all a bit cheerier. After bread and coffee in the morning, we decided to explore the city before seeking out Mr. Wycliff. Wrapping our jackets and cloaks against the city's chill, we made our way to *Rue Notre-Dame.* The large houses of the wealthiest sat on this street. The stone buildings had steeply pitched, cedar-shingled roofs. Dead in the center of the street, like an island in a river, was Our Lady's church. The building was small compared to the European churches, yet it was asymmetrical with a single spire like the cathedrals in Strasbourg and Québec. No one could have an excuse for missing mass on Sunday, as walking on that street would put one right at the church's front door. I could not restrain Anna from entering the dark interior to light candles. When we left the church, we wandered down the avenue to the nearby Seminary of Saint-Sulpice. Two by two, a phalanx of black-cassocked seminarians emerged through wrought iron doors to the street. They passed under a pediment adorned by a coat of arms surrounded by two upright lions. A short tower held a large brass clock under a belfry with four bronze bells. As the clock struck eleven, the bells' peals reminded me that time was fleeing.

We were not tourists in the city. Montréal was another way station on our journey where we needed to locate affordable lodging. Mr. Wycliff's address, folded in my pocket, was perhaps a way to find it.

We made our way to *Rue Saint-Paul*. This street was closer to the river and echoed with the sounds and bustle of the harbor. The inhabitants of these wooden houses and curbside shops were the city's laborers, tradesmen, and shopkeepers. I immediately felt more comfortable on this street. An imposing building on the corner was occupied by the West Indies Company, a large trading firm that was putting individual traders out of business. Canoes and *bateaux* bobbed near a wharf bearing the company's name.

Several doors down, we found Mr. Wycliff's establishment.

When I saw the items displayed in the window, I cautioned the children not to touch a thing. As insurance, I carried Rosie inside, and Anna held Delia. A bell above the transom jingled as we opened the door. The interior was awash with the finest goods I had seen since we had strolled down the *Champs Elysée* with Klaus Fischer months ago. On the left were fine highboys, sideboards, and carved mahogany chairs from England; on the right was an array of fine china, blue and white transferware, sparkling, cut-glass wine decanters, and fluted stemware, but the real treasure was the silver. Tea services, spoons shaped like shells with twisted handles, nutcrackers, footed egg cups, sugar bowls, cream ewers, inkwells, and so on. Light from the windows danced on the silver objects. This world was far from my dreams.

"Welcome, Mr. Klem, Mrs. Klem, I'm glad you accepted my invitation," Barnwell Wycliff said as he stepped from behind a draped curtain of an adjoining room. As he spoke, he polished a tarnished serving fork. I imagined he spent quite a lot of time on this chore.

As Anna and the children chattered about the beautiful display, Wycliff pulled me aside.

"Mr. Klem, you told me you were engaged as a tailor."

I nodded.

"And that you have recently come from Paris?"

I nodded again.

"Perhaps then you might be interested in making me an outer coat in the latest Parisian style. I'd be prepared to pay you dearly."

I sighed before answering. Yes, I was well aware of what the Parisian men wore, and I could easily sew another coat, but it seemed that it was impossible to leave that part of my life behind. I had no choice if this barter would buy the wagon and oxen we needed.

"Certainly, I will do it," I said, "and I know exactly what will suit you. Unfortunately, I have no fabric with me."

"That's not a problem, Klem. A cloth merchant in the next block has a wonderful selection."

"Mr. Wycliff, before sewing, I need to find accommodations for my family for the winter. I've been told to wait until the river freezes to cross it and when a good part of the foul weather is through."

"Sound thinking. It's a delicate balance. You do not want to leave in the dead of winter when you might freeze to death, but you must leave before the thaw or the silver frost. Some call it the hoar thaw."

I must have looked bewildered, and it was not only because Wycliff and I were talking in our second languages. He continued.

"If you don't leave before the thaw, you'll be ankle-deep in sucking mud. And it must be before freezing rain comes and everything refreezes. Quite beautiful but dangerous."

"And when will this happen?"

Wycliff shrugged his shoulders. "Who knows?"

The importer of fine goods was interested in something other than the weather.

"About my coat..." he continued as if I had not interrupted him.

I paced around him, appraising his body and touching his back, shoulders, waistline, and neck thickness.

"I can imagine a stunning coat. It shall be a full coat of dove-colored wool, with two inverted pleats in the back set off by silver buttons, a cutaway lapel, and, because of the cold, a sheared beaver collar. Calf-length breeches will show off your fine boots." When I finished, Wycliff seemed to salivate at the image of the garment I described.

"Let's go now to purchase the fabric," he insisted.

"First, tell me where my family and I might stay. I'll need good light to sew a splendid coat."

"Would you fancy a room above a tavern?"

Although I could manage that, I knew Anna would disapprove.

"Have you other ideas?"

"Klem, have no worries; I will install you in a place that you will find cozy. Let us make haste to the drapers to find suitable fabric."

A week later, I sat by the window in the back room of an abandoned chandler's shop, trying to entice as much light as possible through the rippled glass. I stabbed my needle between the warp and weft of the wool fabric Wycliff had selected. The coat was turning out well despite my reluctance. At least the coat on my lap kept me warm as I sewed in the uncomfortable lodging that Wycliff had found. The single room contained a sooty fireplace, the small window I sat beneath, and a drafty door. We stuffed rags and newspapers in the crevices to keep out the chill. Yet, it was a room all to ourselves. Anna swept and scoured it, determined to bring our accommodations to her cleanliness standards.

Our scarred wooden trunk became our bench. Bernard and I found an old door that we perched on two tree stumps for a table. Wycliff procured an old rope bed sorely needing new ropes and a turning. Anna placed a straw-filled pallet on the ropes, and on top of that, she put the bearskin from Pierre. She bargained for two cream-colored Hudson Bay blankets with cheerful red, green, yellow, and indigo stripes for us to snuggle under. We slept crosswise on the bed so all six of us could fit. My feet hung over the edge, so most nights I spent on the floor beside the lingering embers of the fire.

It was not only cold feet that kept me awake. I counted the

bells chiming from the belfry at Saint-Sulpice. At the two o'clock bell, I was in turmoil. *Will we have enough money, what about the weather, are the roads dangerous, will there be enough land?* To calm myself, I would imagine planting fields of cabbage with dill, potatoes with carrots, strawberries with onions, wheat, hops, rye, and so on.

As soon as I completed the coat for Wycliff, Mr. Cooper showed up with his newly purchased tall hat and a yen for a navy-colored coat. The color he described was Prussian blue. It was the color on the backs of the occupying Prussian soldiers on the streets of Kittersburg. Cooper's request was followed by one from his nephew, a barrister, ordering a black wool cut-away frock coat with long back tails and a velvet collar accompanied by a double-breasted, white silk waistcoat. I had become so busy tailoring that I needed Anna's help. She basted and sewed the inner linings as she'd done with Captain Burbank's coat. When Anna was not helping me, she served in the kitchen at *Château Ramezay,* an old house on Notre Dame Street that had once housed the French and then British governors. She returned home with the remains of a covered dish the resident's family had rejected, yet we devoured.

Chapter 43

Silent Night, Holy Night

Anna

Despite the bone-chilling cold, I was enjoying Montréal. Johann was inundated with clothing orders, and I had a chance to cook decent food for my family on an unshared fire. In the late afternoons, it was often possible for Johann to quiz Bernard and Katja in arithmetic. Bernard attempted to teach the rest of us English. This mean little room was becoming comfortable. Despite missing my mother and Magda, I felt almost settled. Although we were miles from our future farm, I tried daily to look forward rather than behind.

I'd also made the acquaintance of Mrs. Cooper, the wife of our stagecoach companion, the portly and pleasant Mr. Cooper, owner of the smashed hat. Although Cooper described his wife as loose with his money, I found her delightful. Denise

Cooper was much younger than her husband and had come from a large French family with deep roots in Montréal. Her deep-set brown eyes pooled with mischief. The saucy dimples on her cheeks emphasized her radiant smile. She confided in me that she could not conceive, so she was delighted to share her substantial Rue Notre-Dame home with the children and me. When we visited, she invented games for them as if she were their older sister. Denise was much more fun than I, the mother who constantly cautioned the children to be careful. On the days when I was required to serve at the *Chateau Ramezay,* Denise offered to care for them.

"Anna, let me take them; we will have fun." It was a great relief and freed Johann to continue his tailoring undisturbed.

Including Denise in our German traditions felt natural, even in this British/French enclave. She accompanied us as we hiked to Mount Royal to cut a small evergreen tree to lend Christmas cheer to our meager room. Denise insisted that she, too, would have a tree in her parlor to celebrate the season. We decorated our fir with small apples and nuts, and Katja placed a paper star on the top. We wired candles to the branches and lit them briefly to see their sparkle. When we added the evergreen boughs to the mantle, their fragrance filled the room with freshness and vigor.

On the sixth day of December, St. Nicholas Day, we surprised the children with simple gifts—hair ribbons for the girls, even one for Delia, who now had a fine tuft of curls on the crown of her head. For Bernard, we found a copy of The *English Reader* by Lindley Murray at a used book dealer in the market. We continued to prepare for Christmas while we watched the St. Lawrence transform daily with ice and snow. In Kittersburg, we had a foot of snow for the whole winter season, but in Montréal, the white fluff piled high despite the citizens' attempts to push it to the side of the streets.

Johann and I woke the children on Christmas Eve to attend midnight mass. Our breath strung out in volcanos of vapor in the frigid night as we carried candles and sang *Stille Nacht, Heilige Nacht,* Silent Night, Holy Night on our way to *Notre Dame* church for mass. The lovely church was lit with torches, and a small choir sang French carols. Priests from *San-Sulpice* processioned through the church carrying a wooden Christ child, which they placed in a *creche* at the foot of the altar. After the service, we returned to our room over the crunching snow and under a dark velvet dome with glistening stars and a smiling crescent moon.

The following morning, the children opened their gifts: apples and oranges for everyone, bonnets for the girls, and a wooden sword for Bernard. We drank cups of sweet, dark chocolate—a special treat—and munched the *stollen* I'd baked filled with raisins, candied citrus, and almonds. I'd made an extra loaf and gingerbread for the Coopers, who had invited us to their holiday celebration. We walked from our riverside room to the Coopers' elegant home ablaze with a Yule log. The holly branches and the small tree Denise had cut on our trip to Mount Royal decorated their parlor. Mr. Wycliff, Mr. Cooper's nephew, and others we did not know were there. All wore their most elegant attire. Our simple clothing embarrassed me, yet the Coopers made us feel welcome.

Venison, cold meat pies, and bowls of roasted vegetables covered the table. After eating our fill, Denise marched in with a large plum pudding centered on a scrolled silver tray. White *crème anglaise* dripped from the pudding's crown. Mr. Wycliff emerged from the parlor, cradling a violin. Although he was not as talented as our Irish sailor friend, he played a few familiar songs, and the children and some adults danced along. I understood none of the English songs, but given the howls from the adults, I assumed some were a bit bawdy.

After several tunes, Johann edged up to me.

"Anna, if I have one more glass of port, I must be carried home. I'd love to stay longer, yet Cooper's nephew has told me he expects his garments this week."

"Go, Johann. The children and I will soon follow."

This did not occur. Denise insisted that I stay even when other guests were departing. She had gifts for the children. Denise presented the younger girls with dolls in lace dresses with *papier mâché* heads. Bernard and Katja received wood and steel ice skates to be buckled onto their shoes. The children squealed with delight. I protested to Denise that she had done enough already.

"Nonsense, Anna. Their smiles are my medicine. I thank you for sharing your children with me. Tomorrow, I will hire a sleigh, and we will take the children to skate on a frozen pond. Please, tell me you will stay the night!"

"I could not hope to do that. Johann will think we have abandoned him."

"You go back and tell him, but please let the children spend the night. It would please me and Mr. Cooper so."

Reluctantly, I agreed. I would return to tell Johann. Katja assured me that Delia would sleep right next to her. Her hazel eyes told me she needed a night in a splendid house rather than our austere room.

Dusk was settling when I returned to the former chandler's storeroom. Johann was, as usual, sitting under the small window, a lit lantern by his side and Cooper's nephew's ivory waistcoat on his lap. Without saying anything, I approached him and removed the sewing from his crossed knees.

"Johann, it's Christmas. We must thank Jesus for coming and giving us this joyful day."

I took his hand, guided him to the door, and opened it.

From there, we could look across the nearly frozen St. Lawrence to the trees on the opposite bank. They wore an interwoven ribbon of silky white.

"What do you see, Johann?" I asked.

"An icebound river."

"And what is on the other side of the river?"

"Lots and lots of trees."

"And in what country do these trees grow?"

"America."

"Exactly. And do you remember what our bargain was all those months ago in Kittersburg?"

"Anna, must you remind me of my monastic life?" he teased.

"Well, if you can confirm that there are no more boats to ride and that we will soon be in the promised land, our bargain may become invalid." I rejoined.

His silver-blue eyes looked directly into mine.

"If only I can hope..."

"Not all hungers are satisfied by a big meal," I said.

He answered with his generous smile as I closed the door and crossed to our bed.

"Denise has kidnapped our children for the night. Only you and I need to keep each other warm."

"What, no cold feet or sleeping on the floor?"

"Not tonight. Merry Christmas."

Johann put another log on the fire. With great tenderness, he began to unlace the dirndl at my waist. My lips found his.

Later, with my head nestled on his chest, I felt restored. The constellations ruled the heavens; the sword found its sheath;

the breath returned to my lungs; the heart to its center. The song played without end.

Silent night, holy night.

Chapter 44

Preparation

Johann

Anna stood before me three days later as I hemmed Mr. Cooper's coat cuff.

"Johann, I have something important to tell you."

"What could be so important?" I said, puzzled by the anxious look on her face.

"I have sold Mama's candlesticks to Mr. Wycliff."

"What?" I croaked. I was stunned.

"*Ja*, I sold them to him." She reached under her apron into her pocket and pulled out a combination of pounds, shillings, and pence. A few shillings fell from her hand to the floor, rattling over the swept boards.

"Anna, whatever possessed you? You love those candlesticks. You said they were your link to home."

"You're right. I love my Mama's candlesticks. But I love my

children more. You want to leave here and cross that river while it's frozen. And no one knows when it will start to defrost. A clock is ticking in my head, too. We need a wagon, oxen, supplies, food, and everything else. I want to ensure our children always have food and a cover over their heads if needed. If we are in the wilderness, what good will fancy candlesticks do if we have no candles or food to put in the children's bellies."

Words failed me as I realized the enormity of her sacrifice. At the same time, I felt a profound shame that she thought it necessary. My pride was knocked a little off-kilter.

"Do you think that I can't provide for you, that I'm not doing enough?" I said when I found my voice.

"Yes, you do enough. You're awake before the rest of us to sew, and you are stitching when we are ready to blow the candles out. I want to do my part. I can do more than stir a stew, you know."

"*Liebling,* you have always done so much." I would have pulled her onto my lap if it was not already occupied by Cooper's coat filled with pins. Then, I thought, *Coat be damned!* I jumped to my feet and tossed the jacket on the bench. I drew her into the circle of my arms and rested my head on hers.

"Thank you for that gift," I said. "I hope Mr. Wycliff gave you a fair price at least."

"I told him he needed to give me a generous sum because he could never find such fine German craftsmanship in the wilds of Québec. And, if he imported such beautiful candlesticks from Britain, he would wait months and pay a tax."

"And what did he say?"

"He said I was right."

I spotted the candlesticks the next time I went into Wycliffe's shop. They were perched in the center of a rosewood gaming table with carved legs and brass inlays. I'd always admired that table when I stopped at his shop to deliver a garment. The silver candlesticks reflected on the highly polished surface. I felt a catch in my throat—how Anna loved us.

Wycliff would sell them to another Canadian who had roots in Britain, like himself, and had grown rich from the recent war with the United States; nevertheless, I could not be concerned with that. My only concern was crossing to American soil, getting out of others' houses, and stitching other peoples' wardrobes. My unselfish wife gave me that chance. I had to search everything possible about traveling south of the Canadian border. Unfortunately, this time, there was no *Herr* Remmelin to find maps for me or my brother George to build a sturdy wagon. I would need to discover it on my own.

Mr. Cooper and Mr. Wycliff were of little help. "We just fought a war with that country," they said. They didn't add that they had profited from that same war. Cooper connected me with a farmer who sold his wheat across the border. He told me where to cross to avoid officials looking for bribes or a reason for keeping the Klems out of America.

I found a cartwright who had a wagon for sale. After he agreed to make substantial repairs, we made a deal. He knew a cattleman willing to part with a team of oxen. They were raw-boned, but I was happy to see they had developed the long, coarse hairs of a winter coat. I would be sewing capes for Anna and Katja and small jackets for Rosie and Delia; I did not want to think of one more creature that needed protection from the cold.

I trained with the oxen for a week so they would be familiar with the touch of my ox prod and German-accented commands. They were used to an English-speaking team driver, and they needed to hear my voice commanding them to "Step up," "Gee," and "Haw."

Chapter 45

Letter to Grandmother

Katja

Liebe Oma,

I have not written in so long because my fingers have been frozen to the bone.

We left Montréal weeks ago, and there has hardly been a moment when I haven't been cold. Papa bought a wagon and two more oxen. (Rosie named them Little Turtle and Liam. At least they have boys' names this time.) Everyone said that we had to leave while the river was frozen and before it got too muddy. We crossed the big river. It was very hard because all the waves had frozen, and the oxen could hardly pull us over. Some men were fishing in holes they cut in the ice.

This wagon is smaller than the one Onkel Georg made for us, but we all manage to squeeze in with the barrels of food and our trunk. We only have one trunk now. It doesn't matter because we wear all our clothes to stay warm. People told us to bring lots of food because we would not see many towns or forts to buy it. We brought fresh water, too, but it froze. Mama put a bearskin and blankets in the bottom of the wagon in case we needed to sleep in it at night. Bernard and me and the little girls ride in the wagon while Mama and Papa walk in snowshoes. Sometimes, Papa has to go first and stomp on the snow with his snowshoes so the oxen are not up to their knees in the snow. You don't know anything about snowshoes, so I will draw a picture at the bottom of this letter. Papa said maybe he should have bought a sleigh instead of a wagon, but what would we do when the snow melts? Sometimes I walk too, but someone needs to be in the wagon to mind Delia. Mama says Delia is the slowest of her children to walk because she never has a floor under her that's not moving.

We crossed some mountains, which was awful. We don't see many people, but sometimes we see Indians who look at us and say nothing. Once, an

Indian man gave us a rabbit he shot with an
arrow. He had a bunch of them tied by their legs
to his belt. We saw a whole encampment of
Indians sitting by a half-frozen waterfall. They
built a fire and let us warm ourselves. Papa
traded turnips for their corn seeds.

If we cannot find an inn, or barn at night,
we all sleep crunched together in the wagon and
keep each other warm. We put a covering on the
wagon when it snows. Mama is nervous when we
stay at a Gasthaus because she thinks we will get
bugs in our hair. Sometimes, she brings our blankets into the hotel. We stayed in a town named
Ogdensburg. They call them towns here, but they
have fewer houses than Kittersburg, and most
houses are made from logs. A few are made of
brick, but none are as nice as the houses in
Montréal or Québec.

Once, we stayed in Watertown—I thought it was
funny because it wasn't too much of a town, and
there is water everywhere here in America, not just
in that place. Rivers and streams and waterfalls,
you can't get away from all the water. We were
there for a few days because there was a big
snowstorm. Mama wouldn't want you to know that
we all got sick. Even though I felt sick, I was
happy to be out of the wagon. After Mama's
tonics, we felt better. And we thawed out. We see

many deer but no bears because they sleep all winter—I am happy about that. Once, we saw a red fox with a very bushy tail. Papa whistled loudly to scare the fox away because it made the oxen jumpy. Rosie wanted to run after it.

Now, we are close to a big lake called Ontario. Papa said we must go south of this lake to buy our land. The lake looks as big as an ocean, but at least we are not in another boat.

When we get to where we are going, I never want to travel ever again unless I am coming back to Baden to see you. I have to end this letter because Papa says," Paper costs money." Mama says, "Leave her be." Papa is always worried about money.

I am sick of seeing trees.

I miss you so much.

Your best granddaughter,

Katja

P.S. Mama sold your candlesticks. I was mad, but Papa said you wouldn't mind if it made our life better. I don't think it has. Bernard wanted to sell his gold watch too, but Mama wouldn't let him.

P.P.S. I pray for you every night. I hope you pray for me.

Chapter 46

Canandaigua

Anna

After a month on the road, we were closer to our goal, the fertile Genesee Valley. The soulless, miserable journey confounded us with icy stops and starts. Although I sold Mama's gift to keep us moving, I questioned why we left the comfort of the cozy chandler's room and the friendliness of Denise Cooper in her elegant house to mash ourselves together in the slow, lumbering wagon. No one was happy. Tears fell with the snow. Despite the icicles on his beard, Johann chose to look ahead, soldier on, and keep up our spirits. Sometimes, I met his encouraging words and attempts at cheery songs with a stony glare. I tried to keep the needles out of my voice. I knew it was better to see him happy while we walked than to glimpse his eyes narrowed with worry and concern. I dreaded hearing him jangle the thimbles in his pocket. Even he was relieved when we spent an evening at an inn with a blazing fire and a bowl of meaty broth before us. While we sipped our supper, Liam and Little Turtle were tucked in a barn with a trough full of hay. Like us, their hooves needed rest from the narrow path and the relentless, rimed landscape.

In the past week, we traded the daily snowflakes for a scrim of rain. No evergreens wore snowy white dresses anymore. Instead, a scud of clouds brought an onslaught of spring showers. I could not decide which was worse: the slippery path of ice and snow or the muddy road that sucked at our feet.

When we finally reached Oswego at the mouth of a river by the same name, we had exhausted our food and were footsore and despairing. A crumbling stone fort was before us, perched on a high bluff. The American flag snapped on a pole tall above the fortress, its ropes twisted in the wind off the lake. We stopped at the sentry box to ask for directions. To our great luck, one of the soldiers spoke enough German to point us to the village road where we could find shelter.

Bernard, always fascinated by a man wearing a uniform, looked up and saluted. The skinny soldier wore a tattered uniform with elbows jutting out of the crook of his wool sleeve. I hoped that Johann would not volunteer once more to mend the jacket.

"Private Wilhelm Piper of Herkimer, New York, Third U.S. Regiment, Artillery," he introduced himself. His Adam's apple bounced up and down as he spoke.

"How is it you speak German?" Johann asked.

"Great-grandparents settled in the Mohawk Valley a hundred years ago. I don't speak it good, but most farmers and merchants in Herkimer speak some German. People around here only speak English. Probably, it's the same at the tavern in town as well. Never stayed there, but it's a good place to get me away from these stone walls and that miserable weather off the lake."

Once again, I hated hearing that English would be our only option.

Private Piper interrupted my thought when he offered to take us to the inn when his watch was over.

In an hour, we reached the hotel in Oswego. Johann settled the oxen in the stable, and we left our damp outer garments in the second-floor room at the top of the rickety staircase. We sat in a keeping room before the usual roaring fire, eating a mutton stew and drinking pints of an inferior ale. Private Piper, who insisted we call him Will, regaled us with stories of the Battle of Oswego, which occurred less than two years before.

"Yup, the British troops landed in deep water and ruined all their ammunition," he said, "but that didn't stop them. Major Mitchell, our commander, had us pitch tents in front of the village and marched us back and forth to make it look like there were more of us soldiers than there were. Their ammo was dead, yet the Brits came at us with fixed bayonets. We fought them off as long as we could. We skedaddled out the back of the fort when we knew our goose was cooked. They took us that day—all our supplies, cannon, and even a schooner. But in the end, look who won the war? You won't see the King's flag flying in these parts."

Bernard was as taken with Private Piper's soldiering stories as with Klaus Fischer's. I prayed that my son would be a farmer and not at the target end of anyone's gun. We spent the next few hours talking about life in this rustic area where houses were few and wolves roamed at night.

Johann produced the folded, raggedy handbill from the Holland Land Company he'd been carrying for years. It announced that he needed to inquire about the land from Mr. Oliver Phelps of Canandaigua.

Will scratched his scruffy beard as he considered the notice.

"Canandaigua, huh? Heard of it, but I've never been there. My family's all scattered about Herkimer, which is considerably east of here. You'll need to follow the path south along the Oswego River 'til you get to the Genesee Road. They tell me it's a turnpike now, so you may be paying tolls. The road is an old Indian path worn deep from thousands of Iroquois feet tramping it down for hundreds of years. Most roads here were their trails first. You'll probably be sharing the road with animals and lots of New Englanders who are moving west for the frontier land just like you. I'd judge that not any of them speak German."

He stopped to take a deep draft of his ale. I watched, fascinated, as the knob in his neck appeared and disappeared with his swallow.

"Pity that you're here right now—though I am glad to have met you—but if you waited five years, a canal would take you to your destination. It's all the talk. Albany to Lake Erie. That will be something all right. You'll be taking the path General Sullivan's men walked back in 1779 during the revolution. Burned up all the Indian villages that weren't on the American side of things. He..."

Before he could start another war story, I interrupted him. Except for my silent father, I was convinced that every German-speaking man I met thought the stage was his alone.

"Will, I'm sorry to barge in on your history lesson. Nevertheless, I would be pleased if you could point us to a Catholic

church. We haven't been to a mass since we left Montréal a
month ago."

"Well now, Mrs. Klem, sorry I can't help much with that.
Not a church man myself, and most of the folks around here
would tell you they're God-fearing yet not church-going
because there're so few meeting rooms about."

My face must have fallen because he started to reassure me.

"I bet there's a Catholic church in Albany. *Ja*, I'm sure
that's the case. Must be a priest and bells and all that there. But
so far in these woods, I doubt it. Most folks going west to where
you're headed are Massachusetts or Connecticut men. Probably Congregationalists, if anything. They wore out their soil,
so they're moving to cheap frontier land. If I were a betting
man, I'd put a coin on it that, when they're settled, some of
those men will plant little white chapels along with their wheat
and corn. But believing in the man in Rome, I would doubt."

"And tell me, Will, how far is this Albany that is sure to
have a church."

"Southeast from here. If the roads are passable, 175 miles
or so. Opposite direction from where you're headed."

I felt something inside me somersault and collide with the
ground. Underneath my cloak, my hands gripped Mother
Joséphine's gift, the left-behind silver cross.

"Thank you, Will."

I scowled at Johann, who had been silent throughout this
conversation. Even though it was not Johann's fault there was
no Catholic Church, I barely said a word to him for the rest of
the night. Will nattered about Herkimer and generals and snow
as deep as a cow's eye. I watched Will's bobbing Adam's apple,
but my ears had stopped listening.

As I fell asleep that night, I clutched the shawl my mama
had wrapped around her candle sticks close to my chest. It
caught my tears.

The sun peaked a pearly pink over the horizon early the following day. With a promise of dry skies, we rested the oxbow on Liam and Little Turtle's shoulders, hitched the wagon, and set off along the rutted road that followed the wide river path leading us to the Genesee Road. Although the weather was warmer than in the mountains, ice floes clogged parts of the river. Each turn of the wagon's wheels brought us closer to our destination—a destination without a church or a mass. I thanked God that we were well and that the journey was pulling to a close. I vowed to be a better wife.

Will was right. The Great Genesee Road, called the Seneca Road by some travelers, carried more traffic. Teams of six horses pulled covered wagons, and drovers moved cattle or sheep. Mail stages passed, as well as tin peddlers and emigrants like us. In the swampy parts, men lay logs horizontally across the road. The corduroyed road was bumpy but saved the cart from being pulled in by the greedy mud. If someone's wheels got stuck, another traveler usually lent a shoulder to heave it out.

And there were tolls. Johann had exchanged British pounds in the inn in Oswego, but he was uncertain of the American money's value. He watched what other travelers were giving. Sometimes, he was right, and sometimes, there was an extra charge for something we did not understand. Every country we trekked through had its bewildering currency.

The small taverns in the towns consisted of a center

entrance with a small hallway and a steep staircase to the rooms above. A kitchen and keeping room sat on the right side, and a parlor on the left. We avoided the parlors because the drovers and teamsters settled themselves for cards and rum in the evenings. Up the staircase, a guest room lay on each side of the landing. I was wary of these spaces and rubbed the children with the clove oil I found in an apothecary in Montréal to keep the bugs away. I had washed our linens with vinegar and lavender and hung them in the sun to dry before we left Montréal. Now, a month in, I doubted their cleanliness. Instead of the canvas top, I strung the linen sheets over the wagon's hoops when the sun shone.

Although most of the road was deeply forested on either side, we saw the land where the trees had been cut, the brush burned, and the stumps yanked. A farmer with reins tied over his shoulder followed behind two well-muscled draft horses clearing a field. They left behind furrows of freshly turned earth. Johann halted the oxen. I watched as he waved to the farmer, walked over to a small berm, and grabbed a chunk of the sweet-smelling soil.

He brought the dirt to where I stood near Little Turtle's shoulder.

A smile spread across his face, beginning at his eyes and extending over both cheeks. A whoop erupted from his mouth. He was enveloped in joy and vindication.

"Anna, this is it. This is thousands of years of the earth folding in and covering itself with dead leaves, worms, and everything that makes it rich, dark, and ready to grow." He threw it in the air like a child with a pile of leaves.

"This is why we have traveled all this way—for this beautiful fertile ground. It will be ours."

He threw his arms around me and lifted me from the ground. He twirled me around so quickly that a shoe flew from my foot. He pressed his lips to mine and gave me such a long kiss that the farmer in the field applauded. Bernard and Katja covered their eyes. He placed me back on the ground and laughed aloud. Johann was a happy man who had clutched his dream and found it even bigger than he imagined. His holy grail had gloriously spilled through his fingers, saturating him to the bones.

He circled to Liam's side, picked up his goad stick, and yelled, "Haw." The oxen pair picked up their pace as if they caught his enthusiasm.

In the late morning of that day, we saw a wooden sign nailed to a tree with a pointing arrow: CANANDAIGUA - 2 miles.

Johann glanced at me with the same contagious smile.

"We are almost there, *Liebling!*"

In an hour, we rolled into a small town at the edge of a long, narrow lake surrounded by sloping, tree-covered hills. The deep green water shimmered under the afternoon sun. Several one-masted boats caught the wind mid-lake. The chunky clouds reflected in the smooth water looked like someone had crumpled white silk and tossed it into the sky above. In the town's center was a village green with a stone fountain. The children jumped from the wagon and rushed to a pebbly beach near a wooden pier without asking. Delia giggled and joyfully shrieked as Katja ran, bouncing the laughing baby on her hip. Knowing the children would be safe under Katja's watch, I pulled the pail from the wagon and headed to the fountain to get water for Liam and Little Turtle: a reward for their swift walk.

Across from the green was a series of stores. The center

building had gold leaf words painted on a nailed-on sign: Hawley's Dry Goods and Supplies.

Johann smiled and dug the Holland Land Company circular from deep in his waistcoat pocket, where he kept it folded and wrapped in waxed cloth. He called Bernard, who was skipping stones with his sisters by the lake.

"Bernard, *komm bitte hir.*"

At his father's call, Bernard came running.

"You and your mother and I are going into that store to see if we can find Mr. Oliver Phelps to buy our land."

"Yes, Papa," Bernard replied. I thought it was too much to place on the shoulders of a seven-year-old, but I was no help with English. Every day, I felt I knew more, yet still, I was content to listen and hesitant to speak.

We walked into the store crowded with barrels, their staves held together by steel rings. A canopy of metal oil lamps hung from hooks nailed to the ceiling. In the corner were stacked shovels, axes, hatchets, saws—everything needed to change this wilderness into towns and farms. Tables held stacks of homespun fabric and every size knife imaginable. In the center was a cast iron stove, and behind that, at a large desk – its cubby holes stuffed with papers and envelopes – sat a full-bearded man on a ladder-back chair. His mouth twitched as if it was deciding to smile or frown at us.

"How can I help you?" he said. His voice was as gravelly as parts of the road we'd walked.

"We want...find...Mister Oliver Phelps," Johann said, trying his best to say the words clearly, pronouncing the w's and v's in the right places as Bernard instructed. A fine film of sweat covered his upper lip.

"Oliver Phelps?" The storekeeper repeated.

"*Ja,*" said Johann until Bernard poked his back.

"Yes," he corrected.

"Can't," the storekeeper said.

"Can't?"

"Nope, can't see him."

Johann looked puzzled. Bernard squeezed his father's hand until Johann stooped to his son's mouth. "*Kann Nicht*," Bernard whispered. Father and son quickly conferred.

"Why...we cannot see...Mr. Phelps?" Johann said slowly and carefully.

"Dead."

"Dead?"

"*Er ist tot, Papa.*" Bernard translated.

Johann, perplexed, pulled out the flyer he had shown Private Will Piper days before.

The merchant carried the handbill to the chaos on the desk, cleared a spot, and smoothed out the wrinkles. He placed small eyeglasses on the bridge of his nose. The glasses made his red-veined eyes look immense. He looked at the paper as he shook his head.

"This handbill's old. Phelps died several years back. His house still stands on the other side of the square." He gestured through the window to a two-story, white-washed house on the far side of the green. "Yup, Phelps was a good man. Built a grist mill here and a school, even made friends with the Seneca *sachem*, but good men die, too."

I knew Johann did not understand all that the merchant had said. The man removed his glasses and repeated his words louder as if that would help. Johann and Bernard whispered again. Johann nodded at our son.

"I want land," Johann said, looking into the bearded man's face. Johann's face was clouded with anxiety. I read the anguish in his eyes.

"Well, Mister, there may be land around here, but the farther west you go, the cheaper it will be. May I suggest you go to a place called Rochesterville. They're hungry for new settlers. I hear they have the town divided into 100 quarter-acre plots. It's about 29 or 30 miles from here."

"How I go to Rochesterville?" asked Johann haltingly, as he attempted to speak in English.

"Keep going the way you were headed. With oxen, you can make it in two days, maybe three. When you get there, ask for Colonel Nathaniel Rochester. Unlike Phelps, he's very much alive." The storekeeper picked up one of the crumpled envelopes and wrote down a name with the stub of a pencil. He handed it to Johann, who traced the letters with his finger.

"With all the talk of the canal and such, Rochesterville might be a good place for a homestead. Fertile land, the river's right there, and, of course, the lake's there too. You'll have to cut down trees, burn stumps, and so forth..." I was sure he would keep talking, but Johann had turned toward the door.

"*Danke schön, danke schön,*" Johann murmured. He stopped and corrected himself, "Thank you."

We followed him out the door until the merchant called Bernard, "Hey, little fella." Bernard stopped, and the merchant dropped a scoop of dried apples into Bernard's open hand from a barrel near the cluttered desk.

Johann walked to the lovely lake without looking back at us. I kept the children near me, sensing Johann needed time alone. He pulled his hat from his head and flung it, only missing the lapping water by inches. Pacing back and forth along the shore, Johann muttered to himself. After what felt long but was probably only ten minutes, Johann picked up his hat, slapped it on his pant leg, and put it back on his head. He turned slowly and walked back to us.

We all gathered around him in the grassy square; the children lined up next to each other on the bench near the fountain. Johann's face, joyous only hours ago, gleaming in the delight of the farmer's freshly plowed field, was dark and troubled. I reach my hand out to touch his cheek. His eyes avoided mine. He wiped his nose on his cuff. It was something that Johann, always careful with his clothing, rarely did.

When he tried to speak, his voice cracked. Clearing his throat, he tried again. This time, his voice was as husky as the shopkeeper's.

"Anna, children, I'm sorry. I have asked so much from you. You have been my brave soldiers, always putting up with your papa's crazy plans. We all know we have come too far to give up. We need to go on. We need to find a home that will have us."

"Papa, how much farther do we have to go?" Katja asked, her voice beginning to quiver.

"Two days, perhaps, three."

When she heard his words, Katja's face screwed up, and her sobs began. The tears cleared a path down through the dust on her face. Though this improbable journey had lasted almost a year, it felt like two more days might break us. Rosie's tears followed her big sister's. Putting my arms around them, I hugged them tightly. Even Bernard could not eat his dried apples; he let them dribble to the ground. Delia clutched at my knee, begging to be held.

The tears running down my cheeks were for my poor children and bereft husband. I think we all had cried more in the past year than we had done in all the years put together before leaving Kitterssburg. I felt so bad for Johann who had carried the name Canandaigua in his pocket for years. Oliver Phelps had become his religion. This strange name was always on the tip of his tongue. Oliver Phelps had died and was not resurrected. Redemption eluded us. How much more did we need to endure? Had God played one more trick?

I felt the hard edges of Mother Josephine's cross press into my chest. I knew she and people everywhere prayed for us. We could not give up. With Little Turtle and Liam's help, we would follow the birds until we built our nest.

Chapter 47

Relentless

Johann

I replaced the name of Oliver Phelps in my mind with Rochesterville. I practiced saying it repeatedly, trying to remember precisely how the shopkeeper had said it. I needed to pronounce the last part, the *ville*, in an English way, not in two syllables as in German or drawn out as in French. "Phelps" had been much easier to say.

After we left Canandaigua, I could hardly speak to Anna or the children. I felt shame and determination—they deserved much better than my mistakes. The only direction I knew was the dirt road in front of me. I was unrelenting with Liam and Little Turtle, but the good beasts sensed my urgency. They pushed into their yoke as hard as they could.

Fortunately, the road was relatively flat, the hills rolling, unlike the steep slopes of the Adirondacks on the far side of the frozen St. Lawrence. And the weather was fair. The late spring sky burst with silvery light, a ceiling of perfect blue. I had once lined a waistcoat for Holbauer in expensive silk of the same shade. I would not let thoughts of him weaken my resolve.

Despite my mood, I was not blind to the jumble of wild-flowers—violet, pale pink, and white—that bobbed and danced on the sides of the road. The children grabbed handfuls and deposited them into Anna's apron pockets. We came across a few log houses and cleared fields, but dense forest stood on either side for the most part. If we were still on the *Stalwart,* the learned *Professeur,* undoubtedly, would have found a book to describe how glaciers or rivers had scoured out the terrain of this land. I was not interested in how it came about but only in pushing forward until some of this beautiful valley could be ours.

Determined, resolved, stubborn, dogged, unshakeable. I felt all this as I guided the creaking wagon and lumbering beasts. My jaw ached from clenching it so tightly. My calculations told me we could finish the final leg to Rochesterville in two days. I could coax the oxen to six more miles today, giving them an extra hay bale and more grazing time when the sun melted crimson through the trees.

That night, we made it as far as Avon, a fetching little town on the banks of the broad, slow-moving Genesee. Several plank houses roosted on its banks around a main street. This was the river that, according to Will Piper, had given this valley its dark, loamy soil. A newly constructed wooden bridge crossed the river in the middle of the town. At the foot of the bridge was a tavern run by an elderly woman with sausage curls protruding from her linen mob hat. We stayed the night at her well-scrubbed inn. When the owner, Mrs. Berry, realized we spoke little English, she drew a picture of the rope ferry she and her husband ran there before the bridge was built.

A gracious light broke through the shutters the following

morning. I awakened Anna and the children. With Mrs. Berry's hearty bread and strong tea in our bellies, we were ready for another day on the road. Before we left, I dug into my pocket and pulled out the envelope with Mr. Rochester's penciled name. She pointed the direction over the bridge, through the rest of the peaceful town. We would be following the river north as it made its way towards its mouth in the lake called Ontario.

The weather continued fresh and spring warm. Liam and Little Turtle stepped up as I touched their shoulders with my stick. The rest of the family walked or rode in the wagon. There was no inn by nightfall, and we pulled the wagon into a wooded clearing. We all fell into an exhausted sleep. I awoke once at night to hear tiny animal feet scrambling underneath the wagon.

The following day was a repeat of the last: few stops and me encouraging the oxen to step it up. Once, we were approached from behind by a woman on horseback with a leather pouch on either side of her horse's saddle. As she moved past us, I motioned for her to stop. I pointed to the name on my paper and asked her in my miserable English, "Where is?"

She counted out eight on her fingers. She patted the sacks on her mare's back.

"Mail," she said before she kicked her mare back to a trot.

Eight miles. We could do it by evening.

If light is in your heart, you will find your way home.

— Rumi

Chapter 48

Rochesterville

Anna

The sun was setting when we heard the roar of the falls. Before we heard the noise, we encountered recent clearings and scattered houses on each side of the Genesee River's path. Once the sun set, it would be impossible to go further. Johann commanded the oxen to "stand." Liam and Little Turtle must have been as relieved as the rest of us when the creaking wheels stopped their spin. A mill dam and a rough but sturdy-looking sawmill were on our left. The resiny odor of freshly sawed planks scented the air. Piled-up tree trunks waiting to be milled sat beside it. A newly built frame house sat across from us in a clearing. A bridge, higher than the one in Avon, crossed the river. Several buildings with steeply pitched roofs lined up in a row on the far side of the river, none higher than one story. Light filtered through small windows. I saw no church spires among the buildings. We could not distinguish if one of the structures were a tavern or an inn. We felt reluctant to knock on doors in the dusk.

The noise from the river pulled us closer. Leaving the wagon in the gap between the mill and the foot of the bridge, we followed our ears. In the last rays of light, we saw luminous spray leaping from an enormous broad waterfall. From the safety of a rock ledge, we peered at the white water cascading down to a carved-out gorge. Johann thought the gushing falls must be a hundred feet high and perhaps even wider. The rushing river hit the rocks so hard that the spray leaped up, half the height of the falls. I imagined a beautiful rainbow would emerge in the morning when sunlight danced on the droplets. Rosie put her hands over her ears to block out the fall's thunder. Delia, my always happy baby, was delighted. She waved her hands and tried to touch the rising spray. Before the daylight was completely gone, we returned to the wagon.

As the children ran ahead, I caught Johann's elbow.

"We are here."

"Yes," he said. "We are finally, *finally* here." He placed his arm around my shoulder and pulled me to him.

"What do we do now?"

"I'm not sure," he said, looking around. "We can't find Colonel Rochester in the dark."

We decided to spend one more night sleeping in the confines of our cart. Our steadfast animals and our faith had brought us hundreds of miles. We ate a quick meal of bread and sausage before falling asleep, exhausted, but comforted by the wagon's embrace. As I fell asleep, I heard the soft, deep sound of an owl and a wolf's mournful howl.

Early the next morning, a loud knocking on the wagon's side woke us. Bernard pulled aside the canvas curtain at the front of the wagon. A crowd of people surrounded the wheels.

A man stepped forward. From the practical cut of his clothing, I presumed that he was a working man. Taking off his leather hat and tucking it under his armpit, he looked directly at Johann when he spoke.

"Good morning, sir. I'd be Enos Stone, and that mill there, near where you hobbled those oxen, belongs to me." He pointed to the mill on the river we'd seen the night before. "And that log house across the way is mine, too."

Bernard told us as much as he could of Mr. Stone's statement.

Johann cleared his throat. "I am John Klem. This is *mein* family," Johann said. We descended, one by one, from the wagon's high sides to the ground.

Mr. Stone scratched his chin, puzzling out Johann's spotty English. "Looks like we might need some help here."

With an embarrassed look, Johann pointed to himself and said, "I speak *Deutch*,"

As in other encounters we'd had, Enos Stone said, "Dutch?"

Someone in the back of the crowd yelled, "That's German. He speaks German. So does Jacob Hau, the baker."

A woman's voice joined in. "The Colonel's wife, she speaks German."

Enos Stone, the apparent leader of the citizens, said, "Someone, go tell Colonel Rochester that we have visitors. And kindly tell Mrs. Rochester that she is needed. And get Hau, as well."

A man in the back holding the reins of a sway-backed mare shouted, "I'm on my way." He and his horse clattered over the wooden bridge.

The men checked out the wagon's axles and commented about the horns on the oxen. The few women in the group came close, clucking over the children, especially Delia, who snuggled in my arms. Within ten minutes, an aristocratic-looking couple strode over the bridge. The man, at least sixty, was tall, maybe six feet, with a slight stoop. In his left hand was a silver-topped cane. White hair was visible under a beaver hat. Tiny gold wire spectacles sat on the bridge of an aquiline nose. His handsome wife, considerably younger, had dark curls tumbling from the back of a lace-trimmed bonnet. Her eyes were blue and kind.

The Colonel walked up to Johann and extended a gloved hand. His wife spoke first.

"*Willkommen,* I am Sophia Beatty Rochester, and this is my husband, Colonel Rochester," she told us in German. She quickly explained that although she was born in Maryland, her parents had emigrated from Mainz on the Rhine. German was her first language. Johann squeezed my hand at our good luck.

Johann told her we also were from a *Stadt* on the Rhine. We had traveled far to buy land for farming and to settle in Rochesterville. When she repeated this to her husband, the eminent gentleman shook Johann's hand again and patted the children's heads.

By now, Mr. Hau, the baker, had arrived on the back of a flopped-eared mule.

Mr. and Mrs. Rochester, Mr. Hau, and Johann engaged in a four-way conversation.

Did we need land in town? No, we needed space for fields.

Did we need the power of the river and falls? No.

Did we need access to a creek? Yes.

The Colonel, who started his career as a surveyor, said he knew a likely spot for a wheat farm. We did not need land in town among his 100-acre tract. We needed flat land outside of the village to raise crops. He hastily called to some men milling about to bring two horse-drawn gigs to take us to prospective land.

While we waited, we walked to the middle of the new bridge. The stone bridge we had crossed from Baden to Strasbourg a year ago was built by the Romans centuries earlier; this wooden structure could not be more than a few years old. On either side of the river were budding trees, which I later learned were dogwood, birch, and choke-cherry. Looking north between the bridge's wooden trusses, we spied a swampy area where a doe and her fawn paused at a deer lick. As they drank from a spring, the white flag of their tails twitched back and forth, delighting Rosie and Delia. We were told that beyond the great falls we had seen the previous night, two more cascades interrupted the Genesee before it reached its mouth in Lake Ontario.

Mr. Hau and the Colonel pointed out the people and buildings past the river. On the east side of the river, Issac Stone's tavern was not far from where we had parked the wagon—if only we had known the night before. On the west side of the river lay Silas Smith's store, the physician, Orin Gibbs' house, the millwright, David Cartter's house, the saddle maker, Abelard Reynold's house and shop, Hervey and Elisha Ely's store, Hamlet Scrantom's new house, the cabin belonging to brick maker, Abram Stark, the tailor, Jahial Barnard's shop, John Mastick's law office, Ira West's store, the lime kiln, the ruins of old Allen's mill, Aaron Skinner, the school teacher's, house, and the schoolhouse. Beyond the clearings for the homes and shops, dense forest continued.

When Katja heard that there was a schoolhouse, she bravely asked Mrs. Rochester, "May I go to that school?"

The stately woman smiled at Katja's eager question, "Certainly, dear. Mr. Skinner would love to have an eager new student."

Katja beamed. Since we were at the Ursuline Academy, she told me how she wanted to return to school.

By now, the gigs with fresh horses were brought. When I looked toward the children, a woman with a sun-worn face came forward. After a few words from the colonel's wife, I was confident the children would be well cared for in our absence.

Mrs. Rochester and I climbed into the small carriage with a dappled gray horse; Johann and the Colonel were in the other. Mr. Hau rode beside them on his mule. We made our way on another narrow road surrounded by deep woods.

While Mrs. Rochester drove the gig, she recounted the trip she and her husband and six of their ten children, ages four to twenty-one, took from Hagerstown, Maryland, five years earlier. Two family carriages and three Conestoga wagons accompanied them.

"My husband was a prominent man in Maryland, a state legislator, in fact," she said. "He also had interests in grist mills, banks, and rope factories, but like your husband, he was drawn to the frontier. Leaving my civilized life in Hagerstown was hard, yet I have learned to love this land. It won't be easy, my dear. I must confess that the winters are long but beautiful. The summers bring fevers and agues. And there are snakes and wolves. Yet, we both know life is much easier when our husbands are happy."

How well I knew what Mrs. Rochester said was true. I would try to forget about the winters and wolves.

After a two-mile drive east of the infant town, we arrived at the property the Colonel had suggested. Johann leaped from the gig and stood beneath a cathedral of colossal ancient trees. Tangled grape vines and ivy interlaced the tree canopies. The land was flat, and if there were swampy patches, we did not see them in the underbrush. To the right, a creek flowed, convenient enough to water crops if rain failed. Johann grabbed a broken limb and scratched the earth near a fallen log. As the previous day, he grabbed a hunk of soil and crumbled it between his fingers. Joy beamed from his face. Johann had found his treasure. I walked to his side and lay my head on his shoulder. I intertwined my fingers in his dirt and all.

"*Liebchen,* clearing this land will be tremendous work. We will need to sacrifice these magnificent trees. We will need to chop and burn all these brambles and undergrowth. We will need to build our own house. Are you with me? Can I possibly ask more of you?"

I did not need to consider this. I nodded. A smile spread wide across his face. In the reflection of his eye, I could imagine fields bursting with grain and orchards drooping with fruit. He bent his head near my ear. "How I love you, Anna Maria Klem," he whispered.

When I squeezed his hand, Johann looked across the creek at the Rochesters, who stood near the bay horse.

"Colonel, we want this land," Johann said as he pulled the leather money pouch from his inner pocket. Mr. Hau began to translate, but no interpretation was needed for two men who revered the land.

"All in due time, all in due time, my man. The land will be yours. We can discuss the terms and a mortgage if that's what you need with Enos Stone, my land agent." When Jacob Hau finished his translation, Johann's sigh released decades of dreaming, planning, storms, fevers, frozen feet, mud, and unintelligible words.

"Nathaniel, I suggest we all go to Mr. Stone's tavern to celebrate the Klems' arrival and the prospect of their new farm," said Mrs. Rochester, clutching her husband's sleeve.

"Absolutely, my dear," Mr Rochester replied as he helped her into the gig.

The reins snapped on the horses' backs, and they turned back toward the developing village. The Rochesters rode in the first gig this time, and Johann and I followed in the second. I lay my hand on his knee.

"We have done it, *Shatzi*, we have done it," he said.

I was silent as I watched a small brown bird land on the horse's harness. In her beak was a snippet of dried grass. We, too, would build a nest. We had found our home.

Chapter 49

Letter to Grandmother

Katja

Dear Grandmother,

We are in Rochesterville. Mama and Papa bought the land. Papa is so happy, and he doesn't have to pay all the money at once. The colonel said he trusts that Papa will pay him. We are staying in the log house of Mr. Hau, a baker. His bread is as good as Mama's.

Papa and some men are cutting down the trees on the land. Liam and Little Turtle will bring them to the mill. Mama does not want a log home but says even a house made of logs is better than sleeping in a wagon. The houses here are very different from the houses in Kittersburg. Everything is different.

There is a waterfall bigger than you can ever imagine. Papa wanted to throw all his silver thimbles over the waterfall, but Mama wouldn't let him. Instead, he gave one to each of us and said, "Use them to sew only your own clothes!"

There is a school, and I will be allowed to go even though I am twelve and a girl. That makes me so happy.

Delia is finally walking. Mama says, "That little girl never slows down." Bernard is annoying, but he is helping me with English. Only two people in Rochesterville speak German, so we must all learn the new language. I understand a lot, yet I still feel too shy to say it to anyone but Rosie.

Mama is sometimes sad because there is no church here. She says we must go to Albany for mass at Easter. I don't know where that is, but I never want to walk anywhere far again.

I continue to miss you every day. You can write to me because there is mail delivery. I don't know if you ever got my other letters, but now we have a real place, we are not going anywhere else.

Love,

Katja

P.S. Mama no longer calls Papa, Johann. She only calls him John.

Epilogue

Bernard
1879

"Dad, it's time. You need to write some of your stories down before you can't," my oldest son admonished me after my last short illness. He was right. If my days here on the Lord's blessed earth are numbered, I need to record as much as possible so my many children and their children will know their past. I sat at my oak desk with my dip pen, inkwell, and a stack of paper before me and began to sort through a lifetime of memories. I began, "I, Bernard Walter Klem, born in Kittersburg, in the Duchy of Baden in 1809..."

Most of my memories are American memories. I recall only snippets of my life in the Rhineland. I know there was a teacher who was kind to me, and Katja always talked about our grandmothers. Although it happened over sixty years ago when I was just a lad, I recollect bits of our long journey. I know there were storms, big boats, English lessons. Papa told me how he almost died and how Mama would not give up on him. I can feel the delight of skating on a frozen lake somewhere. I remember my belly never being full. On the night we arrived at the great Genesee Falls, we rejoiced because we knew the long journey was finally over. We slept in the wagon under the stars, and the next day, there was a crowd of people around us. That was a story that Papa loved to tell when we gathered at Christmas and sat by the fire, shelling walnuts.

Papa told me he hired men to help fell trees and build a log house. He was late planting a crop, but it would come to no avail. In 1816, there was hardly a summer. It was rainy, and the winds blew cold. Eventually, we learned that a volcano in far-off Indonesia put so much ash in the air that the sun was blocked, even as far east as our corner of North America. So, despite all his efforts, Papa had to go back to tailoring until the following spring, when he could plant a decent crop. It was a hard go. Things were never easy in those days.

Mama had another baby two years after they started the farm, giving me one more sister. Papa named her Anna Maria after Mama. Anna Maria was such a big name for such a tiny baby, so we always called her Annie. A week after she was born, Mama announced at breakfast that it was high time baby Annie was baptized. I'd hardly finished my eggs when she said she was ready to find that church in Albany. Papa said it could not happen. He was too busy toppling trees and burning stumps. Mama insisted she would go by herself. I volunteered to go with her. I was only nine when Mama, Annie, and I walked two hundred miles to find a priest. It took us two weeks. Walking with Mama and taking turns carrying the baby was more fun than helping Papa chop and turn the soil. As we walked, we saw men digging the trench that became the canal.

She told me stories of elves and goblins and fairies and our old home in Kittersburg.

When we finally reached Albany, there was no priest. We couldn't go backward because we knew there was no priest where we came from, so we kept going. Two weeks later, we arrived in New York City. The bishop baptized Annie and praised Mama for her faith. Since winter was coming upon us, we spent most of the winter there, too. I sold vegetables on the streets to make the trip home a little easier. I'll save the rest of that story for another day.

What about my other siblings? We were all distraught when my older sister, Katharina, or Katja, as she liked to be called, died at the age of seventeen. Some say she died of a fever, but I always thought that Katja was lonely in America. Can a person die from a broken heart? Mama said she couldn't believe that God had taken a third daughter. She grieved for months; it took my brother's birth the following year to get her out of wearing black. My only brother, John Baptist, was named after Papa. To my parents' delight, he became the learned man my parents hoped I would be. He even became a Jesuit priest. Unfortunately, my baby brother died in George-town, Maryland, when he was only 27. Mama said the saddest thing in her life was losing so many of her children.

Some might ask what of my other sisters. Rosalia never married and remained living with Mama and Papa. She was happiest with them and the chickens and cows. Delia married Anthony Lintz and moved to Chicago. Mama and Papa's first *American* daughter, Annie, married Balthazar Minges. She passed away just a year ago. It was heartbreaking to know that my sister, who I helped carry so many miles when she was an infant, was gone before me.

One thing I remember as clearly as if it was yesterday was my parents' fiftieth anniversary. January 2, 1853. It was so cold that day. Living in Rochester, we knew cold. And we knew snow. Being snowbound and shoveling a path through shoulder-high drifts to get to the barn was not unusual. But on that January day, when our breath hung in the air like angel wings, it felt like paradise. We watched Mama and Papa's sleigh, decorated in pine boughs and scarlet ribbons and drawn by a big bay mare with icicles on her mane, pull up to the church's front doors. My sisters, the grandchildren, and scores of our fellow Rochestarians—German, Irish, and otherwise—were there to celebrate. Fifty years together. Can you imagine? It was quite an occasion for all of us. I felt so proud to be their son.

Before that big day, I convinced them to sit for daguerreotype portraits. When Mama saw the results, she insisted that Papa was still the most handsome man she ever met. In the photograph, Mama is wearing that silver cross she never took off. There was a story behind it, but I can't recall it anymore. The daguerreotypes still hang in my parlor over the mantle. I hope my oldest son will cherish them as much as I do.

It's a good thing we gathered then because three years later, we buried Papa. He was the hardest-working man I ever knew. That man just loved farming his land. He would sometimes take me by the shoulder and say, "Bernard, buy land when you can—the good Lord is not making any more of it." Papa's fields and orchards were so productive that they fed the best houses in town. Once the Erie Canal was dug, he had plenty to sell and ship to far-off places. He never had to go back to tailoring, but he did take time to sew my first wedding suit.

What a sad day for me when Mama passed six years after Papa. But she was ready. She said she wanted to be with her "angel" children and her mother once more. She wanted to greet all those people who helped us get to America. She couldn't wait to see "Johann" again. After he died, Mama started to refer to Papa as Johann again and not John. Mama was a wise and loving woman. She frequently told me, "Always love first; when you think you're done, love more."

When the Irish came to our town, they started a church on Platt Street called St. Mary's. We attended the church, but it never felt quite right; we German speakers wanted our own church. So when Father Joseph Prost passed through in 1835 and delivered a sermon in German, we begged him to stay. Six months later, 600 of us German speakers bought an old Methodist building to use for a Catholic church. Papa and I contributed money. We became trustees for a beautiful stone church that opened on Franklin Street eleven years later. It's the same church where Mama and Papa celebrated fifty years together.

And what of me? I know my time on this blessed earth is passing. It's been a challenging but good life. I married my darling wife Elizabeth Aman in 1831. She was my helpmate in building our home together. When we could not farm in the winter, we made sausages together. They were so delicious, flavored with a bit of paprika and mustard, that there was quite a demand for them. Elizabeth birthed our twelve children. I understood Mama and Papa better after we lost two of them. After twenty-two years of a very happy marriage, I lost my dear Elizabeth. Like Mama and Papa, we were always good friends and tried to laugh even in the worst times.

The following year, I married my sweet second wife, Elizabeth Meier, a widow. She brought two children to our marriage. We had two children together, although God took them both to Heaven before their time.

After my second wife's passing, I married once again. My third wife, Beatrix Feller, a good soul and very good mother, was considerably younger than me. We had nine children, but only seven survived. There was a thirty-eight-year span between the birth of my first son and my last. That must have broken some record. I have seventeen surviving children, and I am proud of every single one.

In the ebbing of my life, I can say that God has favored me. Like Papa, I thirsted for land and farming. I was successful enough to leave Beatrix and the children a bit of something to tide them over. Like Papa and Mama, I want to leave this earth a little better for having been here. I'll leave these pages to be passed on to my descendants so they will know something about the people who came before them and found a good home in America.

Author's Notes

The city of Rochester—its name was changed from Rochesterville in 1822—grew and prospered like the Klem family. From a population of approximately 330 people when the Klems arrived, it increased to 162,800 people by 1900, twenty-one years after Bernard Klem's death. It was considered a boom town.

Nathaniel Rochester, Charles Fitzhugh, and Richard Carrol's idea of investing in the wilderness of western New York proved sound. Of the three original investors, only Nathaniel Rochester lived in the settlement. Rochester and his wife built a brick home on the corner of Spring and Exchange Streets, where they lived until he died in 1831 at age 79. His public service in the frontier Genesee Valley was extensive. He helped create Monroe County, was the first County Clerk, and represented the county in the State Legislature. More recently, controversy arose regarding Col. Rochester's involvement in the purchase and sale of enslaved people in the 1790s before the founding of the city.

The city exported both lumber and flour via the new man-made transportation system. In the canal's first ten days of operation from the Rochester port, it is estimated that 40,000 barrels of flour (3,600 tons) made their way to Albany and New York City. This gave Rochester the epithet "The Flour City, " later changed to "The Flower City," when the city housed numerous seed nurseries. In addition to agricultural products, the city became famous for photography, clothing manufacturing, and optical products. It was an early center for both political and social reform. Both Frederick Douglass and Susan B. Anthony resided in the city for a time. The Underground Railroad had several stations in the Rochester area.

John Baptiste Klem died on January 26, 1856, at age 76; his wife, Anna Maria, survived him by several years, dying on March 31, 1862, at age 83. The Klems' property was at the southeast corner of South Goodman Street and East Avenue, across from the present Rochester Museum and Science Center.

Like his parents, Bernard remained a devout Catholic and contributed land for the original Catholic cemetery on Goodman and Main Street East. St. Joseph's Church, which the Klems helped found, was in use until it was seriously damaged in a 1974 fire. The façade still survives within a city park.

When Bernard Klem died on January 21, 1879, at age 69, he left considerable fortune and property to each of his seventeen surviving children. He also bequeathed $1,000 (equivalent to $30,000 today) to St. Joseph's Orphan Asylum and another $1,000 to the Catholic Men's Organization.

Bernard Klem's two-story frame house homestead was initially located on Goodman Street and was moved to 1223 Main Street. The building was later the home of the cemetery caretaker, a bicycle shop, a fireworks company, the Beechnut Packing Plant, and the Unit Parts Corporation. When it was razed in 1928, it was said to have the original hand-split lathes in the walls; the basement supports were hand-hewn trees, several bearing their original bark. Some of the interior walls were constructed with stone.

In 1934, Rochester celebrated its centennial as an incorporated city. Residents were asked to complete a form to determine if they were descendants of the early residents. Certificates were given to more than 835 Klem family members, stating they were descendants of a pioneer family. It was the most extensively certified family. The family was so large it had its own float in the centennial parade.

The author is the great, great, great, great-granddaughter of John Baptiste Klem and his wife, Anna Maria.

Acknowledgments

If it takes a village to raise a child, it may take a city to write a novel. I appreciate all the people who have helped me lay the infrastructure, pave the streets, and erect the libraries.

I want to give special thanks to Stephanie Larkin and her staff at Red Penguin Books, who guided me through the publishing process. She patiently advised me through decisions, offered choices, and calmed my hesitancies.

Many thanks to my sister, Barbara Hall, the family genealogist, for providing me with names, dates, charts, and numerous articles on the Klem family. It was enormously helpful. Thanks to my parents, who provided opportunities and were models for my siblings and me to become a family of readers. Also, thanks to cousin Mark Shallenberger, who continues to find lost family members and located a photo of the purported trunk the Klems used on their journey.

Heartfelt gratitude to my Spirit Writer sisters for their encouragement and willing ears. Special thanks to Katherine Tandy Brown, our leader, mentor, and prompter. Longtime members Ellen Kelley, Susan Madison, and Donna Armer have been with me for the long haul. New members Erin Ryan, Michelle Jerome, Cookie Brown, and Beth Macdonald gave me critical advice and motivation. My kissing cousin, Donna, inspired me with her creativity, introduced me to Red Penguin Books, and even gave me cooking advice.

I sincerely thank my beta readers, Joan Wylie Hall, Kathy

McShane, and Karen Warner-Schueler, for catching my inconsistencies, correcting my French, and giving me so much of their time by reading and editing my novice work. You made me feel my writing was not in vain.

Thanks to the WOW group, especially Jane Adams, John MacIlroy, and Vernie Singleton, for advice and encouragement and for setting an example. Thanks to Tim Johnston for mentoring and gathering us in his living room.

Thanks to Frank Birman for continuing to herd the ever-changing cats of Dataw Island's Writers Group.

I am indebted to Klaus Justen, Ursula Barrett, and Julika von Stackelberg for their translations of Chronicles of the Homeland by Josef Schäfer (© 1964), a history of the Kittersburg area of Germany.

My gratitude to Pat Stolte and Gene Ciccone for their medical advice.

I live in a supportive and generous community. Although I cannot mention everyone personally, I want to express my gratitude to the members of my book club, the historic foundation, and my fellow croquet players for giving me joy when I am not writing. I also want to thank my good friend Laura Riski for her generosity and for being a model of organization.

I love and appreciate my children (Jolie, Luke, Hope), their spouses (Greg, Katherine, Dave), and my grandchildren (Mira, Wylie, Beau, and Sunshine) for their love and kindness. Special thanks to Hope for her creative and technological assistance to her old-school mother. I hope you can be as proud of me as I am of you.

Great thanks to Guy for everything, but also for realizing that, like Virginia Wolfe, I needed a room of my own.

About the Author

Before Virginia (Ginny) Hall-Apicella began her second career as a writer, she spent thirty years as a counseling psychologist. She was a senior psychologist in the New York City court system, a consultant for mental health agencies, and had a successful private practice. Her profession gave her great insight into her fictional characters and left her with thousands of personal life stories in her head. Besides editing a local history foundation's newsletter, she has published several short stories. She enjoys being a docent at a historic church and the ruins of an antebellum mansion. In addition to being a history nerd, Ginny enjoys gardening, poker, reading, and competitive croquet. She lives with her husband in Beaufort, South Carolina.

Printed in the USA
CPSIA information can be obtained
at www.ICGtesting.com
CBHW032102300524
9299CB00004B/12